LISA,
IF YOU MADE IT THIS
FAR, YOU MUST LIKE WHAT
YOU'RE READING, SO THANK
YOU!

Necrophobia

Publisher's note: This is a work of fiction. Names, characters, places, and incidents either are the product of the author's imagination or are used fictitiously. Any resemblance to actual events, locales, or persons, living or dead, is entirely coincidental.

Printed in the United States of America
Edited, formatted, and interior design by Stephanie Lomasney Levert.
Cover art design by Emily Johns

First edition published 2018
10 9 8 7 6 5 4 3 2 1

Finley, Justin
Necrophobia / Justin Finley
p. cm.
ISBN-13: 978-1-7919597-6-0

For Love

Necrophobia

A novel

Justin Finley

Saturday Afternoon

Chapter 85

Tiffany Melancon's right hand rested in her boyfriend's lap as the two relaxed in Adirondack chairs on the shaded deck in her mom's backyard. She sipped on a vodka and cranberry, while a can of Guinness sat on a table to the right of Brett. Both drinks were heavily collecting condensation in the afternoon July heat.

"You feel like going swimming?" Brett asked his girlfriend.

Tiffany raised her Ray-Ban Aviators onto the top of her head before staring into her boyfriend's dark, smoldering eyes. His dirty-blonde hair, clipped tight on the sides and not quite two inches long on top, was pushed upward and to the left. It was styled just how she liked it. Within a month of dating, she had convinced him to cut his nearly shoulder-length hair, claiming he looked like a stoned-out surfer. "Maybe later."

"Do you mind if I jump in? I'm sweating bullets."

"Not at all."

Brett removed the cell phone and wallet from his khaki cargo shorts before taking off his t-shirt. Tiffany was proud of the arduous work her boyfriend had put into the gym over the last six months. When they first met at a mutual friend's bar-b-que, Brett had love handles, along with skinny arms and legs. Upon asking her on a date, she told him he wasn't her type. When he asked why, her reasoning was she wasn't attracted to his body. He admitted he only exercised when it was convenient, and it was usually just cardio. She told him if he committed to five days a week in the weight room, she would consider going to dinner with him. Three months with a personal trainer added fifteen pounds of muscle and dropped his body fat by five percentage points. Tiffany then agreed to a first date. Over the next nine months, he rarely missed a training session. His love handles had withered away, his legs became muscular, his arms grew in circumference, his chest no longer looked flat, and his butt finally took shape. The last thing she was waiting to see

2

develop was a full six-pack. The top four muscles were visible, but the last two still had a thin layer of fat covering them. She was confident all six would be noticeable by the time they embarked on their week-long beach trip with his friends at the end of August. He kissed her forehead before telling her, "I love you."

Her lips remained closed as she smiled. The three-word phrase had been proclaimed three times since breakfast. Twice she repeated them but chose to remain quiet as he kicked off his sandals. A talk was inevitable about his repetitive phrase that was starting to lose its luster. As he walked towards the saltwater pool, she told him, "Please don't splash me."

The 6'4" Brett stepped onto the edge of the diving board. He raised his arms while eying the water below. Several bounces ensued as Brett, so far, had form comparable to an Olympic diver. He jumped high into the air, flinging himself forward. His body was parallel to the horizon as he hit the water—a perfect belly-flop. Tiffany grinned as her boyfriend's head emerged from the water. "Ouch," he said with closed eyes. He looked to be in pain.

"That must have hurt."

"It did."

"Why'd you do it then?"

He opened his eyes, continuing to tread water. "To make you smile."

She again grinned. "Thank you, honey."

As Brett began to swim laps, the back door opened. Onto the wooden deck stepped someone Tiffany had been eager to see. His arm was interlocked with her mother's. "Look who's here, Tiffy."

She jumped to her feet. "Hey, Mitch."

"Hey, Tif." His hair was parted down the middle, with his bangs tucked behind his ears.

"Can I get you something to drink, Mitch?"

"A water will be great, Victoria. Thank you."

"You got it." She let go of Mitch's right arm before heading inside.

"Did you find out anything?" Tiffany asked the federal agent.

"Is that Brett swimming?"

"Yes. What did you discover?"

He subtly nodded while staring at the pool. "He's got a good freestyle stroke."

"He's been swimming with me. What did you find?"

He continued to stare towards the pool. "I'm not sure you're going to believe me."

"Try me." She grew uneasy while waiting to hear what he had to say.

"Do you want to hear this now?"

"Yes, I do."

"In front of Brett and your mom?"

His question only furthered her uneasiness. "I don't know. Do you not want to tell me in front of them?"

The back door opened. Victoria walked towards the two, extending a bottle of water to her guest. "What brings you by, Mitch?"

"I just wanted to see how my two favorite women are doing."

Victoria frowned. "I've been better. I miss him dearly."

"Mom, can you check on the roast? I don't want to burn dinner."

Victoria nodded before walking inside.

"Tell me everything you know right now, Mitch."

He chuckled under his breath, shaking his head side to side. "You're not going to believe me."

Tiffany was quickly growing frustrated by his procrastination. "Just tell—"

"Hey, Mitch." Brett began to climb the ladder in the deep end of the pool. Tiffany walked towards her boyfriend, placed both hands on his chest as he stood on the top rung, and then pushed him into the pool. As water splashed into the air, she made her way back to Mitch.

"Tell me what you—"

"What was that for?"

Tiffany turned around. Her anger was increasing by the second. "Keep swimming or no sex tonight!" She watched as Brett gave her a look as to say 'what's your problem' before submerging himself underwater. "Tell me what's going on, Mitch, or your ass is going swimming too."

With a grin, he told her, "So feisty. You remind me of your dad sometimes." He then grabbed her arm, directing her to the side of the house.

"Mitch, if you don't start—"

"How do you feel about your ex-fiancé?"

"Jackson?"

4

"How many ex-fiancés do you have?"

"What does he have to do with anything?"

A smirking Mitch ran his hands through his hair several times, eventually tying it into a ponytail using the rubber band around his wrist. "Everything, actually. Now, answer my question. How do you feel about him?"

"I…" she looked to the backyard and then back to Mitch, telling him, "care about him. I'm glad he didn't die in the plane crash. Why?"

"Do you wish you would have married him?"

"What does Jackson have to do with Dad's death?"

"Quite a bit."

Tiffany grabbed Mitch's t-shirt, squeezing it into her fist while gritting her teeth. "Tell me what the hell is going on!"

"I think Jackson was responsible for your father's death."

"Bullshit!" Her fist remained tightly clutched to his shirt. "Jackson wasn't even around him when he died…of a heart attack, nonetheless."

"It's true, Tif. I just got confirmation a little while ago. I'm almost certain he was with your dad the moment he died in the Ferrari."

She eased her grip, soon letting go. "Jackson was several states away while Dad had a heart attack. He was having doubts about marrying the slut he was with because he still has feelings for me. That's why he didn't get on the airplane."

"I hate to burst your bubble, but he was not out west. It's all a lie. He and an unidentified female were with your dad the night he died. The blood on the doorway belonged to a man in Mobile, who Jackson may have killed less than a day before killing your dad."

With a subtle shaking of her head, she told Mitch, "You're saying that Jackson, my ex-fiancé—who had never been in a fight in his entire life—killed a man in Mobile, and then a day later made it look as if my dad died of a heart attack—all while fooling the entire world into thinking he was in the western part of the country? Can you see, Mitch, how I might have trouble believing you? I'm done here." She began to walk toward the backyard. Mitch grabbed her arm, spinning her around.

"The marks on the bed were from someone other than your dad being handcuffed to it. The knife under the couch was from a struggle inside the house. The misplaced roll of duct tape was used to tape your dad's wrist to his own steering wheel. The blood on the doorway was transferred from a crime scene in Mobile. Jackson's fingerprints were found inside an eighteen-wheeler in Mobile—whose owner was found dead at that very crime scene—thus proving Jackson was not fifteen hundred miles away. I need you to believe me, just as I believed you when you called me over here two days ago. I swear on your dad's grave I'm not making this up."

Tiffany's suspicion that Mitch may have been telling the truth gained some momentum with his last remark. Her dad was almost like a father figure to Mitch. She knew he wouldn't have made the comment if he didn't believe it to be the truth. Still, she found difficulty in believing his far-fetched story. "I'm going to need something else to persuade me that what you're saying is the truth."

"And when I do convince you Jackson was responsible for your dad's death, what would you want me to do to him?"

"Prove this ridiculous story first, and then we'll talk." Tiffany lowered her sunglasses over her eyes. "Why don't you go out the side gate? I'll tell Mom you got called out on work."

"Jackson killed your dad, Tif."

She was at a loss for words as Mitch walked backwards towards the gate.

"Once I prove it, he's going to pay for what he did. Justice will prevail."

Once Mitch shut the gate, Tiffany began to tear up. *Jackson didn't kill Dad. He wouldn't do such a thing. It's not true… It can't be true… Is it true?*

Chapter 86

Logan stood next to Marcus at the back of the cathedral Jackson was to secretly wed Delain. Neither the bride nor the groom was present, but close to one-hundred guests were in attendance at ten minutes to seven o'clock. The pews were lopsided; so much so Cecile Fabacher asked family members to sit on the bride's side.

"Your mom is not going to take this well," Logan mumbled to Marcus.

"No, she's not. Between last night's events and now this, she'll be back in sedation mode again."

"It's about time to break the news to everyone. How are you going to do it?"

"Me? You're the one he talked to. Shouldn't you do it?"

"You're his brother. Plus, he said he wanted you to do it; something about you being more mature than me. You've got to admit, he's got a point."

Marcus shut his eyes, lifting his head upwards. "Why did he just leave town like that? And what did those F.B.I. agents want with him?"

"I don't know. What I do know is you need to make an announcement, and right now."

"Damnit." Marcus opened his eyes before beginning his hobbled walk down the aisle.

"Imagine yourself naked," Logan mumbled to him. "It'll help with your nerves."

Halfway to the altar, Marcus approached his mom as she talked to her cousin. She placed her hand on his shoulder and whispered into his ear, "Is he here?"

"You should go have a seat next to Dad." He leaned against his cane, waiting until she took her seat in the first pew.

"Marcus," a male's voice called out. He glanced to his right, making eye contact with Al. "Have you seen Caroline?" Marcus shook his head, prompting Al to appear confused.

Once his mom was seated next to his dad, Marcus continued his journey towards the altar. Melanie next caught his eye. She flashed a smile that wasn't one of joy, but rather concern. Marcus earlier told his wife about his parents' infidelity, about Jackson's biological father and twin brother, and the gangster he killed in order to save Jackson's life. They both agreed to have their twin boys stay with Melanie's parents in Baton Rouge for a few days. As he passed his wife, his gaze shifted to his parents. Their smiles weren't joyous either, but rather hinted at guilt. Instead of his dad holding his chin high, it was noticeably lower. His mom's cheeks were not nearly as pronounced when smiling big and proud. Marcus was certain they were ashamed by their actions that had recently been brought to light. While he still loved them dearly, he wasn't fully ready to forgive or forget what they had done to him, and especially to Jackson.

Father Peter, holding a Bible held against his chest with both arms, smiled at Marcus from atop the altar. Marcus couldn't smile back, instead choosing to nod before turning around to address the crowd. He cleared his throat, placed his cane behind him, and looked straight ahead to the back of the church. Logan held his right thumb up while nodding. There was no need to procrastinate any further.

"Firstly, I'd like to thank everyone for coming out to witness the union of my brother and his fiancée." He paused, waiting for a lengthy swallow to pass before saying," Unfortunately, there will be no wedding this evening. Thank you for understanding."

Nearly every head in the church turned, while several people gasped. Chaotic mumbling ensued until someone spoke up. "What do you mean? Where's Jackson?" a relative of Marcus asked.

"He's not here, Uncle Charles."

"Well, where is he? I drove 200 miles for this so-called 'secret wedding' and you're saying there won't be one?" Charles had been Marcus' least favorite family member since childhood. His mom's older brother drove a $120,000 car, lived in a 7,000 square foot house, and owned a private plane. Despite being wealthy, every Christmas his gift to Marcus and Jackson was socks. His cheapness, constant rudeness, and his 'I'm-wealthier-than-you-so-I'm-better-than-you' attitude made it justifiable to joke about the patch of hair covering his Adam's apple that seemed impervious to razor blades for the better part of ten years.

"We're not quite sure where Jackson is at the moment. I apologize."

"This is twice now he's done this to the family. This is getting ridiculous."

8

"There's no need to get upset, Uncle Charles," a calm Marcus spoke.

"I put everything on hold to attend this impromptu wedding, and no one even knows where the groom is?"

Marcus was growing furious with his uncle's selfish comments. 'Shut the hell up, Uncle Charles' would have felt awfully satisfying crossing his lips, but Marcus didn't want to create more friction in the cathedral. Before he could come up with a lie as to Jackson's whereabouts, someone else spoke.

"Keep your socks on, Chaz." Logan walked down the aisle, staring Charles down. "Remind me to give you a razor on your way out."

Charles snarled his lips. "Don't you—"

"Everyone," Logan addressed over Charles, "Jackson and Delain just want to make sure what they are doing is the right decision. Given the events that took place in the last week, I think we can all agree there's no reason to rush into something as sacred as the institution of marriage without knowing for sure it's the right path. I can assure you they love one another greatly, and they thank you for your understanding and cooperation. Now, how about a round of applause for Jackson being alive." He began to clap. Marcus did as well, followed by most everyone else in the church. "And how about a round of applause for how handsome I look this evening, ladies."

Andrew Fabacher approached his oldest son. "Where is he?"

"I don't know."

Andrew's head immediately hung low. "It's my fault. We shouldn't have hidden the truth from the two of you."

Marcus couldn't help but notice how tired and defeated his dad looked. Never had he seen the look before. "He'll be back soon. One thing about Jackson, he always comes back."

"I don't know if he is this time, Marcus. He told me he was leaving New Orleans after the wedding. He said he wanted to start over someplace far away."

"You really think he's not coming back?"

Andrew shrugged his shoulders. "If I had to guess, I would say yes."

Marcus had never heard his father talk so despairingly at any point in his life. Andrew was the rock, the foundation, the glue that kept the Fabacher family together. He couldn't lose hope, or else the family would crumble. "Dad, Jackson will be back. I need you to believe that with me."

While Andrew subtly nodded, Marcus took notice at how his mom was still sitting in the pew. Her frozen gaze appeared to be aimed at the statue of a crucified Jesus high atop the altar. Marcus took to the pew, placing his arm around her. "You okay, Mom?" She neither answered nor acknowledged his presence. Marcus waived his hand in front of her eyes several times. She eventually turned to him. "Mom, are you all right?"

Cecile stared at her oldest son in a way he had never seen from her before, a stare as if she was under some sort of spell or hypnotic trance. "It's over."

"What's over?"

"Us. Our family. We will never be the same again. We were so…perfect."

"We will be normal again," Marcus told her, not quite sure if he believed himself.

"It's not. I knew this day would come. I just didn't know it would be this catastrophic."

Andrew sat on the opposite side of his wife. "Honey, it's going to be okay. Jackson is coming back."

"There's no going back to the way things were," she somberly declared, shaking her head back and forth. "Our family is broken. It can't be fixed."

Marcus grew frightened by the glazed-over look in his mom's eyes, and the bleak and ominous words crossing her lips. It was as if she was someone else completely. "I'm going to get him back here, Mom. We're going to be okay."

"The beginning of the end," she murmured.

Andrew grabbed his wife's hands. "Why don't we get home? Jackson may already be there."

"He's gone, Andrew. It's my own fault."

Marcus had never heard his mom call his dad by his real name unless she was introducing him to someone. "Dad, why don't you get her home? I'll take care of damage control here."

Logan walked up as Andrew said, "Yep."

"What's going on?"

"We need to get my mom out of here now. You're right. She's not taking this well." Charles was quickly approaching his sister, along with several other family members behind him. "Shit. Everyone's coming this way."

"I'll distract them." Logan approached Charles in the aisle, falling to the ground like a limp noodle before violently shaking in front of him. "I'm…having…seizure!"

Andrew helped his wife to her feet, quickly escorting her to the back of the church via the side aisle. Once they were safely outside, Marcus approached and nodded to the seizure victim.

Logan jumped to his feet. "I'm okay. The seizure has left me. It's a miracle!" he shouted with outstretched arms. "A round of applause for my miracle, ladies."

"Where's your parents, Marcus?" a disgruntled Charles asked.

"They're just getting some fresh air." Marcus then leaned towards Logan, whispering into his ear, "We have to find Jackson. Where the hell can he be?"

Chapter 87

"Are you freaking kidding me?!" a wide-eyed Caroline shouted as we sat in my 4-Runner on the shoulder of the interstate, about twenty miles west of the Texas/Louisiana state line.

With a partial grin about my face, I nodded.

"But the news report didn't mention anything about someone rescuing them. The reporter said they escaped on their own, and then called 911."

"I told them not to tell the police because…" I thought it best not to tell Caroline exactly what I told Rebecca and Maria as they sat on Hank's couch—that the woman I love (Delain) may be in danger, "I wanted to get back to New Orleans and confront Davis. Luckily, no one knows I was in Hank's house except for those two girls, and they didn't see my face."

Caroline grinned as she shook her head back and forth in the passenger seat. "I can't believe it. Why didn't you say anything, silly?"

"I didn't want you or Delain to become anymore nervous or upset."

"Upset? Why would I be upset you saved those two girls from that creep's sex dungeon? You're a hero."

"Because of the circumstances leading up to it, and what the three of us went through with Davis."

During our nearly four-hour drive, I told Caroline everything. I confessed to stealing a car in Denver, having to hitchhike with Cliff to avoid the police, killing him after he had just shot Hank, using Hank's truck to get back home after hiding in the attic for hours, the discovery of my twin brother, who my real father was, the mobster killed in my kitchen by Marcus and why he had come to shoot me, and why the F.B.I. agents showed up at my front door. I told her everything because I couldn't keep it in any longer. I feared something tragic looming in my near future, and if something were to happen to me, Caroline could reveal the truth.

"It's a bit much, I know."

"A bit much? Jackson, I…I…"

"Don't believe me?"

"No, I believe you. I'm just in awe of how normal you've seemed over the last few days."

"If I appeared normal, I assure you it was just a façade. The panic attack you witnessed a few hours ago in Delain's living room was, I think, the fourth one since Wednesday."

"I had no idea. Perhaps it's a good thing you didn't get married tonight," she said with a straight face.

"It did feel like we were rushing into it— with everything going on."

"Do you think the wedding was part of the reason for the panic attacks?"

I told her what I thought she wanted to hear. "Yes."

"And being where you are right now, do you still feel…scared?"

Again, I told her what she wanted to hear. "Not as much. Telling you everything that has happened is helping to relieve some of the stress."

She placed her left hand on my thigh. "I'm glad you told me. I want to be here for you. There's no way I'm leaving you."

"Let me remind you not only does a Las Vegas mobster want me dead, but two F.B.I. agents are currently looking for me as well. Someone is most likely going to make a second attempt to kill me, while two others probably want to arrest me. I'm not so sure you should be with me right now."

"There's nowhere else I want to be."

"If anything were to happen to you, Caroline, I don't know how I'd be able to live with myself." As her lips began to turn upward, I told her, "And that's why we need to go our separate ways. We're about two hours from Houston. I think it's best if we drive to the airport there and you fly home. I'll pay for your ticket." I was torn by my decision. I didn't want to be alone, but at the same time I wanted her out of harm's way.

Her lips reversed directions. "I'm not going home. I'm staying in this car with you."

"It's not safe for you to be with me. You could end up either dead or arrested for aiding a criminal. Is that really what you want?"

She stared into my eyes, emotionless for several seconds, before subtly nodding. Her gaze then shifted onto the interstate. A short moment passed before she said, "I guess you're right. How about I drive us to the Houston airport?"

"I'm okay to drive."

"Let me do it. You're going to be driving by yourself for God knows how long. You can get a little rest while I drive." She opened her door.

"Okay." I opened my door. Caroline stepped onto the shoulder of the road. As I walked around the front of the car, she jumped back into the passenger seat, shut the door, climbed into the driver's seat, and waved goodbye. I watched in disbelief as she veered onto the interstate. "What the hell?" My 4-Runner soon disappeared in the distance.

I covered the setting sun with both hands, waiting to see reverse lights coming back towards me on the shoulder of the interstate. Several minutes later, I realized she wasn't coming back. Caroline had left me in the middle of nowhere with no cell phone or wallet. I couldn't believe it.

To my right, two horses grazed in a large field. In the distance, I could see a house at the end of a dirt road behind the field. My only option (since I would never again hitchhike) was to walk to the house and ask to use the phone. Logan and my brother were the only two people I would call. Nighttime was fast approaching. As I walked towards the dirt road, still shocked by Caroline's actions, I heard the honking of a horn. I turned around to see Caroline driving east on the interstate. She drove past me before making a u-turn in the median of the interstate, nearly hitting a westbound car as she drove across both lanes of the interstate. "Holy shit!" She came to an abrupt stop on the shoulder of the road where she had left me. I hurried toward her. The passenger side window was partially rolled down.

"What's wrong with you?!" I attempted to open the door. It was locked.

"Did you like being without me just now?"

"I can't believe you left me like that? Unlock the door."

"How did it feel?"

I told her the truth. "Scary. Open the door."

"Good, because that's how I felt when you said you wanted to get rid of me. Now, are we in this together?"

"Caroline, I don't—" She took her foot off the brake. As my vehicle started to roll away, I walked alongside with it. "Yes, you can come along! Just open the door!"

She pressed on the brake. "What's the magic words?"

"Please unlock the door, Caroline."

"Those aren't it. The magic words are what you told me on my last day of work with you in the break room. Remember?"

"Yes."

"Say them."

"Caroline, please open the door." She again took her foot off the brake. "I think I'm falling for you!"

"Louder," she demanded while continuing to roll forward. "You know I can't hear that well."

"I think I'm falling for you, Caroline!"

She finally unlocked the doors. I jumped in. "I'm driving."

"Okay. Get out and walk over here."

"You're driving." I shut the passenger door. "Don't go over the speed limit. The last thing we need is to get pulled over."

She grinned merrily while merging onto the interstate. "Yes, sir."

"You have no idea what you're getting into, Caroline. This ordeal is far from over." I glanced at the gas gauge on the dashboard. Less than a quarter of a tank remained. "We should get gas pretty soon."

"I don't care what happens. I'm staying with you. I'm not leaving you like Delain did."

I again recalled the last moments with Delain. She seemed just as excited as I did about leaving town together. Since there was no sign of struggle, and a note left behind, I ruled out an abduction. She appeared to have left at her own will. "Can you call her again?"

Caroline grabbed her phone. "Yes, but she's not going to answer." She turned the speaker on while holding her phone between us. Again, Delain's voicemail picked up without ringing. "Delain, it's Caroline. Call me back. It's an emergency." She hung up.

"Something had to have happened while I went home to pack my suitcases. She was all gung-ho about leaving town."

"Do you think she left with Tyler?"

"She told me she met with him in his hotel room this morning and claimed she no longer felt anything for him. She confessed to finding closure with him."

"Do you think she was telling the truth?"

"At the time, yes. Now, I'm not so sure."

"Delain just so happens to run into an ex-boyfriend one day before she was to wed you—an ex-boyfriend she profoundly loved and was going to marry until Davis intervened. That's some coin…cidence." Caroline then flashed a puzzling, concerned look.

"What?"

"I just remembered something when I was briefly talking with Delain and Tyler yesterday at the airport. At one point, I was nearly certain he called Delain either 'Christine' or 'Christina'. I nearly forgot about it until just now. Do you think 'Delain' isn't her real name?"

"At this point, I wouldn't be surprised."

"I think she changed her name to hide from Tyler, so he couldn't find her."

It made sense. "Whatever her name is, I'm done with her and all the lies."

Caroline stared straight ahead while asking, "Are you sure about that?"

"I knew she was forced to date me, yet I thought she had fallen for me. I'm an idiot for thinking she was in love with me. How could I have been so stupid? I killed a man for her. I should have backed out once I knew of Davis' plan." I grew angry, not so much at Delain, but myself for thinking I could convince her to stay with me. With my left forearm resting on the console, Caroline grabbed my hand.

"She's the stupid one for not staying with you." The palm of her right hand was soft and comforting as it grazed the back of mine, and her French-manicured fingernails provided chills as she gently glided them along the palm of my hand.

Just as it did the last time we were in a car together, something dawned on me— and it was much stronger than the previous feeling three days earlier. I turned to my left. "No. I'm the stupid one for not realizing what has been in front of me this whole time."

"What are you—"

"You."

Caroline turned to me, smugly grinning while asking, "What do you mean?" Her eyes returned to the road.

"I've had a crush on you since the first time you walked into the clinic. If Delain had never killed a man, met Davis, and was forced to date me; if our relationship was a

16

normal one, I still would have had doubts about marrying her because of you. You have never lied to me, and you're currently putting your life and freedom in jeopardy just to be with me. I told you something in the back of the Mustang three days ago, but I wasn't quite sure if I meant it then. And I shouldn't be saying this now, especially since," I glanced at the clock, "I would possibly be saying my vows at this very moment to Delain if she didn't run off, but I really do love you, Caroline. I'm saying this with absolutely no hesitation or doubt in my mind. And by the way, I didn't want to drop you off at the airport in Houston."

Her eyes remained fixed on the interstate, almost dazed, as she continued driving at 70 miles per hour. Even though she had yet to respond to my confession, thus causing doubt that her feelings may have lessened or changed completely by my admission, I didn't regret telling her how I felt because it was the God's honest truth.

"And, yes, I had to hide my smile when you told me you had broken off your engagement to Brock."

Caroline slowed down before pulling onto the shoulder of the interstate. Once the car came to a stop, she hurriedly unbuckled her seatbelt. "Get out the car."

"Are you leaving me again?"

She opened her door, stepped out, walked in front of the car, and with a look of utter determination in her eye, opened my door. I stepped out. She shut my door, pushed me against it, and then planted her lips to mine. I shut my eyes while engaged in a kiss that had been building for months. 'Sweet' and 'innocent'—words often used to describe most first kisses—would be highly inaccurate descriptions of ours. A documentary on the last days of Pompeii intrigued me as a teenager. One story told (whether it was true or not, no one really knows) involved two people so much in love that instead of attempting to flee the erupting volcano, they remained in each other's arms and passionately kissed one another as lava encompassed their bodies and preserved their love for centuries. I imagined the only heat felt as they passed away was from their kiss. As Caroline pulled away, the only word I could find to suffice in describing our first kiss was 'Pompeiian'.

"Holy shit," I mumbled.

She shook her head back and forth while saying, "I don't think I can drive right now. My legs are trembling. I can honestly say, Jackson, I've never felt this way after a kiss."

I felt a little wobbly myself. The last kiss shared with Delain was the most passionate and intense of all our kisses. At the time, it was one I thought could never be eclipsed. The kiss with Caroline on the side of the interstate was on a whole different level, surpassing the aforementioned kiss. "To be honest, I don't know if I have either."

"Maybe it was a fluke." We again kissed. It was no fluke.

I wanted to keep kissing her, but the sudden image of Vincent's ugly mug incited a gentle nudge. "Not to kill the mood, but we need to keep moving."

"Do you know where we're going?"

From the time we left Delain's house until the moment Caroline and I kissed, I had no idea. It then dawned on me where we were headed. "Yes."

Chapter 88

Andrew shut the door to the bedroom as his wife lay asleep in their bed. Cecile had relapsed into the same behavior following Jackson's funeral—pill dependant. During the ride home from the cathedral, Cecile ingested Prozac and Ambien before Andrew could talk her out of it. While walking down the stairs, he came to the realization his wife and youngest son shared something very much in common—both seemed to run away from dramatic events in their life instead of facing them. Whereas Jackson physically strayed from his problems, Cecile's escapes were pharmaceutically induced. He wished both were a little less avoidant when a crisis presented itself.

"How are you doing, Angelo?" Andrew asked the young man upon walking into the portrait room.

Angelo stood to greet him. "Good. How was wedding?"

"Sit. Sit," Andrew said, motioning for him to do so. Angelo returned to the velvet couch. Several photo albums were stacked next to him, while one sat in his lap. "No wedding tonight." Andrew took to the other couch.

A frown appeared on Angelo's face. "No wedding?"

"It got…postponed."

"Postponed?" Angelo looked puzzled.

"It got…cancelled."

"Cancelled? This is common?"

"More than you think."

"Jackson—he is okay?"

"He's going to be okay."

Angelo closed the album in his lap. "I'm sorry for surprise visit. I hope no one is upset. I think Jackson maybe so."

"He's a little…surprised, but he'll come around soon."

"He's coming around tonight? I can talk to him?" Angelo flashed an eager grin.

Andrew shook his head "Probably not tonight."

Angelo's smile lessened. "I hope soon. I want to talk to him. I never had brother or sister. When I see him on American T.V. channel I was most excited I ever been. I realize I not alone anymore. I had family again."

Andrew's heart went out to the young man seated three feet in front of him. Even though he had known him for less than a day, he wished Angelo could be part of the family. Unfortunately, doing such a thing would land him and his wife in legal trouble. "I'm glad you finally got to know the truth about where you came from, Angelo."

"Me too. I very happy right now. Is Mrs. Cecile feeling good? She looked tired when she came in."

"She is tired. She should be better tomorrow."

Angelo again smiled. "Good. I want to know her more if that's okay."

"I'm sure she would like that." Andrew glanced at the stack of albums. "What are you looking at?"

He opened the album he had just closed, smiling while pointing at a picture. "Jackson looks very happy as child."

Andrew partially grinned while nodding. "He was."

"He must like to dress up." Angelo pointed to another picture of his twin brother. "Superman."

"He loved to dress up and fight the bad guy. He even had a superhero name."

"What is name?"

"Captain Incredible."

"Captain Incredible. I like." Angelo's smile was eerily similar to Jackson's. About the only physical difference Andrew so far noticed between the two was the tiny mole on the left side of Angelo's nose. It was small enough to almost go unnoticed.

Andrew stood. "Angelo, please excuse me for a few minutes. I need to talk with Marcus and Logan. Can I get you anything to eat or drink?"

"I'm okay. I keep looking at pictures while you gone. Thank you very much."

Andrew patted Angelo on the shoulder on his way out of the room. As he made his way down the hallway, he recalled the night he and his wife said goodbye to Angelo. His wife took it especially hard, losing nearly thirty pounds over the next six months. The guilt was so great, Andrew didn't know if she would ever fully recover. Twenty-nine years later, he believed she had yet to recover.

"Is Mom asleep?" Marcus asked Andrew once he stepped into the parlour. His son sat on a bar stool, while Logan stood behind the bar. Both of their cell phones lay on the counter.

Andrew closed the sliding doors behind him. "She'll be out for a while."

"It's so weird seeing a clone of Jackson," Logan spoke at a low decibel. "How much longer is he going to be here? It's kind of freaking me out."

"Should we try to get him back to Italy?"

"Not now. The safest place for him is inside this house. And while he's here, we're going to make him feel like he's part of this family. He has every right to know the truth too."

"You want a drink, Mr. F?"

"No, thank you, Logan." Andrew sat next to his son. "Any idea of where Jackson could be, fellas? Do you think he's doing the same thing he did after the last wedding?"

Marcus glanced at Logan. "Tell him the message Jackson left for you on the dry erase board."

"What message?"

Logan cleared his throat before telling Andrew, "Jackson left a note saying he was leaving town before the wedding due to the recent events. He didn't say where he was going."

Andrew experienced a sharp pain in his chest. It passed following a few deep breaths. "He told me this morning he was leaving town, but not until after the wedding. I thought he would come to his senses and stay. I guess he and Delain wanted to take off sooner." Andrew then reached in his pocket.

"You know what I just remembered?"

Andrew placed two cell phones onto the bar. "What's that?"

"While I was walking down the aisle, Al asked me if I had seen Caroline. I don't think she showed up at the cathedral either."

"She wasn't there and," Logan continued while grabbing a glass from the shelf behind the bar, "it's interesting you just mentioned her."

"How so?" Andrew asked him.

21

Logan waited until after placing ice cubes into the glass in his hand to answer. "First of all, I want to make sure, Mr. F., you don't have cancer."

"No, and you're the second person to ask me that in the last week. Delain mentioned it at Jackson's funeral before retracting it and claiming she confused me with someone else named Andrew."

"Delain was lying to you. She very much believed you had cancer."

"What makes you say that?"

Logan inverted a bottle of Jack Daniels over his glass until the copper-colored liquid covered the ice cubes. "I caught Jackson in a little lie the other day." He placed the whiskey back on the shelf before opening a can of Coke.

"What lie? And can you make me one as well?" Marcus asked him.

"It began a few months ago. Jackson was noticeably down. When I confronted him about it, he told me you, Mr. F., once again had testicular cancer. He told me not to mention anything about it to anyone, especially you." Logan mixed the Coke into the whiskey before handing it across the bar.

Marcus grabbed the drink. "Why would he make the cancer thing up?"

"His reasoning was because he was having doubts about marrying Delain, and he didn't want anyone to know why he was down."

"I don't get it. When he told his mother and me about proposing, I had never seen him so proud and excited."

"I thought the same thing when he told me. I suggested to him he should wait, but he managed to convince me he was madly in love with Delain. I believed him."

"Why did his feelings change?"

"Because of the intern he spent twelve weeks with."

"Caroline?" Andrew asked.

"Yes, sir. He was having doubts about Delain because he had developed strong feelings for Caroline." Logan grabbed another glass as he continued. "Jackson was, or I'm assuming still is, in love with two women."

Andrew stood from the bar stool, placing his hands in his pockets as he stared at the floor. "Why would Delain lie about saying someone else had cancer when she thought it was me? Why wouldn't she just tell me Jackson told her I had cancer? Why cover it up?"

Marcus took a sip of Jack and Coke before setting in on the bar. "You said she mentioned it at the funeral. How did it come about?"

"Well, now that I think about it, it wasn't at the funeral, but here following the funeral. She told me good luck with the cancer, then Cecile came over and Delain mentioned something about Valentine's Day."

Logan snapped his fingers. "Right around Valentine's Day—that's when Jackson told me you had cancer. What happened around that time?" Logan set the empty glass on the bar.

"Cecile said something about balloons when Delain mentioned Valentine's Day. Then, I remember her getting kind of nervous. I thought she was just experiencing the same sadness we all were, but maybe it was something else."

"I remember him talking about doing the balloon thing for Delain a few days before Valentine's, but now that I think about it, he never mentioned how it turned out. I'm now starting to think it never happened because one of them would have surely mentioned it afterwards, but neither did. That could explain why we were both told around the time of your cancer, Mr. F. Something happened on or around Valentine's Day."

"Delain told Cecile and I that Jackson did do something special for her on Valentine's Day, but I'm not so sure she was telling the truth. She seemed flustered and then immediately left."

"I noticed the same thing," Logan added, "and I even told Jackson two days ago how it was weird she left here last Sunday and didn't say goodbye to me or Marcus. Something happened on Valentine's Day, Fabachers, and Jackson and Delain are both covering it up. Maybe it has to do with why two F.B.I. agents knocked on our door this afternoon."

"What?" an even more concerned Andrew asked. "Two agents knocked on the door this afternoon and were looking for Jackson? To arrest?"

"Not to arrest him. They said they wanted to talk to him but didn't say what it was about. They then asked me his whereabouts when he was thought to be dead and if I had communication with him. I told them the truth—no. I saw them outside the cathedral earlier tonight. I wouldn't doubt it if they're outside this house right now."

Andrew grew more paranoid by Logan's revelation. He knew F.B.I. agents didn't stop by a civilian's residence just to ask a few innocent questions. Jackson was in trouble. "I need to talk to him immediately."

"He said he was going to call me tomorrow from a payphone."

"I don't like the idea of F.B.I. agents talking to him without me or at least another lawyer present." Andrew grabbed his cell phone from the counter and began to dial. "Why won't he just answer—" His attention was diverted to the other cell phone recently removed from his pocket as it vibrated on the bar.

"Is that Ralph's phone?" Marcus asked.

Andrew stared hypnotically at the screen. The incoming call had a 702 area code. "Yes."

"Answer it."

"That's not a good idea."

"Dad, answer it! It could be about Jackson!"

"And put it on speakerphone, Mr. F."

Without further contemplating his actions, Andrew grabbed the cell phone and pressed the 'talk' button followed by the 'speaker' button. "Hello?" There was no reply. "Hello?" he again asked.

"Who is this?"

Andrew lowered his mouth towards the phone. Before he could speak, Marcus did. "Officer Smith. Who is this?"

"Where is he?"

"Who are you referring to, sir, and what is your name?"

"Why am I on speakerphone, Officer Smith?" The man's accent hinted that he was from New York, and possibly of Italian descent.

Marcus looked up for help. Logan slowly mouthed a word to him. Marcus repeated the word towards the phone. "Protocol…sir."

"As to who I am, I'm someone you don't want to get involved with. Now, where is the owner of this phone?"

"Sir, I'm going to need your name before this conversation can continue."

"Why is that?"

"So I know who to arrest."

The man on the other end of the phone chuckled before saying, "Arrest me for what?"

"Murder." Andrew tapped him before mouthing two words. Marcus repeated them. "Attempted murder."

"I don't know what you are referring to. I didn't attempt to kill anyone."

"If you're looking for Ralph, you may want to call the morgue." The man on the other end of the phone grew silent. "Hello?"

"Tell Jackson he made a deadly mistake."

"If you come after him, I'm going to fucking kill you myself!"

"You're no officer. Who are you? A relative of Jackson? Your voice doesn't sound like it belongs to that of a sixty-four-year-old male, so this isn't Andrew Fabacher the Third. Marcus, is that you?"

A look of shock was broadcast all over Marcus' face. He glanced at his dad and then Logan. After covering the phone with his hand, he asked them, "How does he know that?"

"Judging by your silence, I will assume you are Marcus Fabacher— husband to Melanie, father to Dylan and Daniel."

"If you come near my family, I'll kill you the same way I killed Ralph, you son-of-a-bitch!"

"I've never killed brothers before. This should be fun. See you boys soon." The call ended.

"Shit!" a red-faced Marcus shouted.

Logan pounded his fist onto the bar. "We gotta find Jackson before that asshole does."

Chapter 89

Vincent stood from his desk chair, cocked his right arm backwards, and hurled his cell phone against the wall, narrowly missing one of the ten television screens before him. "Fuck!" The phone lay in several pieces on the concrete floor.

"Is Ralph okay?" Anthony asked him. Whereas Ralph was Vincent's right-hand man, Anthony was Ralph's.

Vincent shot a cold stare at Anthony while saying, "I just threw my cell phone against the goddamn wall. Do you think Ralph's okay, you dumb shit?!"

"No?" asked the dark-complexioned, twenty-five-year-old who had just recently joined Vincent's organization. He ran his hand through his slicked-back, jet-black hair while awaiting an answer.

"He's dead, Tony…which means you just got promoted."

"Dead? Was he murdered?"

"I think so."

"By who?"

Vincent grabbed the remote control from his desk with the number '10' drawn upon it in white. He aimed it at the bottom screen on the far right, pressing a button. A still image of Jackson Fabacher appeared from a newscast recorded three days earlier. "Either him or his brother."

Anthony read the screen while asking, "Who's Jackson Fay…Fab…"

"Fa-bach-er. It's German."

"Who's Jackson Fabacher?"

"A soon-to-be dead man."

Anthony stepped closer to Vincent's desk, leaning towards him while mumbling, "You want me to, um, take care of him, Boss?"

Vincent laughed. "You kidding me? You wouldn't know where to begin to kill someone."

Anthony leaned even closer, pointing with his thumb towards the couch while softly asking, "Shouldn't we keep it down in front of the girls?"

"Stop whispering, Tony. They're not gonna say nothing. Ain't that right, girls?"

"I don't know what you're talking about," spoke a young black girl.

Vincent then stared at the blonde-haired escort that had been a regular fixture in his office over the last few days. "What about you?"

"I don't know what you're talking about either, Vincent."

Vincent pointed his finger at her. "You been in here a lot this week. What's the matter? Got evicted from your apartment?"

She cracked a smile. "I like it in here."

"You better start getting some more customers, or I'm going to evict you myself."

Her smile vanished as she nodded.

"I can take this guy out, Vincent. Please give me a chance to prove myself."

"Shut up." Vincent aimed his pointer and middle fingers at the tenth television screen as if they were a gun, and then made a gesture as if pulling the trigger. "I'll take care of him myself."

"What can I do to help? I want to help," Anthony begged.

"Book me a flight to New Orleans."

"For when?"

"First thing tomorrow morning."

"You going alone?"

The blonde escort stood from the couch. "Can I go?"

"Can you go where?"

"With you—to New Orleans."

"I thought you weren't listening."

With a shrug of her shoulders she told him, "I may have heard a little bit."

His stare towards her was lengthy and one of deliberation. "You wanna go to New Orleans with me?"

"Yes."

He walked towards the couch, standing just inches from her as he asked, "Why?"

"I have family I want to visit. Plus, I could be your alibi if anything were to happen."

Vincent again deliberated before finally nodding. "Clever girl. Tony, book two first-class tickets to New Orleans.

"You got it, Boss."

"Go home and pack a light suitcase," he told the escort. "We're going to the Big Easy,   baby."

Chapter 90

"Would you prefer a queen-sized bed or two doubles?" the woman behind the check-in counter of the Carefree Inn in Flatonia, Texas asked us.

I looked to my left. Caroline shrugged her shoulders and raised her eyebrows while a smile she failed miserably to conceal surfaced. During our road trip earlier in the week, Caroline insisted she had no choice but to rent a motel room with one bed to avoid any speculation she was traveling with a companion. While sharing a bed on both of those nights, a pillow separated the two of us and there was no physical contact at any point throughout the night. Four nights later, things were different. Delain appeared to want nothing to do with me, while Caroline was adamant about staying by my side. I turned to the woman behind the counter. "Two doubles." Caroline looked disappointed, but I didn't think it moral to sleep in the same bed with someone when, twelve hours earlier, I thought I'd be sharing a bed with my new wife.

"Will you be paying with a credit card or cash?"

I adhered to the same method from a week earlier of using cash instead of a form of payment that could pinpoint my whereabouts to federal agents, pissed off mobsters, or curious family members. Caroline walked with the key ahead of me while I carried the suitcases to our room. It was nearing midnight. I was both physically and mentally exhausted.

While Caroline showered, I leaned against the headboard of the bed closest to the window. A wave of déjà vu soon overcame me. I was once again in a motel room while embarking on a road adventure on the day of my wedding. The difference the second time around, however, was I felt less scared and depressed. I was very much paranoid, and my anxiety levels were far from minimal, but Caroline's presence helped incite a strange feeling of calm. It was as if I was on a life raft that was slowly leaking air in the middle of a shark-infested ocean, yet believed I was going to be rescued soon.

My thoughts then drifted to the conversation shared with Logan the day before I proposed to Delain. He didn't try to sugarcoat the fact I had very little "me time" between relationships. I was curious if my 'autophobia', as Dr. Blanchard called it, was the reason I had developed even stronger feelings towards Caroline since our second road trip began. As my eyes grew heavy, I convinced myself my attraction towards her had nothing to do with Logan's and Dr. Blanchard's claim that I feared being alone.

The clearing of a throat awakened me. Steam exited from behind Caroline as she stood just outside the bathroom door. "Sleepy?" she asked with a subtle grin. A white towel was wrapped around her torso. Her hair, darkened from being wet, draped over the left side of her face.

"Maybe a little."

"I used all the hot water," she playfully frowned. "You may want to wait a few minutes."

The five steps it took for Caroline to reach her bed were four steps more than I needed to notice a swagger about her. It was very similar to the way she strutted from the Mexican restaurant to the hotel our first night in Denver—a confident walk suggesting everything in her life was perfect. She fell onto the bed, lying on her back. Her feet remained in contact with the floor, while her head rested in the middle of the comforter. A glance to my right revealed a direct line of sight down the top of her towel. Beads of water glistened on the top half of her breasts as she stared at the ceiling. I took my time looking away.

"What's on the agenda for tomorrow?" she asked.

"Eat breakfast and then keep heading west."

In front of us was a rectangular mirror hung above the three-foot-high dresser. With both hands resting beneath her head, she gazed upon my reflection in the mirror. "Where are we going?"

"I'm not sure why, but I want you to meet someone tomorrow."

"Who?"

"I'll tell you on the way there." I could see her smiling as our eyes remained locked with one another. "Are you having second thoughts yet about getting in the car with me?"

"No, sir."

"You're not the least bit worried after everything I confessed in the car?"

"Nope. Are you?"

"Nah." I was lying through my teeth.

"So…the fact that the F.B.I., the police, or a mobster who has two reasons to want you dead could knock on the motel door at any moment doesn't scare you?"

I glanced at the door, making sure both locks were fastened. "Maybe a little."

She placed her right hand on her towel as she turned to me. Lying on her side and with her left hand supporting her head, she asked, "Do you think someone could really find us out here?"

"I hope not."

"Could they track us with our phones? I saw that in a movie recently."

My suspicions on government phone tracking was heightened as she became the second person to mention such a thing. "Not through mine. My phone's more than likely in the belly of an alligator right now." As she squinted at me in confusion, I told her, "I threw it into a canal earlier today because I wondered the same thing."

She sprung to her feet, clutching the towel to her chest while reaching her available hand into her purse on the dresser. She removed the back panel from her cell phone before taking out the battery. "Are we safe now?"

"I would think so."

She returned to one of the two beds, only it wasn't the one she was lying on seconds earlier. "Doesn't it kind of feel like we're Bonnie and Clyde?" Once again lying on her back, her head was next to my knees. Both of her arms rested on the bed. She had to have known I could see straight down the top of her towel.

"A little bit," I answered, my voice cracking like a fourteen-year-old boy's at the onset of puberty. After a subtle clearing of my throat, I told her, "But hopefully we don't start robbing banks."

"Do you know how old Bonnie Parker was when she died?"

"Um…" It was difficult to concentrate. I scooted down until we were lying next to each other. Both of our gazes were aimed at the ceiling. "Thirty-something?"

"Twenty-three—the same age as me. Do you know when her birthday was?"

"The same day as yours?"

She gasped. "How did you know?"

"I'm starting to see a trend with your questions."

"And on what day was Bonnie Parker and I born?"

"October 1st."

"You remembered." She held her right hand up. "They were killed in Louisiana. Did you know that about your home state?"

"I do now." I high-fived her right hand with my left. Neither one of us bothered to pull our hand away.

"She was so in love with Clyde that she didn't care what he did. She didn't care he was a criminal, and that they had to look over their shoulder wherever they went. Their love was so pure and honest, and they died together. That's how I want to go."

"You want to be riddled with bullets? That's how you want to die?"

"No, silly. I want to die in the arms of my lover."

"Even if you're only twenty-three years old?"

"If I'm in the arms of my love, then yes."

"You wouldn't rather live to be eighty-five?"

"Sure, but if I had to choose between dying alone in a nursing home at eighty-five or dying in my lover's arms at twenty-three, I'd choose the latter. What would you choose?"

"Dying at eighty-five in my wife's arms."

"That's not an option, Fabacher. Would you rather die at the age you are now in the arms of the woman you love or die alone at eighty-five?"

Discussing when I wanted to die wasn't helping with the crippling fear of death that had haunted my thoughts since Ralph was killed in my kitchen, but I also didn't want to hurt the feelings of the woman next to me by ignoring her question. "Eighty-five. Just because I would die alone it wouldn't mean I was alone for all those years. Plus, I'm not ready to die just yet. I still have things to do."

"Such as…?"

"For starters, I'd love to wake up on my wedding day and actually be married when I go to bed."

"Third time's a charm," Caroline spoke with a chuckle. "What else is on your bucket list? World traveling? Skydiving?"

"I've already been skydiving with…"

"Delain."

As Caroline mentioned her name, I didn't think about how she deserted me hours earlier. Instead I thought about our first date. I remembered how scared I was and how

Delain's touch calmed me on the airplane. I again experienced tightness in my chest as I recalled our first kiss in front of Jax Brewery and how hopeful it made me.

"Do you miss her?"

"No."

"You can be honest. Today was your wedding day. I know you're a little upset with her lying, but I would hope you wouldn't be over her after just a few hours."

"It's hard to miss someone when you don't know what was real and what wasn't."

"Do you think she loved you?"

"If I had to guess, I'd say…I don't know."

"I think she did."

I let go of Caroline's hand as I turned to her. Her stare, still aimed at the ceiling, lacked any sort of emotion. "Why do you think that?"

"When I went to her house after the funeral, she told me she loved you and missed you dearly."

"How do you know she was telling the truth?"

"I just assumed she—"

"Don't be so gullible, Caroline. She lied. Everyone lies—even family."

"Not everyone lies," she said before sitting up and glancing back at the nightstand. "It's almost one o'clock. Why don't you go take a shower? We probably need to rest up for whatever you have planned for us tomorrow."

Chapter 91

Scott Melancon's elbows rested on the phone list atop his late brother's office desk. He shut his eyes and rubbed both temples in a circular motion with his pointer and middle fingers. On Friday, he had placed fifty-eight phone calls to anyone who had worked at the Fleur-de-Leans at the time of Davis' death. Thirty-six of the employees were eager to return to work, while seven had already found employment elsewhere. He left voicemail messages for the fifteen remaining staff members, informing them of a meeting to be held Sunday afternoon in the dining room of the restaurant for those interested in resuming their positions at the Fleur-de-Leans. Scott was optimistic he would have a successful turnout.

Upon opening his eyes and taking deep, relaxing breaths, the mild headache that surfaced earlier had begun to subside. Before reviewing Davis' last menu, Scott decided to make himself a drink. He walked beneath the opulent chandelier centered high above the dining room on his way to the dimly lit bar. The wrought iron chandelier, the largest of five in the dining room, was as big as the eight-seat circular table over which it hovered. It was the only chandelier in the dining area currently illuminated, as it was enough to brighten the entire room when turned to its highest setting.

He slid his hand over the thick cypress planks that made up the bar's countertop on his way to the bottles of liquor located behind it. Scott didn't drink often (about once a month), and when he did it was only one drink. An alcoholic for eleven years of his life, Scott quit cold turkey when he lost his restaurant, his first wife, and visitation rights with his daughter all within one month's time. Very few knew of his alcohol-fueled past, and even fewer knew of his previous marriage and nine-year-old daughter. Eight years had passed since he last felt the effects of alcohol. Scott partook in the occasional drink to prove to himself he could control his demons. He poured Bombay Sapphire and a splash of tonic water over ice, garnishing it with a wedge of lime. While sipping on the cocktail, he listened to what was sure to be one of the last quiet moments in the restaurant.

Scott's thoughts eventually shifted from the restaurant to the meeting held earlier in the day with the Krewe. He was still in disbelief that Jackson—a young man he grew fond of while dating his niece—was responsible for the death of his brother. Jackson seemed nothing like the murdering type, thus causing concern with Scott. The only reason he sided with the rest of the Krewe was to avoid being the odd man out. More evidence, he felt, was needed before convicting Jackson of murder. As the idea of meeting with and talking to him came to mind, someone knocked on the entrance door. He approached the oversized wooden door, curious as to who was knocking on the other side. *Probably just a drunk pedestrian.* "We're closed!" he shouted.

"Even for your good friend Charlie Guichet?" the muffled voice asked.

Scott unlocked and opened the door. "Hey, Charlie."

"I had a feeling you might be in here." Charlie, wearing a suit as white as the hair atop his head, asked, "Is that bar of yours open?" So far, Scott had yet to see Charlie wear anything but a lightly colored suit.

"For you, anytime."

Charlie let out another of his belly-jiggling laughs as he stepped inside the restaurant. "And that's why I'm so fond of you, Scottie."

Scott led the way to the bar, where he stepped behind the counter. "What can I get you?"

"I know it's hard to believe," he said with a rub of his belly, "but I skipped dessert tonight. I could use something on the sweeter side."

"Grand Marnier?"

Charlie took to the stool. "You are reading my mind, Scottie."

Scott poured the cordial into a snifter, sliding it across the bar. Charlie set a hundred- dollar bill on the counter. "It's on the house, Charlie."

"No, sir. I want to officially be the first patron of the re-opened Fleur-de-Leans."

"I'm not charging you, especially eighty-five dollars more than the price of the drink."

"Consider it a tip." Charlie held the glass to his nose, inhaling deeply. "I dearly love the smell of a fine liqueur." He then placed the glass to his lips, slowly tilting his head backwards while ingesting the first sip.

"I thought you were headed to the Gulf Coast with your wife earlier this evening."

"That was our intention, but Mrs. Guichet developed a bit of a headache. She retired for the night, so I decided to take a walk after dinner and ended up here at your fine establishment."

Scott grabbed his drink from the counter. "You live close by?"

"Three blocks away. Mrs. Guichet and I bought a little condo here in the Quarter almost thirty years ago. We've seen a lot of change here in those three decades. Either we're getting older or the kids today are getting louder and more rambunctious."

"You haven't changed a bit, Charlie. Every time I see you, you look like you haven't aged a day."

Charlie belted out another laugh. "Scottie, you need to schedule a visit with an optometrist as soon as possible, for I fear you may have developed severe cataracts." He swallowed another sip before asking, "How's everything coming with the restaurant? Still hoping to open next weekend?"

"That's the plan. I'm having a meeting tomorrow with most of the former employees. I'm feeling good about it."

"That's incredible. The Krewe is proud of you, and you have our support. If you need something, anything, everything, just ask any of us."

"I will. Thank you." Scott took a sip, as did Charlie.

A brief moment of silence passed. Scott tried to think of something to say that wouldn't make it seem like he was slightly uncomfortable by Charlie's late-night surprise visit. Before he could mention how hot the weather was earlier in the day, Charlie asked, "How's little Thomas doing?"

"He's doing well. He was a little fussy earlier today because he didn't have his favorite teddy bear. Bridgett couldn't find it, so we had to go buy him a new one."

Charlie grinned. "Children and their toys. Thomas reminds me a lot of my son."

Scott couldn't recall Charlie ever mentioning a child. He assumed he and his wife never reproduced. "I didn't know you have a son."

"Had," he told him as the grin remained on his face. "He died very young."

"I'm so sorry, Charlie. I never knew."

Charlie's grin lessened. His eyes left Scott's as he looked off to the side. "He died many years ago. His immune system was very fragile. He got pneumonia at six and never recovered."

"My condolences, Charlie. I know that's very difficult to live with."

"The loss of a child is one of life's cruel misfortunes. Not a day has gone by in the last thirty-five years that I don't think of Charlie Guichet, III—or 'Trip' as Mrs. Guichet and myself called him. Trip was a handsome little devil." Charlie took a deep breath and exhaled before returning his gaze to Scott. "I don't want you to experience what I have suffered through, my dear friend."

"If Thomas gets so much as a sneeze, Bridgett has him at the pediatrician's office."

"I'm not talking about an illness for Thomas. I'm talking about you losing him."

Scott grew concerned as soon as the words left Charlie's mouth. "What are you talking about?"

Charlie crossed his arms above his stomach as he leaned back in the bar stool. "Your brother was a very loyal man. There is nothing he would not do for those close to him. Would you agree?"

"I would."

"Before I can proceed, I need you to tell me what you already know about how Thomas came to exist in your and Bridgett's life."

A feeling of numbness overcame Scott. He set his drink on the bar. "What's going on, Charlie."

"I need you to focus for a minute, and tell me what you know, Scottie. I assure you I am here to help. You have my word."

"He's adopted. We don't try to hide the truth from those close to us."

"What else do you know?"

"I know my brother might have arranged for the adoption to take place."

"Yes, he did. And do you know what he did to bring Thomas into you and your lovely wife's life?"

"I know my brother wasn't a saint. He probably did some things in his life I would have done differently. When my wife and I got the call from the adoption agency telling us they had a newborn baby for us after only four months of being on a list, I thought it was too good to be true. When I was told the baby was here in the New Orleans area and that Davis knew the woman from the adoption agency, I thought my brother may have been involved. I imagined a sum of money may have been exchanged as well. I suspected something, but I never approached Davis about it. To be honest, if dirty politics were involved, I don't want to know anything about it. But, now that you're sitting here and asking me about my son, I'm very concerned and a bit scared. If we were to lose him…"

Scott balled his hand into a fist, hovering it just above the bar. Tears were on the verge of streaming down his face. "We love him so much."

Charlie grabbed his hand, gently shaking it while telling him, "You're not losing him, Scottie. There is no need to worry."

"How do you know?"

"Have you forgotten about your friends? We protect and look after one another. We're not going to let anything happen to you, your wife, or that handsome son of yours."

"Are you sure about that?"

Charlie again laughed. "Scottie, think about the professions that encompass our little… networking group—as you call it. I don't want to sound too conceited, but we are untouchable in the great city of New Orleans, my good friend."

Scott managed to prevent from shedding any tears. "I hope you're right."

"There is no need to hope, Scottie, because yours truly is right, or my name isn't Charles Woodrow Guichet, II. Now, are you sure there's nothing else you know about your son's adoption, such as who the birth mother is or anything of that nature?"

"I know nothing else, but something tells me you may know more than me."

Charlie swallowed the last sip of his drink. After setting the empty snifter onto the bar, he wiped at his mouth with the handkerchief from his pocket. "I do, and I'm telling you this now—per Davis' request."

Chapter 92

Tiffany opened the door to the guest bedroom of her mom's house following a bedtime shower. She was none-too-pleased by the sight of a dozen or so flickering candles on the dresser and nightstands. Whenever Brett lit candles in the past, it meant one thing and one thing only.

She was in no mood for sex. The death of her father was still sinking in, while the ridiculous assumption that Jackson was responsible for his death had been on her mind for hours. "If you're trying to get in my pants, it's not happening."

A shirtless Brett lay on the king-sized bed with an open book resting upon his chest. "I don't want to have sex tonight."

"Liar. I know what lit candles mean." She crawled into bed.

"And I know what sweat pants to bed means—you're not interested in sex. You see how well we know each other." He leaned over, kissing her forehead before focusing his attention to the book in hand.

"I've never seen you read a book anywhere but on an airplane. What are you reading?"

"A romance book. Your mom loaned it to me."

Tiffany, to make certain Brett didn't attempt to make any moves on her, placed her backside against the left side of his body as she lay in the fetal position. "Those books are so cheesy. Why are you reading it?" she asked with shut eyes.

"I love romance."

The only book she had seen him read was a biography on the life of Kurt Cobain. "Since when?"

"Your question has me wondering whether or not you find me to be romantic." She didn't respond. "Tif, am I romantic?"

"Yes."

"Am I the most romantic guy you have ever dated?"

"Sure."

"That didn't sound very reassuring. You didn't find the poem I wrote for you to be romantic? Or the lobster dinner I prepared last month? Or how I surprised you by painting your living room while you were at work?"

"Those were all very sweet and romantic."

"But not the most romantic?"

Instead of answering, Tiffany remained shut-eyed and nestled in a ball. The mattress shifted. She could feel Brett peering over her body. She tried not to but couldn't help smiling at her envious boyfriend. Tiffany found delight in bringing him to a jealous state, as it meant he was still infatuated with her.

"Who was more romantic than me?"

"Nobody. You're number one."

"Was it him?"

She knew exactly to whom he was referring. "I have no idea who you're talking about."

"Your ex-fiancé?" Again, she didn't answer. "What was the most romantic thing he did?"

"What does it matter? And why are you so competitive all the time?"

"Did he ever write you a poem too?"

"Once."

"What was it called?"

"It was titled 'shut up and go to bed.'"

"Come on, tell me."

"If I tell you, will you go to bed?"

"Yep."

"Infinite love."

Brett laughed. "Are you serious? That sounds like a Celine Dion song. Did it win a Grammy?"

"Shut up. It was good."

"You're defending the guy who dumped you on your wedding day."

Tiffany, yet to tell Brett the truth of her nuptials, was determined to never let him discover her indiscretion. So far, he had not heard about the video played at her wedding. Friends and family members were instructed to never mention it again. Part of the reason she still resided in Dallas was because Brett was less likely to discover the truth. If he were to ever find out, she was prepared to tell him the entire video was staged. Jackson, she told him, was addicted to cocaine. Following the wedding, she was going to bring him to a rehab center to get help. He refused, walking out of the ceremony before it was complete. "I'm just saying he was romantic."

"Who would have thought a crackhead could be so romantic?" Brett's tone had shades of jealousy. "I'm going to finish reading this book."

Silence filled the room, causing Tiffany to feel slight guilt for making her boyfriend envious of a past relationship. "What's the name of the book?"

"The Proposal."

"I'm sure the title says it all, but what's it about?"

"A man who falls madly in love with a slightly younger woman, who was left at the altar by her cocaine-snorting ex-fiancé two years prior. He has been dating the woman for only nine months and he wants to propose, but he's worried she may think it's too soon."

Tiffany opened her eyes, slowly turning onto her back.

"The woman, who is the most beautiful woman the protagonist has ever seen, just lost her father, and the man feels she needs him more than ever. He wants to propose, even though it's not the ideal location."

A nervous Tiffany glanced at the book cover. Nowhere on it did the word 'proposal' appear. In fact, no words appeared on what looked like a book, but was instead a hollowed out decorative piece. Her mom had something just like it on one of the shelves in the living room armoire. "That's not a book you're holding."

"I know."

"And the synopsis of what you just said sounds..."

"Awfully familiar?" he asked with a grin.

She sat up. "I hope you're not doing what I think you may be doing right now," she told him, sans smile.

His face had a glow about it as he asked, "So, if I were to tell you there was an engagement ring currently sitting on my chest right now, you wouldn't want to at least look at it?" She glanced at his chest, yet the fake book blocked her view. She attempted to move it, but his grip was overpowering. "What are you looking for, dear?"

"I want to see if you're telling the truth." She tried to move the book for a second time. Her strength proved useless against his. Frustrated, she lay back down.

"What if I am?"

She shut her eyes once more upon coming to a realization. "You're not."

"Why do you say that?"

"Because you wouldn't propose in bed. It's not very romantic. Besides, you know where and when I want to be proposed to."

"I don't give a shit about where and when and how. When I'm ready, I'm going to do it wherever I want to. And if I want to pop the question right here in the same bed you used to dream about your Prince Charming, then I'm going to damn well do it."

Tiffany had never heard Brett act so assertively. "Are you feeling okay?"

"I will if you answer 'yes'."

She opened her eyes to find something shiny hovering inches in front of her face. After focusing on it, she grew shocked at what Brett held in his hand. "What is that?"

"What does it look like?"

"An engagement ring."

"You're so smart, Tif."

She again sat up. Her eyes remained fixed on the ring. The center diamond on the platinum band looked to be at least two carats. It was cut just the way she wanted it (princess) and it was beautiful. "Why do you have it?"

"Because I love you and want to prove to you for the rest of your life I'm the most romantic person you've ever dated."

"Brett, that's an engagement ring. Are you asking me to marry you…right now?"

"I sure am."

"Baby, I'm in my pajamas. Besides, we're not at—"

"I know we're not in New York in Central Park, and I know it's not Christmas and there's no snow on the ground, but I can't wait that long. Yes, you are in your pajamas and I don't have a shirt on, but I can't wait any longer. I already asked your mom and she gave me her blessing." Brett stood, walked around the bed, and then knelt next to her. "Tiffany Melancon, will you marry me?"

Her heart was nearly pounding out of her chest. "Are you really doing this now?"

"The sermon the priest gave during your dad's funeral really got to me. When he talked about treasuring the moments you have with loved ones, I couldn't stop thinking about you. I thought about the memories we've so far shared with one another, and how I want to make several more unforgettable memories with you—starting with this one."

"But we're in bed and—"

"Stop saying that, damnit," he spoke behind clinched teeth. "I don't give a flying shit about how you want to be proposed to. I'm tired of you having everything always planned out. I'm being spontaneous because that's how I like to do things sometimes. Now, stop your whining and answer the damn question. Tiffany Melancon, will you marry me? The next word out of your mouth better be a 'yes' or 'no'."

She found his domineering behavior to be quite a turn on. Widely grinning, she answered, "Yes."

He shut his eyes and lifted his head upwards. "Thank God." Upon opening his eyes, Brett slid the ring on the appropriate finger. "If you would have said no, I probably would have punched a hole in the wall."

Tiffany glanced at the ring by candlelight. She found it to be the most gorgeous ring she had ever seen—even more spectacular than her previous engagement ring. "I've never seen you so aggressive, baby. I kinda like it."

"Good, because I've kinda been holding back."

She placed both hands on his cheeks while kissing him. "I love you so much, baby."

Sunday

Chapter 93

With her bare feet resting on the dashboard, Caroline asked me, "Why are we getting off in El Paso?" Her toenails, like her fingernails, were French-manicured.

"I want you to meet somebody."

"Who? A friend?"

"More like an acquaintance."

We soon pulled into the parking lot of the same motel where I resided for nearly a week, twenty months earlier. Nothing had changed. The exterior of the building looked like it was still in desperate need of a fresh coat of paint, the parking lot was nearly empty, and the shrubbery could use a green thumb's touch.

"Your acquaintance is at this motel?"

"Close by." I parked in front of room 128. "Wait here. I'll be right back."

A young Hispanic woman sat behind the counter. While glancing at the dozens of keys on the wall behind her, I discovered my old room was available. I handed the woman $57.00 in cash.

Caroline, with her back to me as she stood next to the 4-Runner, stretched her arms overhead while bending backwards. The afternoon sun shined down upon her, creating a sight that was almost heaven-like. I was ready to pin her against the car and again kiss her with Pompeiian intensity.

As I grew closer, she turned around, smiled, and then asked me, "Are we staying here tonight?"

I quickly realized it wasn't time for another Pompeiian kiss. That type of kiss can't be planned; it must happen spontaneously and follow a confession of pent up emotions that could no longer be held inside because they were too honest and too combustible to be bottled. Instead, I only imagined kissing her while again asking myself if I was moving too soon. "Yes, but just for the night."

"This place looks a little rundown."

I placed the key in the lock. "Yes, it still does."

"You've been here before?"

I nodded, pushing the door open. The room looked just as it had when I left. The carpet, television, bedspread, lamps, and lighting fixture above the table were still outdated. I was certain if I looked under the bed, I might find one of the sleeping pills I threw onto the floor nearly two years earlier.

Caroline set her purse on the table next to the window. "I don't mind chipping in if you want to stay someplace a little more…updated."

After placing the car keys next to her purse, I sat on the bed. "I almost died right here."

"Come again?"

"I almost died on this very bed, six days after my first wedding."

"How?" Caroline looked genuinely concerned while sitting on the bed to my right.

"After playing the video of Tiffany confessing to cheating on me, I got in my car and started driving west. I found myself here in El Paso on Sunday night. I lied on this very bed, turned off all the lights, threw a blanket over the window, and ingested sleeping pills. Whenever I woke up, I swallowed more sleeping pills." She squeezed my left hand as I stared at the ground. "I had this very vivid dream I was just moments away from death. I woke up gasping for air. It felt so real."

"How long did you sleep?"

"Five days." She squeezed my hand tighter. "I didn't realize it, or maybe I did but just couldn't admit to it at the time, but…."

"What?"

I couldn't say the words. I was worried it would make me look weak and pathetic. "Nothing."

"You can tell me anything, Jackson," she softly spoke into my ear. The warmth of her breath sent chills throughout my body. I was putty in her hands.

"I think, subconsciously, I was attempting to…end it all."

As it had done over the course of the last four months, Caroline's embrace comforted me. "I'm glad you didn't succeed. Really glad."

"After waking up on that fifth day…" I grabbed her hand, pulling her up from the bed as we both stood, "and stumbling across the parking lot…" I led her outside before pointing in the direction of the diner, "I ended up over there."

We soon stepped into Edie's diner. Just as it was the last time I had visited, hardly any patrons filled the diner. A familiar face emerged from the kitchen. Edith smiled, but I couldn't decipher if it was a 'hi, stranger' kind of smile, or an 'I remember you' kind of smile. Hank Williams' *There's a Tear in my Beer* played in the kitchen.

"Welcome to Edie's. How y'all doing?" A smiley face sticker was still attached to her nametag.

Hoping she would remember me, I even sat on the same bar stool. Caroline sat to my right. "We're doing great."

Edith placed two menus in front of us. "What can I get you two to drink?"

"Iced tea please," Caroline spoke.

"Same for me, Edith."

Edith squinted briefly at me before walking away. Perhaps she was starting to remember.

"When do I get to meet this acquaintance of yours?"

I gave a nod in the direction of Edith. "That's her."

"The waitress?"

"Yes."

"You know her?"

I could see Edith's husband—whose name I couldn't recall—in the kitchen. He still had his thick beard and was again singing along to a classic country tune. It felt nostalgic to be back in the diner. "I met her last time I was here. She gave me some uplifting advice."

"What did she say?"

Edith approached us and set the glasses on the counter. "Two iced teas." While staring intently at me, she said, "Pardon me for prying, but you look familiar, young man."

I don't know why it was so important for Edith to remember me, but I was glad she did. I smiled while saying, "About twenty months ago—"

"I got it," she said with a snap of her fingers and a widening of her eyes. "You're the man from the news. You were the one they thought died on the airplane. Am I right?"

47

She knew who I was but didn't remember me. "Yes, ma'am."

"You sure are lucky to be alive. Can I ask your name?"

"Jackson. And this is Caroline."

Edith, while leaning across the counter, said, "I was so intrigued by your story, Jackson. My husband and I followed it until…wait a minute. Are you the fiancée?" she asked Caroline. Her smile was as big as her eyes.

We looked at one another. Before I could speak, Caroline held her left hand up. "Yes. My ring's getting resized as we speak."

"I'm glad to see you two are together. You make a beautiful couple."

Caroline flashed her infectious smile. "Why, thank you, Edith."

"You're welcome." She was beaming. "Did you two decide on anything yet?"

"What's good here?" Caroline asked.

"The burger is the best you'll ever have," I told her.

Edith winked at me before telling Caroline, "Your fiancé's right. Al makes a darn good burger."

"I've never been one to turn down a darn good burger," Caroline said. "Medium-well with a side of fries please."

I handed Edith both menus. "The same for me, Edith."

"You got it." Edith walked toward the kitchen, looking back along the way and offering a smile.

Caroline cleared her throat. "I apologize."

"About what?"

"Proclaiming to be your fiancée. I figured it would bypass minutes of head scratching explanations."

"If you didn't say yes, I was going to."

After tucking her hair behind her ear and grinning, she glanced at Edith through the kitchen window. "Not to be a Debbie Downer, but I don't think she remembers you in the way you were hoping."

"It seems that way." I watched as Edith pointed towards us through the kitchen window while talking to her husband. Al smiled, waving before returning his attention to his wife. I recalled Edith's story from twenty months earlier—how her first husband left her, and she then met the man who appeared to be the best thing to ever happen to her. I wondered if my life was starting to somewhat parallel Edith's.

"They look happy," Caroline told me.

"That they do." As I looked into Caroline's eyes, I realized I didn't care anymore. I didn't care I almost married someone else the day before. I didn't care if Logan, Dr. Blanchard, my parents, or anyone else thought I moved too quickly between relationships. I didn't care about anyone's thoughts or opinions except Caroline's. I leaned towards her, placing my lips directly on hers. Our kiss wasn't Pompeiian, but it still gave me goosebumps. "I couldn't wait any longer to kiss you again," I told her upon pulling away.

Her face lit up. "Me neither."

Just as I had experienced the last time I was in Edie's diner, I felt at peace even though chaos surrounded me.

While eating our burgers, we couldn't stop smiling at one another. The tingling sensation lasted throughout lunch. No longer was I involved in a love triangle. Caroline was the only woman I wanted to be with. It was just me and her. I was ready to start my life over in a new city with someone I was certain would never lie to me—unlike most everyone else who was important in my life had done.

Edith placed a small tray containing twenty quarters on the counter in exchange for the $5 bill in my hand. "Even though I saw you on the news channel this week, Jackson, I still feel like we may have crossed paths before. Or maybe you just have one of those faces."

She was finally starting to remember. "It was about twenty months ago. I had a rough week, and it was pretty noticeable. I sat in this exact spot and ordered the same meal you just brought us. I asked if you were married, and you told me how you found the love of your life back there." I pointed to the kitchen.

After appearing to be in deep thought, Edith soon nodded. "You looked lost and confused when you came in here. I thought you were on drugs. Turns out you had just gotten out of a relationship."

"I was going through one of the worst moments of my life. You gave me some advice I still carry with me. You said—"

"'Don't give up. True love is out there waiting for you to sweep her off her feet.' I think it was something to that effect."

She had remembered perfectly. Once again, Edith helped in lifting my spirits. "You're exactly right. It wasn't any kind of earth-shattering advice, but it stayed with me for quite some time."

She pointed at Caroline. "And was I right?"

I made eye contact with the blonde next to me. "Very much so."

Caroline blushed while grabbing and squeezing my hand.

"I'm glad I could help. Now, if I'm not mistaken, the wedding was supposed to have been yesterday, correct?" Edith must not have seen the interview with the reporter outside of Delain's house.

"Correct," I told her.

"I don't want to step on any toes, and please tell me to mind my own business if I'm prying, but are you two gonna actually…?"

"Tie the knot?" Caroline asked.

Edith nodded, eagerly awaiting an answer while flashing her comforting smile.

We again looked at one another. Caroline's lips began to move, but I answered before she could. "I'd be stupid if I let this one get away."

"I saw the kiss you two shared a little while ago. The both of you lit up as you lovingly stared into each other's eyes. You two looked like you just shared a first kiss or something. I think the future's very promising for the both of you."

Caroline again blushed. "You really think so?"

Edith's smile was as big as Caroline's. "I do—no pun intended. And I think the both of you need a piece of cherry pie— it's on the house. I'll be right back."

Caroline grabbed my hand. "I like Edith. I see why you wanted me to meet her."

Even though I was hopeful about my future with Caroline, I became concerned about my past while glancing at the quarters on the counter. I didn't want to do it, but knew I had to check in to see what had transpired since we had been away.

"Here you go, one piece of homemade cherry pie." Edith placed the golden-crusted pie on the counter along with two forks. "Now, every slice of complimentary pie at Edie's comes with a piece of advice. This is for the both of you, so listen closely—Never go to bed angry, never leave for work angry, never hang up the phone angry, and never forget to say 'I love you' because you never know if it's the last time you'll get to say those words to each other. That's Edith's advice for this visit."

"You always give great advice. We'll be sure to remember that."

Edith smiled. "Y'all enjoy."

We finished the pie, said our goodbyes to Edith, and walked outside to a nearby payphone. Before calling Logan, I dialed my cell phone number to listen to the messages. The first message was from the person I still had difficulty in calling Dad, asking of my whereabouts. Marcus and Logan called as well, also inquiring about my location. A second message from my brother was placed after midnight.

'Jackson, Mom's not doing so well. She's in a comatose state right now. I've never seen her this way before. I think everything that's going on is too much for her. She needs to see you. Also, Vincent called Ralph's cell phone a little while ago. I hate to be the bearer of bad news, but I think he's coming for you. Call my cell as soon as you get this. We're all very concerned about you. Call me a.s.a.p.'

I skipped to the next message, wondering if El Paso was as far west Caroline and I would make on our trip.

"Is everything okay?"

"My mom's not doing well."

"What's wrong with her?"

"Marcus says she's in a comatose state."

"Do we need to go back?"

"I don't know if it's safe to do that. He said Vincent is looking for me."

"The mobster guy?"

"Yep." I felt sick to my stomach as I continued listening to the messages. The next call was placed at 2:35 in the morning.

'Jackson Fabacher, this is an old friend of yours.' I recognized the voice as the person Caroline and I had just discussed. *'Not only did you invade a very personal property of mine, but you then killed my best friend. I'll be seeing you soon, Loverboy.'*

After hanging up, I imagined Vincent standing over not only my body, but also Caroline's as we lay in a hole with dirt being shoveled over us. The thought of Caroline and I being buried alive after getting beat to near death with a baseball bat caused my throat to constrict. The gut-punching feeling I experienced moments earlier after hearing from my brother that Vincent was looking for me was nothing compared to the uneasiness felt upon hearing the demented man's voice. Feeling light-headed, I squatted, placing all my weight on my toes while resting my forearms on my thighs.

"What's wrong, Jackson?"

I closed my eyes. Caroline and I were suffocating to death beneath a mound of Texas dirt as Vincent belted out his big Italian laugh several feet above us. It was difficult to breathe. "I need to sit down." A bench was a few feet away on the side of Edie's diner, but I chose the concrete beneath my feet instead.

Caroline knelt in front of me. "I'm here for you," she told me while rubbing my back. "Now, what's wrong?"

I soon realized she and I weren't being buried alive, yet I still panicked. "Vincent left a message. He said he was coming for me. You have to get as far away from me as possible, Caroline. This asshole already tried to kill me once. If he was pissed off before his partner was killed, you can only imagine how angry he is now."

"I already told you I'm not leaving."

"If something were to happen—"

"I'm not leaving you! Get it through your thick head!" The resolute look on her face was enough confirmation for me to shut up because I wasn't going to win the argument.

"We have to be careful and protect ourselves."

"I have a gun."

"Al's gun?"

She nodded.

"Delain said you returned it."

With a shrug of her shoulders, she said, "She wanted me to return it, but I wasn't ready."

"Al doesn't know it's missing?"

"He's got like twenty guns. He probably doesn't know yet."

A car sped by the diner at a speed well past the 35 mph limit. I momentarily froze, fearful it was Vincent. Once it passed, I thought it wise to get the gun in one of our hands. "Where is it?"

"In my purse." Caroline's attention shifted to the motel. "Over there in…" Her face was one of bewilderment as she rose to her feet. From where she stood, she could see our motel room. My vision was blocked by the corner of Edie's diner.

"What is it?"

"A black SUV with tinted windows just pulled up next to your car."

I jumped to my feet, pulling her out of sight from whoever was in the vehicle. I wasted no time in peering around the corner. Two men dressed in dark suits I had a feeling I would see again exited the S.U.V. One was white and the other black. "Shit," I mumbled. "How did they find us?"

"Who are they?"

"F.B.I. agents. They're the ones who interrogated me in Arizona after you dropped me off, and the same ones at my house yesterday."

She grabbed my hand. "Do you think they're here to arrest you?"

Agent Parker knocked on the motel door of room 126 while Agent Williams scanned the parking lot. Once his gaze was nearly aimed in the direction of the diner, we scooted back against the wall. "I don't know. They don't have their guns drawn."

"What are we going to do? Should we keep running?"

Across the street was a liquor store. I handed Caroline the room key. "Go back in the diner and wait a few minutes for me to get the agents out of here. After we drive off, go in the room, get the car keys and get out of here. First, I need to get something from the liquor store."

"You're giving yourself up? What if they arrest you?"

"At least you won't be arrested."

"That's the dumbest thing you've ever said." Caroline grabbed the room key. "How about you go wait behind the liquor store? I'll be there in a few minutes to pick you up." She took a step toward the motel. I pulled her back.

"What are you doing?" I frantically whispered.

"Getting them away from the motel so I can get my purse and the car keys from the room."

"Are you nuts? You can't get the car from under their nose. They know it's mine. If they see you drive off in it, they're going to know you're with me."

"I better be careful then." She removed my hand from her arm. "You have about one minute to get across the street. Whatever you do, don't go back in the diner. See you soon." Before I could again grab her, she began her walk towards the agents.

Chapter 94

Caroline nervously twirled the room key around her finger while approaching the federal agents. *Deep breaths. It's not the first time you've done something like this. Jackson needs you.* Both men stared at her from behind sunglasses as they stood in front of room 128. She smiled before saying in her Australian accent, "G'day, gents."

"How are you, ma'am?" the bald white gentleman asked.

Since the agents had knocked on another door before knocking on the one she and Jackson were staying in, she assumed they didn't know which room they were staying in. "Well, I'm a little nervous since two men are standing in front of my room, mate."

"I apologize, ma'am." The white gentleman reached into his back pocket, telling her, "My name is Agent Parker, and this is Agent Williams." He then held up a black wallet containing his identification. The letters F.B.I. were easily visible.

"May I see that please?"

"Sure." Agent Parker handed her his identification.

After inspecting it, she handed it back. "Thanks. I've heard stories about men pretending to be federal agents, and then abducting women. It looks real to me, mate."

Agent Parker returned the wallet to his pocket. "You never can be too careful. You're a smart young woman."

"I know. Now, how can I help the two of you?"

"We're looking for the owner of this black 4-Runner. Did you happen to see him, Ms…I'm sorry. I didn't get your name."

Chloe was on the tip of her tongue, but before it could come out, she answered, "Bonnie. And I haven't seen who the vehicle belongs to."

"Nice to meet you, Bonnie. Are you staying in this motel?"

She held up the room key. Her stomach was in knots as she told him, "Yes, in the very room you're standing in front of."

"By yourself or with someone?"

"With my fiancé." She held up her left hand. "My ring is getting resized."

"May I ask his name?"

"Of course." Caroline contemplated not saying it, but couldn't resist. "Clyde."

Agent Parker grinned. "Bonnie and Clyde?"

With a shrug of the shoulders, she told him, "I know. We hear it all the time. But I can promise we haven't, nor plan to, rob any banks or kill anyone. He was named after his grandfather. In actuality, we were introduced to one another by a mutual friend because of our names."

"Is Clyde available? Perhaps he has seen the driver of this vehicle."

"He's at a job interview right now with the border patrol. Do you have a picture of the person you're looking for? Maybe I've seen him around."

Agent Parker looked to his partner. "We do."

As Agent Williams walked to his vehicle, Caroline asked, "Can I ask what he did, mate? Should I be concerned if someone staying in this motel is dangerous?"

"No, ma'am. He's just needed for questioning." Agent Williams returned, holding up a 4"×6" picture. Even though Caroline had anticipated it, she grew even more nervous while staring at an image of Jackson. "Have you seen him, Bonnie?"

She nodded, pointing towards Edie's. "He's in that diner right over there."

"Are you sure?"

"Yep. He was heading towards the bathroom as I walked out. He smiled at me. I smiled back. He's kind of cute."

Agent Williams briskly walked across the parking lot towards the diner with the picture in hand. Agent Parker nodded to Caroline while saying, "Thank you, Bonnie." He then followed his partner.

Once the agents were out of sight, Caroline quickly grabbed her and Jackson's belongings from the room. After locking the room and bringing the key with her, she threw her purse in the passenger seat of the 4-Runner and started the ignition. Before backing up, inspiration struck. She hurried to the agents' vehicle. Not only were the doors unlocked, but the keys were still in the ignition. She removed them, hiding them under the driver's seat, before locking and shutting the door.

While reversing out of the parking spot, she assumed the agents were probably questioning Edith at that exact moment. It would only be a matter of seconds before they discovered she wasn't Australian, her name wasn't Bonnie, and Jackson wasn't a stranger.

She drove around the motel to avoid driving in front of Edie's, soon finding a street leading her to the liquor store. Caroline pulled behind it. She watched as Jackson peered around the side of the building. His back was to her. She rolled down the window, whistling to him.

Chapter 95

"I'm pretty sure I just committed a crime," Caroline confessed once I shut the passenger door.

"What did you do?"

"Told a few lies before locking their keys in their car."

"Holy shit!" I was equal parts scared and impressed by her actions. After hearing what Caroline did to get Davis back to his house, and what she had just done to two federal agents' car keys, I realized there was more to her than meets the eye. "You got a little rebellious side, don't you?"

She smirked while pulling onto the highway. "It just comes out of me sometimes."

I opened the glove box and began rummaging for a brochure. "What did you say to the agents?"

"My name was Bonnie, my fiancé was away on an interview with the border patrol, and that I saw you eating in the diner. Once they hurried over, I ran inside and got our things."

"We may have to get rid of my car."

"Why?"

"Because of this." I showed her the brochure of the device that more than likely led the agents to the motel.

"LoJack?"

"It's how they find stolen vehicles. There's a device somewhere on this car."

"Can we take it off?"

After skimming through the brochure, I grew discouraged. "It says there are about fifty places it could be hidden. We don't have time to look for it." I turned around to make sure the agents weren't following us. Paranoia was setting in yet again. "Start looking for a rental car company. We need another car, and quickly."

We headed north on Highway 180. While I dug in her purse to retrieve the pieces of her phone, a sign caught Caroline's attention. "An airport's close by, which means rental cars."

"Good thinking. Head that way." I put the phone back together then powered it on. "I need to call my brother and see how my mom's doing."

"Do you think he's making it up to get you home?"

"I hope so, but I doubt it." As I dialed my brother's cell number, I noticed the battery was running low. "Do you have a car charger for your phone?"

"No."

"Hello?"

"Marcus."

"Jackson! Where the hell are you?" He sounded like he was in a car as well.

"Texas."

"Are you okay?"

"Yes. How's Mom?"

"We had to rush her to the hospital early this morning."

"What happened?" Vincent's face came to mind as I awaited an answer. I was on the verge of vomiting.

"Her eyes are open, but she can't talk or move. She hasn't eaten since the party on Friday. Whatever part of Texas you're in, you need to get home now."

I found slight relief knowing Vincent wasn't involved. "We're in El Paso."

"You and Delain?"

Caroline pulled into the parking lot of an Enterprise. "No. Me and Caroline."

"What the hell are you doing with her, and why are y'all in El Paso? Where's Delain?"

"It's a long story. I'll explain when I get home. We're turning the car around as we speak."

"Did you get my message about Vincent?"

"Yes. He left me one as well."

Caroline put the car in park. She grabbed her purse from the backseat while whispering to me, "I'll be right back."

"What did he say?"

I scanned the parking lot as she walked into the building. "In a nutshell—that he was coming to kill me."

"That's what he said in front of me, Dad, and Logan last night. I have a gun with me at all times now. I told Melanie to join the boys at her parents' house until this blows over. I just wish we knew what Vincent looked like. Dad's got some of his friends trying to figure it out as we speak."

"He's big, ugly, and has a thick moustache and thinning black hair. You'll know when you see him. Where are you going now?"

"Back to the hospital to see Mom. I think there's an airport in El Paso. It's going to be better if you can fly here and see her as quickly as possible. I think you may be the only one who can bring her back to normality."

I was worried the agents would have the means to find me if I flew back home. "I can't fly, but we're heading that way now. We'll take turns driving. I'll be there as quickly as I can. Which hospital?"

"Ochsner."

"I have to turn the phone off because the battery is almost dead, so if anything happens, call this number, and I'll check it later tonight."

"Get here as quickly as you can, Jackson."

"I will." I hung up and again dismantled the phone.

Caroline soon returned with car keys in her hand. "Got us a new ride."

"We have to go back to New Orleans now."

"Then get your ass out of the car."

Chapter 96

After hanging a framed picture of her dad on the wall near the entrance of the Fleur-de-Leans, Tiffany stepped back to make sure the 8"×12" picture—taken the morning the restaurant first opened—was level. After straightening it, she wiped at her eyes. Tiffany—barely a teenager—remembered how excited her father was for the photo shoot. It was the only moment of the day, however, she saw him smile. The dates at the bottom of the picture marking his birth date and the day he died, made her once again think about what Mitch had told her on the side of her parents' house. It was hard to fathom that Jackson may have been the catalyst for her father's death. Still, the allegations had crossed her mind several times in the last twenty-four hours. Also in her thoughts was the notion that, for years, Mitch had an attraction to her. A pass was never made at her and nothing inappropriate had ever crossed his lips, but her gut feeling was that if she were to kiss him, he wouldn't pull away. *Could he have just made those allegations up about Jackson because he's been jealous of him all this time?*

"Your father was the most nervous I had ever seen him that day," Victoria proclaimed, "and so was I." She wrapped her arms around Tiffany, resting her chin on her daughter's right shoulder. "Nothing went as planned. The produce truck delivered only about half of what we originally ordered, so I had to run to Schwegmann's and buy two buggy's worth of fruits and vegetables. The newspaper article put the wrong opening date. There was barely anyone here when we opened. Your father had to go outside and round customers up. Before the night was over, we had a small fire in the kitchen. It was a mess," she said with a chuckle. "I thought for sure we were going to lose every dime we invested. But, your father said he was going to be successful, and he was right. He created a legacy here in New Orleans."

"He did good…and so did you. I remember how much you helped out in those early years— hosting and making sure all the employees were in good spirits."

"Don't exclude yourself, missy. You were the most beautiful and charming hostess in the whole city. Everyone said so." Victoria grabbed her daughter's hand, turning her around. "He would have liked Brett very much. I know he would have given his blessing for Brett to marry you."

"I think so too."

"And I'm certain he would have liked him a lot more than that idiot you almost married," Victoria spoke with a deadpan stare aimed over Tiffany's shoulder at the picture.

"Are you bringing him up again?" She let go of her mom's hand. "I thought we weren't going to talk about that any longer."

"It just came out. I'm sorry."

With gritted teeth, she told her mom, "I swear to God if you mention him one more time…" Shaking her head, she told her, "I'm going to see if Uncle Scott needs anything else done before Brett and I leave." Tiffany stormed off in the direction of the kitchen, passing her fiancé as he stood atop a ladder in the bar area.

"Can you hand me another dust rag, babe?"

She turned around, grabbing a folded rag from a box before handing it to him. "Here," she affirmatively told him.

"Are you okay?"

All she could think about was Jackson and the accusations. "Just tired. We're leaving in a minute." She continued to the kitchen.

Scott, wearing a white, double-breasted chef's coat, stood behind a metal table while preparing a dish. "Hey, Tiffy." His smile was noticeably absent.

She glanced around the kitchen. "Where's Aunt Bridgett?"

"She went to the airport to pick up our babysitter from back home. We've been so busy with the restaurant, we needed an extra hand with Thomas."

Tiffany pulled a stool up to the table. While sitting directly across from her uncle, she proceeded to tell him what she had observed throughout the afternoon. "You've been acting different today."

His focus remained on the dish before him as he asked, "How so?"

"You're quieter than usual, and more distant."

"I apologize. There's a lot going on."

Tiffany rested her elbows on the table and her chin upon her hands. "Anything you care to talk about?"

Scott drizzled a copper-colored sauce over a large scoop of ice cream before saying, "Your father…"

"What about him?"

"He was…something special."

"How do you mean?"

Scott slid the oversized bowl in front of Tiffany. "He was a great man, and I wish he was still around so I could talk to him—that's all." He then finally made eye contact with his niece. "Now, onto business. This is my newest creation." He placed a spoon next to the bowl.

"What is it?"

"Banana bread pudding doused in a brown sugar and rum sauce, served beneath a scoop of slow-churned, bourbon-enhanced vanilla ice cream drizzled with a sea salt infused caramel sauce. I'm calling call it bananas foster bread pudding. Tell me what you think."

Tiffany slowly picked herself up from the table.

"Speaking of not being themselves today, you seem a little off yourself. You just got engaged. Aren't you excited?"

"I guess."

"Your dad's passing still on your mind?"

"Yes, but that's not the only thing."

"What else is—"

"She keeps bringing him up and it pisses me off."

"Who and who are you talking about?"

"Mom keeps bringing up Jackson and what he did at the wedding. She keeps calling him names and it makes me mad."

"Can I ask why it angers you?"

"I don't know, it just does. I've finally gotten over what happened, but she still brings it up. I hate it."

"Are you sure you're over him?"

"Yes."

"Positive?"

"I think so."

"Let me ask you this: how did you feel when you heard he died in the plane crash?"

Tiffany was on the way to her Saturday morning Yoga class when a friend called to tell her the news. She had to pull onto the shoulder of the highway. "I was numb at first. I couldn't believe he was dead. I hate saying this, but a small part of me was relieved I would never see him again. I wasn't sure how I would react if we ran into one another. I didn't know if I would curse him, slap him, or cry in his arms and tell him I still loved him." Tiffany looked over her shoulder, making sure Brett hadn't snuck into the kitchen. "I truly did love him, Uncle Scott, and I still hate myself for cheating on him."

"Well, time travel doesn't exist yet, so all we can do is learn from our mistakes and try not to repeat them."

"I hated him for so long, but once I saw him on the news, old feelings started to resurface."

"If you don't want to talk about him any longer then you can tell me to mind my own business, but can I ask you something else?"

As her uncle aged, Tiffany noticed how similar he and her father looked like one another. Scott's hair was identical to Davis' before he shaved it off, and their smiles were mirror images to one another's. Even the way they talked was eerily similar. In a way, it felt like she was talking to her dad. She reached for the spoon, inserting it deep into the dessert. "You can ask me anything." She placed the bite into her mouth. "Oh my. This is amazing, Uncle Scott."

He grinned. "You're the first to try it. Should I put it on the menu?"

"This is going to be the signature dessert; I have no doubt about it." She took another bite before setting the spoon down. After swallowing, she asked him, "What were you going to ask about Jackson?"

Scott began to unfasten the first of twelve buttons on his chef's coat. 'Melancon' was embroidered on the right breast and 'Fleur-de-Leans' graced the left side. "This was your dad's. I hope you don't mind if I wear it."

"Not at all, but you're the only one who can."

"Thank you." His grin lessened before he cleared his throat. "When you and Jackson stayed with me a few years back, my opinion of him was that he was a very respectful and genuinely good guy. Am I correct?"

"Yes."

"He doesn't seem like a violent person."

"I've never seen him get angry with anyone. He's never been in a fight to tell you the truth."

"That's the impression I got about him too."

Tiffany grew apprehensive by his questioning, especially since it was coming off the heels of Mitch's accusations. "Why are you asking this?"

He grabbed his left ear while telling her, "Just curious. Do you think Brett and your mom would like to try my new creation?"

"You and Dad are different in many ways. Whereas you are laid back, reserved, and easy going, he was much more extroverted, louder, and uptight than you. However, the two of you share some similarities and mannerisms. For instance, whenever he was lying to me, he would grab his ear—like you just did. So, let's have at it, Uncle Scott. Why the peculiar question about my ex-fiancé?"

Scott hung the coat on a hook fastened to the wall behind him. "It's nothing important."

Not believing him, she decided to bring up a name and watch for his reaction. "Mitch Hennessey."

His eyes squinted together and there was slight hesitation before he asked, "What?"

"Nothing."

"Why would you mention your dad's former partner?"

"Just wanted to. It's nothing important."

"What's going on, Tiffany?"

"Nothing," she casually replied with a subtle smirk.

"And speaking of your father's mannerisms, you have the exact grin he flashed whenever he was up to something sneaky."

The smirk remained on her face as she reached for another bite of the dessert. "I have no idea what you're talking about."

"Okay. You win. I will tell you why I asked the earlier question, but only if you tell me why you just mentioned Mitch's name."

Before she could answer, the kitchen door opened. "All the chandeliers have been dusted, Scott. Anything else you need me to do?"

Tiffany stood, walked towards Brett with the bowl of bananas foster bread pudding, and handed it to him as she said, "Go have a seat in the dining room and try this. We'll be out in a minute for your opinion."

"Can I eat it in here?"

Tiffany shot her fiancé a cold stare. "Dining room, honey."

"Be nice," Brett softly spoke before stepping backwards into the dining room.

Tiffany returned to the table, waiting for the door to stop swinging before continuing. "Mitch came to my parent's house yesterday to inform me that my ex-fiancé was responsible for Dad's death. I found it a little hard to believe, but since you're asking me if I think he is a violent person, I'm inclined to believe Mitch's claim. Now, please tell me why you just asked about Jackson."

Scott sighed before telling her, "What if Mitch was telling the truth? What if Jackson caused your father to have a heart attack?"

"Why does he think that?"

"Mitch found enough evidence to place Jackson with your dad when he died, and not out West. I found it very hard to believe at first, but everything seems to align for him to have done such a thing."

"And why would he want to kill my dad? We both agree he's not a violent person."

While grabbing his ear, Scott told her, "I'm not exactly sure why he would do it either. I'm afraid the only person who may know is Jackson."

Tiffany's belief that Jackson didn't kill her father began to dissipate. The hatred she felt towards him immediately following their wedding started to resurface as she told her uncle, "I'm gonna need to talk to that asshole then."

Monday

Chapter 97

We drove at a constant speed of 75 miles per hour in a Chevy Impala, stopping four times along the way—three stops at gas stations and a four-hour 'layover' at a motel in Katy, Texas. We arrived at Ochsner Hospital shortly after 12:30 in the afternoon. Stopped in front of the emergency room doors, Caroline asked of me from the driver's seat, "Call me as soon as you can and let me know how she's doing. Do you have my number memorized?"

"I do. Please be careful."

She pointed to her purse in the backseat. "I'll be fine."

We leaned towards one another. Her kiss made me not want to get out of the car. "I wish we didn't have to come back here. As soon as I talk to my mom and she appears to be okay, I say we get back on the road. You can pick where we go next."

"Count me in. I'll be at my uncle's, smoothing things over until I hear from you. I imagine he's not too thrilled I left town without telling him or Betty."

"I'll call you soon."

After vacating the car, I scanned the parking lot for either a suspicious vehicle a Las Vegas mobster may be hiding in, or a darkened SUV containing two pissed off F.B.I. agents. I didn't see signs of either during my leery walk inside the hospital, but was mindful of the fact the agents would have the resources to know my mom was in the hospital.

I approached a receptionist behind a desk. "I'm trying to locate Cecile Fabacher."

After scanning her computer, she told me, "We don't have anyone by that name checked in here."

A light-skinned black nurse stood behind the receptionist. She looked young, perhaps fresh out of nursing school.

Confused, I asked the receptionist, "Are you—"

"Jackson?" the nurse asked.

"Yes?"

"Follow me please."

My immediate thoughts were perhaps she worked for Vincent, or even for the agents. "Where are we going?"

She walked from behind the desk, directing me to follow her with her pointer finger. I reluctantly followed, staying several feet back as she led me down a hallway. Upon noticing I wasn't directly behind her, she waited for me to catch up to her. "Your mother is down the hallway, second to last door on the right. Your father wanted us to admit her under an alias for safety reasons."

I could see my brother standing in the doorway as we approached the room. "Thank you," I told the nurse. She left my side.

Marcus turned towards me. Whatever minute feelings of optimism remained that my mom was going to be okay quickly escaped me as I saw his expressionless face. He hobbled towards me. Instead of greeting me with a hug in the hallway, he grabbed my right arm.

"Get in there now," he demanded with a forceful push towards the room.

A doctor and two nurses stood in the room. The man who raised me held my mom's hand. His back was to me. No longer was I thinking about the past and the secrets my family held for decades. "Dad."

He turned around. After gently setting my mom's hand on the bed, he held both arms out to me. As we embraced, I felt I could cry. As I had done for the better part of twelve years, I held it in. "Go talk to her," he whispered into my ear. "She needs to hear your voice."

My mom's eyes were shut. She looked to be peacefully sleeping. I leaned towards her. "Mom, it's Jackson. I'm home now. You need to wake up." My dad placed my hand on hers. I grabbed it as one might grab an injured bird from the ground. "I just want you to know I love you very much, Mom." I could ever so slightly feel her hand trying to squeeze mine. Again, I was on the verge of crying, but managed to control it. The monitor next to her bed revealed her blood pressure to be abnormally high. I looked to the doctors and then to my brother and dad. "What's wrong with her?"

A doctor of Indian descent entered the room as Marcus answered, "She suffered a stroke."

My entire body went numb. "What? How did this happen?"

"Gentlemen," the Caucasian doctor spoke, "we need to get her to the O.R. now."

"Why does she need surgery?" I asked.

"She has a clot. Not enough blood is reaching her brain. We need to perform a thrombectomy as soon as possible," the doctor answered, handing my dad a clipboard and a pen. "We need your signature, Andrew, to proceed with the operation."

My dad wasted no time in signing the papers. "How risky is this procedure, Paul?"

"With any surgery, there are risks. But I can assure you Dr. Sanjay is one of the best in the nation at this procedure. I will be assisting him."

The nurses dislodged the brakes from the wheels and proceeded to roll my mom out of the room. I grew fearful I may never see her again. "Should we be nervous right now?" I asked the doctor.

"We're going to take good care of her."

My dad shook the doctor's hand. "Let me know as soon as she comes out of surgery."

"I will." Both doctors stepped into the hallway.

My dad flashed a smile that looked forced and uncertain. "She's going to be fine. Are you okay, Jax?"

"No." Several of my physical therapy clients over the years had suffered paralysis caused by a stroke. The possibility that my mom would be partially paralyzed and/or have slurred speech worried me greatly, as did the surgery she was about to undergo. "Who knows what side effects she may have from this stroke, and that's if she even makes it out of surgery."

My dad put his hand on my shoulder. "They're going to take good care of her. She's not going to have any complications from this. Why don't we go to the waiting room?"

Ever since witnessing my grandfather's death in a hospital, I hated stepping foot in them. I hated the smell, the sights and sounds of other human beings in pain, as well as the coldness not only in the air, but also from the doctors. There was nothing pleasant about being in a hospital, especially when a loved one was undergoing a life-saving surgery.

"How did this happen?" I asked once we all sat.

"We don't know."

"Of course we do, Dad." Marcus stared intently at me. "Your selfishness did this, Jackson. When are you going to understand you're part of a family?"

My dad, seated between my brother and me, put his hand on Marcus' shoulder. "Stop."

Marcus nudged his hand away. "Anytime something doesn't go as planned, what do you do? Run away. Mom had a stroke because of your actions. I had to kill a man because of your actions. My wife and kids had to leave the city and are living in fear because of your actions. The lives of everyone close to you are now in danger because of your actions."

"Marcus," my dad sternly stated, grabbing him with both hands, "stop it now."

Marcus nudged his hands away. "You stop! Stop babying him and treating him like he does no wrong! Look at how he's affected everyone's life! We're all constantly looking over our shoulder now, and who knows if we'll even see mom conscious again!" Marcus' shouting caused the only other person in the waiting room, a Latino woman holding an infant in her arms, to cast her eyes upon the three of us.

I could find nothing to say to defend myself because he was right. Since Mikey's death, I was well aware my actions had negatively affected someone close to me. I had just hoped no one would realize it.

"Why don't you go home, Marcus? I'll call you in a bit."

"I'm not going home while Mom is about to go through surgery."

"Go get some fresh air then. You're not helping things right now. You're the one acting selfishly."

Marcus stood. The look on his face just before he turned around and walked outside was one I had never seen on him before. Never in twenty-nine years had I felt any semblance of hostility from my brother. The bridges between those close to me were crumbling. I felt like nothing could be done to stop them.

"Don't pay any attention to him right now. He doesn't mean what he just said. He's just—"

"He's right."

"No. He's just upset because he's worried about you."

"He's right though, isn't he?"

He looked away as he told me, "No."

"You do act as if I do no wrong. I made some mistakes in life, and now loved ones are in harm's way because of them."

"No one is going to be harmed."

"What about Mom?"

"Especially your mother. She's going to make a full recovery." His optimism didn't comfort me as it had done in years past. "Her stroke had nothing to do with your actions. If anything, it's because of what I did thirty years ago. If anyone is to blame, it's me."

My eyes felt incredibly heavy as I leaned back in the chair. During the layover in Katy, I slept no more than forty-five minutes.

"You look tired, Jax."

"I didn't sleep much last night." An even more truthful answer would have been I hadn't had a good night sleep in about two weeks.

"How about I drive you home so you can rest up?"

"I want to stay here until Mom is out of surgery." It wasn't long after the words left my mouth that I rested my head against the wall behind me and shut my eyes.

The sight of a doctor walking into the waiting room was the first thing I saw upon waking up. The deadpan stare in his eyes and the fidgeting of his hands suggested he was about to be the bearer of bad news. I watched breathlessly as he made his way across the waiting room. I felt a slight reprieve as he stopped next to the Latino woman.

"How long was I out?"

My dad looked at his watch. "A good hour."

My brother had returned to the waiting room at some point during my nap. He sat several chairs away from us, bent over with his head hung low. It was if we were strangers to him.

"How long has Marcus been sitting over there?"

"About thirty minutes."

His aloofness only added to the guilt I held for my mom's condition. I wasn't sure how much longer I could hold it all in. I tried not to focus on the conversation between the Latino woman and the doctor, but I could hear every word.

"We tried to revive him several times. I'm sorry, but your husband didn't survive the surgery." The woman began to cry. I then imagined a doctor soon telling us the same news about my mother. I couldn't have felt much worse.

Once the doctor stepped away, my dad approached the young woman, offering his condolences. She cried on his shoulder for several minutes. I admired him for doing something I would have never done. Death was something I was never comfortable with. I never knew what to say to someone who had just lost a loved one.

"Do you have someone you can call to pick you up? Family or a friend?" my dad asked her.

The lady shook her head. "No familia."

He reached into his back pocket. From his wallet he removed some cash. I could see a $100 bill wrapped around a few other bills as he handed them to her. "Taxi."

The woman continued to cry while refusing the money. A plastic grocery bag in the seat next to her served as a diaper bag. Holes were visible in her shoes. The blanket swaddling her baby could use a good washing. My heart went out for the woman not only because her husband had just died, but because she appeared to have fallen on hard times. I wanted her to take the money. After refusing the money again, my dad placed the money in her hand. "Por favor."

She soon gave in. "Gracias." The woman continued to cry as my dad helped her to her feet.

Marcus assisted my dad in bringing the woman to the desk. After signing some papers, they escorted her outside and waited with her until a taxi arrived. The only reason I didn't help was because I was afraid of my own brother.

When they returned to the waiting room, my dad sat to my right and Marcus to his right. Very little was spoken between the three of us.

Another couple of hours passed until the Caucasian doctor my dad was on a first-name basis with emerged from behind a set of doors. "Andrew."

We all stood. My heart pounded, my knees wobbled, and my stomach was about ready to empty what little food was in it.

"How is she, Paul?"

"She's awake."

"Can we see her?"

"She's asking for him." The doctor pointed at me.

I wasted no time in walking towards the doors. Upon entering the hallway, I hurried to where I last saw my mom, leaving the doctor behind me. He said something, but I was too focused on seeing my mom to comprehend it.

Her eyes were open. I smiled while looking down upon her. "How are you feeling, Mom?"

She smiled, but only the right side of her lips, along with her right cheekbones, moved upward. "My…baby… boy." Her speech was slow and slurred. I grabbed her right hand as she attempted to reach for me.

"She suffered paralysis on the left side of her body," the doctor spoke from behind me.

It was greatly upsetting to hear that was my mom was paralyzed. "Is it permanent?"

"We don't know yet. Only time will tell. She's going to start rehab immediately."

"I…knew…you…be…back." She squeezed my hand. I wanted to lean over and hug her, but was afraid I'd injure her or accidentally dislodge one of the several tubes emerging from her frail-looking body.

"Mom, I'm sorry I left."

As she swallowed, it was not only slower than a normal swallow, but looked like a struggle as well. "It's… okay. Promise…you…won't…leave…again."

"I won't."

"Where…did…you…go? Where's…Delain?"

"I don't know where she is."

Her smile waned, giving way to an uneasy stare.

It dawned on me she didn't know what had happened. There was no need to upset her any further. "I don't know where she is at the moment. She dropped me off here then had to rush home. She could be on her way back as we speak."

The right side of her lips and her right cheekbones again lifted. "Good. I…love…her." All I could do was smile. "Why…didn't…you…get…married?"

I looked into her eyes, telling her, "It wasn't time yet. We want to wait, to make it more special."

Her eyes slowly shut.

"Mom. Mom, are you okay?" Her head fell to the side. I began to panic. "Mom!"

"It's okay," the doctor informed me. "She needs her rest. I'm amazed she had the energy to talk to you just now. She's a fighter."

"When will she be awake?"

"I imagine in a few hours. We'll let you know when she's up again."

While walking back to the waiting room, I recalled the previous conversation with my mom. She tried to hug me on the eve of my wedding, yet I refused. It was something I immensely regretted and hoped I would get another chance to do very soon.

My dad and brother nervously paced about the waiting room. Marcus was the first to see me. "How is she?"

"She talked to me briefly before going back to sleep."

"Was everything normal?" Marcus asked.

I shook my head.

"What's wrong?"

I didn't want to tell them. It was all my fault. "She's paralyzed on the left side of her body."

Marcus swung his cane against a chair. "God damnit!"

"Calm down, Marcus. We don't know how bad it is. It may just be temporary."

"That's what the doctor said."

"What if it's not? What if mom is paralyzed forever?"

"She won't be. Jackson, did she tell you anything?"

"She asked if Delain and I were still together. I told her yes."

"And that was a lie, correct?"

"Yes, sir."

"Where is she?"

"I don't know. She left me."

"When?"

"Saturday—a few hours before the wedding was to take place."

"Why?"

"I wish I could tell you, but I don't have an answer for that either. I didn't want to tell Mom the news just yet. She seemed happy when she asked about Delain."

"I have to admit, Jax, I'm very worried about you. Vincent's looking for you and Logan said two F.B.I. agents are doing the same. I think it's safer if we all stay together right now. Don't you agree?"

"I suppose."

"I take it you drove here?"

"Caroline dropped me off."

"You can ride home with me. I'm going to talk to Paul for a minute." My dad left, leaving me and Marcus alone in the waiting room.

I had never seen, or thought I would ever see, a side of Marcus suggesting he was resentful of me. To say I was feeling uncomfortable in my brother's presence was a vast understatement. Truth be told, I was scared.

"What's going on between you and Caroline?" he asked.

I wasn't ready to admit she and I were more than just friends. "Nothing."

"Then why was she with you in El Paso?"

"She wanted a ride back home."

"So…you started a long-distance taxi service for women you have crushes on? And not only that, you start the service on the day of your wedding?"

"What are you—"

"What happened on Valentine's Day? How come you didn't blow up the balloons for Delain like you were supposed to? Why did you tell Logan that Dad had cancer? What the hell are you hiding?"

No one knew what happened on Valentine's Day except for me, Caroline, and Delain. I wasn't physically or mentally ready to tell Marcus the truth. "I'm not hiding anything. I overheard Mom and Dad talking in the study one night about Dad's cancer. I thought he had it again, but they must have just been talking about his past bout."

"What about the balloons you were supposed to blow up for Delain on Valentine's?"

"Why do you think I didn't blow them up for her?"

"Logan said you never mentioned anything about it after you were supposed to do it, and Dad said Delain acted weird when he and Mom mentioned it to her at your funeral."

"Could Delain have been acting weird because she was grieving my death?"

Marcus said nothing as he took to one of the chairs.

"I'm not hiding anything."

"Then why are F.B.I. agents looking for you?"

"I don't know."

His head hung low as he repeatedly tapped his cane against the ground. "Vincent knows my wife's and sons' names." No longer did he sound angry, but more exhausted than anything. "He said it would be fun to kill brothers. Do you know how miserable it is to be scared for not only yourself, but also loved ones every second of the day? I've been

75

carrying a gun in the back of my pants for the last two days. When's it going to end, Jackson?"

I couldn't do it any longer. I was ready to throw in the towel. "Right now."

"How?"

I removed a business card from my wallet. "Can I borrow your cell phone?"

He looked up. "Who are you calling?" I showed him the card. "It's about time you came to your senses." After patting his pockets, he said, "I must have left it at Mom and Dad's."

"I saw a payphone outside. I'll be back in a minute."

While reaching for some quarters from my pocket, a car door slammed behind me. Paranoia incited a jolt, preceding a look over my shoulder. Since a blonde-haired woman didn't fit the description of a balding, overweight Italian male, I turned around and proceeded to place several quarters into the phone. After dialing the number, I turned to face the parking lot once more. The woman grew closer.

"Hello?" the man on the other end of the phone asked.

I suddenly found it difficult to speak. Breathing wasn't any easier to do, nor was the simple act of moving my arm to hang up the phone. I grew paralyzed while looking into the eyes of the woman from the parking lot.

"What are the odds of this?" the woman spoke from a few feet away. She flashed the same grin that I, at one time, found to be the most gorgeous smile I had ever seen on a woman.

All I could get out was her name. "Tiffany."

"Hey, stranger."

I was well aware I wasn't dreaming, but wished I had been. I wasn't physically or mentally ready to engage in conversation with my ex-fiancée. "What are you doing here?" I felt out of breath, as if I had just run a four-minute mile.

"Hello?" Agent Parker again asked on the other end of the phone.

Tiffany wore a khaki mid-thigh skirt and a white tank top that accentuated her cleavage. "Visiting a friend. What are you doing here?"

Before giving an answer, I pictured Tiffany the last time we saw one another— in tears on the altar of the St. Louis Cathedral. "My mom had a stroke."

"Is she okay?" She appeared concerned.

"She suffered paralysis. We don't know yet if it's permanent."

She placed her right hand against her chest. "That's terrible."

Upon realizing the phone was still in my hand, I hung it up. "I can't believe I'm running into you like this."

"Me neither." While smiling once more, she stepped closer. "Can I have a hug?"

An interrogation with two F.B.I. agents didn't have me as nervous as I felt while hugging Tiffany. Not seeing her for almost two years was part of the reason, as was the uncertainty of whether or not she was bitter about how our courtship ended. The majority of my nervousness, however, was brought on by the fact I was responsible for her father's death.

She stepped back. "It's been a while. You look good."

It was hard to admit, but she looked as gorgeous as ever. "You too."

"You do look a little skinnier than normal, though. You been fasting or something?"

"Low carbs."

"I don't know what you have planned right now, Jackson, but I was about to grab a cup of coffee just up the road. I would love to catch up. I know you don't drink coffee, but I could use some company for a few minutes."

Her reaction, so far, wasn't how I envisioned her to be during our first meeting since the wedding. Even though she was much calmer and friendlier than I had anticipated, I was still hesitant about being alone with her. "I would love to, but I was just about to catch a ride back to my parents' house with my dad. I don't have my car right now."

"I can drop you off there afterwards. I still remember where they live." Her smile had yet to wane.

"Can I take a raincheck, Tiffany?"

Her smile finally vanished. "My dad just passed away, Jackson. I could sure use a familiar face to talk to. It will only be for a few minutes."

A helicopter approached the hospital. There was a good chance a patient was on it, yet I couldn't help but wonder if it was Agents Parker and Williams. Despite thinking I was ready to talk to the F.B.I., I no longer was due to the woman standing before me. "I need to be home in an hour."

Again she smiled. "Thank you. You're still the best."

If the helicopter was headed for the hospital, it looked to be a good two minutes away from landing. "I need to let my dad know I'm not going home with him."

Tiffany pointed to the payphone. "If he has his cell phone on him, why don't you call him and save yourself a minute or two?"

I reached into my pocket for a quarter.

"I'll pull the car up. See you in a second, Mr. Fabacher."

Chapter 98

As if agreeing to have coffee with Tiffany wasn't already anxiety-inducing enough, watching her pull up to the curb in Davis' Ferrari had me second guessing if I was experiencing a stroke as well. Numbness suddenly occurred in my left arm, quickly spreading over the entire left side of my body. My breathing became heavier while my legs grew weak. I felt that climbing into the vehicle in which I watched Davis suffer a fatal heart attack at the hands of my doing might be my demise. I placed both hands on my thighs while leaning over. Tiffany, I sensed, was staring at me. I looked upward. The passenger-side window was rolled down.

"What are you waiting for? Climb in, Jackson."

I was certain that having a stroke, heart attack, or panic attack in front of Tiffany was a sure sign that I was guilty of something.

"Are you okay?"

I nodded while slowly standing. As waves of numbness and tingling occurred in my arm, I grimaced while telling her, "My lower back's been bothering me. I slipped in the shower last week. It comes and goes."

"Ouch. You need help?"

"I got this." I took deep breaths while gingerly walking towards her. Along the way, something told me not to get in the car. "Can I meet you at the coffee shop, Tiffany?"

"I thought you didn't drive here."

"I'll have my dad drop me off. Which coffee shop?"

"Have your dad drop you off?" Tiffany laughed. "What are you, in junior high? Get in here, silly."

"I don't—"

"If you're wondering if I'm upset about the wedding," she held her left hand up, "I'm not. I just got engaged to an incredible man."

I wasn't sure I believed her about not being upset by the wedding fiasco. Tiffany always had trouble letting go of grudges. I remained outside of the Ferrari, contemplating my decision.

"Come on, Jackson. Please don't make me beg to chat with an old flame."

I looked up to see the helicopter slowly descending onto the top of the hospital. I reluctantly lifted the door and buckled myself into the very seat I sat to check her father's pulse.

"If Dad knew you were in here, he'd be turning in his grave."

Before I could unbuckle and climb out, Tiffany slammed on the accelerator. My head and body slammed against the seat as we raced out of the hospital parking lot. She slowed down seconds later. "I love doing that," she said while grinning.

"Can we not do that again? My stomach's halfway up my throat."

Tiffany laughed. "It takes a little getting used to. I'm still on the learning curve, but I'll be getting lots of practice since Dad left it to me in his will. Is this your first time in it? I can't remember if he bought it before or after our wedding." We came to a stop at a traffic light. Tiffany turned to me while awaiting an answer.

"Before the wedding, and no, I've never been in it." I began to gently rub my left arm, trying to get some feeling back in it while changing the subject. "Tell me about your fiancé."

"Well, after I was…embarrassed at our wedding," she said with a smirk and a roll of her eyes, "I moved to Dallas. Needless to say, I was a little heartbroken and thought I would never find love again. Then, I met Brett backstage at a U2 concert, right next to Bono. We actually just got engaged this past weekend."

"Congratulations."

"Thank you. It was quite the proposal. Following Dad's funeral on Thursday," she turned onto Jefferson Highway as she continued, "Brett said he had a business meeting in New York on Friday and asked if I would accompany him. Stupid me actually believed him, so you can imagine my surprise when we not only stepped onto a horse-drawn carriage in Central Park, but also came to a stop at the most beautiful and secluded part of the park, where a waiter held a picnic basket for us. We sat on a plush blanket and ate foie gras, caviar, and gourmet cheeses while drinking Dom Perignon. Then, as the sun set, he got down on one knee and popped the question. Obviously, I said yes."

There was no reason for her to tell me the story of how he proposed other than an attempt to make me jealous. I knew her too well. I was far from jealous. "Sounds lovely."

"It was magical—straight out of a fairytale. We then stayed in a suite at the Crowne Plaza before flying back home last night on Brett's private jet."

"You like those park proposals, don't you?"

"That's right," she spoke while nodding. "You proposed to me at City Park, didn't you?"

Her comment had me biting my tongue. I wanted to tell her how much of a controlling bitch she was, but used great restraint. "Yes, because that's where you told me to propose to you." Her laugh led me to believe she thought I found it funny that she told me when and where to propose. In reality, I was reminding her how horrible of a person she was.

"Speaking of proposals, I hear you're engaged as well."

Technically, I still was since neither of us had told the other we wanted out. The less Tiffany knew, the better. "I am."

"How did you do it?"

"Propose?"

"Yes."

"Last Christmas I created a winter wonderland in my backyard using thousands of white lights and a truckload of snow. Next to a real snowman, I dropped to one knee and proposed. Obviously, she said yes."

There was no semblance of a smile upon her face. "Huh. Sounds…"

"Magical?"

"Um…maybe." Jealousy, as expected, was easily detected in her tone. "What's her name?"

I was 100% certain she knew her name, but played along with her little game. "Delain."

"This Delain must be thrilled you didn't go down with that airplane a week-and-a-half ago."

"She was."

"I still can't believe you were believed to be dead for…how long was it?"

"Five days."

"That's incredible." We came to another stop at a traffic light. Tiffany turned to me. "Where were you for those five days?"

"Out west."

"What where you doing out there?"

"Thinking about things."

"Such as…" The traffic light changed. She didn't notice.

"It's green."

She looked forward, pressing on the accelerator. Again, my head slammed against the seat as we raced down South Claiborne Avenue. "Sorry. I forget how powerful this thing is. So, what were you thinking about for those five days?"

"Things."

"What kind of things?"

"Private things."

"I see. Where did you stay? How did you get around? Did you rent a car or something?"

"In cheap motels. I didn't rent a car because I didn't want anyone to find me. I hitchhiked a couple of times."

"That could have been dangerous."

"I know, but I'm alive and well."

"Were you having doubts about marrying your fiancée?"

I got the impression saying yes would make her feel as if she had one up on me, but telling her no could lead to questions I didn't have an answer for. "Yes, but I don't have doubts anymore."

"That's good. May I ask you something, Jackson?"

"Sure."

"Was I ever a thought while you were out there?"

Actually she was, but more so what her reaction would be if she knew the truth of her dad's death. "How do you mean?"

"Like…did you think about how life would have turned out if we would have gotten married? I think about that sometimes."

"You mean what life would be like if you didn't have intercourse with your ex-boyfriend a couple of weeks before our wedding?"

"Yes," she answered as if she didn't notice the verbal jab sent her way.

After picturing her dad begging for me to unfasten his hands, I told her, "The thought may have crossed my mind."

Tiffany smiled while patting my thigh. "Me too, Bumpkins." The pet name she bestowed upon me three months into our relationship resurfaced. I wasn't so sure her fiancé would approve of the thigh patting or the pet name calling. It certainly wasn't the first time she did something inappropriate behind a fiancé's back.

"But, I've learned not to dwell in the past. Nothing comes from it. Besides, I found somebody and so did you. It sounds like we've moved forward, and we're both doing just fine."

She removed her hand from my leg. "Except for the fact that I lost my dad. It's been hard, Jackson. Seeing you again, though—it's like he's still with me. He liked you, you know."

"Bullshit."

"I'm serious."

"He tried to attack me, Tiffany. I have three-hundred witnesses."

"That was just an impulse reaction to his baby girl being embarrassed on her special day. He told me a few months later he regretted his actions that day. He was very remorseful for what happened in the cathedral."

"You just said he'd turn over in his grave if he knew I was in this car."

"I did say that...but only because he didn't want any other male in his Ferrari but him." Tiffany was lying through her teeth, yet I didn't see fit to call her out on it. We came to another stop. "Too bad you didn't get to see him before he died," she said while peering in my direction. I stared straight ahead. "Have you not seen him since the wedding?"

The image of her father just moments after his death was impossible to not think about. I was nearly certain I could still smell the pungent, lingering odor of Davis' vomit in the car. "No."

"Too bad. He would have loved to make amends with you. Would you have forgiven him for something he didn't mean to do?"

I again had to bite my tongue as I told her one of the biggest lies to ever cross my lips. "Yes."

She grinned as the light turned green. "That makes me feel a little better. I bet he's smiling down on us right now."

If anything, he was looking up at us, and I was certain he wasn't smiling. "Yep." If she knew the truth of Mikey's death, she might have thought differently about her father. "Speaking of people who are smiling down on us, I'm sure you heard about Mikey."

"I did. That was very sad to hear. I know the two of you were close."

"What did you hear about how he died?"

"That he was with a married woman, and her husband—a police officer—walked in on them having sex and shot him," she said with a straight face.

"Something like that."

With her eyes still focused on the road, she turned her head slightly towards me. "What does that mean?"

"Who told you?"

"Dad. Why did you just say 'something like that'?"

"Your dad told you over the phone?"

"Yes. Why?"

"How did he sound?"

She briefly glanced at me then back at the road. "What are you doing right now?"

"Mikey broke your dad's hand after he yelled at my parents. I'm sure he wasn't saddened by my best friend's death."

"I'm sure he—"

"Who were you going to visit at the hospital a few minutes ago?"

"A friend."

"What's this friend's name?"

"Rebecca."

"Last name?"

While turning onto Poydras Street, she answered, "White."

"That name doesn't ring a bell."

"I met her after you and I broke up."

"While you were in Dallas?"

"Yes."

"Why was someone from Dallas in a New Orleans hospital?"

"She moved here a few weeks ago."

"Why were you going to visit her?"

"Jackson, you're acting kind of weird right now." She again briefly glanced at me then back at the road. "But if you must know, she just had a baby and I was going to see her. Why does talking about Dad make you so uneasy?" She turned left onto Carondelet Street.

No longer did I feel pain in my arm or chest. "I don't see why you're trying to cover for him by saying he liked me."

"I'm not. I'm telling the truth."

I desperately wanted to tell her how he blackmailed Delain, more than likely raped her, impregnated her, kidnapped her son and gave him to Scott after telling her he had died, blackmailed her again, tried to kill her with a knife, and then drugged and tried to kill Caroline. Davis Melancon was a monster. Although she might not have known how horrible he was, she certainly knew he had a devious side to him. We came to a stop next to an antique store on Royal Street, directly behind the St. Louis Cathedral. She turned the engine off.

"Why are we parking here?"

"Because people park their cars before getting out of them and walking to their destinations." Her laugh was a sarcastic one.

"Where's the coffee shop?"

"A few blocks that way." She pointed behind us, in the direction of the Chick-ory. "But I wanted to show you my new condo." She leaned across the steering wheel, glancing upward at the balcony above the antique store.

"You live there?"

"Yes. On the second floor."

"Since when?"

"Yesterday," she emphatically smiled. "Dad bought it and left it to me in his will. The delivery truck is on its way from Dallas with my belongings. I'll be all moved in by tomorrow. It was supposed to be a surprise to get me back to New Orleans, but he passed away before he could tell me. I remember how often you spoke about living in the Quarter, so I wanted you to see it. Isn't the balcony to die for?"

The balcony looked like it could easily hold fifteen people, if not twenty. "It's quite big."

"I know," she eagerly spoke. "I can't wait for Mardi Gras. Now, after we see the condo and before we head to the Chick-ory, I thought I'd take you to the restaurant."

"What restaurant? The Fleur-de-Leans?"

Tiffany nodded. "The grand re-opening is this coming weekend. Uncle Scott is taking over. He's in there right now. He'd love to see you again."

"I'm not going in there."

"Why not? It's only five blocks away."

"Because after the wedding, I swore I would never step foot in that restaurant again. Your dad hated me after what I did. I don't believe for a second he was remorseful for his actions."

"Why do you say that?"

"Because I know your dad, Tiffany, and so do you. You know damn well he did some illegal, screwed up shit over the years. While we were dating, you told me you thought he was involved with some corrupt people."

She sighed before saying, "I did tell you that one time, but I was wrong. He wasn't a bad person. He was my dad, Jackson, and now he's gone." The whites of her eyes had become red. "Why are you bringing this up now?"

I was too worked up to feel bad for making her cry, especially since she purposely brought herself to tears several times during our relationship when things didn't go her way. I couldn't stay in the car much longer, listening to blatant lies about Davis. "I just find it odd Mikey was killed by a man who was a notorious swinger, and who just so happened to be on the police force the same time as your dad."

Her crying ceased. "What are you saying? That my dad was part of some conspiracy theory with Mikey's death?"

"I'm not saying anything. I'm just stating facts."

She reached across my lap, opening the glove compartment. "You see that prescription bottle."

I stared nervously at a bottle of nitroglycerin pills.

"You want to talk conspiracy theory. Dad died right where I'm sitting because he couldn't get to this bottle I'm easily reaching for. Don't you find that peculiar?"

The anxiety was returning, as was the pain in my chest.

"Maybe if his hands were bound to the steering wheel by, I don't know—duct tape—then I can see why he wouldn't have been able to reach his pills."

I was convinced she knew something, but hopefully not everything. "Duct tape? Steering wheel? What the hell are you talking about?"

"A forensics report just came back and it said Dad's wrists were bound by duct tape to the steering wheel. That—along with a kitchen knife found under my parent's couch and blood from another crime scene on the base of the door leading from the garage into the house has the police about to reopen his case and search for another cause of death. Someone else was in the house when he died. Dad was murdered, Jackson."

Sweat had gathered on my forehead and palms. I wiped my hands against my shirt. "Murdered?"

With a cold stare aimed into my eyes she repeated, "Murdered."

I opened the door. "I don't know what to tell you about that. I hope they find whoever did it."

"They have a pretty good idea who it was. I was told they're just waiting for the warrant to come through, which shouldn't take too much longer to get."

My entire body began to tremble. "I need to get to my parents' house." I stepped onto the curb. Tiffany exited the car as well.

"I hope Mrs. Cecile makes it out of the hospital. Losing a parent is an awful feeling, Jackson."

"I would imagine so." A woman exited a taxi cab two blocks away.

"It's much worse than losing a fiancé."

"Good luck with everything, Tiffany." I headed towards the taxi cab.

Before I could make it to the corner of the street, Tiffany yelled, "I'm sure we'll be running into one another real soon, Bumpkins!"

Chapter 99

Since Davis' death one week prior, my crippling fear of being incarcerated grew with each passing day. Still, during those seven days, a part of me was convinced there was no way to connect me to Davis' death. I believed I was thorough and didn't leave evidence behind. Apparently, I wasn't thorough enough. The blood from the other crime scene Tiffany spoke of was either Cliff's or Hank's, and it must have been on my shoe. I grew even more nauseated as I again wondered if my fingerprints were found inside Cliff's rig, and if that's how I was being linked to Davis' death. It seemed to only be a matter of time, according to Tiffany, that a warrant would be issued for my arrest.

As the taxi approached my parents' house, I noticed across the street a black SUV with tinted windows that looked very much like the SUV in El Paso. If it wasn't Agents Parker and Williams in the SUV, then it was maybe fellow agents of theirs, waiting to inform them of my whereabouts.

"Driver, can you continue to the next street and take a left?"

"It's your dime."

I ducked in the back seat until the taxi drove past my parents' house and turned left. "At the next street, take another left. It's the fourth house from the stop sign."

I waited until the taxi was out of sight before walking into the backyard of the house, in the midst of a massive renovation, located directly behind my parents' home. The owners, friends of my parents, had been living in their Florida condo until the construction was finished. Dusk had arrived. No workers were on sight. I carefully scaled the six-foot-high rod-iron fence hidden beneath a thick blanket of ivy, passing through the pergola on my way to the backdoor. Using my key, I unlocked the door and quietly stepped into the dimly lit kitchen. I shut and locked the door before leaning against it. The house was eerily quiet. I removed my shoes before stepping across the hardwood floors of the kitchen. It didn't appear my dad or brother were home. I wondered if they were still at the hospital because something had happened to my mom. I dialed my dad's cell phone using the kitchen phone. Five rings later, I was directed to his voicemail. "It's me. I'm home. Call me and let me know how mom is."

After hanging up, a sound I hadn't heard in decades echoed from the hallway. It was the sound of something heavy being hinged open. Fairly certain as to who was making the sound, I hid behind the kitchen island until I knew for sure who was in the house with me. I soon heard footsteps in the kitchen.

"Jackson?" the person asked in broken English.

I stood from behind the island. Angelo flashed his big, Italian grin at me. I couldn't smile back while making eye contact with someone I was very much uncomfortable being around the first and only time we had been in one another's presence.

"Brother!"

"Have you seen my dad or Marcus?"

"They came home, but go back to hospital. Mom was awake. Mr. Andrew said to call when you come home. When I heard keys in backdoor, I hide."

I wasn't a fan of someone other than me and Marcus calling Cecile Fabacher 'Mom'. "I just called him."

"I have been praying all day for her. She will be home soon. I know it."

As my stomach rumbled, I could only nod. I wasn't hungry but needed to fuel my body for whatever lay ahead. The tail-end of the conversation with Tiffany had me wondering if it would be my last meal before being branded a criminal. "Hungry?"

Angelo smiled. "Always."

From the refrigerator I grabbed hummus, a bowl of red grapes, and a block of cheddar cheese before grabbing a box of Wheat Thins from the pantry and a knife from a drawer. Angelo sat on the wooden bench at the elongated kitchen table while I sat across from him in one of the padded chairs. When my parents revealed the truth about their past in the portrait room three days earlier, my back was mostly to Angelo, as I found it difficult and disturbing to face him directly. As I sat with him at the kitchen table beneath the soft glow of the chandelier, I got my first real look at him.

"This is so trippy."

Angelo looked on with confusion. "Trippy?"

"Weird. This is so weird— looking at someone who looks exactly like me."

Angelo nodded. "Si, but we're not exact." He turned his head to the right and pointed. A mole about the size of a pen point was visible on the left side of his nose. I probably wouldn't have noticed it if he didn't point it out. It had me wondering if we had any other differences.

"Where's your birthmark?"

"Birth…mark?" He appeared confused.

I stood, lifted my pants leg and pointed to the darkened spot on my calf about the size of a half-dollar. "Birthmark."

"Voglia. Si. I have." He stood, removing his shirt. Working out must have been just as common in Italy as the U.S. because his muscles were well-defined, probably more than mine at the time being. I hadn't stepped foot in the gym in two weeks. Lack of exercise, along with a drastic dip in my daily caloric intake, had me feeling as if I was becoming weaker by the day. Angelo's birthmark was located on the back of his shoulder. It was darkened and similar in size to mine.

I cut a piece of cheese, placing it on a cracker before handing it to Angelo. "Cheese and crackers. American snack."

He smiled while placing his shirt back on. "We have same in Italy."

My stomach again rumbled. I placed a handful of hummus-dipped crackers into my mouth to shut it up. "You must like to workout."

"Not so much," he confessed with a shrug of his shoulders. "I do it so ladies look at me more."

Sure, weightlifting helped to release endorphins, burn fat, increase bone density, and improve overall health, but my predominant reasoning in lifting weights for nearly fifteen years was the same as Angelo's—to appear desirable to either the woman I was with or, if I was single, desirable to other women. His response had me wondering what else we had in common. "I take it you're not married. I don't see a wedding ring."

"No."

"Girlfriend?"

Angelo beamed while nodding. "She is very beautiful. Most beautiful girl I ever seen. She makes me happiest man in Italy."

"Are you going to marry her?"

"Si. When I return to Italy, I ask her to marry. First, I come here to see you."

"Do you have a picture of her?"

Angelo removed and handed me a picture from his wallet.

Her hair—the color and sheen of black silk—draped past her shoulders; her olive skin appeared smooth and flawless; her eyes were dark and captivating. But what initially caught my attention was her smile. She had one of those effortless and natural smiles. A smile that didn't look like one was posing for a photograph but smiling because life couldn't be better. I imagined she and Angelo were madly in love with one another. "She is very pretty. What's her name?"

"Isabella."

"She has a very pretty smile."

"It made me weak first time I see her. When I get home, we go to Venice and I ask her to marry on gondola."

"Congratulations."

Angelo placed the picture and wallet back into his pocket. "My father like her very much. He would be happy." After mentioning his father, his smile lessened.

"Were you mad at your father because he didn't tell you about me until recently?"

"No. I was happy to know about family."

We may have looked alike, but our reactions to a nearly thirty-year secret were night and day. "What job do you have back home?"

"I paint houses. My father, I mean our father, was great painter. I hope to do museum paintings like him one day."

"So, when he wasn't having sex with married American women, he was painting?"

Angelo subtly nodded.

He probably didn't like my comment. I could care less if I offended or disrespected him. I still knew very little about Angelo's father, but judging by his actions of not only separating twins shortly after birth—and doing so by using violent threats—I concluded he was a horrific person. "What was he like?"

"He was fun and...pretty?"

"Handsome."

"Handsome. Handsome. He was fun and handsome." He again reached into his pocket and removed his wallet. "I have picture of him when he our age." He handed me another picture.

Chills shot up and down my spine as I looked at the picture. Angelo and I were the spitting image of the man in the picture. "This is so…"

"Trippy?"

I nodded. "Yep. Trippy indeed. What else can you tell me about him?"

"Everybody loved him, especially women. He had lots of girlfriends. Always he was with one of his girlfriends."

I handed the picture back. "Would you say he hated to be alone?"

Angelo wasted no time in giving an answer. "Very much so. If he had no girlfriend, he come stay with me. He and I very different."

One trait, so far, I shared with my birth father. "Was he ever married? What was his name again?"

"Dominick. Three times. Like I said, he had lots of girlfriends."

Even though I hadn't been married three times, I was nearly married twice. "You said he was in a coma for weeks. How did that happen?" Angelo looked down at his clasped hands as they rested on the table. He looked uncomfortable. "You don't have to say anything if you don't want to."

"He was shot with gun two times."

"Who shot him?"

Angelo slowly lifted his head. As he reached for a napkin, I discovered something else that separated the two of us. "A man who was husband to one of my father's girlfriends. He was angry at my father. He shot him in the head."

While Angelo wiped at his eyes, I pictured Vincent pointing a gun at my head and pulling the trigger. A wave of nausea overcame me. With elbows resting on the table, I placed my face against the palms of my hands. "What happened to the man who shot him?"

"The police catch and put in jail. My father told me about you before he went into coma. He never wake up. Are you okay, Jackson?"

The more I got to know about my birth father, the more I was starting to sound just like him. "Like father, like son."

"Like father, like son?"

I lifted my head. "I did something a while back and now I'm in trouble—a couple of things actually."

"Vincent?"

I perked up. "How did you know that?"

"I hear Mr. Andrew and Marcus and Logan one night. Some person named Vincent called on the telephone. He wants to hurt you. It made me upset."

It seemed my secrets—all of them—were spreading like wildfire. My fling with Krista, my actions that were the catalyst in Davis' death, my involvement in the deaths of Hank and Cliff—all were separate events finally merging to form one perfect storm. Going to jail no longer seemed like the worst thing that could happen to me. It was nearly impossible to get the notion out of my head that death was inescapable. If not by Vincent's hands, then perhaps by a vengeful ex-fiancée whom I was certain placed me with her father when he died. Something told me if she did know and had yet to go to the police, then she may already be involved with the same corrupt people her father was involved with. "I had sex with Vincent's wife, and now he wants to kill me."

After a few passing seconds, Angelo's eyes grew big. "Just like papa."

I nodded. "Just…like…papa."

"I get now—like father, like son." He then momentarily grinned before probably realizing the severity of the situation. "Mi dispiace. Um…Sorry."

"No need to apologize."

"How do you stop him?"

"It doesn't matter. If he doesn't get me, someone else will. There's no escape for me, Angelo." I truly believed there was no way that I would be either alive or not in jail in the next twenty-four hours."

"No escape?"

"I've done some bad things, Angelo. I'm not a good person."

He shook his head. "I no believe it."

"Well, it's true. Your twin brother has broken pretty much every commandment as of late, along with quite a few laws."

"You not give up. You not die. You have fiancée that loves you, no?"

"No," I told him. "She deserted me." Angelo looked perplexed. "She left me. I don't know where she went."

"Was she taken?"

"No. She left a note behind saying she was sorry. She left me, Angelo. She go bye-bye."

"Why?"

"Not sure," I told him with a shrug of my shoulders.

"Maybe we find her and you marry?"

"I don't think so."

Angelo's face grew sad as he reached for another cracker and slice of cheese. "Do you miss her?"

I was too upset with Delain to miss her. "I don't know."

"Maybe she knock on door today; come back for you."

"There was knocking on the door earlier?"

"Si, but I not see who. I stay hidden until Mr. Andrew let me out. There was several knocks last few days."

The ringing of the house phone caused me to flinch in the chair. I considered letting it ring, as it was perhaps an F.B.I. agent, police officer, or someone who wanted me dead, but then wondered if it was my dad returning my call.

"Hello?" I asked in a voice deeper than my own.

"Is Jackson Fabacher in?" The voice belonged to a female.

"No, he's not. Can I take a message?"

"My name is Officer Brandi Jordan with the New Orleans Police Department. We were calling to let him know the man we believe to be Vincent Dichario has been captured. We were wondering if he could come to the station to identify him. Legally, we only have four hours to book someone for a crime or we have to let him go. He's been in our custody now for three hours."

I closed my eyes, deeply inhaling. A considerable amount of stress seemed to leave me upon exhaling. It seemed the perfect storm was starting to disperse. "Can't you verify his identity with his fingerprints?"

"Unfortunately, we can't. It seems his prints have been permanently scarred. There's no other way to identify him except by a lineup."

In all of my excitement, I couldn't help but wonder if the corrupt people Davis was associated with was behind the call. "Officer Jordan, how do I know I can trust you?"

"I don't follow, Mr. Fabacher," she immediately told me. "Why would you think I was not telling you the truth?"

Based on timely response of her previous answer and because there was no fumbling with her words, I suspected she wasn't working for Davis' group. "Just making sure, Officer Jordan. Where is the station?"

"If you like, we could pick you up."

I forgot I wouldn't have a vehicle until my dad or brother came home. I didn't want to wait any longer to have Vincent incarcerated. "Actually, that would be great. Can I ask how he was captured?"

"We caught him at the airport trying to use a fake passport. In his suitcase we found two guns."

"What an idiot. When can you be here?"

"An unmarked white Crown Vic will be in front of the house in exactly five minutes. Officer Henry Jones will be the one picking you up."

"Sounds good. Thank you." The black SUV with tinted windows parked across the street came to mind. "Wait. Is there any chance you could pick me up at another location?"

"Sure. What is it?"

"Prytania Street. There's a house being renovated on the 2600 block. Meet me there."

"You got it, Jackson. We'll see you in just a minute."

Because I was about to converse with police officers, I was nervous. I needed something to drink. I motioned for Angelo to follow me into the parlour.

"Good call?"

"Very good call, Angelo. The guy we were just talking about, Vincent, was caught by the police. I have to make sure they found the right guy." Behind the bar, I poured tequila into a shot glass. "Tell my dad I'm at the police station when he gets back." My nose crinkled and my eyes shut as if bright light was being shined into them as warm tequila trickled down my throat.

"Si."

"Are you going to be okay by yourself?" I asked, pouring another shot.

He nodded. "I go back into hiding place if someone comes to door."

"You don't find it constricting in there?"

Again, he looked confused by my choice of wording. "Con…stricting?"

"You like hiding in tiny room?"

He nodded, subtly grinning. "It's like hide and…hide and…."

"Seek. Hide and seek. That it is, Angelo."

He pointed to the shot glass. "May I try?"

I grabbed another glass from beneath the bar, pouring Mexico's finest into it. "Do you like tequila?"

"Maybe. Never taste before. You look like it tastes not so good."

"Not so good is correct." I slid one of the glasses to him. "Cheers, Angelo."

"Cheers." He waited until I tilted my head back and shot the tequila before doing the same. After a forceful cough, he grabbed his throat while making a face as if he had just swallowed shards of glass.

"You like?"

He shook his head in disgust. "Not so much."

"Me neither." I stepped from behind the bar. "I'll be back soon."

"Be careful, brother."

I headed out the backdoor, jumped the fence, and while hiding behind a portable toilet, grew upset with myself for suddenly remembering I had yet to call Caroline. I told myself I would call her as soon as I got back from the police station. It didn't take but more than a minute for a white Crown Victoria to pull in front of the house. The windows were tinted. As I tried to peer through the driver's side window, the back window rolled down no more than in inch. "I'm Officer Henry Jones. Climb in back here, Jackson." I cautiously opened the door. The dome light inside the vehicle was turned off, but the street light behind me offered enough illumination that I could see someone wearing a police uniform seated in the back seat. Even though I couldn't see the person's face, I could tell it was a male due to his larger frame. As I stuck my head inside the door, I was grabbed by my shirt and pulled into the vehicle. The car sped off.

Vincent flashed his smug, ugly grin while pointing a gun at my head. "Hello, Loverboy."

Chapter 100

I stared past the barrel of Vincent's pistol and into his dark, vengeful eyes. My life was about to end in the backseat of a Crown Vic at the hands of a goddamn mobster.

"No sudden moves, or I end you right here. Now, sit up slowly." It took several seconds to do as he asked. "That was way too easy," he spoke with a sinister smile. "I've had to abduct two other men before, and they put up more of a challenge than you did. I love how gullible people can be. Who's the idiot now?" He threw handcuffs into my lap. "Put those on."

I placed the cuffs around my wrists, yet loose enough that I could slip my hands out of them.

"You think I was born yesterday? Squeeze them tighter!"

I tightly bound each cuff to my wrist. With the gun still aimed at my head, my eyes wavered to the driver's seat before me. The driver was Caucasian and wore a black baseball cap. "The police have been circling my parents' house for the past few days. I'm sure they're following us right now."

"I surveyed the house for hours and didn't see any police cars," Vincent proclaimed. "I do my homework. Any more bluffs you want to throw my way, Loverboy?" The car turned back onto St. Charles, heading in the direction of the river.

"You were gonna have someone shoot me because I slept with your wife, whom I had no idea was married?"

Vincent nodded. "That's only half the reason I was going to kill you."

"What's the other half?"

His smug grin finally disappeared. "You lied to me in the elevator. I hate being lied to. You thought you got the better of me, didn't you, you piece of shit?!"

I slowly moved my hands toward the door handle. "How does killing me make things even with what I did to you?"

"You killed my friend and had sex with my wife! That's my property! You had your hands all over it and your dick inside of it—right under my nose!"

My hand was nearly to the door. "I didn't know, Vincent. If I would have known, I would have never done such a thing to…it. I swear to you."

"She's got a rock on her finger the size of a fucking golf ball! How did you not know?"

"She didn't have it on."

"You lying fuck! I saw it on her hand when I got back to the room! She never took it off!"

"It was off when I met her." My hand was on the door handle. In just a few more seconds I would be a free man. Bruised and perhaps a broken arm from the fall, but I would be alive. "When you say 'took it off' it sounds like you talking about her in the past tense. Is she…?"

"Dead? None of your damn business. Tell me something, Loverboy. How did you two meet?"

It was time to go. I pulled on the handle. My plan of escape had been foiled by the child safety lock. Within seconds, my adrenaline had run its course, allowing the effects of the tequila to take over. "At the blackjack table."

"She came on to you?"

"What does it matter?"

"Because I want to fucking know!" He looked to be gripping the gun tighter.

"I don't remember. I was drunk. So was she."

He cocked the gun before telling me, "You better try to remember. And before you answer, just know I asked her the same questions. If your answers are different from hers, your brain's going to be decorated all over this backseat. Did she come on to you?"

"Yep."

"How many times did you fuck her?"

I knew I couldn't get to the gun before Vincent pulled the trigger, especially with bound wrists. "Four or five."

"Not yet, Vincent," the driver spoke immediately after I gave my answer. The voice belonged to a woman. "Stick with the plan."

Vincent's hand was shaking as the gun remained pointed at my head. He wanted to kill me right then and there.

"Where are we going?"

"Swimming," he answered behind clinched jaw.

"Where?"

"The mighty Mississippi."

At the age of six, I attended the World's Fair several times with my parents and brother. The only memory I could recall from the months-long event was riding the gondola high across the Mississippi River. I remembered it so vividly because I was scared to death of being in a small glass box as it came to a stop in the middle of the river. When a teenager complained to another of being scared, his friend laughed and said the fall wouldn't kill them; it was the current of the river that would be their demise. He said that not even Jesus would survive if he fell into the Mississippi. I believed him.

"Anything else you want to confess, Loverboy?"

Death by gunshot sounded less agonizing than drowning in the Mississippi. "Krista—your wife—said I was the best sex she ever had." My smile was the only one in the backseat. "She came five times then told me that she faked most orgasms with you because she wasn't attracted to you. But let's be honest, can you blame her? Have you looked in the mirror lately?" Vincent sat as lifeless as a statue.

"Vincent, don't listen to him."

"If you didn't have money, do you think someone as attractive as Krista would have even gone on one date with you?" I held my breath in anticipation for the gun to be fired. Nothing happened.

Vincent finally showed signs of life, smirking as he asked, "Do you think what you're telling me is something I didn't already know? I don't look like Sinatra or Deano, but I have something women are attracted to—power. I've committed more crimes over the last two decades than Al Capone did in his lifetime. I'm untouchable, you meaningless shithead."

"I bet Ralph thought he was untouchable too. Did you know he slipped on my kitchen floor and shot himself? The gunshot woke me up. I walked into my kitchen to see that assclown bleeding all over my floor. Do you even bother to screen your employees to see how incompetent they are?"

Vincent transferred the gun to his left hand, before balling his right into a fist. I didn't have time to react. Numbness came and went in a split-second, preceding a sharp, intense pain I had never experienced. My jaw felt as if it were broken, a loud ringing occurred in my left ear canal, and vision in my left eye was blurred. As seconds ticked by, the pain seemed to only intensify. I had managed to last twenty-nine years without being punched. The pain was god-awful.

"How 'bout we just do this right here!" Vincent shouted.

"Vincent, we're almost there. Follow the plan," the driver spoke. "How are we going to explain the mess to your friend? We'll get caught if you do this here."

"Then hurry up. I don't know how much longer I can go without pumping this asshole full of lead."

The car accelerated, continuing towards the mighty Mississippi.

Vincent's right hook kept me silent as we crossed the Mississippi River via the Crescent City Connection and passed through the small suburb of Algiers, located on the west bank of the Mississippi River. As I had done while handcuffed inside of Cliff's rig, I thought about those close to me. In only a week, so many truths had come to life. Truths I wished I had not known about. It upset me I would never get to make amends with my brother, tell my dad one last time I loved him, embrace my mother, thank Caroline for her support over the last few months—especially the last couple of days, or that I would never discover the truth behind Delain's disappearance. By my count, I had eluded death five times in my life. I feared my luck was about to run out.

We came to a stop in a darkened, secluded area next to the river. The driver shut off the engine and the headlights. I looked out of the window, hoping a bystander was around. Not a soul could be seen. The driver was the first to exit. She opened my door before Vincent told me, "Get out."

I didn't move. From behind, a hand grabbed a chunk of my hair and pulled me backwards. I stepped out. The driver's hand shifted to the back of my neck.

"Don't turn around or I'll snap your neck," she told me.

"You're an accessory to murder. They won't have mercy on you just because you're a woman."

"Shut your mouth, asshole."

Once Vincent stepped out of the car, he looked to the woman behind me, telling her, "I knew bringing you along would be a good idea."

To my left was the bridge we had crossed minutes earlier. I had lived in New Orleans all my life and crossed the bridge at least a hundred times. I had never seen it from the underside. The bridge was colossal. One of the nearby concrete pillars supporting the bridge had a circumference greater than the length of a large car. To my right was an abandoned Mardi Gras float warehouse. I considered running toward it, but the female's grip on my neck was unyielding.

"Why don't you walk him to the river, Vincent? I think he's itching to run."

"I think someone's gonna be moving up the ladder at Dichario Enterprises when we return to Vegas." Vincent grabbed my right arm, pushing me up the grass levee and towards the river. Being handcuffed would make it more challenging to get the gun from Vincent's hands, but I wasn't going down without a fight.

"You should have heard Ralph beg for his life before he died. He cried as he took his last breath." Vincent raised his right arm. I lunged forward, heaving my shoulder into his torso. He didn't budge. I watched as he lifted his right arm once more, ramming the butt of the gun into the right side of my face. The impact knocked me to the ground. Blood dripped onto my hands as I rested on all fours. Before I could attempt to get to my feet and run, Vincent grabbed my right foot and proceeded to drag me a few yards to the river's edge.

"Any last words?" he breathlessly asked.

I closed my eyes. It wasn't my parents, older brother, twin brother, Delain, or even Caroline that I pictured. It was something else completely.

"Goodbye, Jackson. This is for Ralph." With shut eyes, I anticipated a shoe being pressed firmly against my back before succumbing to the undertow of the Mississippi. While holding my breath, I heard a gunshot. After flinching, I waited to feel an intense pain. I felt nothing. Upon opening my eyes to examine where the bullet had struck me, I realized I wasn't the victim. I looked upward. Blood oozed from a hole in Vincent's chest. His eyes grew large as he slowly turned around. His legs blocked my view of the shooter's face, but I could see smoke emerging from the gun held in her hand. She hastily approached Vincent. As he lifted his right arm, she again fired her gun, piercing Vincent's chest once more. He staggered backwards, tripping over me before falling into the river. As water splashed onto my back, I couldn't believe who stood before me.

Chapter 101

Even though vision in my left eye was still blurry and blood continuously dripped into my right eye socket, I could clearly see the woman before me that had been an occasional thought over the last nineteen months.

"Jordan! What are you doing here? What the hell is going on?"

She wiped the gun with her t-shirt before throwing it into the river. "I'll tell you in the car. We need to get out of here now." She grabbed my bound hands, helping me to my feet. I felt light-headed upon standing, but the sensation quickly passed.

I jumped in the passenger seat while Jordan returned to the driver's seat. She handed me several napkins from her purse, telling me, "Hold these tight against your gash. Try not to get too much blood in here." She then sped off.

I probably should have felt a throbbing sensation radiating from where Vincent struck me with his pistol, but I was too distracted by the person next to me to pay any attention to my pain receptors. "There are a dozen questions floating around my head right now."

"Is one of them 'why did the escort from Las Vegas that I paid to not have sex with me just save my life?'"

"That's on the top of the list."

"Vincent is my boss—or was my boss."

"He's your...pimp?"

"We call him our manager, but yes. He wasn't always my manager, though. His wife was initially. I believe you met Krista."

I remembered from our night together that Jordan's husband cheated on her with her best friend. I feared Jordan may have thought less of me knowing I slept with a married woman. "I swear to you I had no idea she was married. If I had known, I never would have...done what I did."

"I believe you." Her eyes remained on the road as we headed back towards the city. "Krista ran the escort side of Vincent's empire. We all loved her. She treated each of us like we were her own daughter. Once a week she would take me to breakfast. She was the closest thing I had to a mom. Then, just before Christmas of '05, she was gone. It didn't take long for rumors to spread about her disappearance. Most of us believed Vincent had something to do with her sudden absence, but we couldn't prove it. Even if we could, I doubt any of us would have said something to the authorities for fear of being killed. It wasn't until I saw the newscast last week of you that I discovered the truth. I was taking a nap on my friend's lap in Vincent's office when I was awoken and asked if I knew the man on television. Before I could answer, Ralph came in and said something about them being in an elevator with you. They came to the realization you slept with Krista. They said something about a missing shoe and a handkerchief with your initials."

"After she told me she was married, I hurried out of the room and left those two items behind. I never thought it would get me caught."

"When I found out Ralph had left to go to New Orleans, I was worried about you. I eventually got your house phone number from information and tried calling you, but all I got was the voicemail. I left a message to call me, but I guess you never got it."

"I haven't checked my messages since I've been back."

"I thought you were dead. I then grew upset with myself for not trying harder to contact you. Once I found out you were alive and Ralph was dead, I felt so relieved. That is until Vincent said he was coming down here to take care of you himself. That's when I volunteered to go with him."

"You came down here with intentions of killing Vincent?"

Jordan merged onto an on-ramp leading to the Crescent City Connection. "I don't know what my intentions were. I just reacted. Do I think Vincent deserved to die? Yes. Not only am I certain he killed his wife and at least one other man, but he was physically abusive to some of the other girls. Am I upset and scared that I just killed him? Absolutely."

"Did he ever hit you?"

She glanced in my direction then back at the road. "Once. Slapped me right across the face. I should have left then, but I was scared to leave."

The shock of escaping death and being reunited with Jordan was starting to wear off. Pain had begun to radiate on the right side of my face. I pulled the napkins away. They were completely doused in blood. "Do you have anymore napkins?"

"No. Take off your shirt and use that. I don't want you to get involved with Vincent's death."

"It's too late for that," I told her while removing my shirt. "Besides, I don't want you to get involved with it. It's my fault he came down here and you had to shoot him. I'm taking the rap for his death."

"No. Besides, you have a fiancée. I'm certain she—"

"I don't have a fiancée," I told her as we approached the toll booth.

"You don't have to lie to me."

"I'm not."

"But I saw the newscast— the runaway groom."

"I had a fiancée, but she's gone."

While rolling the window down, Jordan flashed a perplexed stare at me. "Pretend you're sleeping. Hide the gash on your head, and the handcuffs too."

I leaned back, my hands nestled between my thighs as I closed my eyes and rested the right side of my head against the window. My shirt—I hoped—was collecting every drop of blood dripping from the gash that was growing more painful with each passing minute. After Jordan paid and began to roll up the window, I sat upright.

"What do you mean she's gone?"

"I have no idea where she could be."

"I don't understand."

"Neither do I. We were secretly leaving town this past Saturday, but when I went to her house to pick her up, she wasn't there. A note that read 'I'm sorry' was left behind."

"How do you know she wrote it? Was it her handwriting?"

"It was definitely her handwriting."

"Why would she just leave you like that? Was there someone else?"

Even though I had no idea what he looked like, I pictured Tyler. I imagined Delain wrapped in his arms as the two passionately kissed one another. The thought hit me like a punch in the gut. It was apparent I wasn't over her, and I wouldn't be until I found her. "Maybe. She ran into an ex-boyfriend at the airport a day before the wedding. She was different after that."

"And you don't think he has something to do with her disappearance?"

"She swore she no longer had feelings for him. I believed her." I turned my shirt around, using a dry spot to soak up more of the blood.

"This ex of hers shows up a day before the wedding and she mysteriously disappears. I'd bet my money if you found him, you'd find her as well. First things first, we need to get you to a hospital."

"No hospital. They're going to ask questions, and the last thing I need right now is more cops or federal agents questioning me. What we need to do is make sure nothing happens to you. Whose car is this?"

"Vincent called a guy he knew down here and asked that he specifically have a white Crown Vic with tinted windows waiting for him at the airport, along with a police officer outfit in the trunk."

"We need to get rid of it, and then get you someplace safe. Do you still have family in Kansas City?"

"You remembered where I was from."

"I remembered everything from our night together, Brandi/Jordan. Your first…oh my God. I'm so stupid. That was the name you used when you called me a little while ago. I missed it—Officer Brandi Jordan."

"And you also missed the name of the officer who was picking you up—Officer Henry Jones."

"I don't get it."

"What movie did you tell me you were watching when you called the escort service in Vegas, thus providing you with your alias."

"*Raiders of the Lost Ark.* I told you I was Dr. Jones. But his first name is Indiana."

"What's his real first name?"

I suddenly remembered Sean Connery saying his birth name in the third movie of the series. "Henry. Damn you're good, Jordan."

"If I would have said Officer Indiana Jones, Vincent would have thought something suspicious was going on. I tried to warn you, but I guess it was a little too subtle."

"I should have caught it."

"Now, what were you saying about our night together? My first…?"

My headache intensified greatly. I closed my eyes as I told her, "Your first kiss was in the fifth grade with a boy named Mikey, who then tattled on you and got you in trouble.

Fiji is where you want to go on your second honeymoon. Your worst date was with a man whose name I can't remember, but the night ended with him running into his ex, whom he proceeded to make out with right in front of you before the two cried and climbed into a taxi together." Jordan was quiet. I opened my eyes, glancing to my left. Her face was blank. "Are you okay?"

"I'm fine."

I got the impression she wasn't. "Are you sure?"

She was slow to respond. "That night with you was probably the last time I felt…safe. I'm just a little taken aback you remembered all those things."

I again closed my eyes before telling her, "I was in Las Vegas for six weeks. That night with you was the only night I didn't feel alone. I chased you down the hall after you kissed me. You had already gotten into the elevator. I wanted to track you down and ask you on a date, but I convinced myself you were pretending to care about me only because I was paying you."

While staring at the road, she told me, "I wish I could tell you I was pretending, Jackson…but I'd be a liar."

When I first saw Jordan in the hallway of the hotel nineteen months earlier, I was instantly attracted to her. Her hair was nicely styled, her make-up looked as if it was meticulously applied, and her dress appeared to have been purchased from a high-end clothing store. While driving the Crown Vic, she wore jeans and a t-shirt, had her hair tucked into a baseball cap, and her face lacked any make-up. I found her to be more attractive dressed down then up. "I thought about you a lot when you left my room."

"You were in my thoughts for several months, Jackson. I was finally able to forget about you— until a couple of days ago."

Jordan's claim that I was a fixture in her thoughts gave me chills. "I'm sorry."

"Why are you apologizing?"

"Krista. It's my fault she's dead."

"It's Vincent's fault."

"But if I didn't sleep with her, she would still be alive." I grew angry upon reminding myself she was dead because of my actions. And not only Krista, but Mikey, Davis, Brad, Hank, Cliff, Ralph, and Vincent were all dead because of me. Eight people were no longer alive because of me. Eight people were dead because I chose to play a video of my ex-fiancée cheating on me. Never did I think it would have gone as far as it did.

"Don't blame yourself. Vincent killed her, and now he's gone. Justice has prevailed."

I agreed Vincent's death was justified—along with Ralph, Hank, Davis, and Cliff's. Krista, Mikey, and Bradley, however, were innocent victims. "Justice may have prevailed in our eyes, but not the authorities. His body will most likely be found, and if so, an autopsy will be administered. Soon they will find out who he is and that he was shot and…did you fly down here together?"

"Yes."

"They'll be looking for you too. I'm sure some of Vincent's associates will want to talk to you as well."

"They can't talk to me if they can't find me. I'm not going back to Vegas."

"What are you going to do?"

Jordan shrugged her shoulders. "I haven't gotten that far yet."

Yet again, someone else's life would be forever affected because of me. "What about Kansas City? Do you think you would be safe there?"

"Only one of the other girls knows where I'm from and my real name. If they ask Ginger, she might be scared enough to tell them the truth."

"You can't go there."

"For how long?"

"I'm not sure."

"Now I'm starting to get a little nervous, Jackson."

"You don't have anywhere safe to go?"

"Not really."

An idea then came to mind. "Unfortunately, you won't be any safer hanging around me right now, but I know someone who will be eager to help us."

"We need to get those cuffs off of you too."

"I think my friend will be able to help with that as well."

Chapter 102

After wrapping the seatbelt around my right arm several times and gripping the console tightly with my left hand, I nodded. Jordan dabbed several hydrogen peroxide-soaked cotton balls against the laceration on the right side of my forehead. "Shit!" My face felt like it was both paralyzed and on fire.

"I'm sorry." Her apology preceded the blowing of cool air upon the open wound. It momentarily lessened the burn. "The good news is the bleeding is slowing down."

"How deep is it?"

She leaned closer, squinting while answering, "The Grand Canyon comes to mind. You're going to have a pretty nasty scar. Are you sure you don't want to make a trip to the E.R.?"

"Positive. I think we can do this ourselves."

"It's your call, Scarface."

I grinned at a stone-faced Jordan as we sat in the Crown Vic in the parking lot of a grocery store abandoned since Katrina. Something else I remembered from our night together was she didn't smile much, even when telling a joke. She sat on the edge of the passenger seat with her feet on the cracked pavement and her back to the dashboard while digging through a plastic Walgreens bag. She removed a tube of Neosporin, squeezing a large glob onto her pointer finger and then applied it to my face.

"Are you sure you can't tell me why it's not safe to be around you right now?"

"For your own safety—yes."

"Just so you know, that only makes me more curious. Maybe I'll be able to get that information from your friend when he gets here."

"He doesn't know much more than you."

"Can't you give me a little hint or something? I think it's only fair since I just saved your life."

"Thank you again for that. I owe you big time."

"And you can start by letting me in on some of your secrets."

"Fair enough. Do you remember the reason I went to Vegas?"

She placed the tube of Neosporin back in the Walgreens bag. "At your wedding, you played a video of your fiancée cheating on you. You wanted to get away." Jordan then removed a box of butterfly closures from the bag.

"That same fiancée isn't happy with me right now."

"Because of the video?"

"Something else. Something much worse."

Jordan placed a closure over my wound. "Are you going to be okay?"

Even with Vincent dead, I still feared for my life. The conversation a few hours earlier with Tiffany was the new catalyst for my pessimistic outlook. "I don't know."

"Can you go to the police?"

"My predicament involves a former police officer. I don't know who I can trust there."

Jordan applied another butterfly closure. "I'm scared for you, Jackson. I don't want anything to happen to you."

"I don't want anything to happen to you either. That's why you need to get out of here soon."

"Do you trust him?"

"Who?"

"Your friend who's meeting us here— Logan."

"With my life. You're going to be in good hands."

"How long do you think I'm going to have to hide out?"

Before I could answer, truck headlights flashed on our faces. Jordan leaned across me, grabbing another gun from her purse.

"How many guns do you have?"

"The one I threw in the river was left in here by Vincent's New Orleans associate. Remember during our night together how I told you I always carry a little firepower in my purse?"

Once I could see Logan's face, I motioned for her to put the gun away. Logan's eyes hinted at excitement as he pulled up next to us. I knew my friend well enough to know he was pleased by Jordan's appearance.

He rolled the window down. "Hello, Jordan. I'm Logan and I'll be your bodyguard for the next few..." His eyes grew even larger upon finally glancing in my direction. "What happened to your face?"

"Vincent hit me."

"With what? A piano?"

"A gun."

"Where is he?"

"Somewhere in the Mississippi River."

Logan grinned. "The son of a bitch is dead?"

I nodded.

"Then it's over, right?"

I shook my head. "Not yet."

"What the hell else is there?"

"He won't say," Jordan told him.

While pointing to Jordan, he asked, "Is she right?"

"Yes. I don't want—"

Logan slammed his left hand against the door of his truck. "You're still not going to tell your best friend the shit that you've gotten yourself into?!"

"I can't. It's for your own protection."

"What about your protection? I don't want to lose another best friend."

"I'll be okay. I have it all under control."

He snickered. "You have it under control? Let's see..." He began to count on his fingers as he said, "Your mom's in a coma, your brother is currently pissed to high hell with you, a hit-man was killed in your kitchen, a mob boss is floating in the Mississippi, the F.B.I. is looking for you, your face is swollen and bleeding, your fiancée is nowhere to be found, and this lovely lady right here now has to go on the lamb for God knows how long with your best friend who wants nothing more than to help you. Jackson, how in the hell do you have this under control?"

Jordan and I both stood from the passenger seat. "You're helping me by looking after Jordan. Please can we not talk about it right now? It's been another long day. Can you just get out of here before something happens to either one of you? Please, Logan."

"God damnit." With a roll of his eyes, he asked Jordan, "Are you ready?"

"I guess so." She grabbed her purse as she turned to me. "Will I see you again?"

110

"Yes."

"When?"

"Very soon." My gut told me otherwise. Jordan briefly placed her lips onto mine before climbing into the truck. I walked to the driver's window, placing my hands in front of Logan. "Where are you gonna go?"

Logan inserted a key into the handcuffs, unfastening them with one attempt. "Would you leave your best friend if he was in obvious danger?"

"If he told me to—yes."

"Where did you obtain a handcuff key?" Jordan asked Logan.

Logan turned to her. "Let's just say I once dated a girl who was into the kinky stuff, and we'll leave it at that." After turning back to me, he said, "You look pale."

I felt light-headed and weak. "I'm fine."

"You're lying. Is Texas far enough away?"

"It should be."

"I figured a little adrenaline might distract us for the time being." He turned to Jordan, asking her, "Have you ever been bungee jumping?"

"Not since yesterday," she spoke with enough sarcasm for me to detect.

"Good." He pointed to the bed of his truck. "I got an extra bungee back there with your name on it."

"Y'all be careful."

Logan nodded. "We got this. Call me as soon as you know something, you secret-having, non-sharing bastard."

"I will. You take care of her."

"Will do," Logan said with a wink of his left eye.

"Jordan, hit him if he comes on to you."

She flashed the gun from her purse. "I'll do more than hit him. Don't forget the ammonia. It's in the bag."

"This should be interesting," a grinning Logan spoke. "Be careful, Jackson. Don't do anything stupid."

"I've made it this far, haven't I?"

"Barely."

Chapter 103

A common phenomenon as of late, déjà vu, struck me once more as I drove the Crown Vic beneath the same interstate overpass I parked Hank's truck one week earlier. His truck was nowhere to be seen. Since it was in good condition and still operable, I imagined it was stolen before the police could find it. After wiping any place Jordan or I could have touched, and spraying the entire inside with ammonia, I ditched the Crown Vic before hailing a taxi outside of a nearby bar. I had the taxi driver drop me off on the 2600 block of Prytania Street.

I was a different person walking through my parents' backyard than when leaving hours earlier. Even though I had been hit on the head and lost a significant amount of blood, I felt lucid. I was exhausted, but my thoughts were becoming more rational. Lights were on in the kitchen, but no one occupied it.

"Anybody here?" I asked at a decibel just above a whisper.

"Jackson?" My dad's voice echoed from the study. I walked into the room to find him standing from one of the two leather chairs. He looked as exhausted as I felt.

"How's Mom?"

"She's…my God! What happened to your face?!" He placed both hands on my shoulders while leaning towards the gash I had yet to see for myself.

"Vincent."

His jaw dropped. "He did this to you?"

"Yes."

"Where is he?"

"Dead."

"How?"

"He was shot, and then his body plopped into the Mississippi River."

My dad appeared transfixed by my revelation. "You shot him?"

"No. Someone else." I sunk into one of the leather chairs. Even though I was far from relaxed, resting in a familiar place was the calmest I had felt in days, if not weeks. I could have fallen asleep in seconds if no one was in the room.

"Who?"

"A prostitute from Las Vegas."

My dad slowly lowered himself into the adjacent chair. "Is she dead too?"

"No. She's with Logan." The ibuprofen Jordan purchased earlier from the drug store was quickly wearing off. The pain felt like it was intensifying with each tick of the grandfather clock in the hallway. I placed both hands on my head while leaning forward.

"Are you okay?"

"My face is hurting again. Can you grab the Walgreens bag on the kitchen counter and some water please?"

In the short moment it took for my dad to retrieve what I had asked for, I dozed off. I awoke to him nudging me. "Jax, are you sure you're okay?" He handed me the bag and a bottle of water. "Do you need to go to the hospital? What if you have a concussion?"

"I'm fine. I'm just tired. It's been another long day."

"Who's the prostitute, and why is she with Logan?"

I placed four pills in my mouth before chasing them with a large gulp of water. "She worked for Vincent. She came down here with him and shot him before he could throw me into the river. Logan's looking after her until all of this is over." I leaned back, resting my head on the back of the chair while shutting my eyes.

"Until all of what is over?"

"You never did tell me how Mom is doing."

"She's stable—in and out of consciousness. Marcus is with her right now. We decided one of us should be there and one here for when you got back. All of what, Jackson? What else is there?"

My eyes remained closed as I asked, "How did you do it for so long?"

"Do what?"

"Pretend everything was normal? Act like giving away my twin brother didn't have any kind of impact on your life?"

"Your mother, your older brother, and you," he immediately answered. "The thought of losing any one of you is what kept me together. Your mother felt the same way.

Angelo's father was bad news. When your mother confessed to having an affair with Dominick, I confronted him."

I opened my eyes and turned to my left. "Did you hit him?" I never imagined my dad engaging in fisticuffs at any point during his lifetime.

"That was my intention. I met him at the restaurant your mother was to meet him. A heated argument ensued, and we were kicked out of the establishment. Before I could take a swipe at him, he threw me into an alley, where he pulled a knife from his boot and pressed the blade against my throat." He lifted his chin, pointing to the white horizontal line just above his Adam's apple. "This was a gift from Dominick."

"All these years I thought you got it from shaving."

"I didn't think a seven-year-old needed to know the truth about my scar. Don't you agree?"

I nodded. "I guess."

"What do you think goes through my head every time," he again pointed to the scar, "I look in a mirror and see this?"

I imagined he didn't see his wife engaged in sex with another man during his daily shave in the bathroom mirror, but instead he and another woman in a hotel room during his campaign.

"Dominick stuck the blade into my neck. Blood trickled down my throat. He said he had killed a man before and was prepared to do it again. I believed him."

Another trait my biological dad and I shared was just revealed to me—murderer. "Were you scared?"

"Yes, and even more so when he pulled a gun from the back of his pants and held it to my forehead. He had this look in his eyes. For the few seconds the gun was pressed against my forehead and the blade to my neck, I thought I was taking my last breath."

Four times throughout my life, I had a gun aimed at me. With each, I felt something different. At nine years old, without knowing the true meaning of death, I didn't know to be scared while a gun was pointed at my head. Instead, I was angry at having to give my parents' Christmas present away. In Cliff's truck, I never feared he would shoot me. I was more bothered and annoyed by Cliff's antics than anything. Hours later in Hank's living room, was the first time I was truly scared and thought death was forthcoming. I envisioned either Cliff accidentally shooting me or Hank strangling me to death. I didn't want to die, mostly because I feared Delain would never discover the truth about her son.

114

When Vincent tried to kill me by the river, I was by all means afraid, but it was different than the previous incident. "What did you think about for those few seconds?"

"The woman I cheated on your mother with—Clementine. I know they say your life flashes before your eyes when death is imminent, but I pictured Clementine. The biggest regret of my life flashed before my eyes."

"How did you get away?"

"A group of people saw what was going on. Dominick backed down, but not before saying he would kill me if he ever saw me again. He was bluffing because I saw him a couple of months later when your mother and I confronted him about the pregnancy."

"Were you scared when you saw him again?"

"Terrified, but," he looked me square in the eyes as he straight-faced told me, "if he would have touched or threatened your mother, I was going to kill him."

I didn't think he had it in him to kill another person. "Were you worried about going to jail if you would have killed him?"

"I didn't care. I loved your mother just as much then as I do now, and I know she felt the same about me. When you're madly in love with someone…"

I pictured Davis bound to the steering wheel of his Ferrari as I told him, "You'd kill for them."

"Love makes even the most timid of men feel like they're Hercules—like nothing in the world can stop him. I was ready to tear him limb from limb with my bare hands. Love makes you do crazy things."

"Tell me about it."

"Speaking of…have you heard from Delain?"

"Not a peep."

"It's so strange she would just leave like she did."

Just seconds before Jordan saved my life, I came to the realization that I was to blame for my multiple near-encounters with death. I was also to blame for the death of eight people. I was a virus that was infecting others. I had to be stopped before someone else died. "I killed Davis."

My dad shook his head while squinting. "He died of a heart attack."

"A heart attack I caused."

"You're not making sense, Jax. You weren't even around when he died. Your head injury might be worse than you think."

"I wasn't out west. I was in Davis' house when he died. I taped his wrists to the steering wheel and held a gun to his head. He had a heart attack and begged me to grab his nitroglycerine pills in the glove compartment. I let him die." Speechless, my dad looked on. "The F.B.I. agents that have been looking for me, I'm going to tell them the truth tomorrow morning. I'm going to tell them everything."

"Are you…are you serious?"

"Yes, sir."

"Why?"

"Love makes you do crazy things."

"I don't understand."

"You will tomorrow. I can barely keep my eyes open." I stood. My dad grabbed my arm before I could head for the stairs.

"You're not going to bed yet, and you're not going to confess anything to the F.B.I. without talking to me first."

"The longer I wait, the more people's lives are in danger. I can't keep it in any longer. I'm tired of running. I'm doing the right thing by telling the truth now instead of later." He let go of my arm. "I'll see you in the morning." I walked upstairs to my old bedroom, falling asleep within seconds of my head hitting the pillow.

Tuesday

Chapter 104

The fact that I had the best sleep in weeks only helped to convince me I was making the right decision by telling Agents Parker and Williams everything that had transpired in the past week and a half. It was possible the pain relievers aided my restless sleep, but I truly believed my decision to come clean had more to do with it. A glance into the bathroom mirror revealed the side of my face to be very much swollen, and the bruising had become darker surrounding my right eye and cheek. After a few dabs of an alcohol-soaked cotton ball onto the wound, I made my way downstairs. It was not quite eight o'clock. My dad and twin brother were seated at the table.

"Morning, y'all."

Angelo turned around. As he had done so often in my presence, he was eagerly grinning. "Brother."

My dad lowered the front page of *The Times Picayune*. "How did you sleep?"

"Very well."

Angelo frowned while pointing. "What happened to the face?"

"I had an accident," I told him while scanning the table. "I'm okay." Both were drinking coffee. No food was on the table. "I'm going to make an omelet. Do either of you want one?"

My dad set the newspaper on the table. "I'll make it. Have a seat." As he walked to the refrigerator, I sat across the table from Angelo.

My brother looked on with concern from behind his coffee mug as I asked him, "You like coffee?"

"I drink every morning. Are you good?"

I reached for the newspaper. "Yes. Are you?"

"Si."

"Jax, is there anything else you want to say regarding the tail end of our conversation last night?"

"No, sir."

"Are you still proceeding as scheduled?"

"Right after breakfast."

I watched my dad crack several eggs into a large mixing bowl. With whisk in hand he asked, "As a lawyer, but more so as your father, I would advise you to talk to me before meeting with the feds. I can help you if you will let me."

If I were to tell him everything, he might try to stop me from talking to them. I came up with a compromise. "What if you were to be there when I talk to them? We could invite them over and do it right here at the table." His subtle nod led me to believe he was somewhat pleased. He placed the whisked eggs into a skillet, followed by a handful of chopped ham and green onions.

"Are you going to mention…everything?" He pointed to Angelo, whose back was to him.

"I don't see the need to talk about something that happened thirty years ago." My dad nodded. "Any word on Mom yet?"

"I just got off the phone with Marcus. She's sleeping, and her vitals are still stable. I think you should go to the hospital with me after breakfast. She needs to hear your voice again."

"I will, and then I'll make the call."

"Since I stay here, tell her I pray for her and hope to see her soon."

"Will do, Angelo."

Tuesday's edition of the newspaper always seemed thinner than every other day of the week's editions. It was as if there wasn't much going on in the world on Mondays. It didn't take long, however, to discover on page five of the main section that something very interesting did indeed take place on Monday two states away.

Mobile, Alabama— Authorities have re-opened the case involving two Mobile women, Rebecca McGovern and Maria Sanchez, who were held captive in the basement of Hank Bowery, also of Mobile, for six weeks. The two women—who were forced against their will to engage in sexual acts with as many as ten different men—were discovered by the police in the early morning hours on Sunday, July 1st. Hank Bowery and another gentleman, Cliff Robertson, were found shot to death in the living room of Bowery's house in what was originally thought to be a shootout between the two men. Evidence has now come forth that another person was in the house during the shootout. The first police officer on the scene, Officer Robert 'Spud' McKenzie, originally...

'How did you know about this place?' Hank asked as I stared at the barrel of his shotgun on his doorstep nine days earlier.

'Spud. Spud told me.'

"Maybe we can talk more after trip to hospital," Angelo suggested. I didn't respond to him. My mind was elsewhere. I was back in the attic, beneath the insulation as Officer McKenzie scanned the attic with his flashlight. To say that the officer was 'good-looking' would have been a very generous compliment. The birthmark surrounding his left eye was distracting, and I'm sure many women found it unattractive; so much so I began to wonder if he had to force women to have sex with him—and perhaps those women just happened to be the prostitutes chained up in Hank's dungeon. My gut told me Officer Robert 'Spud' McKenzie was the same 'Spud' that would have known about the sex slaves. I then recalled the details of when the police cruisers first arrived at Hank's house.

"Angelo just suggested something, Jackson."

I stood from the table. "I'll be right back." I slipped back into my jeans, threw on a clean t-shirt, and brushed my teeth, all while thinking about Officer McKenzie's birthmark. I imagined he was nicknamed after Spuds McKenzie, the famous dog used in Bud Light advertisements in the late eighties. The dog, like Officer McKenzie, had a birthmark surrounding his eye.

I returned to the kitchen table. An omelet awaited me. I pushed it out of the way to get another glimpse at the newspaper. At the bottom of the article, I found what was needed. *Anyone with information pertaining to the involvement of a third party is instructed to call the Mobile Police Department at...*

"Are you going somewhere?"

I ripped the entire article out of the newspaper. "Yes, and I need to borrow the car."

"Where are you going? And don't you want to eat your breakfast?"

I was never one to do much of anything without first eating breakfast. I grabbed the plate. "I'll eat on the way. Where are your keys?"

"Where are you going, and what did you just rip out of the newspaper?"

"I can't tell you."

"Then I can't give you the keys."

"I can't play this game right now. I think someone is getting away with a major crime."

"Then tell me about it."

"Not right now."

"Of course not." For the first time I could ever remember, my dad looked and sounded agitated with me. I couldn't blame him.

"If you let me borrow the car, I'll tell you everything when I get back, and then I'll call the agents after that. How's that sound?"

"Like you're starting to come to your senses. How long will you be gone?"

"Fifteen minutes."

He handed me his keys.

"Thank you. Can I borrow a couple of quarters too?"

Payphones, it seemed, had become more and more elusive as I drove around the city in search of one. The gas stations I passed either had no payphone at all or contained the vestiges of once was a payphone. Twenty minutes into my search, I spotted one outside a diner.

A man wearing a mesh trucker's hat watched from inside the diner as I deposited several quarters into the payphone. After dialing the number from the newspaper article, I turned around as the man's constant staring from the other side of the window created an air of uneasiness.

"Mobile Police Department."

"I need to speak with Officer Robert McKenzie."

"Hold please."

Part of me wondered why I was calling him, while a much larger part of me wanted justice to prevail. If the police officer was the same Spud that was part of Hank's sex ring, I wanted him behind bars.

"Officer McKenzie."

"Is this Spud?"

"This is Officer McKenzie."

"But the newspaper article included Spud in your name."

"That was a misprint. Can I help you with something, sir?"

"I need to find Spud. I have a very important message to relay from an old friend of his."

"What's the message?"

His inquiry led me to believe he was indeed Spud, but I wasn't sure if he was 'the' Spud. "Sic semper tyrannis."

With each second of silence that ensued, I grew more confident my hunch was right. A good five seconds passed before I could hear the clearing of his throat. "Who is this?" His tone grew much more authoritative.

"Someone who knows all-too-well about secret phrases used to get into underground sex dungeons." There was no response. "You still there, Spud?"

"I'm glad someone from New Orleans knows about secret phrases."

I wasn't surprised he knew where I was calling from, as it was the reason I searched for a payphone. "I'm guessing your nickname is Spud because of the birthmark around your eye."

"How do you know about my birthmark?"

"I saw it."

"When?"

"Nine days ago…in Hank's attic." I held the phone tighter to my ear. Heavy breathing was all I could hear. "The light from your flashlight passed in front of your face as I hid beneath the insulation. You were right, Spud—the air conditioner wasn't on so there was no reason for the rope hanging from the attic door to swing other than the fact I had just gone up there."

"Is that right?"

"Cliff instructed me to tell Hank that Spud sent me to his house with two one-hundred- dollar bills. Hank then asked if Spud told me the rules. Someone named Spud knew about the chained girls. Someone named Spud was the first to enter the house after the shooting took place—and so quickly. Tell me, Spud, why wasn't your siren on while the other police car sirens were when they arrived after you?"

"You're making a very bold accusation, friend."

"An accusation implies there is some uncertainty. I have no doubt you are just as guilty as Hank and his buddy Cliff. They told me all about you."

"Is that so? Well, let's just pretend for a second that I am who you say I am. What is the purpose of this phone call?"

So far, it was just to inform him I knew who he was. I wasn't sure of my next step. "To let you know you have about ten minutes until the Feds arrive at your station."

"Good to know." He didn't sound fazed. "My turn, friend. Why are you waiting until nine days later to come forward? Why not sooner?"

"Guilty conscience."

Officer McKenzie laughed before saying, "Doubt it. I think you're part of something too. Why didn't you stay behind and take credit as a hero? Why were you at the house with Cliff to begin with? Why is an F.B.I. agent reopening a case that was already closed?"

Agents Parker and Williams came to mind. I wondered if they discovered the truth because of my fingerprints. "I'll ask Agent Parker as soon as I hang up with you and tell him about your involvement with Hank."

"Agent Parker?" The uncertainty in his tone led me to believe Agent Parker wasn't the agent he was referring to. My gamble of making him think I already knew about the F.B.I. agent involved backfired. "Whoever you talk to, don't forget to remind him you stole Hank's truck after you shot Cliff because you were trying to avoid the police. What are you guilty of, friend?"

"Cliff kidnapped me and forced me to go to Hank's house." I waited for a reply, but instead received a dial tone. I hung up, more nervous than before making the call.

As I inserted more quarters into the payphone, I could feel the man in the mesh hat inside the diner continuing to stare me down. After dialing Caroline's cell phone number and while waiting to hear her voice, I glanced at the middle-aged Caucasian gentleman as he sat alone in a booth. His weathered face and dark tattered clothing, along with a pronounced underbite as he chewed, invoked feelings of sympathy. He reminded me of Cliff.

"Hello?"

The person's voice on the other end of the phone didn't belong to Caroline or any another female. I wondered if I dialed the wrong number. "Um...is this Caroline's phone?"

"Yes, it is. She's in the shower right now. Is that you, Jackson?"

I then knew to whom the voice belonged. "Brock?"

"Hey, fella. How's it going?"

I became shocked and even more apprehensive upon hearing his voice. "What are you doing with Caroline?"

"I flew down last night to be with her."

"Y'all broke up."

"Who told you that?"

"Caroline."

I could hear Brock excessively breathing before saying, "We took a little break, but it looks like we're going to work on things."

The familiar feeling of betrayal overcame me. The phone nearly fell out of my hand. "What?"

"It took a little time apart for the two of us to realize how much we really love one another. The engagement is back on."

I found myself leaning against the payphone, as standing under my own strength became increasingly difficult.

"Did she tell you anything else, Jackson? Did it sound as if she missed me?"

The only time his name was mentioned in the last week was when Caroline told me she had called off the engagement. She didn't miss him all too much. I was certain Brock was lying. I was tired of being lied to and tired of lying to everyone. "No."

"No, she didn't miss me?"

"She didn't mention you at all."

"Are…are you sure?"

I no longer cared what Brock thought of me. "Why are you answering her phone? Did she tell you to answer it, or did you take it upon yourself to see who was calling her because of your insecurity?"

"I bought the phone for her, and she's my fiancée, Jackson. I'll do what I damn well please. I don't appreciate your condescending tone right now."

"Caroline doesn't love you."

"How the hell would you know?"

"She told me. Why don't you do us a favor and go back to California."

"Listen you little piece of…what do you mean 'us'?" His tone was becoming more aggressive by the second.

"Have you noticed how distant she feels around you now? Why can't you let it go and move on? You're a good-looking guy. You'll find someone who loves you back."

"There's something going on between you and her, isn't there?"

"I want to speak to her now."

"I knew it. You two have had a thing since she first came down here. I sensed it when the four of us went to dinner."

"Ask yourself this, Brock: was she excited when you surprised her last night, or was her expression similar to that of a deer caught in headlights? I'm betting on the latter."

"If having sex a few minutes ago means she wasn't excited to see me, then I'd love to know what we would have done if she *was* excited to see me. And it was the craziest sex we've ever had, my friend." The image of Brock inside of Caroline as they kissed one another caused my queasiness to return.

There was no goodbye as I slammed the phone onto the ringer. The 'feeling' that had occurred over the last few days was again encompassing me. I closed my eyes while inhaling deeply. Before the attack could worsen, Jordan came to mind. I thought about our conversation the previous night, and how she revealed I had been in her thoughts for several months. I placed another quarter into the payphone. I needed to hear her voice.

"Hello."

"Logan, are y'all okay?"

"Thank God you called." He sounded panicked.

"What's wrong?"

"Jordan's gone."

My chest tightened even more. "What do you mean?"

"Once we left you last night, I think reality set in for her. She started freaking out about shooting Vincent. I tried to calm her down and even gave her a Xanax. She was convinced she wasn't safe around me. I woke this morning to find both her and my Mustang gone. The only reason I didn't report the car stolen was because I wanted to check with you first."

"Do you have any idea where she could have gone? Did she talk about anything else?"

"Besides you— no."

"Besides me?"

"She told me about the night you two had in Vegas."

"What did she say about that night?"

"How it was one of the very few nights she enjoyed while living out there. She said you were a perfect gentleman and never tried to take advantage of her."

I visualized Jordan driving on the interstate in Logan's Mustang, heading someplace far away from New Orleans and Las Vegas. I envisioned her giving up prostitution and soon finding someone with a good heart that would treat her nothing less than amazing. Our paths would never cross again.

"Are you still there, Jackson?"

"I'm here."

"You sound upset. You okay?"

"I'm ready for all of this to be over."

"Are you finally going to tell me what you've been up to?"

"Yes. Where are you now?"

"I went back to our house last night. I figured since Vincent was dead we were safe there. I was going to drive Jordan to Texas this morning, but she was gone."

"Go to my parents' house. I'll tell you and my dad everything before going to the Feds."

"It's about damn time. I'll be there soon."

"I'm sorry I got you into this, Logan."

"Stop saying that. I finally have some excitement in my life. See you soon, Outlaw."

I took a seat on the curb, placing my head between my knees while gasping for air. Even though it was barely 9 o'clock, the air was thick and warm, thus making breathing even more of a challenge. Only adding to my distress was the realization everything around me was crumbling. Even though I had avoided dying in a plane crash eleven days earlier, I felt as if I was on an airplane that was out of fuel and quickly descending. I feared before the day was over, a fiery crash would occur.

I knew she wouldn't pick up, yet I couldn't resist the urge to call Delain and leave her a message telling her goodbye. While dropping another quarter into the payphone, a black SUV pulled into the diner parking lot. I dialed her number. The darkened windows on the SUV caused immediate apprehension. No longer wanting to talk to a federal agent until telling my dad everything, I was ready to hang up and run if Agents Parker and Williams were to exit the SUV—but Delain's phone started ringing. Every other time I had called since Saturday afternoon, Delain's voicemail picked up immediately. My heart pounded as the anticipation of hearing her voice overpowered the need to quickly flee. With my left arm leaning against the phonebooth—shielding my face from whomever was in the vehicle—I peeked beneath it to see the vehicle slowly passing my dad's car. It came to a stop. I couldn't see who was in the SUV, but I was certain they were looking at me.

"Hello?"

I gasped. "Delain!"

"Jackson!"

Both the driver's and passenger's doors opened. "Where the hell have you been, Delain?!" While awaiting an answer, two men I had been hoping to avoid for a little while longer made eye contact with me.

"He's gone!" she cried.

"Mr. Fabacher." Agent Williams smirked as he and his partner approached me. "We found some irregularities with your previous statements. You're going to have to come with us I'm afraid."

Agent Parker's face was one without emotion. He nodded as if to say 'listen to my partner'.

I ignored them, instead asking Delain, "Who's gone?"

Agent Williams reached for the phone in my hand. Instinct caused me to slap at his arm. Using his other hand, he reached for the firearm holstered at his side.

"Where are you?" Delain asked.

Agent Williams stared at me from behind his Glock. "Drop the phone now!"

In a fit of anger, I threw the phone. As it swung back and forth, Agent Parker removed a set of handcuffs from his belt. "Turn around, Jackson."

"Why?"

"You just assaulted a federal agent!" Agent Williams yelled. "Turn around and place your hands behind your head!"

I turned around. Agent Parker's reflection in the diner window grew larger as he approached then grabbed my right hand. "This is bullshit and you know it."

"I'm afraid the statement you gave us was bullshit, Jackson. I'm sorry it's come to this."

He placed my left hand behind my back just before the sound of metal clicked into place, officially making me a criminal. I stared into the diner, particularly at one of the patrons. The man in the mesh hat continued to stare at me with no emotion. I shot him a cold stare just before Agent Parker turned me around.

Agent Williams reached for the dangling phone and placed it against his ear while asking Delain, "Who is this? This is a federal agent. Who is this?" He soon hung up. "Who were you just talking to, Jackson?"

"The fucking tooth fairy!"

He grew closer, gritting his teeth as he again asked, "Who were you talking to?"

"I will not say anything further until my lawyer is present."

Agent Parker escorted me into the back seat of the SUV. He sat to my left while Agent Williams drove.

"What happened to your face?" the agent next to me asked.

As promised, I didn't open my mouth during the entire ride. Instead, my thoughts were centered on one thing and one thing only—where in the hell had Delain been?

Saturday Afternoon

Chapter 105

Delain sat on her living room couch, her knees bouncing anxiously as she stared at the packed suitcase next to the front door. *Am I making the right decision? Will Jackson and I be okay? Where are we going to go? How are we going to get Caleb back? When is this going to end? When do I tell him the truth about everything?* After placing a piece of gum into her mouth, she glanced down at her phone. It was 3:05. If Jackson was on schedule, he would be arriving to pick her up in about fifteen minutes. In her hand, she held a white envelope containing her entire savings. *I hope you know what you're doing, Jackson.* As she stood up to place the envelope into her suitcase, a car door shut. It sounded as if it was in her driveway. *That was quick. He must have been speeding all the way back here.* Before Delain could peek through the blinds, there was a knock on the door. Even though she anticipated Jackson to be on her front step, she peered through the peephole. A man about two decades older than she, dressed in a light gray suit, stared directly at the peephole as though he could see right through it. Delain grew frightened. *Is he an undercover policeman? A detective? Someone associated with the person that tried to kill Jackson the previous night?* She imagined the man holding a knife or gun, waiting to stab or shoot her once she opened the door. He again knocked. *Maybe Jackson knows who it is.* Delain pressed the 'talk' button on her phone. Jackson's number appeared as it was the last person she called.

Before she could again press the button, the man on her doorstep loudly spoke, "Delain, I need to speak with you. It's a very urgent matter. I know you're in there. Please open the door."

How does he know my name?! "Who are you?"

"Someone with information you desperately want."

"What information?"

"I'd rather tell you face to face."

"That's not happening."

130

"Please open the door. I'm not going to hurt you."

"I'm calling the police," she told him, not actually wanting to do such a thing.

"Delain, open the door. If not for me, then do it for Caleb."

The phone fell out of her hand. She reached for the knob, pausing to lock the chain in place before cracking the door open. "Who the hell are you?"

"Someone who is going to help you get your son back—if you will allow me." There was no smile on the gentleman's face, just a look suggesting he was speaking the truth.

"How do you know Caleb?"

"I know a lot about you."

"How?"

"I'd rather tell you on the road. We have to leave now."

Delain then remembered what was in her purse. She shut and locked the door, reached into her purse, and then reopened the door while aiming her gun at the mysterious man with salt and peppered hair and a nicely tanned face. "Start talking or I start shooting. Who the hell are you?" Delain's heart pounded. Her body began to tremble as she waited to hear something to validate his claim. To disguise her shaking, she placed both hands on the gun, squeezing the handle as tightly as possible.

"My name is John. I have information regarding Caleb—or Thomas Melancon as his adopted parents call him—which you may like to know." John seemed unfazed by the gun aimed at his chest. "I also know of a way for you to claim him as your own." He glanced down at his watch and then back at Delain. "If you want this information, you have to come with me now. I'll tell you everything in my car."

Delain grew speechless as she pictured Caleb next to her in the elevator four days earlier. The teddy bear he dropped was packed in the suitcase at her feet.

"We have to go now, Delain. Or do you prefer I call you Christina?"

Her secrets, it seemed, were no longer secrets. "How do you know all of this?" She was on the verge of crying.

"Come with me and I'll tell you everything. I realize I'm a stranger and you're scared to go with me, so how about this: you sit in the backseat and keep your Rossi .357 Magnum aimed at me. Once you feel comfortable and realize I'm an ally and not a threat, you can lower it."

"I'm going to follow you in my car."

"I'm afraid that's not an option."

"Why?"

As a car approached Delain's house, John hastily turned around, watching until the Toyota Camry drove past her driveway. "It's not safe. That could be one of them now." His attention returned to Delain.

"One of who?"

"Them. The bad guys. They also know the truth about your son. You're no longer safe here."

"I'm about to leave town with—"

"Jackson. I know. If you leave with him, the window to get Caleb back will more than likely close for good."

"How did you know I was leaving with him?"

"I already told you—I know everything about you. Now, I'm leaving here in thirty seconds. If you're not in the car, you will never see me again and you'll be on your own in reclaiming Caleb as your son. Do you have any idea how you're going to get him back without going to jail or getting killed?"

"But I have to tell Jackson."

John began to walk backwards. "You have twenty-five seconds to get in the car, Christina Delain Foster, or say goodbye to Caleb." He turned around. "Don't forget your luggage. Twenty seconds."

While frantically grabbing her cell phone from the floor, Delain noticed a pen and piece of paper on the coffee table. She had enough time to write two words upon the sheet of paper, before grabbing her suitcase and unfastening the chain lock. Using the gum in her mouth, she stuck the note to the back of the door before closing it, not even bothering to waste time by locking it. The trunk of the black Chrysler sedan popped open. Delain threw her luggage into it, alongside several metallic boxes and suitcases, and then climbed into the backseat. While aiming the gun at John in the driver's seat, she tried to catch her breath, all while processing what was taking place. *I'm in the backseat of a car with a stranger who seems to know all my secrets. And I just left Jackson without saying goodbye. What in the hell am I doing?!*

As John began to reverse out of the driveway, he asked, "Do you have your cell phone with you?"

"No."

"Please don't lie to me, Delain."

"What does it matter if I have it or not?"

"If you do have it, please remove the battery and place it in the front seat."

"Why? So I can't call for help?"

"No. So the bad guys can't track you."

"I'm not giving you my battery."

After backing onto the street, the car came to an abrupt stop. "Goodbye, Delain." The locks on the door popped up. "Good luck getting Caleb back."

"Shit." With the gun in her lap, Delain removed the battery and slid it down the passenger seat.

"Thank you. I assure you it's for the both of our safety." He began to drive.

I Doubt it. "Start talking, John."

"What do you want to know?"

"Everything."

"Yes, ma'am. Now, before I begin, would you feel more comfortable if I call you Delain or Christina?"

"Let's start with how you know my real name."

"I was hired to follow you."

"Hired by who?"

"Davis Melancon."

Delain grabbed the gun from her lap, gripping it tightly while aiming at John's torso from behind the driver's seat. "Why?"

"For several reasons. Did you decide?"

"On what?"

"Delain or Christina?"

With the exception of the occasional phone call with her parents, and the two conversations with Tyler within the last twenty-four hours, Delain had yet to hear someone call her by her real name in nearly three years. Hearing it brought back memories of a time in her life when everything seemed just about perfect. "Delain."

"Firstly, Delain, Davis wanted to make sure you weren't getting cold feet about the wedding. Secondly, he wanted me to let him know if you went to the police. Thirdly, he had to make sure you didn't find out the truth about Caleb."

"And what were you instructed to do if I did any of those things? Kill me?"

"No. I don't kill people, Delain. I'm just a private investigator. I merely follow the subject, and then report to the person paying me."

"What did you report to him?"

"Nothing. He died before I could present to him what little information I had at the time."

Delain grew even more anxious as John stared at her through the rearview mirror. *He's been following me? What if he was there when Davis died?!* "It's a shame he died from a heart attack."

John's eyes continued to gaze upon her in the mirror. "And not from carbon monoxide poisoning as originally intended."

He was there?! "Well, I read carbon monoxide was the original cause of—"

"Jackson watched him die, Delain, and did nothing to help him. If all the facts were presented to a jury, he would be convicted of second-degree murder. You were there as well, and so was an unconscious Caroline—I mean Chloe."

He knows everything! How is that possible?!

"You don't remember me, do you? We've met before, but it was a very quick meeting."

Delain found it difficult to recall where she might have met John, since most of her thoughts were still consumed by the fact that he knew so much about her life over the past few days.

"It was in the bar of the Fleur-de-Leans six nights ago, the night Davis died. You brushed me off, so I engaged in conversation with your Australian friend. By the way, her accent was quite believable."

"Let me guess—you're driving me to the police station, so you can turn me in."

"Why would I do that?"

"An accessory to murder."

"That's the last place I would bring you."

He's going to kill me himself! Delain pressed the gun against the seat. "You think I'm responsible for your boss's death."

"On the contrary. I know private investigators aren't known for being the most scrupulous human beings on the planet, but I believe in justice. When Davis hired me, I had no idea what he had done to you in the past. Once I found out, I became outraged someone would do such a thing to another human being. He truly was an evil person. He got what he deserved."

"How did you find out what he did?"

"This is the part I didn't want to tell you, but I have no choice. I have not only been following you the last few days, but listening as well."

"You bugged my house?"

"No. That's illegal. I do not break the law, Delain."

"Then how have you been listening?"

"Do you know what a parabolic microphone is?"

"No."

"Well, I have one, and it lets me hear things I normally wouldn't be able to hear from a few feet away. If you've ever paid close attention to the sidelines of a football game, you've probably seen someone holding a parabolic mic, capturing the hits of the game."

"How is eavesdropping on me not illegal?"

"I never entered your home. I merely sat in my car outside your house and pointed my special microphone towards you."

"How is that…" she noticed a black 4-Runner fast approaching, "not legal?"

"The streets are public domain."

As the 4-Runner grew closer, Delain could clearly tell a male was in the driver's seat. Once it passed and she could see the driver's face, she grew nauseated. *What did I do? He's going to hate me—and he has every right to.* As John spoke, Delain pictured Jackson walking into her house in the next few minutes, discovering the two-word note on the back of the door. *He's going to be so heartbroken.*

"Judging by your silence and the look of grief on your face, I take it you just saw who passed us."

Delain slowly lowered the gun. "Why can't we go back so I can tell him what's going on?"

"Because you would be putting your life, and his, in jeopardy. If you love Jackson, you can't get him involved."

A thought then popped in her head. "What if one of the bad people, as you call them, are at my house now and Jackson walks in and gets shot?"

"He will be fine. They want nothing to do with him. You're the one they're after."

"And who are these bad people you keep talking about?"

With his eyes focused on the road, John told her, "Associates of Davis. Immoral people."

"How many?"

"I'm not sure, maybe as many as four or five."

A glance at her watch reminded Delain of a visit with a friend she forgot to cancel amid the chaotic and sporadic plan to leave town. "Caroline is on her way over there as well."

"Good. That ought to take Jackson's mind off things for a while."

"What do you mean?"

John looked at Delain's reflection, squinting as he said, "You're joking, right?"

"About what?"

"You had to have noticed the way she lights up around him. When I was talking to her at the bar, she told me she had a husband. Guess what his name was?"

Feelings between the two were undeniable, yet Delain believed those feelings had diminished once Davis was dead and the wedding grew nearer. "Brock?"

With a shake of his head, John told her, "Jackson. She then proceeded to tell me how madly in love with him she was. But, maybe that was Chloe talking, and not Caroline."

So that's why she dropped everything to come to the wedding. It wasn't for me. It was because of Jackson.

"When she was talking to you and your old boyfriend inside the airport yesterday…Taylor, is it?"

"Tyler."

"When she was talking to you and Tyler yesterday, I sensed she couldn't wait to tell Jackson about the encounter. Turns out I was right."

"She told Jackson about Tyler?"

"I'm afraid so—at his parents' house last night. I heard it with my mic. She told him not to tell you. I guess the old saying is true: keep your friends close and your friend's fiancé closer."

Leaving Jackson behind with Caroline, all of a sudden, didn't feel as heartbreaking. "Where are we going?"

John dialed a number before placing the cell phone to his ear. "To see your son. After all, isn't today his birthday?"

Chapter 106

John parked the car next to a curb in the upscale, gated subdivision of Moss Oaks Plantation, located on the outskirts of New Orleans. Delain found the name to be appropriate, given the abundance of centuries-old oak trees covered in Spanish moss located throughout the subdivision. Each house they passed showcased lush landscaping and perfectly manicured lawns, along with either a view of an eighteen-hole golf course or one of three manmade lakes. Delain guessed the smallest home they passed to cost at least half-a-million dollars, if not more.

"Why are we stopping here?"

John pointed towards a house three lots away with a 'for sale' sign neatly staked into the lawn. "Your son and the woman raising him are currently in that house."

She wasn't sure if she believed him. "How do you know?"

"You see that white Lincoln Navigator up there?"

Delain spotted the vehicle several houses away, parked next to the curb as well. "Yes."

"It will be leaving in five seconds." John then flashed his brights twice. The car did exactly as John predicted. As it passed, neither John nor the driver of the Navigator acknowledged one another. "I prefer to work alone, but I can't be everywhere at once. I needed another set of eyes."

"That's who you called a few minutes ago."

"You're catching on."

"Who is it?"

"A fellow P.I. Now, we have two options: wait out here and follow Caleb and Bridgett when they leave, or go in and see them now."

Delain wasted no time in telling him, "I want to see my son now."

"I thought you might say that. Since this won't be the first time you'll be in her presence, we can't take the risk of Bridgett recognizing you or your voice. You were well-disguised in the elevator, but I'm not sure if you spoke while in it."

"You mean you weren't on top of the elevator listening in with your fancy microphone?" she sarcastically asked, still none-too-pleased by his eavesdropping over the past week.

John shrugged his shoulders. "Unfortunately, I lost you for a few minutes that night."

"The only thing I said in the elevator was 'twelve'. Scott asked what floor I needed."

"We should be good then. Can you hand me the briefcase on the floor next to you?"

Delain glanced at her feet, grabbing the leather briefcase and handing it to him. She watched as he removed a pair of thick, black-framed glasses and placed them on his face.

"I'm Dr. John Wiggins. You are my wife, Mrs. Samantha Wiggins. We're very interested in buying this house. Are you ready?"

Just as she was four days earlier when stepping into the elevator, Delain was equal parts excited and scared. "Yes."

"What's your name?"

"Dela...Samantha. Samantha Wiggins. You're Dr. John Wiggins."

"Let's do it, Samantha."

"Wait. What are we going to say?"

John opened his door. "Just follow my lead. You'll be fine, Samantha."

How do I know Caleb is really in there? What if no one is in the house and he's really bringing me in there to kill me and then hide my body? Delain tucked the gun in the back of her shorts, making sure her shirt was covering it as she stepped out of the car.

"Are you nervous, Samantha?"

"A little."

"Please don't take this the wrong way, but I've noticed how composed you've been while hiding things. You're going to do great in there."

'Luxor Realities' was printed on the 'for sale' sign in the front yard. A picture of the real estate agent was shown next to the agent's name—Susan Walker. Susan's dirty blonde hair and makeup in the picture appeared to be professionally done, while expensive looking jewelry adorned her ears and neck. Her smile was inviting.

The only tree in the front yard—a Southern Live Oak—had several branches sprawled across the yard, including one that touched the ground before lifting back upwards. Rays of sunlight snuck through the Spanish moss, casting tranquil shadows upon the lush Bermudagrass. While walking up the lengthy driveway, Delain imagined Caleb climbing on the lowest branch while she held his hand.

"Be strong, Samantha," John told her as they walked up the red brick stairs and between two of the four white columns erected in front of the two-story house. "He's going to be yours soon if you trust me—I promise."

Delain's stomach tightened as John jiggled the door knob. *I'm about to either see Caleb, kill a man I don't know, or be killed!* The door was unlocked. After three repetitive knocks, John pushed it open.

"Hello?" His voice echoed throughout the empty hallway. "Is anyone here?"

Delain reached her right hand behind her back. She brought it forward—empty-handed at the sight of a woman at the end of the lengthy hallway. Delain recognized her from the sign on the front yard.

"Hello." Susan looked somewhat confused while simultaneously attempting to smile.

"Hi," John spoke with a wave of his hand. "I don't mean to intrude, but my wife and I were just passing by and saw the sign outside. I'm Dr. John Wiggins, and this is my wife Samantha."

"Hello, John and Samantha. I'm Susan Walker. I'm actually in the middle of a tour right now."

"We are so sorry to interrupt. My wife and I have been in love with this house for the last few years. You can imagine our excitement when we saw the sign on the front yard as we drove by. Is this a bad time?"

Before Susan could answer, a woman holding a young boy sucking on a pacifier stepped into the hallway. Delain's knees were on the verge of buckling. She grabbed onto John's arm for support.

"Not at all," Bridgett Melancon spoke. With a welcoming grin, the pale, slender brunette said, "The more the merrier."

Delain began to shake uncontrollably at the sight of her son. John tightly held onto her arm as they approached the trio.

"This house," John spoke, "is our Graceland. Isn't that right, honey?"

Delain couldn't stop gazing into Caleb's eyes. "Yes."

"Well, don't get too attached yet. Bridgett, her husband, and her son have the first rights to the house."

"I understand completely." John extended his hand to Susan. "Nice to make your acquaintance, Susan. I've heard through the grapevine you are one of the top real estate agents in the city. If God doesn't want Samantha and I to have this house, perhaps you would help us not only find another, but also sell our current abode as well."

Susan flashed the same inviting smile showcased on the outside sign. "I have no doubt I will be able to help you and your beautiful wife find your dream home."

Delain took notice at how Caleb's eyes had been fixated on her since she approached him.

"Your son, Bridgett, is very handsome," John told her.

Gushing, she said, "Thank you. He's my little angel." She then kissed his forehead.

Delain's grip tightened on John's arm as he asked, "I'm guessing he's around two years old?"

"In one more week he will be."

No! Today's his birthday! Why did she just say that?!

"Samantha and I don't mean to impose, but we're flying to Italy tomorrow for two weeks, and we were hoping to get a quick look around. I doubt this place will still be available when we get back. If you happen to buy this house, Bridgett, we would never get a chance to see what we have been dreaming about for the last few years."

Bridgett squinted her eyes as a smirk appeared on her face. "I see what's going on here."

"I beg your pardon?" John asked.

"I wasn't born yesterday. I know how this thing goes."

"What thing?"

She turned to Susan. "You had these people show up and pretend to be interested in the house, so I would be even more tempted to make a deal on it. Am I right? I bet his name really isn't Dr…" She turned to John, "what was it again?"

"John Wiggins." John reached into his back pocket.

Susan appeared almost insulted. "I have never seen these two in all my life."

"Are you sure?" Bridgett again smirked.

From his wallet, John removed a small stack of business cards. He handed Bridgett the card on top. She spoke while reading the card. "Dr. John Wiggins. Doctor of Internal Medicine." She looked upwards, her cheeks flushed. "I'm so embarrassed."

"Don't be," John spoke. "I would have probably thought the same thing if I was in your shoes. Isn't that right, dear?"

Delain cleared her throat before mumbling, "Yes."

"I apologize to the three of you." Bridgett handed the card back to John. "I believe Susan was just about to show me the kitchen. I don't mind sharing a tour."

Susan's smile returned. She waved her hand to the left. "That is correct. Right this way, and you will see one of the most beautiful kitchens in all of southern Louisiana."

As Bridgett began to walk, the pacifier in her son's mouth fell onto her forearm. She paused to place it back into Caleb's mouth before following Susan. John and Delain closely followed behind.

"Are you new to the area, Bridgett?" John asked.

"I am. My husband lived here several years though. Recent events have brought us back to his hometown."

"I apologize. I didn't catch your last name, Bridgett."

"Melancon."

"Melancon…Melancon…As in Davis Melancon?"

Bridgett nodded. "He was my brother-in-law."

John placed his hand to his heart. "I'm sorry to hear of his passing. He was a good man. I met him on several occasions at the restaurant."

Delain gave John a look as if she was about to hit him.

"He was. He will be missed."

Once everyone stood in the kitchen, Susan said, "And here we are in my favorite room of the house. Isn't it incredible?"

Delain's attention wasn't focused on the six-burner gas stove, the custom stainless steel hood above it, the twelve-foot-long by six-foot-wide cypress island, the stone-washed brick flooring, the limestone backsplash that beautifully accentuated the cream-colored cabinet doors, or the rod-iron chandelier hovering over the breakfast table. Instead, she was fixated on two things: her son as he sat comfortably in Bridgett's arms, and the cool touch of the gun pressed against her lower back. Removing and pointing it at Bridgett and demanding her son back was awfully tempting, yet clearly not the sensible thing to do.

"You're right, Susan, it's gorgeous," Bridgett said while her son squirmed about in her arms. "Okay. I'll put you down." She set her son onto the ground, clutching to his hand. "The chandelier is gorgeous, Susan." She then set her purse on the island.

A shy Caleb clung to his mother's leg while staring at Delain. She smiled at him. He soon smiled back. The pacifier fell from his mouth and onto the floor. Bridgett didn't notice. Before Delain could reach for the pacifier and hand it to her son, someone beat her to it. With a quick swoop, John grabbed the pacifier with a handkerchief before discretely sticking it into his pocket.

What is he doing?! Is he crazy?

John approached the island, standing within an arm's reach of Bridgett. She and her purse were to his left. "Is that a Viking stove?"

"It sure is."

"Could we see the inside of the oven, Susan?"

As Susan opened the oven door, Delain watched John engage in another peculiar act. While Bridgett's attention seemed focused on the oven to their left, John reached into her purse.

Is he stealing her wallet?! Who is this guy?!

John turned his attention to Delain. "Honey, preparing Thanksgiving dinner would be a breeze with that oven. What do you think?"

"It's, um… quite spacious."

"How many turkeys do you think you can put in there, Bridgett? Have you seen an oven that big before?" As John seemed determined in making sure Bridgett's attention stayed focused on the oven, Delain watched as he removed a hair brush from her purse. While slyly sticking it into his pocket, he removed a beeper from the same pocket. After pressing a button, it began to vibrate loud enough for everyone's attention to be diverted to it.

"Oh, darn," John spoke while gazing at the beeper. "I'm on call until this evening, and I just got buzzed." John extended his hand to the woman whose hairbrush he just stole. "Bridgett, it was a pleasure to meet you."

"You as well." She turned to Delain. "Nice to meet you too, Samantha."

All Delain could do was nod.

"Honestly, Bridgett, I want you to have this house. If you choose not to, however, I will be making an offer to Susan." John handed Susan his business card. "You might need this."

"Thank you. I'll be in touch very soon. It was nice to meet the both of you."

John grabbed Delain's hand on the way out of the kitchen. Once they turned the corner and headed down the hallway, John's pace increased. "Don't say anything until we're in the car," he whispered to Delain.

Delain waited until both the driver's and the rear driver's-side doors were shut before asking, "Why did you steal his pacifier and Bridgett's brush?"

"DNA." John reached into the glove compartment, removing two plastic bags. He placed the pacifier into one, and then the hairbrush into another. "Don't you want to find out who the biological parents are of the child in that house?"

"Me and Davis."

"Are you sure about that? Could someone else be the baby's father? Like your ex-boyfriend, Tyler, for example?"

In all the events that took place over the previous few hours, Delain nearly forgot about the last comment Tyler told her as she hurried to the hotel elevator. She didn't have to ask John if he heard Tyler's comment from earlier in the day, as he was most certainly eavesdropping somewhere nearby. "You can find that out from his pacifier?"

"Yes, but I also need hair, saliva, or blood samples from both Davis and Tyler. Unfortunately, Davis is dead."

"What if Tyler is the father?"

John started the car. "Then we don't need DNA from Davis, and the mystery is solved."

"And if Tyler is the father?"

"Once we find out who the father of the Melancon child is, we go to the proper authorities."

"And then what?"

"And then you get your son back."

"But did you hear what Bridgett said about Caleb's birthday being next week and not today?"

"That's not surprising. Davis probably lied about his birthday to further throw you off if you were to ever try to locate your son."

Delain nearly broke down in the backseat of the sedan. The nineteen-month conflict of regaining custody of her son may have finally been coming to an end. "Why are you helping me?"

John didn't at first answer as he drove towards the entrance of the subdivision. He waited until he came to a stop then turned around to face Delain. "Even though I'm nearly half-a-century old and have seen more injustice and corruption in this screwed up world than most people would ever know, I still believe in John Wayne, Superman, and God. Call me old-fashioned, but good will prevail over evil." He turned around and continued driving.

"Thank you, John...Wiggins? Is that your real last name? It was on the business card so I'm assuming..."

John handed Delain a stack of business cards. She sorted through them to find the first name on most of the cards to be 'John', but the last name and profession on each was different.

"Who are you?"

"John. That's all you need to know."

"Well, thank you, John."

"You're welcome."

"Can I ask where we're going now?"

"To visit your ex-boyfriend."

Chapter 107

John pulled into a parking spot outside the Doubletree Hotel. With the engine still running, he turned around, placing his right hand atop the passenger seat. "Did you decide?"

From the backseat, Delain stared at the entrance to the same hotel she had visited earlier in the day. "I'll do it. Plus, your method of securing a DNA sample sounds much too convoluted." John's plan included pretending to be room service and bringing Tyler a tray of food that was laced with a fast-acting and powerful sedative. "Are you sure he hasn't checked out?"

"Yes."

"How do you know?"

"I called before arriving at your house. He answered the hotel phone." John handed Delain a cotton-tipped swab enclosed in a small, plastic tube. "Are you sure you can do this?"

"Yes," she answered, unsure if she could.

"If you don't think you can get a swipe on the inside of his cheek, hair will do too. But it has to have the root on it, and we need at least ten hairs. If either of those is too challenging to obtain, a well-chewed piece of gum could do the trick. Make sure whatever sample you get, you quickly place it in that tube to reduce contamination. Be smart, Delain. Don't do or say anything that can jeopardize you or your son. Are you sure you don't want me in the hallway up there just in case? I can be right outside the door."

"I'm sure. Give me an hour." Delain opened the backdoor.

"Wait. Take this." John handed her a small black device. It was plastic, no bigger than a driver's license, and about half-an-inch thick. Directly in the middle was a red button.

"What is it?"

"Press the button if you get into trouble. It will send me an alert that help is needed."

Delain handed it back. "I won't need it."

"Are you positive?"

"Yep. See you soon." She shut the door as she made her way to the hotel entrance.

What if I tell him to close his eyes, and then kiss him while sliding the cotton swab against his cheek? Delain thought while making her way through the hotel lobby. *He might think it's my tongue. No, that won't work. What if I just tell him the truth?* Before coming to a decision, she spotted Tyler on a couch. He wasn't alone. A woman with slicked-back hair as dark as freshly poured asphalt and lips as red as a ripe strawberry, stared captivatingly into Tyler's eyes while resting her hand upon his knee. The mystery woman's slender and lengthy legs looked like they belonged on the cover of an Italian fashion magazine. But what stood out the most to Delain was how the woman's smile alluded to the fact that she was quite pleased to be in the presence of the gentleman in a white dress shirt, black slacks and a tie seated before her. Tyler's continuous grinning led Delain to believe he was just as excited to be talking to the attractive woman touching his leg. The woman was the first to make eye contact with Delain as she approached and stood behind Tyler. Delain's subtle clearing of her throat caused Tyler to turn around. His smile waned, giving way to a look of disbelief.

"Christina." He then glanced curiously at his watch. "Aren't you supposed to be getting married right now?"

"I decided not to go through with it."

Tyler stood from the couch. "What?"

"Cold feet, I guess."

Tyler appeared dumbfounded before subtly shaking his head. "Where are my manners? Christina, this is Adrianna. Adrianna, this is Christina."

Adrianna stood from the couch, pushing down on her snug, mid-thigh skirt before extending her right hand. "Nice to meet you. I don't mean to be forward, but you are very beautiful." Her accent hinted that she was from somewhere in Eastern Europe—Russia, Romania, or Poland came to mind.

"Thank you. And you as well." Adrianna was tall, thin, thick-chested, and despite having a pale complexion, Delain found her to be strikingly beautiful and a dead ringer for a model in a Robert Palmer music video.

"What brings you here?" Tyler asked Delain.

"I was wondering if I could talk to you."

"Sure. What's going on?"

Delain quickly glanced to Adrianna and then back to her former boyfriend. "I was hoping we could do this in private— if that's okay."

"Um…" Tyler turned to Adrianna.

"We can finish this stimulating conversation later tonight, no?" Adrianna asked with a grin.

"Of course we can. You don't mind?"

"Not at all. I will go have a drink in the bar across the street and you come meet me shortly." Adrianna extended both arms. Tyler hugged her.

"I'll see you soon."

Delain noticed the subtle rubbing of Adrianna's hands along Tyler's back as the two embraced. She found herself becoming not only uncomfortable by the touching, but quite jealous.

"I have your number," Adrianna told Tyler while pulling away, "so if something happens and my friends force me to go out with them in a bit, I'll text you and tell you where I'll be."

"Sounds good."

"Christina, it was pleasure to meet you. Take good care of this American beefcake for me." Adrianna smiled while patting Tyler's chest.

Delain flashed a forced smile towards Adrianna. "I'll try."

Adrianna walked off, but not before turning around along the way to offer Tyler a goodbye smile and wave.

"Before you say anything, I want to apologize if you thought I was implying you were a gold-digger this morning. I know you're not, Christina. That was stupid of me to say."

"Do you still have your room upstairs?"

"Yes."

"Can we go there?"

"Or course."

As they walked towards the elevator, Delain couldn't help but ask, "Who is Adrianna?"

"I met her after my interview today. I was getting a late lunch across the street. While eating, I noticed she was looking for a place to sit. All the tables were taken, so I offered the other chair at my table. We've been hanging out for the last few hours."

"She's kind of...pretty."

"She's not bad looking."

The elevator doors opened. An older couple followed Delain and Tyler into the elevator.

"What floor?" Tyler, standing next to the panel, asked the couple.

"Seven please," the gentleman answered. Once the doors shut, the gentleman asked, "How was y'all's day?"

"Eventful," Tyler answered.

"You make a beautiful couple," spoke the elderly woman with curly gray hair and a pink fanny pack around her waist. "Are you two married?"

Tyler looked to Delain before confessing, "Actually, we're no longer a couple; just friends now."

The older woman shook her head. "That's too bad. Two good-looking people like you would make beautiful babies."

Delain was overcome with emotion as Tyler thanked the woman.

The doors opened on the fourth floor. Tyler bid farewell to the couple, while Delain simply waived at them.

"Older people are adorable," Tyler spoke as they walked down the hallway.

"Yep."

As they came to a stop in front of room 407, Tyler gazed into Delain's eyes. "Should I be a little nervous right now?"

"Probably, since I am as well."

He opened the door. Delain first stepped into the room, immediately taking a seat on the bed. Tyler loosened his tie while asking, "So...what happened today? Why aren't you in a white dress right now standing before a priest?"

Delain exhaled loudly as she gazed not into his eyes, but at his chest. "I decided not to do it."

"Did you postpone it or...?"

"Cancelled."

"Really," he spoke with a subtle nod. "Is he upset?"

149

Revealing she ran away instead of telling Jackson she couldn't marry him, she feared, would make her look like a heartless bitch. "Yes. I told him I need time to think about things."

"What kind of things?"

She finally looked into his eyes. "You were right this morning—I'm not ready to get married."

Tyler smiled. "I'm glad you came to your senses. Has he been trying to call you?"

"I don't know. I turned my phone off."

"What are you going to do now?"

With a shrug of the shoulders, she answered, "Not sure."

"Not that I'm upset about it by any means, but why did you come here?"

"I wanted to go where no one could find me. And I didn't want to be alone."

Tyler sat to her left. "I'm glad I didn't leave town yet."

"So am I. Speaking of, how did the interview go today?"

"They offered me the job. I told them I need a few days to decide."

"What was the position?"

Tyler unfastened the top button of his shirt as he asked, "Can I get you a drink? I have vodka and some club soda right here on the desk."

Delain felt alcohol would help with not only her anxiety, but the task at hand. "Please."

"Two vodka tonics coming up." Tyler held the empty ice bucket in his hand. "First, we need some ice. I'll be right back."

The door closed behind Tyler. Delain glanced around the bedroom. Her ex's suitcase, closed but not zipped, lay on the floor beneath the window. Not usually one for snooping around, Delain could not resist the urge to see what was inside. Socks, underwear, t-shirts, jeans, a pair of khaki shorts, and workout apparel occupied the orange carry-on. After opening the suitcase fully, Delain spotted a 4×6 picture frame inside the mesh-lined pocket attached to the top of the suitcase. Despite the picture being upside down and partially hidden behind a folded necktie, Delain recognized it. She and Tyler stood beneath the arch, their lips locked with one another. Her hair in the picture was blonde. The smile on her face wasn't forced or one that was hiding something. She was momentarily taken back to a time when innocence was as much a part of her life as was the belief that true love and a fairytale ending awaited her. *Why does he have this picture in his*

150

suitcase? It used to be on his nightstand. Does he bring it everywhere he goes? Is that weird...or romantic? She shut the suitcase before returning to the bed. The door soon opened.

"We now have ice." Tyler's smell as he walked past her was familiar, but even more so, comforting. "To answer your question from earlier;" he said while dropping ice cubes into a glass, "it was with a software company. What I would be doing is trying to find glitches in the programs they create. Somehow my résumé ended up in their hands and they saw some of my work and called me last week. That's why I ran into you yesterday at the airport." Tyler poured the cocktail into another glass and back into the original glass. He handed the mixed drink to Delain.

"Thank you. By the way, I'm sorry about how I acted this morning."

He poured vodka and tonic water into another glass as he told her, "You didn't do anything wrong, Chrissy. There's no need to apologize."

"Yes, there is. I kind of freaked out about everything going on and snapped at you."

"I deserved it. Besides," stirring the drink with his finger he told her, "it was probably my kissing. I've been meaning to work on my technique." He placed the glass to his lips.

"There's nothing wrong with your technique." She grinned. "It was and always has been...perfect."

"You're probably right," he said with a playful wink.

Delain took a sip of the vodka tonic. It was potent. She took another sip before asking, "When are you going back to Atlanta?"

"My flight's tomorrow afternoon."

"What are your plans for tonight?"

Tyler stared into his drink, took another sip, and then answered, "As you heard a little while ago, Adrianna wanted to meet up later on, so..."

Jealousy again overcame Delain as she pictured Tyler kissing a drunk Adrianna in the corner of a crowded, noisy Bourbon Street bar. Adrianna's eyes were shut, and her breath smelled of Red Bull and Vodka. Her tongue whipped around every crevice of Tyler's mouth as she pressed her European breasts against his chest. "What if I wanted to spend time with you tonight?"

"You really want to hangout with this lousy kisser tonig—"

"Amazing kisser."

"Amazing kisser tonight?"

"I'd like that. But, if you want to see Adrianna then I'll go."

"Are you hungry?"

"Starving."

"Why don't we go grab a bite somewhere?"

The thought of running into Jackson, or one of his family members, or one of the 'bad guys' John spoke of worried her. "Can we do room service instead?"

Tyler nodded. "Absolutely."

"Why don't you order some food, while I go down to my car and grab my luggage?"

"Do you want me to come with you?"

She stood from the bed. "No, thank you. I got it."

"What are you hungry for?"

"Surprise me. I'll be right back." Delain felt excitement as she headed towards the elevator.

Dusk had arrived. Headlights from John's sedan flashed as she made her way outside. She hurried to the car, carefully scanning the parking lot along the way. The driver's side window was partially rolled down.

"Did you get the sample?"

"Not yet. I need more time."

"How much time?"

"I need to stay the night."

John looked away, tiredly exhaling in the process. "Well…the DNA sample is important, so I guess we can extend your stay here." His gaze returned to her. "But first thing in the morning, we're out of here. Deal?"

"Deal. Thank you, John."

"No need to thank me. You just be out here at 8:00 a.m. and not a minute later."

Delain nodded. "I need to get my luggage out the back."

John pressed a button on the console. The trunk popped open. After Delain retrieved her luggage, John told her, "Be smart up there. Don't let him know what's going on until we know for ourselves. I'll see you in the morning."

She reached into her luggage, handing John a white envelope. "I want you to have this."

"What is it?" John grabbed the envelope.

"About $3,450."

"For what?"

"Helping me do this."

He handed back the envelope. "I don't want your money."

She attempted to hand it back. "Please take it."

He nudged it back. "You keep it. Raising a child isn't cheap. You're going to need that money."

Delain smiled, holding back tears. "Thank you again, John."

Chapter 108

Delain entered the room to find Tyler hanging up the hotel phone as he stood next to the nightstand.

"I just ordered a bunch of different appetizers," he told her.

"Perfect." She set her suitcase on the ground before plopping onto the bed. After inhaling and then exhaling deeply, she could feel the weight of the day's stress in nearly every muscle in her neck and upper back.

"You had quite an interesting day."

With shut eyes, Delain extended her arms towards the headboard. "You have no idea."

"Do you want to talk about it some more?"

Caleb came to mind. "Actually, I do." She slowly opened her eyes before sitting upright. "When I left here this morning, you mentioned poking a hole in the condom when we last had sex."

His expression hinted at embarrassment as he nodded.

"Did you really want to impregnate me?"

He pulled the chair from beneath the desk. "Out of the blue, you were breaking up with me. I mean," he took to the chair, "I never would have guessed we were going to break up at any time in our relationship. Everything was damn near perfect between us. So, when you said you didn't love me anymore, I freaked out. Once I convinced you to have sex one last time, I looked in the drawer and saw a pen next to the condom. I thought by getting you pregnant, you'd come back to me. Was it foolish? Yes. Would I do it again if we were in the same situation? Absolutely."

"What would you have done if I did get pregnant?"

Staring into her eyes, he told her, "Marry you and then spend the rest of my life as the happiest husband and father on the face of the Earth."

"You would have married me because I got pregnant?"

154

Squinting angrily, Tyler answered, "No. I wanted to marry you regardless—you know that. I even purchased a ring."

"You bought a ring?"

He nodded. "After we went looking at rings, I went back three days later and purchased the one you liked the most."

"I had no idea."

"Good, because I wanted it to be a surprise. But we both know what happened next."

A remorseful Delain lowered her head. "Again, I'm so sorry, Tyler."

"I'm not."

She lifted her head. "You're not?"

"Nope. I've been doing a lot of thinking since yesterday evening, and even more so after you left here this morning, and even more in the last fifteen minutes." He grabbed his drink from the desk.

"Do you care to share some of those thoughts?"

Vodka and tonic water crossed his lips. He lowered the glass, holding onto it as he told her, "I'm glad everything happened the way it did. Not only that, I don't want to know what happened to make you break up with me out of the blue."

Delain was taken aback by his suddenly cool, everything-happens-for-a-reason attitude. At the same time, she was relieved he no longer cared to know what had happened nearly three years earlier. "Are you sure?"

"I am. It's obvious you weren't into us as much as I was. I wanted to spend forever together, but you had other plans. It took three years to finally achieve it, but I finally got it too."

"What?"

"Closure."

As the word crossed his lips, Delain felt a wave of numbness flush throughout her body, followed by a sudden sickness in her stomach.

"Earlier today you admitted to finding closure with me." He sipped his drink before telling her, "Now that I've just said it to you, you appear...uneasy. Is than an accurate statement?"

She scanned the room for her drink, eventually spotting it next to the television. It was just out of her reach. "I didn't expect to hear those words from you tonight."

"What did you expect to hear from me?"

"I don't know."

"How do you feel right now, Chrissy? And please be honest."

She was tired of the lies, tired from hiding, tired from running away. "Sad...lonely."

"Why didn't you marry Jackson tonight?"

"I don't know."

"Do you love him?"

"I don't know."

"Yes or no? You don't have to answer. I don't need to know. Do you love Jackson? Could you see yourself spending the rest of your life with him?"

Delain stared out of the window, pondering the question. She soon had a vision. It was Christmas morning. Caleb sat in her lap. As she helped him open a present, a gentleman looked on. She smiled at him. A feeling of euphoria overcame her in the hotel room. She had found the answer to Tyler's question. "Do you remember the picture I gave you for our one-year anniversary? The one of us kissing beneath the arch?"

Tyler glanced at his suitcase and then back at Delain. "Yes."

"Did you ever take it out of the frame?"

"No."

"So, you never saw the back of the picture?"

His eyes grew closer to one another as he asked, "Is there something written on it?"

Delain shrugged her shoulders. "Perhaps."

Tyler appeared to be in deep thought while staring at his suitcase. "It's weird you're bringing that up right now."

"Why's that?"

Tyler took a sip before telling her, "When you broke up with me, I didn't take that picture down from my nightstand right away. It stayed up for several months. When I started dating again, I took it down and hid it under the nightstand. Once a relationship was over, I would take it out of hiding and return it next to my clock. With my last relationship, it was under the nightstand for some time. Even though it was out of sight, I didn't forget about it. I had trouble letting go of you, Christina. To be honest..." he approached and then opened his suitcase, "and please don't think I'm some pathetic loser, but...." He held up the picture.

Delain pretended to be surprised by the framed picture. "You bring it with you when traveling?"

"No, but for some reason when I was packing for this trip, I decided to bring the picture. I was a little anxious about the interview and having the picture sort of relaxed me."

Delain found comfort in his answer. "That was my favorite picture of us."

"And apparently I don't know everything about it." As he began to unclasp the frame, Delain grew nervous. After removing the glass and setting it onto the desk along with the frame, Tyler flipped the picture over. His lips moved as he silently read the message written four years prior. "Huh."

Delain could only stare at the man who had just admitted to finally reaching closure with her.

"'I know you're the one,'" Tyler read before looking back at her. "Well, I guess things change."

"Sometimes."

He handed her the picture. "Since we've both admitted to finding closure today, there's no need to hang on to this picture any longer. Rip it up."

"What?"

"Tear the picture up so I can throw it away."

"Why?"

"There's no sense in hanging onto it since we're both moving on. Don't you agree?"

Delain stared at the picture. "I...I guess so." She reluctantly grabbed it.

Tyler grabbed the wastebasket next to the desk and held it up to Delain. "Just toss it in here after you tear it up. It was taken a long time ago when things were different."

Delain placed both hands on the picture that, to her knowledge, was the only copy in existence. It was taken with a disposable camera and the negatives were lost. "If you say so." As she held the picture up between Tyler and herself, she saw the five-word message written on the back. She remembered how in love with Tyler she was when writing the message, and how exciting life was going to be once they were married. For their one-year wedding anniversary, she was going to tell him to open the frame and read the message written years earlier. *Don't let me rip it up! I don't want to!* Tyler stared intently into her eyes as she silently begged him to grab the picture from her hand before it could be ripped into pieces. The picture began to tremble in her hands as she realized she could no longer hide the truth. "I can't."

"Yes, you can, Christina. Just rip it up so we can move on with our lives."

"I don't want to."

"Why?"

"Because I lied." Tears began to trickle down her cheeks. She lowered her arms. "I don't have closure with you because I'm still in love with you." Tyler knelt next to her as she asked, "Are you really done with me?"

Tyler, wiping a tear from her left cheek with his thumb, answered, "Not even close."

A relieved Delain smiled. "I was hoping you weren't."

"Last time we kissed, you said you no longer had feelings for me."

Delain grabbed his tie, pulling him towards her before planting her lips to his. She pulled away several seconds later. "I lied."

"I thought about you every day for the last three years," he confessed.

"I thought about you just as much." While again kissing him, a premonition overcame Delain. The feeling was so strong she had no doubt it was true. Just to be sure, she needed validation. "I hate to keep bringing it up, but I'm intrigued by the condom-poking incident from a few years back. Was it a big hole? And are you certain you came inside me?"

Tyler looked away from Delain. "I'm not sure."

"You don't remember?"

"I don't….maybe," he bashfully told her.

She placed her hand beneath his chin, lifting it while telling him, "You can tell me the truth, Tyler. I promise I won't be mad."

"Before we had sex for the first time, you said no one had ever gone inside you, even with a condom on. You said you were waiting until marriage for that to happen. I, unfortunately, was a desperate man, so I kind of broke your rule. I did go inside you. I'm sorry."

"It's okay." She flashed a smile that didn't feel forced.

"Are you sure?"

While grabbing both sides of his face, Delain told him, "I'm glad you did it."

He smiled back. "For weeks, I thought you were pregnant. When I took the condom off, there was barely any semen in it."

Tyler is Caleb's father! He's not Davis' son! I'm certain of it! Relief and joy overcame Delain as she stood from the bed and walked to the television. With drink in hand, she told him, "I'm happy you're telling me the truth. You have no idea how happy I am you're telling the truth."

"I'm glad I'm finally able to tell you."

After experiencing several highs and lows throughout the day, Delain wanted nothing more than to relax. "Would it be okay if I took a bath?"

"Of course. Are you looking for some relaxation?"

"Very much so."

Tyler grabbed a tray containing coffee and tea packets, mugs, and a small coffee pot. "Give me a few minutes." He walked into the bathroom and shut the door. She could hear the water running into the bathtub. While sitting on the bed, Delain again wondered if it was time to tell him everything that had happened, starting with the life-altering bachelorette party and ending with the belief that Tyler was Caleb's father. *Or, should I wait until I know for sure he is the father. I don't want to get him involved just yet. I still need to get his DNA sample without him knowing why. Perhaps tomorrow I'll be able to tell him everything.*

Minutes later, Tyler emerged from the bathroom. "Your bath is ready. I'll see you in a bit."

Delain shut the door behind her. Steam rose from the bathtub. On the counter, a portable speaker connected to Tyler's iPod played classical music. A rolled towel lay on the back of the bathtub and hot tea rested on the side. It wasn't the first time Tyler had prepared a relaxing bath for her, and she was starting to believe it wouldn't be the last. While lying with her head on the towel, the smell of chamomile filled the room. She shut her eyes. In a small Georgia town, she sat on a porch swing. Against her chest, Caleb napped. To her right sat Tyler, his arm around her. It was the first day of fall. Leaves danced across the lawn as a northern breeze made its way through town. Caleb's nose felt cold against her cheek as she held him tightly. She smiled at Tyler. He smiled back as they gently swayed back and forth. *I'm going to get Caleb back, and Tyler is going to be an amazing father.* Just as she was beginning to find herself the most relaxed she had felt in years, she pictured Jackson standing alone in her living room hours earlier. She was no longer able to enjoy her bath.

Delain emerged from the bathroom. Bruschetta, hummus, sliced bread toasts, fresh fruit, various cheeses, and a thick slice of carrot cake sat on a rolling cart.

"Dinner is served," Tyler proclaimed from the desk chair. "How are you feeling?"

"Better." She reached for a slice of pineapple. "Can I ask you a favor?"

"Yes."

"Can you not fly home tomorrow?"

"Can I ask why?"

"I have to go somewhere in the morning, but I will be back in the afternoon. I want to talk to you when I get back."

"I'll call the airline in the morning."

"Thank you."

Sunday

Chapter 109

Due to the sudden influx of optimism that had invaded Delain's thoughts since the previous night, she wasn't surprised to find John waiting for her in the hotel parking lot. *Today's the day!* she thought while approaching the sedan. *It's finally coming to an end!*

The driver's side window slid down. "No suitcase?" John asked from behind the steering wheel.

"I left it in his room," a comfortable Delain answered as she climbed into the front passenger seat.

"Did you get the sample?"

She removed from inside her bra the clear plastic tube John handed her the previous night. "Cheek swipe. Got it while he was sleeping."

"Tyler didn't wake up?"

"He did, but he thought I was kissing him. I did good."

Using a black marker, John wrote the letter 'T' on the tube. "Yes, you did. Are you ready to find out if Tyler is Caleb's father?"

"Yes, but I already know he is," she answered with certainty.

Following a brief drive, John parked the car in the heart of the French Quarter.

"What are we doing here?"

"Waiting for someone."

"Who?"

"A DNA analyst."

With the exception of two middle-aged men walking a French bulldog, Royal Street was eerily empty. "I haven't seen the Quarter this quiet since Katrina."

"It's Sunday morning. Everyone's sleeping off Saturday night's debauchery. This is my favorite time to be down here."

Delain knew nothing about John. She thought a few questions might provide a little more insight as to who he was. "Do you live close by?"

John shook his head. "No, but I used to frequent this beautiful city when I was younger."

"For business or pleasure?"

"The latter." John appeared to be intently staring at a store just outside his window that sold light fixtures and chandeliers. "The love of my life once lived here. Every two weeks I would visit her for a long weekend."

"How long ago?"

"Many moons."

"She lived close by?"

John leaned forward, looking upward as he pointed above the light fixture store. "In the apartment just up there. Whenever I would get out of the taxi, I'd glance upward and see her waving at me through the window. She'd hurry downstairs, jump into my arms, and kiss me like she hadn't seen me in a year." Delain could sense pleasant memories being recalled as the crow's feet surrounding John's right eye grew more pronounced, while a nostalgic smile appeared on his face. "Every time I came to visit, we'd eat someplace different. I don't think we dined at the same restaurant more than twice in the three years we dated. After dinner we'd go listen to Pete Fountain play his clarinet at the Hilton, watch Chris Owens dance on stage at her club, or just walk around the Quarter and talk about anything and everything. I fell in love, not only with a vivacious redhead, but with the city of New Orleans too. As a young man, I had seen none like it. As an adult I had yet to find a city so alive and majestic."

"What happened after three years?"

"We broke up."

"May I ask why?"

"You can," he answered, still staring hypnotically at the apartment. "You see that window to the left?"

Delain looked upward. "Yes."

"On the other side of that window was an olive-green velvet chair. I was sitting in that chair when everything changed on a Friday afternoon."

Seconds passed before she asked, "What happened, John?"

His gaze shifted from the apartment to the road before him. "She told me she was pregnant. I was, at first, shocked and in disbelief. She was barely twenty and I just twenty-one. We were both kids ourselves and didn't know what to do. She cried into my arms well into the morning hours. When we awoke the next day, she was convinced an abortion was our best option. I was strongly opposed to the idea. We went back and forth all day. The discussion eventually turned into a heated argument. She was adamant about terminating the pregnancy, and I wasn't budging on my pro-life stance. Needless to say, it wasn't a pleasant goodbye that weekend. On my return trip two weeks later, she confessed to having an abortion in my absence." John subtly shook his head back and forth. Delain watched as his right hand clenched into a fist in his lap. "I was so furious at her. She claimed it was her body and she could do whatever she wanted. I stormed out of her apartment and took a taxi back to the airport two hours after arriving in town."

"Did you ever see her again?"

Before he could answer, a short, bald gentleman on the thin and pale side appeared on the sidewalk. He was walking in the direction of the sedan. John grabbed another plastic tube containing a cotton swab—identical to the one he gave Delain the previous night—from the center console. "Open up," he told Delain.

"Why?"

"We need physical evidence you're the birth mother."

Delain opened wide. John swabbed the side of her cheek, and then slid the sample into the tube. After writing a large 'D' on the container, he placed a baseball cap on his head and sunglasses onto his face before rolling the tinted window down no more than two inches.

"Do you have the time?" asked the man in khaki shorts, Hawaiian print t-shirt, and sandals.

"My watch is broken," John quipped back.

Delain noticed that John's watch and the car clock were working just fine.

John handed the tubes with Tyler's DNA and Delain's DNA, the plastic baggie with Caleb's pacifier, and another baggie with Bridgett's hairbrush to the bald gentleman, who never looked inside the car.

"Maternity test on the 'D' tube and the brush. Paternity test on the 'T' tube." John then handed the man a white envelope. "How long to get the results?"

After peering into the envelope, the man told him, "Give me about three hours." He turned around and walked off as John rolled the window up.

"Who is he?"

"A forensics investigator."

"How do you know him?"

"I don't. An acquaintance recommended him."

"Why did it just feel like what you did was illegal?"

"It's legal. We need expedited results, so that's why we didn't go to a DNA testing center, and that's why I paid him a little extra. In three hours, we'll not only have proof that you're Caleb's mother, but also know if Tyler is his father."

Delain smiled at the thought. "And then what?"

"I know a few federal agents that can help. Did you eat breakfast yet?"

"No."

"You hungry?"

"Did you ever see her again?"

John started the car. "No."

"Did you ever talk to her again?"

"No."

"She was the love of your life and you never tried to contact her?"

"No."

Delain found herself intrigued by his story. "Did you ever want to?"

"Two years after she had the abortion, I discovered she was living in Dallas. After a little research, I found out she was married. What hurt the most was that she had a baby on the way. Not being married was never a reason she gave me for wanting to abort. I just assumed it was me."

"Or like you said—she was too young to be a mother."

"Maybe."

Delain felt sadness for him. "I'm sorry, John."

"It's okay," he said, putting the car into drive. "That was a long time ago." John gave one last look at the apartment before driving off.

Chapter 110

John, while reaching for his second glazed donut from the Tastee Donuts box on the dashboard, asked Delain, "Were you really going to marry Jackson yesterday?" They were once again parked on Royal Street, in front of an art gallery.

Delain leaned back in the passenger seat with donut in hand. "I'm not sure how to answer that."

"Let's go back three days to Thursday—you and Jackson were walking out of the Chick-ory after he had just told Brittany he was marrying you on Saturday. If nothing out of the ordinary occurred on Friday or Saturday, if you hadn't run into Tyler or if I didn't knock on your door, would you have married Jackson yesterday?"

"I love Jackson—I really do. And if nothing out of the ordinary happened over the past two days, I probably would have married him. But deep down, I knew it wasn't right. We were definitely rushing into it."

"Then why go through with it if Davis was dead?"

Delain recalled the plan of action that came to her while eavesdropping on Scott and Charlie's conversation days earlier in the Chick-ory. "His dad used to work for the D.A. He would have been able to help me get Caleb back. I imagined after the wedding Jackson and I would sit down and tell him everything. Mr. Andrew would have certainly helped his daughter-in-law. However, when Jackson told me yesterday afternoon that his dad wasn't his birth father, I became concerned. When he went home to pack, reality set in. I didn't know if I wanted to leave town so soon. I was going to discuss my thoughts with him once he came back to pick me up. Then, you showed up." Delain set her donut back in the box. The urge to eat had escaped her. "I'm a horrible person. Jackson was so good to me. He doesn't deserve to be treated the way he did. He had just found out his parents lied to him for thirty years, and what do I do? Run away without telling him."

"Your son is the most important person in your world. All your thoughts and actions should be focused on him right now. Besides, don't forget about Jackson's feelings towards Caroline and vice versa. You did the right thing."

Delain nodded upon being reminded of why she was in the car with John to begin with. *He's right. Caleb is priority number one. Once I get him back, I'll find Jackson and tell him what happened.*

"Here comes our man."

Delain's heart raced as the bald gentleman in the Hawaiian-print shirt approached the car with a folded newspaper in hand. John again placed the hat on his head and sunglasses on his face before barely rolling the tinted window down. Without saying a word to one another and without slowing his pace, the man removed an envelope from the folded newspaper, slipping it through the narrow opening. John grabbed the envelope before rolling the window up.

"Are you ready?"

"Yes!" Delain stared intently at the manila envelope.

John opened it and removed a piece of paper. He began to read. "'The test sample labeled 'B' is excluded as the biological mother of Baby C.'"

"What does that mean?"

"Bridgett is not the biological mother of her son."

"We already knew that."

"It doesn't hurt to make sure." John continued to read. "'The test sample labeled 'D' is not excluded as the biological mother of Baby C.'"

"I'm D?"

"Yes."

"What does that mean?"

"That there is a 99.9999% chance Caleb is your son."

The result came as no surprise to Delain. "I know he's my son."

"And now we have definitive proof." A look of bewilderment then graced John's face as he stared at the report.

An uneasy feeling overcame Delain. "What?"

"'Test sample labeled 'T' is excluded as the biological father of Baby C.'"

"Tyler's not the father?"

John shook his head while looking at Delain. "I'm sorry."

Her eyes shut as she sunk lower into the seat. "How accurate is that testing?"

"Accurate enough."

"Maybe the guy did it wrong."

"I doubt it. He's a forensics expert. It's his job."

"Davis is without a doubt Caleb's biological father. Shit." In the blink of an eye, every ounce of hope that had invaded her thoughts since the previous night escaped her.

"We don't know for sure."

"Davis is the only other person who could be the father, John," a disgruntled Delain told him. "I didn't have sex with anyone else."

"We need proof. We need some of his DNA."

"Why? Tyler isn't the father. There's no point. I already assumed Davis was the father for years. It appears I'm right."

"When happens when you assume? You make an ass—"

"He's the father! That lying, blackmailing, asshole that tried to kill me is the father of my son!"

"Okay," John calmly spoke, "but I need you to understand that we need proof before we bring this to light, Delain."

"He's six feet under. What are we going to do? Dig him up?"

"There are other ways to get a DNA sample—hair, chewing gum, a cigarette, a toothbrush, or blood on an article of clothing."

Once the shock of realizing that Tyler wasn't Caleb's father wore off, Delain was able to think clearly. "His condo is a few blocks from here. Maybe there's something in there we can use."

John nodded. "Good thought. His domicile would have lots of potential. But, I'm not sure how we're going to get in there without breaking the law or picking the lock."

"I have a key. If he didn't change the locks since we..." Delain found difficulty in saying the words, "hung out together, then we have a way in."

"I'm certain we can find a DNA sample in there."

"I'm sure you could."

John shook his head. "I can't."

"Can't what?"

"Can't go in his condo."

"Why not?"

"As I said earlier, Delain, I don't do anything illegal."

"Then how do we obtain his DNA?" John's smirk and wide-eyed stare at Delain informed her of what she had to do. "I have to go in?"

"I'm afraid so."

"What if I get caught?"

"You won't."

"And how do you know that?"

"Because I never lose."

"What does that even mean?"

"You're with me. We're a team. We're not losing." John started the car. "Where is the condo?"

"We're going now?"

"Time is wasting. I'm sure the thought has crossed your mind several times over the last few months, but the window is quickly closing for Caleb to not have detrimental effects from being raised by you, and not Bridgett. We could bring this case to light as early as tomorrow morning if we have all of our evidence."

Delain imagined Caleb in her arms. "It's on the corner of Royal and Orleans."

Chapter 111

After removing the red wig from her suitcase and shutting the trunk, Delain climbed back into the passenger seat. John held a thick pair of high-tech looking binoculars to his face as he looked in the direction of Davis' condo.

"The coast is clear."

"How can you tell with just binoculars? You can't see through walls."

"You're right—regular binoculars can't see through walls. Good thing these use thermal readings. No one is currently in Davis' condo. Now's the time, Delain."

"I was afraid of that."

"There's no need to worry. I'll be your eyes down here. If anyone approaches the building, I'll let you know. You'll have plenty of time to get out of there." John handed Delain a tiny, flesh-colored hearing device. "See if this fits in your ear."

Delain placed the device into her right ear canal. It fit snugly. John next clipped a miniature microphone barely an inch long onto her shirt. A small, black box the size of a pack of gum was attached to the end of the microphone. "Should I be scared right now?"

"Nope. You're in good hands. We'll be able to communicate both ways with this." He handed her the small box. "This is the battery for the microphone. Put it in your pocket."

"Do we really need his DNA?"

"Do you really want someone else to continue raising your son?"

Delain shut her eyes, quickly realizing there was no other option. "Please don't let me get caught. I don't want to spend the night in jail."

John handed her a few plastic Ziploc baggies along with a pair of latex gloves. "You won't. If there's anything you think may contain his DNA, put it in a baggie. One item per bag and use the gloves. They will also keep your fingerprints from getting on anything." He next placed a pair of headphones containing a microphone onto his head. "Testing. One, two, three," he whispered. "Do you read me?"

Delain could clearly hear him through the hearing device. "Can you hear me?" she softly spoke into the microphone attached at the bottom of the 'v' on her v-neck t-shirt.

John lifted the microphone from his mouth. "We're good to go. Are you ready?"

Delain glanced into the visor mirror, straightening the wig on her head. "Please don't take your eyes off of the building."

"I won't. I'd wish you 'good luck', but you don't need it. This will be a breeze."

She opened the door. With key in hand and sunglasses upon her face, Delain walked across the street and into the three-story building where she once again believed Caleb was conceived. *You can do this. Two minutes— in and out. You're not going to get caught.*

The building was comprised of only four condos (two each on floors two and three). Davis' condo was on the second floor, the second unit at the end of the hallway. She quietly walked up the stairs, peering around the hallway on the second floor. The coast was clear. While walking past the first condo on the way towards Davis' door, Delain wondered if the locks had been changed since her last visit. "Can you hear me?" she whispered into the microphone.

"Loud and clear. You're doing great."

"I'm at the door." Delain's hand shook as she inserted the key into the lock. After turning the key, the quandary of whether or not the locks had been changed was discovered.

"Are you in?"

Before she could answer, Delain heard the condo door behind her being unlocked from the inside. She hurriedly opened Davis' door, quietly closing it behind her. A glance through the peephole revealed a couple exiting the neighboring condo. The man looked in the direction of Davis' door, pointing at it while talking to the woman next to him. Once they were out of sight, Delain turned around. "I'm in." She placed the sunglasses atop her head.

"Go to the bathroom. Look for a toothbrush."

The walls of Davis' condo were as bare as the day they were erected. A beige couch that could barely seat two people, a 47" plasma television, and a rectangular glass coffee table with nothing atop it occupied the living room, while the adjoining kitchen contained just the basics—refrigerator, oven, microwave, dishwasher, toaster, and can opener. Nothing decorative sat atop the tiled countertops, and nothing artsy hung on the walls. The master bedroom was the only room that showed semblance of someone living in the condo. A framed newspaper clipping of Davis holding one of his signature dishes hung above the dresser. The picture was taken several years earlier when Davis had hair and was a good twenty pounds thinner. It was hard to admit, given the way he treated her, but Delain found Davis to be somewhat good-looking in his younger days. Also on the wall hung a Crescent City Classic poster from the year 1992, as well as a panoramic picture of the city taken from across the Mississippi River. There were no pictures of Davis' wife or daughter on the dresser or nightstands. In the condo, as Delain already discovered, Davis was a bachelor.

In a glass on the bathroom countertop, Delain spotted what John had requested. After slipping on the latex gloves, she told him, "I found a toothbrush."

"How does it look?"

"What do you mean?"

"Does it look like it's new or heavily used?"

She closely examined the bristles. "New, I guess. Why?"

"The more it's been used, the better the chance of extracting DNA. Bag it and see what else you can find. What does his bathroom trash can look like?"

She placed the toothbrush in a baggie, slipping it into her pocket before looking in the trashcan. "Full."

"Good. See if you can find chewed gum or a used condom perhaps."

"That's disgusting."

"Yes, but it would be the perfect DNA sample. You have gloves. Use them."

The bathroom waste basket was comprised of used tissues and floss, toilet paper holders, and empty boxes of Irish Spring soap. She then found something that offered Delain hope. "I found a condom wrapper."

"Good. Now look for the condom." Not soon after Delain began to unravel pieces of tissue and toilet paper, John's voice again spoke to her. "I think we have company."

Delain's scavenger hunt came to an abrupt stop. "What do you mean?"

"A woman approaching the building with a taller gentleman may be Davis' daughter. I've only seen a picture of Tiffany, and I think this is her walking towards the building."

"What do I do?"

"Hold on. Let me see if she goes in."

Delain froze while awaiting the verdict. "Well?"

"They're entering the building," John told her with a sense of urgency in his voice. "Get out of there."

"What about the DNA?"

"We'll have to hope the toothbrush has enough on it. Get out now. Go up the stairs until they get to the second floor, then come down here. I'll let you know when they enter the condo."

"Just a few more seconds. This might be our only shot." She continued sorting through the basket, determined to find another DNA sample. She soon found the contents of the wrapper. "I found a condom!"

"Is there semen in it?"

A liquid substance, milky in color, rested in the tip of the condom. "Yes."

"Put in it a baggie and get the hell out of there! They're heading towards the stairs!"

Delain tied the opening of the condom into a knot and then zipped it up in a plastic baggie. She hurried to the door. Upon cracking it open, she could hear feet clacking against the wood stairs. It was too late to leave. After locking the door, she peered through the peephole to see an attractive blonde-haired woman and a man several inches taller than her walking towards the door. Delain backed up into the living room. Panic set in. "They're coming in. Help me, John."

"Hide and then wait for my cue."

As someone inserted a key into the lock, she hurried into the bedroom. "What cue?"

"You'll know."

Once the front door opened, Delain crawled under the bed. She tightly clutched the plastic bag containing the used condom, while the baggie containing the toothbrush remained in her pocket, pressed against her hip.

"Not a bad little place," Delain heard the man remark. "You had no idea he had this condo?"

"Not until Charlie told me a few days ago," Davis' daughter spoke. "Now we have a place to stay if we move here."

"Do you want to move back home?"

Delain found it difficult to breathe at the sight of four feet next to the bed.

"Well… I believe you told me a few weeks ago that you would have no problem finding a job here if I ever wanted to move back."

"Thirty more seconds," John whispered into Delain's ear.

"Just say the word and I'll start looking," the man told Davis' daughter.

"What do you want to do?"

"Whatever will make my fiancée the happiest woman in the world."

"Good boy. You're going to make a perfect husband."

Delain heard the sound of a quick kiss as both sets of feet faced one another.

"I love that picture of Dad. I was a sophomore in high school when it was taken."

"I bet he was a good man. I wish I would have gotten to meet him."

"Me too."

How am I going to get out of here?! As Delain tried to calm herself by imagining Caleb in her arms in just a few short days, a cell phone rang.

"While I answer this can you go see what we would need for the kitchen?" Tiffany asked. "We probably need to go to the store. Start making a list."

"You got it."

Once the man exited the bedroom, Tiffany walked into the bathroom where she answered the phone. "Hey, Uncle Scott… As a matter of fact we're right by the restaurant…Of course we can…We'd love to help…See you soon."

As Tiffany walked back into the bedroom, a loud and jarring noise sent a piercing jolt throughout Delain's body. John's cue had been activated.

"What is that?!" the man yelled from the kitchen.

"What do you think it is?! The fire alarm!"

"What do we do?"

Tiffany exited the room while saying, "Get out of here for one. Grab my—" Her voice was lost amongst the roar of the alarm.

Not sure if Tiffany and her fiancé were still in the condo, Delain opted not to move for fear of getting caught. Nearly a minute passed until she asked John, "Is it safe?" There was no reply. "John, are you there?" She began to panic even further. "If you're trying to get me caught, then you are—"

"You're clear. They just passed me on the street outside."

Delain pulled herself out from beneath the bed. Even though John informed her the coast was clear, she still peeked into the living room to find it and the kitchen unoccupied.

She hurried to the front door, first checking through the peephole. The hallway was empty. With the wig atop her head and the glasses back on her face, she hurried down the staircase and towards the entrance. Once outside, she made her way through the crowd of about twenty concerned on-lookers.

"Keep walking down Orleans and take a right at the next corner," John told her via the ear piece.

Following his instructions, she soon spotting the sedan. She hopped in as a fire truck sped past them. "Holy shit!"

"You did great, Delain," John gleefully told her. "If you're thinking about switching careers, I think espionage may be in your future."

She held up the baggies containing the condom and toothbrush. "Can we get these analyzed and then go get my son back?"

"Absolutely." John pressed a button on his cell phone before placing it to his left ear. "I'm proud of you. You were amazing in there."

Delain felt a heightened sense of accomplishment after doing something she never thought she'd be able to do. "Thank you."

"It's John again," he spoke into the phone. "I need another test…I'll double what I gave you earlier, if you can meet me within an hour…Same place as earlier…See you then."

"Is he going to do it?"

"Yep. We're well on our way to having enough evidence for you to reclaim what's rightfully yours."

Once the adrenaline began to wear off, an emotional Delain felt she could cry. Somehow, she kept it in.

Chapter 112

"That's impossible!" Delain shouted in disbelief.

"It says it right here. Both test samples—carbon DNA copies of one another—are excluded as the biological father of Baby C."

"If Tyler isn't the father, then Davis has to be. How do we know the toothbrush and condom belong to Davis? Maybe they belonged to someone else…or maybe the samples were contaminated." A flicker of hope overcame her. "Maybe Tyler's sample was contaminated too. He could still be the father."

"You got a clean swipe at his cheek, correct?"

"Yes."

"And you placed it immediately in the tube?"

"Yes."

"It wasn't contaminated. As for Davis', perhaps you're right—maybe it wasn't his toothbrush and condom. There is one way to find out though." John then exhaled, as if displeased with what he was about to say. "And I was hoping to avoid that route."

"What route?"

"If Davis' fingerprint is on that toothbrush, questions will arise as to why someone wants to know about a recently deceased, former cop's DNA. Davis was part of something corrupt, so once word gets out that someone is inquiring about his DNA, those corrupt people—the same people trying to find you—will undoubtedly come for the both of us."

"I have to know if he's the father. You said just a little earlier that we need to be certain before we go to the authorities."

He nodded while picking up his phone. "You're right. That leaves us no choice."

"Which is…?"

"It's me again," John told the person on the other end of the phone. "I need a fingerprint analysis from the toothbrush…I know it is. I'll pay you just as much….Thank you. Call me when you get a match." John closed his cell phone.

"If Davis pops up on his computer screen, and if he was in fact involved with some crooked individuals, can't they trace your phone?"

"They can, but it won't lead them to me. I'm very meticulous at what I do."

Delain glanced at her watch. It was fifteen minutes past five o'clock. "How long will it take to match the fingerprints?

"I'd imagine a few hours."

"What do we do in the mean time?"

"Prepare ourselves. I have a feeling our lives are about to get…hectic."

Chapter 113

Delain anxiously looked on as John paced about the balcony on the sixth floor of the Jax Brewery. For the few minutes they had been alone on the balcony, John had yet to use the binoculars in his hand. Even though nighttime was upon them, the temperature still felt as if it were in the nineties, with the humidity level nearing 100%. A three-year resident of New Orleans, Delain still wasn't acclimatized to the summer heat. Only adding to her discomfort was the increase in body temperature incited by the red wig atop her head. Regardless, she refused to take if off for fear of being identified.

"Can we wait inside, John?"

"I'm afraid not. We need to be ready when he calls."

"Ready for what?"

"Anything and everything."

Despite still not trusting John completely, she felt safe in his presence. "Why are we up here instead of the car where it's nicely air-conditioned?"

"I need a bird's eye view." John finally looked through his binoculars in the direction of Café Du Monde. About two hundred feet and a large, sprawling oak tree separated Jax Brewery and the famous beignet establishment.

"What do you see?"

"If my hunch is correct, we're going to need assistance."

"Assistance from—" Delain's question was interrupted by the ringing of John's cell phone.

John placed the phone to his ear. "Do you have what I requested?" A short moment passed before John nodded to Delain. "Can you give me the information over the phone?" John awaited an answer, soon grinning while nodding to Delain. "I hate that you have to meet me on a Sunday night. Can it wait until tomorrow?" John's grin remained. "I understand. I'll meet you at Café Du Monde in fifteen minutes. Call me when you're close." John closed his phone. "I knew it."

"What?"

"Pete didn't want to tell me over the phone whose fingerprint it was, and he stuttered when I asked if it could wait until tomorrow. He's adamant about meeting tonight."

"He's going to meet us at Cafe Du Monde?"

"No." John pointed in the direction of Café Du Monde. "He's going to meet my accomplice down there."

"You have an accomplice? The guy driving the white Navigator from yesterday?"

"No. Someone who doesn't even know he's my accomplice."

"I'm confused."

"You won't be in a minute."

John's eyes were glued to the binoculars as he and Delain stood above the 'J' that made-up the lighted 'Home of JAX Beer' sign on the side of the building facing Café Du Monde. 'JAX' was the only part of the sign comprised of red lightbulbs, and it was much larger than the three other words illuminated in white lightbulbs. While waiting for the phone to again ring, Delain's thoughts momentarily drifted towards Jackson. Not only did they share their first kiss six stories below, but two stories below from where she stood was where their wedding reception was originally scheduled to take place twenty-four hours earlier. She again felt remorse for leaving him the way she did. Her only saving grace was that she would soon be able to confront him and reveal the cause for her abrupt departure.

"Perfect," John mumbled.

"What's perfect?"

"Our accomplice. He just sat down."

"Who is he?"

"I have no idea, but he fits the bill—all alone and talking on his cell phone."

John's phone again rang. He answered it while continuing to peer through the binoculars in the direction of Café du Monde. "Hello…Good. I have short, dirty-blonde hair, I'm wearing a white t-shirt, and I'm sitting alone at the back, corner table next to the iron railing. Discretely place the envelope on the table and walk away. I will act as if I don't know you. Is that clear?…" John glanced at his phone, pressing a button. "Here we go." There was an air of excitement in his tone.

"Your phone is still open," she whispered to him.

"I muted it."

"What's going on?"

"Pete's walking towards the cafe."

"To meet you?"

"That's what he thinks. If you noticed, I didn't let him see what I looked like today. That's why this is going to work. The envelope's in his hand. He's approaching the table."

Delain stared in the direction of the café. The tree blocked her view. After stepping to her left, she could vaguely see someone approaching the back of the café. "What's going on?"

"Pete just dropped off the envelope and kept walking. The guy's staring at the envelope…Now he's looking at Pete as he's walking down the alley behind the café. The guy looks confused… He's reaching for the envelope while looking around the café….He's opening it and looking inside…There's nothing in it. I knew it!"

"What does that mean?"

"Hold on. Two men just sat at the table next to him."

"I think I see them," Delain proclaimed. "Does one have red hair?"

"Yes. The other looks muscular and has blonde hair tied into a ponytail…The guy just stood up. He has the envelope in hand and he's walking off. They're following him."

Delain could see both men closing in on the third as they walked briskly behind him. "Are they about to hurt him?"

"I don't—shit!"

Delain could no longer see the trio as they passed a darkened stretch of sidewalk. "What?!"

"They just grabbed him and shoved him into an SUV."

"They're kidnapping him?"

"It appears so. The license plate is a government plate."

"What the hell are we getting involved in?"

John lowered the binoculars. "We have to get back to the car now."

Delain grew panicked. "Are we following them?"

"No. We need to get out of here."

Once they were back in the sedan, John wasted no time reaching for his phone. Instead of placing it to his ear after dialing a number, he turned the speakerphone on.

"You're calling the police?"

He shook his head as the phone rang. "No."

"Hello," a man's voice spoke on the other end of the phone.

"Pete, why don't you call your two friends who just kidnapped an innocent bystander and tell them to let him go?"

"I-I-I don't know what you're t-t-talking about."

"You stutter when you're lying, Pete."

"Who are you?"

"The envelope was empty. Where's the information I asked for?"

"I-I-I…"

"Why can't you tell me that the fingerprint on the toothbrush belonged to Davis Melancon?" Silence ensued. "Still there, Peter?"

"If you already knew, why the analysis?"

"I needed to be sure of something."

"What?"

"The truth." John hung up.

"That means Davis isn't the father?"

"Correct."

A perturbed Delain thrust her hands into the air. "That doesn't make any sense at all."

"You don't remember having sex with Davis, do you?"

"No. He drugged me."

"So, you're not exactly sure if you did have sex with him then?"

"He told me the next day we did, and I was sore down there."

John leaned back in his seat. With shut eyes and a shake of his head, he began to smirk. "Man, he's good…was good."

"Who?"

"Davis."

"How so?"

John opened his eyes as he turned to Delain. "Davis isn't the father, and neither is Tyler, but I have a good idea who is."

"Who?!"

Monday

Chapter 114

Sleep was non-existent for Delain as she lay next to Tyler in his hotel room. Although she was closer to discovering the truth, she had never felt more confused, scared, and alone. She experienced some comfort, however, as Tyler didn't inquire about her day any further than asking, 'how was your day?' Her response of 'productive' incited a smile from him followed by a conversational change.

While sipping on a large black coffee, a white Chevy Tahoe with tinted windows stopped in front of Delain as she stood just outside of the hotel entrance. A wary Delain slowly stepped backwards, readying herself to either run inside the hotel if someone suspicious exited the vehicle, or to grab the gun from her purse. Her fear subsided once the window rolled down and she could see the driver.

"What happened to the sedan?"

"Pete knows what it looks like. We have to be careful. Speaking of which, get in."

Delain scanned the parking lot while climbing into the passenger seat.

"Which hospital was Caleb born?" John asked her.

"He was born in a—wait—you mean to tell me that you don't know something about my past? You weren't listening when I told Caroline?"

"When did you tell her?"

"Last Sunday after Jackson's funeral."

"Before the two of you went to Davis' restaurant?"

"Yes. When did you start spying on me?"

John drove away from the hotel. "Monitoring is a more precise word, and I started right before Caroline pulled up to your house that day. I missed part of your confession to her. I bet it was around the time an ice cream truck stopped in front of your house."

"I see." Still not comfortable with the fact that someone had been 'monitoring' her for the last week, Delain couldn't grow mad at the man helping to get her son back. "Caleb was born in a birthing center."

"No wonder Davis was able to do what he did. Let me guess, it was his decision to use the birthing center."

"Yes."

"And did he recommend the doctor too?"

"Yes."

John shook his head. "He keeps getting smarter and smarter."

"Davis?"

"Yep."

"I did some research last night and earlier today. Caleb's, or Thomas Melancon's, adoption papers are nowhere to be found."

"What does that mean?"

"Legally, he was never adopted. Or if he was, the file has been removed. That means what Davis did was highly illegal and also very complex."

"And we'll never know because he's dead."

"I couldn't agree with you any less. He didn't do what he did by himself. The men from last night may have an idea of what happened."

"Even if they did, how do we find out who they are?"

"The blonde-haired gentleman's name is Mitch Hennessey. He's an F.B.I. agent and a former partner of Davis during his time with the police."

"How do you know that?"

"I traced the license plate."

"Great," she sarcastically replied. "Now we can't go the F.B.I."

"Sure we can. We just need proof that one of their agents is corrupt."

"How do we get proof?"

John held up his cell phone. "We just need a little cheese to catch a rat."

"You're calling him now?"

"Procrastination leads to devastation." John pulled into a parking spot on Canal Street, outside of the Katrina–damaged Saenger Theater. After putting the vehicle in park, he attached a device to the phone.

"What's that?"

"A recorder. Don't say a word, and…" he dialed the number, "here we go." The phone rang twice before being answered.

"Agent Hennessey."

"Is this Mitch Hennessey?" John asked, his voice frail and well-aged sounding.

"Speaking?"

"Is this Federal Agent Mitch Hennessey?"

"Who is this and how did you get this number?"

"I need to speak with Agent Hennessey. It's a life or death situation."

"This is Agent Hennessey."

John cleared his throat before continuing. "Mitch, I hope no harm was bestowed upon the innocent victim you kidnapped last night outside of Café du Monde."

A pause ensued before Mitch spoke. "That was a nifty little trick."

"Pete called you as soon as he discovered someone was inquiring about Davis' DNA. Tell me, Mitch, were you part of it?"

"I always prefer to know a person's name when engaged in conversation. I doubt you'll tell me your real name, friend, so whom should I call you?

"John. Were you part of it?"

"Part of what, John? I have no idea what you're talking about. Do you have a last name, John?"

"Wayne. The truth is about to be revealed about Davis and those involved with what he did. He didn't act alone. Unfortunately, I fear you and your redheaded associate from last night are involved with the cover-up as well. That's why you kidnapped the person whom you believed to be me."

"Cover-up?"

"You can play dumb and lie to me all you want, but you are involved. In just a few hours, the truth will be revealed."

"Tell me a little bit about yourself, John…Wayne."

"I can save you the trouble of trying to trace this call. You won't discover who I am or my location."

Another pause, longer than the previous, occurred before Mitch exhaled into the phone. He then snickered on the other end of the phone. "It's funny you're bring up Davis considering it has just been discovered that he was murdered. Unfortunately, I fear you may be involved with them."

"Them?"

"A young man who has been in the news as of late, and a woman—perhaps the woman you're currently with."

Delain scanned her surroundings before facing John. "How does he know that?" she mouthed to him.

"He doesn't," he told her while covering the phone with his hand. "He's bluffing."

"Your silence is answer enough. What are you, John? F.B.I.? C.I.A.? D.E.A.? Something else with letters in it? Between last night's trick, your ability to trace a government vehicle, and this untraceable call, I believe you are or once were part of a government agency."

"Here's what's going to happen, Mitch—Davis' legacy will be tarnished by the day's end. You have two options: go to prison or save yourself."

"Okay, I'll play along with your little game for a moment. What do you want me to do, John?"

"See to it that the kid returns to his biological mother."

"What kid are you talking about?"

"Goodbye, Mitch."

"Wait! Wait! Don't hang—"

John hung up. He then calmly looked straight ahead.

"Is that it?" Delain asked.

John hit the 'talk' button on the phone. "No." The phone rang only once.

"Don't hang up, John," Mitch spoke into the phone.

"You have three seconds to say the kid's name or I'm hanging up for good. One…"

"Thomas."

"Good. Now, if you pretend to play dumb again, the offer is off the table and you're going down with your associates."

"What do you want me to do?"

"I want to talk to the boy's biological father in one hour."

"Why?"

"I want to talk to the boy's biological father in one hour," John firmly repeated.

"I don't know who his biological father—"

John again hung up. He then set the phone on the dashboard.

An anxious Delain stared at the phone and then at John as she asked, "Now are we done with him?"

"Not yet. He definitely knows who the biological father is."

"How do you know? He said he doesn't know who the father is."

"If he would have said that after the first time I said I wanted to speak to the biological father, then I might have believed him, but he said 'why?' first. He knows."

"Are you going to call him back?"

"Eventually," he casually replied. "I'm going to make him sweat a little more first. How are things going with your ex, Tyler?"

"Good." Delain again stared at the phone, as if silently instructing John to grab it. "How long are you waiting?"

"Long enough to where he won't play dumb with me again. Did you eat yet today?"

"I haven't been hungry."

"Ever since last night I've been craving beignets. I'd love some right now."

Delain was becoming impatient with the hold-out. "Finish the phone call and I'll buy you some."

John grabbed the phone and again pressed the 'talk' button.

"Okay. Where?" Mitch frantically spoke.

"Where, what?"

"Where do you want to meet the boy's biological father?"

"At his workplace. Can you arrange that, Mitch?"

"What will be the purpose of this meeting?"

"We want to talk to him. If you can get him there in one hour, your job will be complete, thus saving you from persecution. I want you there as well."

"How do I know I can trust you?"

"I give you my word, Mitch, from one fed to another."

"I knew it."

"To recap, when are we meeting you?"

"In one hour."

"And where?"

"The Fleur-de-Leans."

"There's no need to, Mitch."

"Come again?"

"I was missing just one piece of the puzzle—Thomas' biological father. You just gave it to me. Thank you." John hung up.

"You were right last night. Scott Melancon *is* Caleb's biological father."

"Yep."

Delain was in shock. "But how is that possible?"

"You don't recall having sex with Davis."

"Correct."

"You didn't have sex with him."

Disbelief soon escaped her as she began to unravel the truth. "Davis drugged me…then his brother impregnated me?"

"That's option number one. The other is that you were artificially inseminated with Scott's sperm while you were passed out. Either way, Caleb is his son too. What we don't know is if Scott knows what his brother did."

"I don't think he had sex with me because he didn't seem to recognize me in the elevator."

"You were disguised. Regardless, we have to assume he knows everything and that he's just as guilty and temperamental as his brother."

It was nearly too much for Delain to process. "What do we do now?"

"That's your call. Either we go to the authorities with what we know now or first try to protect your former fiancé."

"Protect Jackson?"

"Mitch's back is to the wall. He thinks Jackson is involved, hence the comment he made about a young man in the news as of late. He's going to go after him. What's our next move, Delain?"

Chapter 115

With five sets of eyes cast upon him, Mitch stood in front of an oil painting of Judge Broussard as it hung in the stately study of the painting's subject. The image of the judge standing beneath a moss-draped cypress tree in a judicial robe with a gold-plated gavel in his left hand and a pure white colonial wig atop his head was a self-portrait, taking three years to complete. Dark colors along with the emaciated and accurate representation of the subject combined to give the painting a feel of the macabre.

"Gentlemen, I'll get right to business. It seems someone outside of the Krewe has partial knowledge of one of our past endeavors."

"Does it involve Davis and his brother's son?" Roger Ainsworth asked from one of the four stools surrounding the bar.

"Yes."

"You say partial knowledge. Define partial, Mitch," Charlie spoke, seated in one of the two dark leather couches in front of the bar.

"I got a call last night from Pete informing me that a man known only as 'John' was paying him a substantial amount of money to get expedited DNA results. It turns out that two of the items being tested had traces of Davis' DNA on them. One was a used condom and the other a toothbrush. Apparently, John was trying to determine if Davis was the biological father of Scott's son, Thomas. He also had Pete perform a maternity test on two samples, with one being a positive match."

"That means *she* found out and is involved with this John guy," Percy, seated next to Charlie, pointed out.

"Yes, it does."

From the bar stool next to Roger, Redmond stood. "Last night Mitch and I apprehended the man we suspected to be this John fellow. Turns out John used a bystander as a decoy to discover who we are."

"I talked to John a little while ago. He called me from an untraceable number. He is more than likely a former Fed. I'm not sure how or why he got involved, but he did, and finding him is our top priority. So far, he only knows my name. Even though he saw Redmond with me last night, he doesn't know who he is or about the rest of the Krewe."

"She probably hired him to get her son back," Roger suggested.

"That's highly probable."

"His name is John. Can't we start from there?"

"I doubt that's his real name, Judge. To be honest, our chances of finding him are slim to none."

"Then we find Christina, or Delain, or whatever the hell she goes by now," an impatient Percy suggested.

"I went by her place. It's empty."

"What about her cell phone?"

"I performed a trace on it, but nothing popped up. It hasn't been turned on, which furthered my suspicion that John is a former Fed."

"What else did John tell you over the phone?"

"He said Davis was going down in a couple of hours."

Percy stood from the couch and walked towards the bar. "Then it's only a matter of time until the truth comes forth and we all get arrested. It's been a good run, guys." He grabbed a bottle of 20-year-old Scotch from a shelf behind the bar. After pouring himself a glass he asked, "Anyone else care for a drink?"

"I'd love a glass, dear friend."

Percy reached across the bar, handing Roger the glass in his hand, who then passed it to Charlie. "Enjoy it because it may be your last."

"Why are you speaking with such negativity? No ill will be brought onto this group of ours."

"Once a DNA test is performed on the child, Charlie, they will discover that Christina is the biological mother. And then what? She somehow found out what Davis did, and now she's going to tell the authorities. They already know Mitch is involved and," he pointed to Redmond, "someone with red hair who will soon be identified by this John person."

"Mitch and Redmond are not involved. They simply questioned a man last night whom they believed was obtaining DNA information about our departed friend. They were merely curious as to why someone was doing such a thing."

"And what if that man comes forward, claiming he was interrogated by two men asking questions about Davis or the child?"

"He was high as a kite," Redmond told Percy, "and very scared."

Mitch nodded. "He thought we were going to arrest him for having weed in his pocket. Trust me, he's not going to be talking to anyone. There's no need to worry about him."

"What about Scott?" Roger inquired. "When they find out Christina's the mother and he's the father, he's going to have some explaining to do. Speaking of, why isn't he here?"

"We thought it best to let him sit out of this particular meeting," the judge spoke.

"The less Scottie knows, the better it is for him, his lovely wife, and that handsome son of theirs."

"And when a DNA test is administered, what will happen to Scott then?"

"Scott is one of us now, Roger, and we won't let anything happen to him or his family." The judge slowly stood. "Gentlemen, what you see is a problem. What I see is a dilemma in which a solution had already been devised."

"And that is…?"

"Gentlemen, I think it's time we call upon an old friend of ours."

"Harley?"

"Yes, Roger."

Mitch knew Harley all too well. During their first encounter, Mitch (a rookie New Orleans police officer at the time) attempted to arrest Harley for disorderly conduct outside of a bar. The misdemeanor turned into a felony in the blink of an eye as a twenty-one-year-old Harley resisted arrest and struck Mitch, knocking him to the ground. Davis and two more officers eventually subdued and arrested a drunken Harley as Mitch looked on with a bloody nose and a broken rib. The incident incited Mitch to begin a training program that included weight lifting and mixed martial arts. The second time the two were in each other's presence was in court on the day Harley was arraigned. The third meeting occurred seven years later when the two ran into each other at a nightclub. Adrenaline coursed through Mitch's veins as the 6'4", heavily tattooed Harley approached him. A partial

191

smile, an extended right hand, an apology that consisted of the words 'Sorry, dude', and two rounds of drinks eased some of the tension Mitch felt in Harley's presence. A fourth meeting occurred when Harley was hired by restaurateur Davis Melancon to recover money owed to him from someone who had been refusing to pay. After successfully retrieving the money, Harley was hired to fulfill tasks for Davis and other members of the Krewe that resided in the gray area between lawful and illegal. Due to the plethora of ink that covered his arms and neck, his towering stature, the lack of hair on his head, the look in his eyes that suggested he feared nothing or no one, and the dirty-blonde handlebar mustache about his face that was groomed in such a way that he constantly looked to be angrily frowning, the idiom 'don't judge a book by its cover' was disregarded by many who came into contact with Harley. Although Harley was considered a valuable asset to the Krewe, deep down and unbeknownst to anyone else, Mitch was still fearful of him. Even with twelve years of martial arts training under his belt, Mitch wasn't so sure he would be able to defeat Harley if the two were to once again engage in fisticuffs.

"And what will we need Harley's services for?" Roger asked.

"As soon as a DNA test is performed on Scott's son," Judge Broussard spoke, "the truth will come to light. Davis' name will be tarnished, and the rest of us will more than likely go down in flames." The judge pointed to Percy. "The doctor who delivered Thomas." He then pointed to Charlie, "And the lawyer who assisted over the adoption process." His hand next moved in the direction of Roger. "And the accountant that presided over Davis' estate." Mitch was the next to receive the pointer finger of the judge's right hand. "The former partner of Davis that was foolishly seen with…" Redmond simultaneously received the pointer finger of the judge's left hand, "my nephew last night, apprehending a man they believed had knowledge of the truth surrounding this ordeal." Judge Broussard, standing beneath his self-portrait, then pressed both hands against his chest. "And the retired judge who not only had knowledge of the elaborate plan, but who also helped to orchestrate it."

"Yes, we're all involved. Tell us something we don't know, Alfonso," Percy irritably spoke.

"They can't perform the DNA test on the boy if they can't find him."

"What are you suggesting?" Roger asked.

Percy slammed his drink on the counter while asking, "That we kidnap the boy?"

The judge nodded.

192

Roger stood from the stool as he asked, "What?!"

"Are you nuts, Uncle?"

"I know it sounds crazy, but we kidnap the boy only until we find his birthmother. Once we find her, Thomas will be returned to his parents."

"He's right, gentlemen. Think about it. It's going to be awfully coincidental if Christina goes to the police and claims to be the biological mother of a boy who had just been kidnapped. All fingers will be pointed towards her."

"And she won't go to the police if he does get kidnapped," Mitch interjected. "And I'm certain John would contact me again and we can finally catch the son of a bitch."

"We're looking at less than twenty-four hours that Scott and Bridgett will be without their son."

"And if we were to do this, would we even tell Scott?"

"We can't, Percy. The less he knows, the better. We need his and Bridgett's reaction to be authentic in front of the police and the press. This can and will work, gentlemen, and very easily too. We have the resources to make it happen, but we have to act now. As always, we need a unanimous decision before we proceed." The judge raised his hand. "For."

"For," Charlie answered from the couch.

"For," Mitch spoke with raised arm.

Redmond cleared his throat before raising his hand. "For."

"How would the kidnapping go down?"

The judge scrolled through his phone before answering Roger. "Scott and Bridgett have been so busy the last few days that they flew in their babysitter from back home. Scott has been at the restaurant all day. His wife dropped him off there and just checked into a Pilates studio on Magazine Street about twenty minutes ago. The babysitter and Thomas are currently in a not-so-crowded movie theater waiting for the movie *Ratatouille* to begin."

"How do you know this?"

"Because Harley is currently sitting directly behind Thomas and the babysitter."

"Jesus! It sounds like a decision has already been made, Judge!"

"Roger," his uncle Charlie spoke, "we have never made a mistake with any endeavor in which we have partook. No harm will come to that child, the babysitter, or anyone else. And no harm will come to any one of us either. Your mother is my favorite sister, and you are my favorite nephew. I assure you that I would not allow any harm to be bestowed upon you either."

Due to the repetitive shaking of Roger's head and the prolonged silence, Mitch felt that the accountant was going to vote 'against' at any second.

"For…God damnit," the doctor spoke with gritted teeth while making eye contact with the drink in his hand.

Roger glanced at the doctor and then into the eyes of the remaining four gentlemen. After hanging his head low, he mumbled, "For."

The judge texted into his phone before flipping it shut. "Now that we got that little dilemma taken care of, what about the other thorn in our side? What will become of the young man who murdered our dear friend Davis?"

"I thought we were waiting on Tiffany. Did she meet with him yet?" Roger inquired.

"She did," Mitch answered. "Not too long ago."

"What's the verdict?"

"Tiffany has no doubt, like the rest of us, that Jackson is the reason her father is dead. To say that she hates him right now is a vast understatement. She was livid as I talked to her. I asked if she thinks his death would be justified." Mitch walked towards the bar, where he poured Kentucky whiskey into a shot glass.

"And…?"

Mitch tilted his head back, swallowing the whiskey before placing the glass on the counter. "She wants his death to be as painful and agonizing as possible."

Tuesday

Chapter 116

The New Orleans F.B.I. headquarters was located across the street from Pontchartrain Park— the same park where I played baseball as a seven and eight-year-old. Some of my fondest memories were summers spent in that park. While being escorted into the red bricked, four-story F.B.I. building, I longed for the days of Big League Chew, sundown curfews, comic books, and the sound of baseball cards flapping against the spokes of my bicycle. Childhood innocence was long gone.

Reality set in as I sat alone in an empty room, still handcuffed. Certain that I was being watched from behind the rectangular mirror to my right, I stared straight ahead— about as motionless as Norman Bates in the final scene of Psycho. I may have appeared cool and collected, but the inevitability that I was going to jail proved impossible to overlook. If incarceration was my final verdict, I would prefer the death penalty instead. I wouldn't last a day in prison.

Not soon after my thoughts shifted back to Delain and the phone call the ill-timed agents interrupted, the door opened. A familiar face nearly brought tears to my eyes. As I had done for well over a decade, I contained my emotions while gazing upon the man I was proud to call my father. Agents Parker and Williams stood behind him.

"Get those cuffs off of my client right now!"

I had never seen the lawyer side of my dad, but from what I've heard over the years—as well as read in newspaper articles—he was damn good at his profession. I was ready to finally see him in action. As Agent Parker began to uncuff me, my dad asked, "And why is he in those to begin with?"

I glanced at Agent Williams as he told my dad, "He assaulted me."

"What is your name again?"

"Agent Williams."

"What is your first name, Agent Williams?"

"Leonard."

"Leonard, in what matter did Jackson assault you?"

Agent Williams hesitated before answering, "He slapped my hand."

With a roll of his eyes, my dad subtly shook his head. "Let me get this straight. My client didn't punch you or assault you with any sort of weapon?"

"No."

"He tried to grab the phone from my hand," I said. "I instinctively swatted at his arm as he was invading my personal space."

"Why don't we all take a seat," Agent Parker suggested. He sat directly across the table from me, while his partner sat to his left.

After taking to the chair on my right, my dad patted my knee and gave me a nod as if to say 'everything is going to be okay'.

"Mr. Fabacher," Agent Parker began, placing the handcuffs onto the table, "Agent Williams and I met with your son last Wednesday in Phoenix. We questioned him about his whereabouts beginning on Friday, June the 29th at 2:00 mountain time until his emergence at a gas station near the town of Kirkland, Arizona on Wednesday, July the 4th at precisely 3:15 in the afternoon. According to his confession, Jackson claimed that upon leaving the Denver airport, he took a bus to a restaurant on Washington Street, just outside the city limits of Denver. It was at this restaurant that Jackson told us he met a truck driver named Bobby Smith, who then proceeded to drive Jackson to Bakersfield, California. Upon his arrival on Saturday afternoon, Jackson informed us that he checked into a Super 8 motel and stayed there until Tuesday, at which time he hitchhiked with another truck driver only known as Marge. She then dropped Jackson off at the gas station outside of Kirkland, Arizona where we first met him."

"And why is he once again in your custody?"

"It seems we found some discrepancies with his testimony," Agent Williams spoke.

"Such as…?"

"First of all, Agent Williams and myself interviewed each employee of the Super 8 motel in Bakersfield that would have worked from Saturday, June 30th through Tuesday, July 3rd. Jackson Fabacher never checked into the Super 8 motel, and none of the employees recognized him after being shown his picture."

My dad glanced at me, and with a subtle wink of his left eye—the same eye that was out of sight from both agents—asked, "Are you sure you stayed in a Super 8 motel,

197

and if so, are you certain it was in Bakersfield? Also, were you intoxicated at any point while you were in California?"

It didn't take long to see his angle. I looked first at Agent Williams, and then Agent Parker. "Now that I think about it, I'm not so sure it was Bakersfield. Bobby offered me some whiskey in his truck. I had a good bit of it. Plus, as I already mentioned in my confession last Wednesday, I took sleeping pills the entire time I was at the motel. Do you remember me saying that, Agent Parker?"

With a nod he answered, "Yes. I have it documented here."

"And I may have had a bit more whiskey at the motel as I was trying to escape the depressive state I was in about Delain and her male friend. That should be documented as well."

"It is. You're now claiming you stayed in another motel, perhaps in another city?"

"It's very possible."

"Okay," he spoke with uncertainty. "Since we're on the subject of your fiancée...are you ready to tell the truth about her?"

"What do you mean?"

"What's your fiancée's name, Jackson?"

"Delain Schexnaydre."

"Her real name, please."

"Delain Schexnaydre." Upon repeating her name, I recalled the conversation with Caroline days earlier in which she thought Delain's real first name to be either Christine or Christina.

"Surely you know her real name."

"What are you talking about?"

"A little less than three years ago, your fiancée legally changed her name to Delain Schexnaydre from Christina Foster. Were you aware of the name change?"

"No," I spoke with inquisitive eyes. Having my dad at arm's length was like having the right amount of tequila in my system. I felt I could even pass a polygraph test if one was presented to me.

"Where is she now?"

"I was hoping you could tell me."

"You don't know where your fiancée is?"

"No."

With a look of confusion about his face, Agent Parker asked, "When did you last speak with and see her?"

"Saturday—early afternoon."

"That was to be the day of your wedding, correct?"

"We decided we weren't going to go through with the wedding ceremony. We thought it would be exciting to just get in our car and start driving. When I went to pick her up around 3:15, she was gone. She left a note behind that read 'I'm sorry'. That was the last time I had any sort of communication with her."

"Any idea where she went?"

"I got nothing. I don't even know where to start."

"That doesn't seem bizarre to you?" Agent Williams asked.

"Very bizarre. I tried calling her cell phone, but it went straight to voicemail every time.

"When we last spoke, Jackson, you said Delain had a relationship with a male friend that you were uncomfortable with. Do you think this gentleman may have an idea where she is?"

During the last conversation with the agents, the male friend of Delain's whom I was uncomfortable with was fictional. That was no longer the case. "It's quite possible."

"Can you divulge his name now?"

The F.B.I. surely had the means to find someone I was interested in meeting for myself. "Yes, sir. Tyler Bennett. That's all I know about him."

After receiving a nod from his partner, Agent Williams removed a cell phone from his pocket on his way out of the room.

Once the door shut behind him, my dad asked, "Why are you so concerned with my son's fiancée and a friend of hers?"

"Well, Mr. Fabacher, within the last hour, Delain Schexnaydre/Christina Foster has been wanted by the F.B.I."

"She's under arrest?" I asked, shocked and suddenly concerned for her safety.

"No. She's wanted for questioning."

"For what?"

"It's not clear. A local agent is leading the investigation."

"Who?" my dad asked.

"I'm not at liberty to say."

"Perhaps if you did, we could help."

Agent Parker glanced at the mirror and then back at us. "If you can shed some light into this next subject matter, I will tell both of you the agent's name."

My dad and I both nodded.

"Jackson, your ex-fiancée, Tiffany Melancon, has an uncle named Scott Melancon. Did you know him and his wife Bridgett?"

"Yes."

"They have a two-year-old son named Thomas. Did you ever meet him?"

I found difficulty in swallowing as I answered, "Once."

"Last night, Thomas was kidnapped from a movie theatre on Prytania Street."

It was hard not to think that Delain was somehow involved. "What?!"

"A Caucasian man heavily covered in tattoos and measuring between 6'2" and 6'4" grabbed Thomas from beneath his babysitter's nose, escaping out the back of the movie theater with him. That's the only information we have at this time."

"Any other description?" my dad asked.

"Bald and possibly a blonde moustache."

"Harley," my dad quickly spoke with conviction.

Agent Parker leaned forward, placing his left ear closer to my dad. "Did you say Harley?"

"A man named Harley Motichek fits that description. He goes by the name of 'Hitman' on the streets."

"Who is he?"

"Several years ago, my office was assigned a case involving Harley. He resisted arrest and assaulted a police officer following a dispute in a bar. He spent some time in jail—less than two years if memory serves me correctly. While he hasn't been incarcerated since, he was arrested on one count of aggravated assault. A man by the name of Larry LeBlanc claimed Harley assaulted him behind Davis's restaurant. Larry was in the hospital for nearly a month. The case never went to court, because Larry was later arrested on attempted murder of Harley. Turns out the man Larry hired to kill Harley was actually a friend of Harley's. They say that's how 'Hitman' received his nickname; that or because he might actually be one as well. Other charges over the years were brought to light against Harley, but nothing came of them. His lawyer, Charlie Guichet, is one of the top defense lawyers in Louisiana."

"What type of charges?"

"Assault with a deadly weapon, carjacking, possession of an illegal narcotic, plus a few others I can't recall at the moment. We kept our eye on him over the years."

"It sounds like he's not the most upstanding of gentlemen."

"He's not but…" My dad's look then became a perplexed one.

"But what?"

"Based on what you said, Harley fits the description of the person who kidnapped the child, but Harley has been loosely associated with Davis over the years. Why would he kidnap his associate's brother's child? It makes me believe that maybe Harley isn't the person who kidnapped him."

"Or maybe it has to do with the fact that Davis illegally helped Scott obtain his adopted son," I blurted out.

"How do you know that?" Agent Parker asked.

"Because I was minutes away from marrying his daughter. I know things about the Melancon family. Things no one else knows. Things they wouldn't want anyone else to know."

"Such as…?"

With my back to the wall, I had no choice but to divulge Davis' diabolical plan to someone that couldn't have known him, thus wouldn't come after me or my family. "For starters—"

The door to the interrogation room hastily swung open. A man I had met on several occasions at the Melancon house and many times at the Fleur-de-Leans stepped into the room.

"Gentlemen," Agent Parker began, "this is Agent Mitch Hennessey, also with the F.B.I."

"We are well acquainted with one another," my dad spoke.

"Andrew, always a pleasure. Jackson, it's good to…what happened to your face?" Mitch's breathing was heavy for someone who would have just casually walked into the room.

I said nothing as I stared intently at the man whom, over the years, I suspected had developed a bit of a crush on my former fiancée. I had suspicions that Tiffany may have had feelings for her dad's former partner as well. The way the two smiled at one another while engaged in conversation, especially when alcohol was being consumed, was hard to ignore—as was the flirting Tiffany claimed was innocent.

"He fell in the shower last night," my dad answered.

"I'd hate to see what the shower looks like," Mitch said with a smirk.

"What are you doing here, Mitch?"

"My job." His breathing returned to normal.

"Which is…?"

He sat on the edge of the table next to my dad. "To discover the truth."

"About your late partner's nephew?"

"Among other things. It's good to see the two of you again, but I wish it was under different circumstances." Mitch's blue eyes peered deep into my soul as he asked, "Jackson, are Bobby Smith and Marge the only two people you encountered on your trip last week?"

"Yes."

"There were no other truck drivers you may have been in contact with between Friday, June 30th and Wednesday, July 4th?"

My dad, pointing to Mitch but looking at Agent Parker, asked, "Why is he here?"

"Because I have every right to be here," Mitch replied with a tap of the badge hanging from his neck. "This means I can ask whatever I want to whomever I want. You are well acquainted with the law, Andrew. Now, Jackson, were there any other truck drivers that you may have been in contact with between Friday, June 30th and Wednesday, July 4th?"

After unclenching my teeth, I told the man I never cared for, "No."

"Are you sure?"

"Yes."

After adjusting himself in the chair, Agent Parker asked, "Jackson, do you know someone by the name of Cliff Robertson?"

My stomach felt as if it was lodged in my throat. "No." My hands, already perspiring, began to shake. I hid them under the table.

"Who is this Cliff Robertson?" my dad asked Agent Parker.

"Cliff was shot and killed nine days ago inside the home of Hank Bowery in Mobile," Mitch spoke. "Cliff's body was found next to Hank's, who was also shot and killed."

Agent Parker placed a picture in front of me. Cliff stood next to a woman with a brunette bouffant hairdo. She wore a pink wedding dress, while Cliff wore a dark tuxedo with a ruffled light blue shirt. "Do you recognize this man, Jackson?"

"Hank Bowery? Wait—was that the same house where those two young girls were being held as sex slaves?"

"Yes, Andrew, it was," Mitch answered while continuing to stare at me. "Jackson, do you recognize the man in that picture?"

I didn't know what to say. I needed time to conjure another lie.

"Do you know him, Jackson?" the other agent in the room asked.

I hesitated before shaking my head. "No."

"Are you certain you don't know him?"

"Yes."

"Guys, what is the purpose of this questioning?"

Mitch, still staring intently at me, told my dad, "According to the police report, Hank and Cliff shot and killed one another around shortly before 5:00 in the morning on Sunday, July 1st. After examining the crime scene further, I determined that a third person was involved in the early morning shootout. Only adding to the mystery is that Hank's Chevy Silverado was found beneath an I-10 overpass here in New Orleans this past Saturday. That same truck was at Hank's house on the morning of the shootout, so sometime between 7:00 pm on Sunday, July 1st and this past Saturday, July 7th, someone stole and drove the truck to New Orleans. I'm thinking it was stolen much closer to Sunday than Saturday."

"And what does this have to do with my son?"

Mitch, flashing the cockiest of smirks, said, "Everything. Eight years ago, your son was arrested for disorderly conduct. Do you remember that incident, Jackson?"

A police officer caught me urinating on the side of a Bourbon Street bar during one of my very few tequila-fueled debaucheries. The officer probably would have let me go with a warning if I didn't mouth off and call him names.

"It's okay if you don't remember, Jackson. That's what police records are for; that and collecting fingerprints of criminals. Andrew, your son's fingerprints were found inside Cliff's rig."

I felt as if someone had hit the pause button on a remote that controlled my body. I couldn't blink, speak, think, or even breathe while staring at Mitch. It felt like every organ in my body momentarily ceased working upon being caught in a lie that could unravel the truth and send me to prison.

Mitch stood, placing his hands onto the table while leaning forward. "Jackson, I'm going to ask you one more time. Were you ever in contact with Cliff Robertson?"

I couldn't lie anymore. I was mentally exhausted. "Yes," I mumbled.

"You were in contact with Cliff Rob—"

"Yes!"

"In what manner, Jackson?"

"I shot him."

"You killed him?" my dad asked.

I place my hands onto the table, staring at them while confessing, "I climbed into his rig at a truck stop in Oklahoma. He kidnapped me at gunpoint, and then forced me to go to Mobile. He said he had a score to settle with his old friend Hank because Hank slept with his wife. I was a decoy. Cliff instructed me at gunpoint to knock on Hank's door. Once I was inside…"

"What happened, Jackson?" Mitch asked.

"Cliff shot Hank twice, and then I shot Cliff."

"Why?"

"Because he was going to shoot me. It was self-defense."

Agent Parker asked, "Did you know about the young girls in the basement?"

I looked up at him. "Not at first. I heard them calling for help on my way out."

"Why did you leave before the police arrived?"

"I didn't. I hid in the attic until they left."

Agent Parker removed and set his glasses onto the table. "You rescued two young women that were being held as sex slaves, and then decided to hide from the police instead of coming forth as a hero?"

"Yes."

"Why?"

During my Norman Bates stare minutes earlier, I had anticipated the question Agent Parker had just asked. "Did you read comic books when you were younger, Agent Parker?"

"A little bit. Why?"

"I loved comic books. I even had a name for myself."

204

"What was it?"

"Captain Incredible."

Agent Parker cracked a smile, and while subtly nodding said, "That's a…heroic name."

"While I was Captain Incredible, I pretended no one knew my true identity. One thing I hated about comic books was when the hero's true identity was discovered by someone. I didn't want Lois Lane to discover that Clark Kent was Superman or for Mary Jane to know her love interest was actually Spider-Man. My favorite part of being Captain Incredible was anonymity."

Agent Parker nodded. "I see where you're going with this. You didn't want credit for rescuing those two girls."

"There's something heroic and noble about someone who doesn't want or need to be recognized as a hero. Also, and probably more importantly, I wanted to protect those close to me."

"I understand. Hank is dead, though. I think you and your loved ones are safe now."

"I'm not so sure. He didn't act alone. When Cliff led me to Hank's house at gunpoint, he said to tell Hank that Spud sent me. The officer in charge of the case was mentioned in the newspaper article this morning. His name is—"

"Robert McKenzie," Mitch spoke, staring blankly ahead.

"He was the first to arrive at the scene. I didn't realize at the time, but neither his lights nor his siren was on. I finally put two and two together when his nickname was included in the newspaper article this morning. I think he was an accomplice to Hank."

"That would explain his behavior."

"I'm sorry?" Agent Parker asked Mitch.

"I met with him Saturday morning. He was short with me and appeared upset when I said I was reopening the case."

"I have no doubt in my mind that he was a part of Hank's sick and twisted business. He needs to be questioned."

Mitch nodded. "And he will be."

"Mitch, why are you reopening the case?" my dad inquired.

"Because we had reason to believe the—"

"I mean *you*. Why are *you* involved with something in Alabama?"

"Well," he stood upright, staring confidently at my dad, "I'm afraid your son is in some very hot water."

"For killing a man in self-defense, preceding the rescue of two women who were being held as sex hostages?"

"No." With his back to me and my dad, Mitch's hands rested on his head as he stared at the rectangular mirror.

"And you're just going to stand there in silence?"

Mitch turned around. "Davis Melancon was murdered."

My dad glanced at me from the corner of his eye, and then flashed a puzzled look at the back of Mitch's head. "He died of a heart attack."

Mitch turned around. "That's what we originally thought, Andrew, but after a second and more detailed search, we found evidence of second-degree murder."

Even though my heart was pounding with such intensity that I could feel it pulsating in nearly every inch of my body, I tried my hardest to appear as composed as possible. I looked at Mitch as if we were engaged in a staring contest. If I were to look away first, he would know I was guilty.

"A second investigation revealed duct tape residue, not only around the cuffs of the dress shirt Davis was wearing the night he died, but on his steering wheel as well. Also, we discovered blood on the base of the door frame leading from his garage into his house. The blood belonged to Hank Bowery."

I couldn't believe I had transferred blood from one crime scene to another. With a lump in my throat I asked, "Hank killed Davis?"

"Hank was killed early on Sunday morning. The autopsy determined that Davis died somewhere around 2:00 a.m.—the following day." Mitch again leaned against the table, his eyes still locked with mine. "Which means someone got Hank's blood on his shoe and then brought it into Davis' house just before he bound Davis to the steering wheel of his own car and invoked such fear into him that a heart attack ensued. Andrew, I'm afraid all evidence points to your son."

"Wait a minute, you son of a bitch! You're saying my son killed Davis?!"

Mitch reached behind his back. As his hand came forward, I grew uneasy by the sight of a pair of handcuffs. "Jackson Fabacher, you are under arrest for the murder of Davis Melancon. You have the right to remain silent." Mitch grabbed my arm, forcefully swinging me around before pushing me against the table. "Anything you say can and will be used against you in a court of law." He firmly placed both hands behind my back. For the second time in two hours, I had been handcuffed by an agent of the F.B.I. "You have the right to an attorney."

"I'm his attorney!"

Mitch led me towards the door. My dad jumped in front of us. "Move, Andrew."

"Why did Harley, the man who attacked you years ago, kidnap your former partner's son? What's going on here, Mitch?"

"Agent Parker, please restrain Mr. Fabacher before I arrest him as well."

As Agent Parker eased my dad to the side, I grew petrified of being alone with Mitch. "Don't let him take me, Dad! Mikey is dead because of—" Mitch placed his hand on my neck in such a way that my body nearly went into paralysis. I physically couldn't speak as we exited the room. While walking down the hallway with one of Davis' closest friends, I became more terrified than I had ever been in my life.

Chapter 117

Delain stared out of the car window in silence. John handed her a tissue. "We're going to get your son back."

"How do you know that?"

"Because we have the upper hand."

She wiped at her eyes, turning to John. "How can you possibly think that?"

"Because I know their next move before they do."

"And what is their next move?"

"To dispose of the truth."

"Dispose of the...you mean they're going to...kill Caleb?!"

He shook his head. "You."

"They're going to kill me?"

John nodded. "A DNA test will prove you are Thomas' mother. Now, we have something they want—you. And they have something we want— your son. Without Caleb, we can't prove what Davis did to you. It would be foolish to go to the authorities now and tell them what's happening because there's no way they would believe your story. If anything, they would be more inclined to think you are involved with the kidnapping."

"It's not fair."

"You're right—it's not. Can you do me a favor though?"

"What?"

"Don't give up. We're so close. I assure you Caleb will be in your arms very soon."

Delain, again wiping at her eyes, had finally reached the point that she completely trusted John. "Okay. What do we do now?"

John handed her an earpiece before attaching a cord to the phone. "I'm going to call Mitch. If I put it on speakerphone, he may think someone else is listening. See if you can pick up on anything he says. Don't say a word." He handed Delain a small note pad and pen. "If you need to tell me anything, quietly write it down on this pad."

Delain placed the earpiece into her left ear. As she had done several times in the last few days, she nervously checked her surroundings for anything or anyone suspicious as John dialed. It rang only once.

"Agent Hennessey."

"That was a nice little stunt you pulled, Mitch."

"You're going to have to be more specific."

"I know how this routine works. You now have my attention."

"That's good to know."

"While I have a minute alone, I want to run something by you. The female you desperately want to locate hired me to discover the truth. I have discovered the truth, yet she wants me to recover what she thinks is rightfully hers. I told her if she wants me to do such a thing, I would require more money for my services. She refuses to pay me another dollar. With that being said, if you are interested in reimbursing me for delivering someone to you, I'm all ears."

Silence ensued for several seconds before Mitch asked, "How much reimbursing do you need?"

"$100,000 sent to a Swedish bank account within the hour."

"That's a lot of money."

"I'm sure you and your friends will have no problem coming up with that amount. When you think about it, though, it's such a small price to pay for freedom. Wouldn't you agree, Agent Hennessey?"

"What would happen once the money is wired?"

"You would be given the whereabouts of the person you seek. I would convince her that I know where her…prized possession is. You, the redheaded gentleman, and whoever else is involved will arrive at the location and proceed with whatever you deem necessary."

"It's a very interesting proposition."

"You have one minute to decide."

"That's not much time."

"Fifty-seven seconds and counting."

"When you commented on my little stunt, John, I assume you thought I was trying to be vague by asking you to be more specific. I wasn't. I wanted you to clarify about whom you were referring."

"I don't follow you."

"You're didn't hear the other news then?"

John looked to Delain. "What do you mean?"

"It seems your client is having a pretty bad day on all levels."

The pen in Delain's hand began to tremble as she looked at John.

"Do you care to elaborate, Mitch?"

"It would be my pleasure. Her fiancé has just been arrested for the murder of someone he was very familiar with."

Delain's eyes shut. A sickening feeling overcame her as she pictured Davis slouched over the steering wheel of his car.

"I'm staring at him right now as he sits in a jail cell. His head is hung low, and I can't quite tell, but I think he's on the verge of crying."

"How does this concern me?"

"I thought it might serve as a vital piece of information for you as it involves your client. Do you think your client would turn herself in for his release?"

"I sure hope not. It would potentially cost me $100,000. You have fifteen seconds to accept my proposal or you won't find the female in time. How long do you think you can hide the boy for?" There was no reply. "Six…five…four…three…"

"Okay."

"Okay what?"

"We have a deal."

"I'll call you back with instructions within the hour." John hung up.

Delain threw the pad onto the floor in anger. "No!"

"I'm sorry."

"It's all my fault. He's in jail because of me."

"We don't know that for sure."

"I want to talk to him. Call him back."

"That's not a good—"

"Please call him back."

"All right, but first tell me what you're going to say."

Chapter 118

I leaned against the back wall of the windowless jail cell in the F.B.I. building, opting not to sit on the paper-thin mattress that smelled of urine, and was stained with what appeared to be blood. Thoughts of getting raped in prison came to mind, as did the embarrassment and humiliation I surely caused my family. Yet the prevalent issue on my mind was the realization that I killed a man for the woman I loved, a woman who probably never loved me at all. What I thought at the time was justice prevailing, might have been nothing more than a not-so-innocent woman manipulating me into murder. I started to wonder if Delain was, in fact, the one to blame for the hell I had been through over the last few days. Thirty minutes into my stay behind bars, I wished Delain and I had never met.

The sound of footsteps clacking against the concrete floor grew louder. While seated on the cold floor with my head hung low, I decided I wouldn't give Mitch the satisfaction of looking at or acknowledging his presence. Once the clacking came to a halt in front of my cell, the person before me loudly cleared their throat. It didn't belong to a male. I lifted my head. A set of blue eyes that I, at one time, lovingly stared into gazed upon me. They say there's a thin line between love and hate. I'm certain Tiffany Melancon was well beyond that line.

With crossed arms and a scowl about her face, she asked, "Is it true?"

I wasn't ready to admit guilt. "He died of a heart attack, Tiffany."

"And were you next to him when it happened?"

"No."

"Then why are you in jail?"

"Because I know the truth about what your dad has done in the past. Mitch is part of it too."

"What are you talking about? Part of what?" She slowly uncrossed her arms.

"Do you think your dad was a good person?"

"He may not have been a saint, Jackson, but he was by no means a bad person."

"Okay," I replied while laughing.

"Why are you laughing? This isn't a joke."

"Davis was a bully who took advantage of people and threatened them if they got in his way."

With squinted eyes, her jaw tightened as she told me, "He was my father, Jackson."

"Bin Laden has children. So did Saddam Hussein and Stalin."

"You're comparing my dad to them?"

"I sure am. He was kicked out of the police department. That doesn't happen to good people."

"He wasn't evil, Jackson. Stop saying that." She looked to be on the verge of tears.

"Did you not tell me a story years ago about how you watched from your dad's upstairs office as he presided over the beating of a man behind his restaurant? You said how you watched a man covered in…" I jumped to my feet and slowly approached Tiffany as my eureka moment occurred, "tattoos beat another man that owed your dad money?" It was starting to look like my dad's guess as to the identity of the kidnapper was spot-on. "What was his name?"

"Who?"

"The man covered in tattoos."

"Jackson, why are you—"

"His name?!" I yelled. Upon realizing Mitch or someone else could have been listening out of sight, I continued in a subdued tone. "I'm sorry for yelling. Being in jail can make you a little angry. What was his name, Tiffany?"

"Harley. What does it matter?"

"Is he tall and bald?"

She was slow to answer. "Yes."

"What's his last name?"

"My dad wasn't an evil person."

I remained calm while biting my tongue. "You're right. I apologize. Again, being in jail makes you say crazy things. What's Harley's last name?"

"Motichek. Why?"

"Just curious." Like my dad, I believed Harley to be the man who kidnapped Thomas. "Why are you here to see me, Tiffany?"

She could no longer subdue her crying. "Thomas has been kidnapped."

"So I've heard."

"We have to find him. Every minute that passes without knowledge of where he might be, our chances of finding him alive diminish. I can't imagine what he's going through."

I pictured Caleb resting comfortably and unharmed. "I wish I could help, but I'm not going anywhere anytime soon."

She wiped at her left cheek. "Where's your fiancée?"

"Why do you ask?"

"No reason. I thought she might come down to visit you."

Tiffany was the third person to ask about Delain in the last hour. Not only did Agent Parker ask during the interrogation, but also Mitch as he escorted me to my jail cell. It only furthered my suspicion that Mitch not only knew of Davis' plan, but was also involved. "She hasn't stopped by yet."

"Do you have any idea where she might be?"

Lying, I assumed, was my only hope of making it out of jail. "I do."

"Where?"

"Get me out of here and I'll tell you."

"Tell me and I'll make sure Mitch lets you go."

"Get me out of here first or I'm not saying anything."

Tiffany grabbed the vertical bars of the cell. "Tell me!"

I stepped backwards. "As long as I'm in here, I'm not telling you shit."

A look soon appeared in her eyes. I was quite familiar with the look, as it caused me to embark on a seven-week adventure. Mascara ran down her cheeks as she yelled, "Did you kill my dad?!"

"Goodbye, Tiffany." I returned to my seated position on the floor.

"You killed him, you piece of shit!"

With bent knees, I wrapped my arms around my legs and lowered my head.

"Where is she?! Where is my nephew?!"

It was the loudest I had ever heard Tiffany yell. If I were to look up, I'm certain her face would have been the same purplish hue as a turnip.

"Fuck you, Jackson! See you in the courtroom! I'll be the one clapping when the judge sentences you to life in prison, you murdering asshole! At first, I wanted you dead, but now I want you to suffer for the rest of your pathetic life! They're going to beat you and rape you in prison! You're never going to make it out alive!"

She was right, yet I couldn't let her know. I kept my head down.

"You stupid fuck!"

I then heard the sound of heels clacking away from my jail cell as my pissed off, first ex-fiancée stormed off.

As I tried to ponder a reason why Thomas Melancon would have been kidnapped by the same men who probably helped in placing him into Scott and Bridgett's custody, I again heard footsteps in the hallway. I looked up to see another set of blue eyes staring down at me. Mitch held a cell phone in his left hand and a pair of handcuffs in his right.

"Come here," he demanded.

"Why?"

"Someone wants to talk to you."

I climbed to my feet, gingerly approaching him. "Who?"

"Put your hands through the bars."

"Who is it?"

"Once I cuff your hands together and place the phone to your ears, you'll find out."

I cautiously extended my hands. With one of the bars separating my forearms, Mitch cuffed my wrists. He then placed the phone to my ear. "Hello?"

"Jackson!"

I didn't need to hear another word to know whose voice it was. I wanted to ask where she had been and why she left me, yet I didn't want Mitch to know we were no longer together. Knowledge of Delain's location seemed like my only option of getting out of jail. I wasn't sure how much Mitch heard of my interrogation with Agents Parker and Williams, and I wasn't sure how much longer he would let us talk. I also hoped he didn't speak the language of love. "Je sais qui a Caleb."

"Qui?!"

Mitch pulled the phone away, placing it to his ear. "Do we have a deal?" His subtle nod preceded the closing of his phone. "What did you tell her, Jackson?"

"How much I love her."

"She must *really* love you."

"She does."

After removing the handcuffs from my wrists he told me, "She must if she's giving herself up for you."

"What do you mean?"

"She agreed to turn herself over to me in return for your release."

"I'm getting out of here?"

"Of course not," he replied, smirking, "but she doesn't know that."

"I want to speak to Agent Parker."

"He's on his way to Mobile to interrogate Officer McKenzie. If you were right about him, perhaps the jury will show sympathy and your sentence in Davis' death may be reduced a couple of years."

"Why do you want to talk to Delain?"

Mitch slowly stepped backwards, shrugging his shoulders before walking away.

"She's not the only one who knows what you and Davis did. You're going down, asshole!" A door shut. Adrenaline coursed through my veins as I tugged on the iron bars. "God damnit! Is anyone out there?!" My voice echoed throughout the empty holding area.

Chapter 119

"He knows who has Caleb!" Delain shouted. "We have to make the fake exchange with Mitch before it's too late."

"It's never going to happen. He's not going to give Jackson up. He wants the both of you."

"But he said he'd trade Jackson's freedom for me."

"Don't be so gullible." John, staring at his laptop screen, then told her, "Jackson's being held at 2901 Leon C. Simon Boulevard. It's the F.B.I.'s building here in New Orleans."

"How do you know?"

"I traced the call. And because of what Mitch said, Jackson is in the holding cell."

"If Mitch won't give him up, then how do we get to him?"

"We can't."

"Didn't you used to be in the F.B.I.? Don't you have connections?"

"Former federal agent and current federal agent are not the same."

"What if we...I don't know...visit him?"

"They'll get you as soon as you step foot in the door."

"What about you? They have no idea what you look like." John's silence and the look of deliberation on his face offered Delain hope. "I'm sure you have the means to get into the building and at least talk to Jackson. I've seen you in action, John. You're quite impressive. I truly believe you can do this."

"I've spent the last seven years trying to remain inconspicuous. I've changed my name and altered my appearance, so I could escape my past."

"Why?" Delain noticed how John subtly moved about in the driver's seat, as if he was growing uncomfortable. "I don't mean to pry. I apologize."

John closed his laptop, placing it in the backseat. "I love my country and everything it stands for, but there are some corrupt individuals running this nation. I, unfortunately, was around some of those people. I saw things that made me question my loyalty. I was in too deep. The way I saw it, I had two options: stand up for what I believed in and be falsely labeled a traitor, or fake my own death to escape."

"You faked your death?"

John nodded.

"How?"

"Shark attack."

"For real?"

"While scuba diving on the Great Barrier Reef, a great white shark attacked and tore me to shreds. No part of my body was found."

"How did you pull that off?"

"It's not as hard as you think. I went on a private scuba dive and my instructor watched as a great white shark ate me. When you hand someone $20,000 cash, especially someone who makes that amount in a year, they'll have no problem telling a little white lie. I already had my fake passport made, so I vanished."

"What about family and friends?"

"I'm an only child, and my parents were already deceased. I had an ex-wife, but I doubt she shed a tear over my death."

It wasn't difficult for Delain to see similarity between John's past and hers. "What about the woman you used to visit down here? The love of your life, as you called her."

"I doubt she heard what had happened."

"And what if she did?"

"It doesn't matter. That's part of my old life. That life is no more."

Delain didn't believe him. She was certain John would want to know his former lover's reaction upon hearing of his death. "Mitch seems like the kind of person that forced you to start a new life. I understand why you wouldn't want to go into that building. It's too—"

"Be quiet for a minute please," John politely asked of her while leaning back in his chair with closed eyes.

Delain's use of reverse psychology seemed to be working. She sunk into her seat. Silence filled the car. Several minutes later, John leaned forward, finally opening his eyes.

"I'm going to need another person."

"For what?"

"To get Jackson out of jail."

A wide-eyed Delain asked, "You're going to do it?"

"I need a male around the age of thirty. If he's clean cut, that would be another plus. Do you know anyone?"

Someone immediately came to mind. "Tyler fits that description, but what do you need him for?"

"To pose as another agent. If I'm alone, it would look awfully peculiar. Federal agents are like lovebugs. We, I mean, they travel together."

"How in the hell do you propose I ask him to do that?"

"We're going to have to tell him some things."

"And you think he's going to pose as a federal agent—which I'm sure is punishable by several years in jail—to help bust my fiancé out of jail?"

John started the car. "I bet my life on it."

Chapter 120

Caroline stared hopelessly at her cell phone as it lay next to her silverware. Across the table sat someone she no longer wished to see. *Please call me back, Jackson. I need to know if you're okay.*

"You keep staring at your phone," Brock told her. "Are you expecting a call?"

Caroline glanced around the café before returning her gaze to him. "Yes."

"From who?"

"Nobody."

"Well, it's got to be somebody." He grinned.

Already irritated by Brock's surprise visit the night before, Caroline wasn't thrilled by his constant pestering about what she had been doing the last few days or from whom she was hoping to receive a phone call.

"When's the last time you've talked to or seen Jackson?"

Hearing his name caused feelings of both pleasantry and nervousness. "Why do you ask?"

"Just wondering. I like him. How about we go see him today?"

"I'd rather not."

"Why? Don't you like him?"

Caroline knew Brock had been jealous of Jackson since their first meeting at Commander's Palace. She was certain his question had no other motive than to start an argument. "What are you doing, Brock?"

"Nothing," he answered from behind a menu. "I just thought you liked him...as a friend."

"I mean what are you doing here? In New Orleans?"

"I missed you."

"We broke up. Last time I checked, a break up implies that two people no longer see one another."

"It typically does, but we are not your typical couple. We have something special between us. Plus, I thought we were just taking a break."

"Why do you think that?"

"Because you said we needed a break."

"I'm pretty certain I added the word 'up' to the end of 'break' right after I gave you the ring back."

Brock lowered the menu, staring hopelessly into his former fiancée's eyes. "I love you so much, Caroline. I love you more than anyone I have ever known. I felt like I was dying by not having you in my life. Please don't do this to us."

"I told you to let me be. Instead, you showed up unannounced at my uncle's house. Do you know how embarrassing that is? Couldn't you at least call or wait until I got back to San Diego?"

"You make it sound like you don't want to see me."

If they weren't in a crowded café, Caroline would yell the words 'leave me alone' at him. "Not to sound mean, but when I told you I needed some time alone, I 100% meant it—every word. I assure you I'm not playing games. This isn't a test to see if you chase me."

Brock's head hung low as he mumbled, "I just miss you. You're the only girl that's ever broken up with me. I don't know how to handle it. It feels like my best friend just died."

Caroline felt a slight influx of sympathy towards him. "That's what break ups feel like."

After lifting his head, he told her, "Baby, we were engaged. What happened? Everything seemed fine until you came down here for that internship."

"Nothing happened, other than the realization that I'm not ready to get married."

"To me?"

The answer was a resounding 'yes', but telling the truth, she felt, would be more painful. "To anybody. I'm only twenty-three. I'm too young to get married right now."

"And there's no one else? No other guy you want to be with?"

While picturing Jackson, she told him, "No."

"And you haven't kissed anyone since we broke up?"

"No."

"You swear?"

Kissing Jackson passionately on the side of the interstate was on her mind as she told him, "No."

Brock leaned across the table. "There's no one you have feelings for?"

"No."

While glancing to her left, Caroline caught a glimpse of a breaking news report on the television behind the bar. *'Amber Alert!'* flashed beneath the picture of a young boy with light brown hair. He looked to be about two or three years old. *Thomas Melancon, nephew of Davis Melancon, has been kidnapped* next flashed at the bottom of the television screen.

"What if I told you I think Jackson has feelings for you?"

Caroline didn't hear a word that crossed Brock's lips. Her attention was focused on the words flashing across the bottom of the screen. *Two year-old Thomas Melancon, nephew of the late Davis Melancon, was kidnapped last night from the Prytania movie theater. His abductor is described as being 6'2"-6'4" tall, Caucasian, bald, and heavily covered in tattoos.*

"I'll take your silence to mean you agree with me."

If anyone has seen either Thomas or a man who fits his abductor's description, they are encouraged to call 911 immediately.

"And how do you feel about that?"

A panicked Caroline reached for her phone. "What?"

"How do you feel about what I just told you?"

Her fingers trembled as she dialed Jackson's cell phone number and placed it to her ear. While waiting to hear his voice, she glanced at Brock. "You really need to leave. I have some things I need to take care of." Once Jackson's voicemail picked up, she remembered he no longer had a phone. *I need to find him immediately!*

"I knew it. You do have a thing for him."

"What are you talking about? A thing for who?"

"Jackson."

Caroline tucked her phone into her bra. Instead of denying his claim, she told him, "I'm begging you, Brock, to please go home. I need to take care of some things."

"You two-timing whore! I knew you and him had a thing!"

A shocked, but mostly embarrassed, Caroline noticed several patrons' stares aimed in her direction. She balled her hands into fists while leaning across the table. No longer did she care to sugarcoat her feelings towards him. "I want you to pay close attention to the words coming out of my mouth, you piece of shit," she calmly spoke. "We will never again be a couple. You are to never speak to me again. If our paths are to ever cross once more and you attempt to talk to me, make sure you're wearing a cup because I will kick you in your dick so hard that you will never be able to pee standing upright again."

"I know you and Jackson have something going on," he quipped back.

"And why do you think that?"

"I just do."

"You know what, Brock—you are so God-damn insecure. On our first date you thought the waiter was hitting on me. Just so you know, he was gay. He mentioned having a boyfriend while you were in the bathroom. And your insecurity has only gotten worse from there." Caroline stood. "I'm through with you. Have a good life, Brock."

"I talked to Jackson this morning. He told me everything."

Caroline was convinced he was lying. "No, you didn't."

Brock nodded. "Remember how you said you heard me talking to someone when you got out of the shower and I told you it was the manager of my gym back home? Well, it was Jackson. Your phone was on the nightstand and I answered it."

An optimistic Caroline returned to her chair. "What did he say?"

"Why should I tell you?"

An older Caucasian man approached the table. Caroline assumed him to be the manager or owner of the café. "Is there a problem here, ma'am?" He then glanced to Brock.

"Is there a problem here, honey?" Brock asked Caroline.

"No problem at all, sir. I apologize for any inconvenience."

"Please keep your voices down or I'll have to ask the both of you to leave."

Brock stood. "The service here sucks. We were just leaving anyway." He threw a twenty-dollar bill onto the table on his way out the door. Caroline followed.

"Why were you answering my phone?" she asked Brock as he hastily walked down St. Charles Avenue towards his rental car.

"Because I bought it for you and I pay for your service. I can do what I want with it. By the way, I'm cancelling your plan as soon as I get home. What the hell—I'll do it as soon as I drop you off at your uncle's."

"Why didn't I see an incoming call from him?"

"I erased the number after our heated exchange."

"What heated exchange?"

"Jackson, your secret boyfriend, told me you didn't love me anymore, and that you and he have something going on. Are you going to keep denying it now?"

"Where did he call from?"

Brock turned around. With a look of disgust, he threw his hands in the air. "I can't believe you did this to us!"

"We are no longer together, and I can do what I please."

"So, it is true."

Caroline wanted desperately to see Jackson. A streetcar with 'St. Charles Ave.' inscribed across the top was fast approaching. His parents' house, several blocks away, would be on the route. *I bet he's there right now.* "Farewell, Brock."

"You're leaving me just like that?"

"Yep. Adios, jackass." Caroline hurried to the median of St. Charles, where others awaited to board the streetcar. While at the back of the line, she watched as Brock continued towards his rental car. His back was to her as the streetcar came to a stop. The slouch in his shoulders and the repeated touching of his right hand to his face led Caroline to believe he was crying. Instead of feeling sympathy for him as she boarded the streetcar, she grew furious as the words 'two-timing whore' replayed in her head. *Good riddance, Brock.* After sitting on a mahogany seat near the back of the streetcar, Caroline grew excited at the thought of seeing Jackson.

Chapter 121

"Christina's on her way up now," John informed Tyler on his cell phone. "She's going to ask you to do something. Agree to do it, but only after slight hesitation."

Tyler hurried to the bathroom mirror in his hotel room, where he ran his fingers through his hair. "What is she going to ask me?"

"If you would assist me in freeing Jackson from federal custody."

"What? Is this for real?"

"No. Its just a façade. Christina thinks Jackson is under arrest, but he's really not. The building he's in isn't a real federal building, and the people inside are actors. I have a camera hidden on me. Christina will watch and listen to everything as it happens. You must act as if what we're doing is real. It's the only way you will get her back. You must trust me, Tyler."

"I don't understand. Jackson isn't really under arrest and pretending to free him will help me get Christina back?"

"That is correct."

"Why is he in...pretend jail?"

"Christina will answer that for you."

"How will freeing him help me get her back?"

"If you didn't hear what I first told you, let me reiterate: Christina is about to knock on your door. She's going to ask you to help me." John's tone was direct and unyielding. "If you want her back, agree to do what she asks."

Tyler didn't understand John's methods, but trusted him. "You haven't let me down yet. I'll do whatever you say."

"Good man. Before nightfall, this will all be over."

"Are you—" Tyler flinched upon hearing a knock at the door. "She's here," he whispered into the phone.

"See you soon. Remember, Tyler—you have never met me before."

Tyler threw his phone on the bed, popped a fresh piece of spearmint gum into his mouth, and then opened the door. "Hey, gorgeous."

"Hey." She smiled back. "Can I come in?"

"Of course."

Delain greeted him with a lengthy embrace before placing her lips onto his. "Thank you for not leaving town yet."

"I had no place better to go."

She stepped back, grabbing both of his hands. "What are you doing today?"

"Not sure, maybe a little sight-seeing."

"You look handsome—as always."

"And you as beautiful as ever," he replied while grinning.

"You still have the sexiest smile of any man."

"Thank you, but why do I get the feeling you're buttering me up for something."

She let go of his hands. "I need to ask you to do something, but I don't know how to ask it. And time is a factor."

"Then just ask."

She again grabbed his hands. "I love you. I always have and always will, even if you agree not to help me."

A knee-weakening feeling of euphoria overcame Tyler. "I love you too."

"And that's why I need you right now."

"For what?"

"This may sound bizarre, but…I need your help in freeing Jackson from jail."

Tyler tried to act as surprised as possible. With a widening of his eyes, he asked, "What? He's in jail? Why?"

"They're saying he killed someone, but it's not true."

"Who's 'they'?"

"A corrupt F.B.I. agent."

"Why is he targeting Jackson?"

She sat on the edge of the bed. "I don't know yet."

"This is some heavy stuff, Chrissy."

She nodded. "I know, but Jackson has information that will bring you and I closer to one another."

"What kind of information?"

She grabbed his hand, pulling him next to her on the bed. "Maybe you should sit too."

"Why is my stomach in knots right now?"

"Remember the talk we had Saturday night about the last time we had sex?"

"I do."

"Well…let's imagine I did get pregnant. What would you think of me?"

"But you didn't get pregnant."

"But what if I did?"

"Then you certainly would have said something by now, right?" Because her eyes were focused on the ground, and because he could see her hands shaking as they rested in her lap, Tyler was beginning to think she might actually be telling the truth. "Christina…do you…do you have a child?"

She stood from the bed, unbuttoned her shorts, and pulled them—along with her panties— to the base of her abdomen.

Tyler stared at the scar in disbelief. "Is that a…?"

"Yes."

"Oh my God."

She buttoned her shorts while telling him, "I'm sorry I didn't say anything sooner."

He grew lightheaded as he stood, grabbing the nearby desk for balance.

"Are you okay?"

He didn't feel the need to tell her about the tightening in his chest or the sensation that his knees were on the verge of giving out. "How long ago?"

"Two years."

Anger overcame Tyler—not towards Christina, but John as he certainly knew of the news. "Boy or girl?"

"Boy."

"Two years? That means he was conceived less than three years ago. We broke up less than three years ago."

Looking away, she nodded.

"Christina, who's the father?"

While continuing to look away, she told him, "I'm not sure."

The pain in his chest subsided. He no longer felt he might faint, as an incredible and joyous emotion overcame him instead. "Are you suggesting I could be his father?"

Delain's stare was still aimed away from him. "It's a possibility."

Tyler, kneeling next to her, grabbed both of her trembling hands. She looked into his eyes as he confessed, "Ever since we broke up, I felt something was keeping us connected. This is amazing, Chrissy." His smile couldn't have been any bigger.

"I know."

"But," his smile vanished, "what does Jackson have to do with this?"

"He knows where my son is."

"What do you mean 'where he is'? Is he lost or something?"

"Kidnapped."

Tyler jumped to his feet. "What?! By who?!"

"I don't know, but Jackson does. That's why we need to get him out of jail."

"Why is he in jail? How does he know who kidnapped…" 'our' was on the tip of his tongue, but he held back, "your, son? Is there something you're not telling me?"

"Yes."

"Will you please tell me?" he begged.

"Everything I'm about to tell you is the honest truth. I'll start from the beginning."

Chapter 122

Delain climbed into the front passenger seat of the Tahoe. Tyler sat in the seat behind her. Once both doors were closed, she began with the introductory duties. "Tyler, this is John. John, this is Tyler."

"Nice to meet you, John," Tyler spoke with a handshake.

"Same to you. That is a sharp looking suit, my friend."

Tyler glanced down at his black suit, tracing his fingers over the matching tie. "Christina told me to look professional."

"And that you do. We're good to go then?" John asked, looking first at Delain and then Tyler.

"Yes," they answered simultaneously.

"Then there's no time to waste. Tyler, open the briefcase on the seat next to you please. In it, you will find various pairs of non-magnified eyeglasses. Find a pair that fits and place them on your face. In the bag next to the briefcase are various movie studio quality wigs. Choose one not your own hair color and place it atop your head. Christina, do you mind helping him?"

"Sure."

"What do I need glasses and a wig for?"

"Anonymity." John stepped out of the car, making his way to the back.

"What is he talking about?"

Delain shrugged her shoulders as John opened the back doors of the SUV.

From the briefcase, Tyler removed a pair of thick, black-rimmed glasses and placed them upon his face. "How are these?"

"Too Buddy Holly. How are you feeling?"

Tyler returned the glasses to the briefcase. "Nervous, but it's worth it." He placed another pair on his face.

"Too preppy. Try something a little more…plain." He reached for another pair as she told him, "I can't thank you enough for doing this."

"Then stop thanking me," he told her while grinning. "Besides, I'm doing this for the both of us, possibly the three of us. How about these?" The lenses, rectangular in shape, were bound by a thin, black frame.

"Those will do."

The backdoor shut. John returned to the driver's seat with a metallic briefcase and a piece of white poster board.

"It's too sunny outside, so we'll have to take the picture in here. You still need a wig, Tyler."

Tyler reached into the bag, pulling the first one he touched. It was dirty blonde and short in length. "How does it look?"

"Crooked," Delain replied before helping to adjust it.

"How about now?"

She leaned against the dashboard. "It looks real to me."

"It will do. You're going to be wearing a hat over it anyway." John next handed Delain an eyeliner dark brown in color. "Give him a mole on his left cheek; large enough to be seen, but not too big so that it's a distraction."

Delain leaned into the backseat and placed the pencil against Tyler's left cheek, making a small circle about the circumference of a pencil eraser.

"That's perfect. Looks like we're ready. Christina, hold this poster board behind Tyler please." From the glove compartment, John grabbed an expensive-looking camera. "You now look like a C.I.A. agent."

"C.I.A.?" Tyler asked.

"Yes, sir. You are about to become an agent of the Central Intelligence Agency."

"I…what?"

Despite knowing he was helping to free Jackson from an imaginary federal building, Tyler still grew nervous at how meticulous John was in his planning. As Delain held the poster board behind him, John leaned against the dashboard, holding the camera to his right eye.

"Up a little higher, Christina…That's good. Tyler, look tough. Don't smile." A flash went off. John inspected the screen. "You look like a deer caught in headlights,

229

Tyler. Let's try this again. Don't look so scared." Another flash went off. John again glanced at the screen. "Much better."

"And this picture is for...?"

"Your identification." John removed the memory card from the camera and then opened the metallic suitcase. Tyler's hunch that the black device in the suitcase was a portable printer was confirmed once John inserted the memory card into it and his image slowly started to appear. The picture was no larger than that of a passport photo. John next connected his laptop to the printer. After typing a lengthy password, he navigated to a folder, where he typed in another password. Once the folder opened, Tyler watched as John entered a few clicks on the keyboard and then hit the print button. Exiting the printer was a piece of paper the size of a driver's license with the letters 'C.I.A.' printed across the top. John grabbed the printed paper, placed Tyler's picture onto it, and then placed it into another device from the metallic suitcase. A short moment later, John handed Tyler the laminated identification card. "You're now officially in the C.I.A., Agent Jack William Tomkins."

Tyler grabbed the card. The C.I.A. logo was stamped on the right side, his picture on the left, his fictional name beneath the picture, 'C.I.A. field agent' beneath his name, and a bar code beneath his job status. He had never seen a federal identification up close, but it looked official. "You did that so fast."

"Years of practice. You'll also need this." John reached into the console, handing a badge to Tyler.

Situated atop the gold badge was an eagle, in the middle was an engraved C.I.A. logo located between the etched blue letters 'U' and 'S', and beneath the logo, the words 'special agent'—also etched in blue—appeared. The badge was heavier than Tyler expected. "Is this real?"

"Let's just say it's not made of chocolate. Buckle up, folks." John backed out of the parking place and turned onto Canal Street.

While inspecting the badge once more, Tyler asked, "Where are we going?"

John reached for his cell phone. "To get Jackson. But first, I have to make an important call. No one make a sound." After dialing a number, he placed the phone to his ear.

From the backseat, Tyler could hear a male on the other end of the phone say 'hello'.

"It seems our girl has had a change of heart. She no longer wants to give herself up for Jackson. I can deliver her to you once the money is in the account. Is the offer still on the table?" Several seconds passed until John said, "Good. I'm picking her up now. Drive across the Crescent City Connection to Algiers and get on Mardi Gras Boulevard. Drive until you see a large alligator head. It will be next to a warehouse with the number 11 written on it. Do you know which one I'm talking about?...That's the one. We will be waiting there. As soon as you pull up, I will take off, leaving her behind. Do not follow me or I cannot be held responsible for what will transpire. If the money isn't in my account in fifteen minutes you will never find her. Here's the account number..."

Once John hung up, Tyler asked him, "What was that about?"

"A distraction. We don't want the man who arrested Jackson to be at the building when we go in. That call will get him out of there for a good thirty minutes or so."

"When you said 'she' on the phone just now, who were you referring to?"

"Me," Delain answered. "The guy I was telling you about who helped Davis orchestrate this whole thing wants me dead."

"Mitch?" Tyler asked.

"Yes."

"We're not going to let Mitch win— are we Tyler?"

Upon hearing Christina's story, Tyler first felt shock and great sadness for what his former girlfriend had been through. He then experienced an odd sense of relief in knowing she had no choice but to cut off all ties with him. The emotion he felt by the end of her story included the desire to rip the heads off of those who orchestrated the appalling and horrific acts against her. "Hell no. John, don't C.I.A. agents carry guns?"

"As a matter of fact they do."

Tyler was convinced if he were to be in the presence of Mitch, he'd have a hard time not shooting him in the kneecaps, before slowly torturing him. "I'm going to need one then."

With a deadpan stare, John gazed at Tyler's reflection in the rearview mirror. "Yes, sir, Agent Tompkins."

Chapter 123

Three blocks away from the F.B.I's New Orleans headquarters, John put the car in park. "Tyler, can you hand me the black, large-framed glasses in the briefcase next to you?"

"The Buddy Holly specs?"

"Those are the ones."

Tyler handed John the glasses. After setting them on the dashboard, John removed a case for holding eye contacts from the center console. Tyler watched as he placed contacts into both eyes, blinking several times while looking in the rearview mirror. No longer were John's irises blue. They were dark—the same color as his pupils. *Why is he doing all of this?* Tyler thought as John leaned his head forward, placed both hands at the base of his hairline behind his neck, and began to pull. Tyler looked on in shock as John held his salt and peppered hair in his hands.

"You're bald!" Delain exclaimed.

"That I am. Have been for years."

"But your hair looks so real."

John placed the glasses onto his face. "It better look real. I paid a pretty penny for it."

Tyler was astonished at how different John looked without a single strand of hair upon his head, eyes as dark as the night, and a thick pair of glasses. His altered appearance not only made him look a few years younger, but also a bit more menacing.

"You don't look like the same person," Delain spoke, "and that took all of twenty seconds."

John placed his laptop in Delain's lap. "I used to be able to do it in fifteen seconds. I'm slowing down in my old age. Are you ready, Tyler?"

"I am, Agent...I forgot your name."

"Higgins. John Higgins. Don't forget it again."

"I won't, Agent John Higgins. John Higgins. John Higgins."

"Christina, we won't be long. Even though the windows are tinted, it wouldn't hurt to stay down until we get back."

"Okay."

"Let's go, Agent Jack Tompkins."

The two stood at the back of the Tahoe with the doors opened. John handed Tyler a fedora, along with a gun and a shoulder holster. John then placed a C.I.A. badge onto his belt before holstering his handgun. Tyler smiled at Christina in the front seat. She smiled back before mouthing the words 'good luck' to him. After Tyler winked at her, John shut the back doors.

As they began to walk, Tyler grew excited—not nervous—about the imaginary jail break they were about to execute. Once they were several feet away from the car, John placed his right hand over the middle of his tie. "The camera and microphone are connected to the tie clip under my hand," he whispered to Tyler. "Remember, treat this as if it's real. Do not screw up and do not break character at any point."

"Remind me again why we're pretending to do this."

"So Christina will think you will do anything for her—even if it's illegal, and because there's nothing like a little excitement to bring a couple back together."

"And this isn't the real F.B.I. building?"

"No. The real one is downtown. This one is used for movie and television show productions." After placing the index finger of his left hand over his lips, John removed his right hand from his chest. "Agent Tomkins, once we get in the building, let me do all the talking."

Tyler adjusted his gun, as it was digging into his ribs. "You got it, Agent Higgins."

As they approached the four-story building, passing two media vans along the way, Tyler was impressed by how much the building looked like an actual federal building. An American flag, a Louisiana state flag, and a flag depicting the F.B.I. logo flew in front of the entrance.

"Here we go," John told him as they made their way towards the front entrance. "Do not say a word."

A blast of cool air welcomed Tyler as he followed John into the building. A large blue seal etched into the floor with the words 'Department of Justice' atop the circular logo and the words 'Federal Bureau of Investigation' inscribed on the bottom appeared quite real.

John approached a desk behind which two security guards stood. "A man by the name of Jackson Fabacher is being held in this building. I need to see him now."

"And who are you?"

John handed his identification to the man with an earpiece and a badly receding hairline.

The man glanced at the I.D., back at John, and then towards Tyler. "I need yours as well."

Tyler handed him the recently made I.D.

After a lengthy stare at both identifications, the man handed them to the other security guard, who then proceeded to scan the bar codes. He soon gave a subtle nod back to the other guard.

"What does the C.I.A. need with someone suspected of second-degree murder?"

"That's classified. Where is he?" John sternly asked.

The guard who had yet to speak stepped forward. "Follow me, please."

John and Tyler followed the security guard through a set of doors and down a long hallway lined with several office doors, most of which were closed. After coming to another set of doors, the man scanned a card in front of a box on the wall. As the doors opened, a Caucasian man wearing dark slacks and a cream-colored dress shirt stood before them. His F.B.I. badge and holstered pistol were easily visible. The security guard left the three men alone.

"How can I be of service?" asked the gentleman no older than thirty with a closely-shaved flat-top.

John flashed his badge. "John Higgins, C.I.A. This is Jack Tomkins, also C.I.A. We need to speak with Jackson Fabacher."

The man appeared curious by the request. "Agent Hennessey gave me specific orders to keep Jackson quiet and away from any visitors."

"Mitch Hennessey," John spoke while smiling and shaking his head, "Does that buffoon still have that ridiculous ponytail?"

"Yes, sir."

"I've been telling him for years to cut that thing."

"I take it you know him?"

"We go a long way back. Unfortunately, this badge means I can do whatever I want and take with me someone who needs to answer questions regarding a plane crash that occurred eleven days ago."

The agent removed a phone from his pocket. "I'm instructed to call Agent Hennessey if anyone comes back here."

"I wouldn't do that if I were you. I need to speak to Jackson ten minutes ago."

"It's my orders."

Tyler, still believing Christina could see and listen to what was transpiring, took it upon himself to ignore John's request and show initiative. "Parris Island or San Diego?"

The agent looked up from his phone. "Parris. First Lieutenant."

"I thought so."

"You?"

"Parris. Best thirteen weeks of my life."

"I had a feeling you were a Devil Dog—even with the longer hair."

"Great minds think alike. What's your name, Lieutenant?"

"Mark Abbott. Federal Agent Mark Abbott."

"Mark, two of our Parris Island brothers were on that plane. Jackson, we believe, may have information leading to the real cause of the crash."

Mark flashed a confused look. "But a flock of geese caused the crash."

"Don't believe everything you see or hear on television, Lieutenant," John told him. "Now, where is he? Please don't make me have to mention in my report that you were insubordinate."

Mark looked at both John and Tyler before closing his cell phone and placing it back into his pocket. "Right through here." He opened another set of doors using a beige unmarked card. Tyler followed John and Mark, passing two empty holding cells before coming to a stop in front of the third and last cell. Tyler recognized the gentleman sitting on the floor from the recent television newscast. Even though he had never met Jackson, he wasn't fond of the person recently engaged to the love of his life.

Chapter 124

None of the three men standing on the 'free' side of the metal bars looked familiar. Judging by their attire, I assumed them to be more federal agents. "Now what?" I mumbled in a tone suggesting I didn't want to be bothered by anymore of Mitch's corrupt co-workers.

"Jackson Fabacher, I'm John Higgins with the C.I.A. I'm afraid you're going to have to come with me."

"Now you're taking him?"

Agent Higgins removed a piece of paper from his jacket, handing it to the man sporting a flattop. "That piece of paper, Mark, means you better comply or face federal persecution. Now, be a smart F.B.I. agent and open this cell."

Flattop looked none too pleased while walking away.

I felt as if I was stuck in a hole that kept getting deeper and deeper. Now that the C.I.A. was involved as well, it seemed my days as a free man were growing scarce. The cell door opened.

"Turn around and place your hands behind your back, Mr. Fabacher."

I remained on the ground. "Where are we going?"

Flattop returned as Agent Higgins told me, "A quiet place, where you can answer questions about the plane crash last week. Stand up please, Mr. Fabacher."

I was hesitant in doing as he asked, but quickly realized it might be my only opportunity to tell someone about Mitch's involvement with Davis' illegal endeavors. I stood. Agent Higgins walked towards me.

"What do I tell Mitch?" Flattop inquired.

"The truth—some boys from Langley came by and picked up Mr. Fabacher." Agent Higgins cuffed and then directed me out of the cell. "I saw some media vans gathering out front, Mark. Is there another exit we could use to avoid pandemonium?"

"Yes, sir. Follow me." As Flattop led us out of the holding cell area and down a lengthy hallway lined with offices, I could feel the third gentleman—who had yet to speak—staring at me as if I had done something to wrong him.

We approached an unmarked door. Flattop waived a beige card in front of a small, digital box on the wall. The door opened. The bright light of the sun caused me to squint as we stepped outside. It felt like days since I had last seen the sun, while, in actuality, it was only a few hours.

"Thank you, Mark," John told Flattop. "We'll have him back in two hours."

The door shut behind the three of us. Agent Higgins and the other agent remained quiet as we hastily created distance between us and the building. "Why are we walking so fast?" I didn't receive an answer. "I didn't cause that plane to crash."

"We know," Agent Higgins spoke.

"Then why does the C.I.A. want to speak to me?"

"They don't."

"What?"

"We're not C.I.A. We're the good guys, Jackson. We're here to help." As we approached a white Chevy Tahoe, my handcuffs were unfastened. The rear passenger door opened from the inside. I climbed in. Before the door could shut behind me, I grew numb at the sight of the person next to me.

"Hey, you."

I couldn't find anything to say as nearly every emotion I had ever experienced overcame me in the blink of an eye. Relief turned to anger, excitement morphed into confusion, and happiness gave way to hatred as I looked into her emerald eyes.

"What happened to your head?"

Both men climbed into the front seats. "Did you see how easy that was, Chrissy?" the man in the passenger seat, who had yet to speak, asked with a grin.

"What do you mean?"

"The video camera on John's tie— didn't you see it?"

Delain appeared confused. "What are you talking about?"

"I have a confession to make, Tyler," spoke the bald man in the driver's seat. "Nothing about Jackson's escape just now was staged."

"What?! That was real?!"

"I'm afraid so."

I pointed to the front passenger seat, asking my fiancée, "What's his name?"

"I just helped someone escape from federal custody?!"

"Tyler," Delain answered.

"Tyler Bennett?"

She nodded. My stomach grew queasy as Delain's former boyfriend continued to freak-out in the front seat. "I just committed a federal crime?! I could go to jail for life!" He removed the fedora from his head before doing the same with the blonde wig.

"Why do you think I disguised you? You're going to be fine."

"That's your ex-boyfriend?" I asked.

Delain nodded.

"Who's back in your life again?"

After hesitating, she nodded. "Correct."

"John, why would you let me do that?!"

"If I told you it was real, Tyler, you never would have gone along with the escape. I needed a partner. Relax. Nothing will happen to you. Mitch is just hours away from being arrested."

"What's your real name, Delain Schexnaydre?"

Looking into my eyes, she told me, "Christina. Christina Foster."

I shook my head in disgust. "Everything between us was a lie."

"That's not true."

I wanted to pound my elbow through the window to my right. "I don't give a shit anymore. I'm tired of being lied to by you. What's it been now—three or four times you've lied to me? I'm over it and I'm over you. Driver, where are you taking me?"

As he began to drive, he told me, "Anywhere you like, but only after you tell us who has Christina's son."

"And why should I tell y'all?"

"How did you like being in federal custody just now?"

I turned my body, placing my back to Christina. My heart was pounding out of my chest. Glancing out of the window, I told him, "His name is Harley Motichek. He also goes by the nickname 'Hitman'. He fits the description of the man who kidnapped Thomas. He was also friends with Davis and Mitch, which makes this whole thing bizarre."

"Or justified," the driver spoke.

"They are now aware that I know I'm the mother of Thomas. They kidnapped him, so I couldn't prove it with a DNA test. Once they kill me, Thomas will reappear unharmed."

"Unfortunately, the only 'evidence' we have to prove she is the birth mother is currently kidnapped. We know at least one other person is involved—a man with red hair. Any speculation as to who it may be?"

I tried to calm myself, to let go of the anger I held towards Delain. It was difficult.

"Any speculations, Jackson?"

"I'm certain it's more than just one person. Right before he died, Davis mentioned he was part of something big. I'm afraid he was right." I pictured Davis sitting in a circular booth at his restaurant. Mitch was at the table. So was a man with red hair and a few others. Several times I had seen the same group of men at the Fleur-de-Leans as Tiffany and I went occasionally on Fridays for lunch. "The guy with red hair—is he kind of short and around his early forties?"

"I would say so."

"If it's the same guy I'm thinking about, his name is Redmond Broussard. He, Mitch, Davis and about three or four other guys would sit together in the same booth nearly every Friday at Davis' restaurant. They would refer to themselves as the 'Krewe', as in a Mardi Gras Krewe. Every year they rode together in the Bacchus parade. Maybe that helps."

"I think it helps a lot. I knew there was a reason we snuck you out of jail. Speaking of which, Jackson, until we find Christina's son, you better lay low. Mitch is going to have every F.B.I. agent looking for you as well. Once we prove what he's doing, you'll be a free man. Until then, you have to hide."

"Take me to my parents' house. It's on St. Charles. They won't find me there."

"That's probably the first place they'll look."

"They will, but they won't find me. By the way, who are you really?"

"He's a private investigator," Christina answered. My back was still to her. "He's helping me to get Caleb back."

"You can call me John. With your help, Jackson, this whole thing may be done before the day is over. Once it's complete, you'll be a free man."

"How did you free me back there, John? I don't think a normal private investigator would be able to do what you just did."

"You're right, Jackson. My previous career provided me with the tools and training needed to be successful at my new career."

I turned to my ex-fiancé. "Delain—I mean—what name should I call you now?"

She looked to the front seat then back to me. "Christina will do."

"How long have you had this investigator, Christina?"

"A couple of days."

"When exactly?"

"Why?"

"I just want to know exactly when you decided to take things upon yourself instead of sticking with the plan you, me, and Caroline came up with. The same plan you promised you wouldn't deviate from. I don't know why I'm surprised, though. Nothing that's come out of your mouth since day one has been truthful."

Tyler turned around. "Go easy on her, Jackson. She's had a rough time."

I locked eyes with the asshole seated before me. "She's had a rough time, Tyler?! I got pistol-whipped last night by a mobster who was about to shoot me in the head and then dump my body into the Mississippi River, only to be saved by a gun-toting hooker. Twelve hours later, I got arrested for killing Davis, a man that was about to stab your ex-girlfriend—my fiancée— to death, even though he was the father of her son. All this occurring just three days after the woman," I again turned to Christina, "I thought loved me as much as I loved her, deserted me at the time I needed her the most." I gazed back at Tyler. "Sorry if I'm not respectful to her at the moment, Tyler. And by the way, why the fuck are you here right now?!"

"Christina and I ran into each other at the airport last Friday when she was picking up Caroline. I came to town for an interview. What do you mean Davis is the father of her son?"

"He impregnated her then…" I threw my hands in the air as I was too exhausted to continue. "Just get me to my parents' house before Mitch finds out I'm gone."

Tyler looked over his left shoulder. "Is that true, Christina? Davis is the father of Caleb?"

Her head hung low. "No."

I didn't think it was possible, but I grew even angrier. "No?! You're saying Davis isn't Caleb's father?!"

She shook her head. "I just found out he isn't."

"Then who the hell is the father?!"

"I don't know. There's a possibility that…" She looked at her ex and then back to me, "maybe Tyler is."

The final blow had been dealt. I wanted nothing more to do with her.

"I just found out yester—"

"Please don't talk anymore," I furiously demanded.

Tyler again turned to me. "Don't get upset with her, Jackson."

"And you neither, jackass! I'm a fucking murderer because you knocked her up! I hope the two of you find your son and live happily ever after! John, please step on it!"

Tyler hastily unfastened his seatbelt. "John, please stop the car so this asshole and I can finish this discussion outside like real men."

John motioned to Tyler to put his seatbelt back on. "Easy, gentlemen. You are not each other's enemy. Mitch is the bad guy. He and the rest of Davis' cronies are the reason all of this is transpiring."

On the verge of tears, Christina asked me, "Would you please let me explain?"

"There's nothing to explain. I saw the look in your eyes on our first date when you mentioned," I pointed to the front, "him. You loved him then and you still do. Am I right?"

She glanced briefly at Tyler, and then back at me. "Yes, but—"

"Please hurry, John!"

The rest of the car ride was silent, except for the few words I spoke to direct John to the house directly behind my parents. While opening the car door, something grazed my back pocket. I didn't turn around as I didn't want to look at Christina. No farewells were exchanged as I slammed the door and snuck through my parents' backyard.

Chapter 125

The backdoor was locked. The keys I left the house with earlier in the day (my dad's keys) were somewhere within the F.B.I. building. I gently tapped on the door. Someone soon moved behind the thin curtain. If it were a police officer or someone else I didn't recognize, I was prepared to run. The curtain lifted. Marcus' eyes grew big upon seeing me on the back porch. He swung the door open.

We embraced as he told me, "What are you doing here? Dad's been trying to get you out for the last few hours."

"I escaped."

"What?!" With both hands on my shoulders, he pushed himself away from me. "How in the hell did you do that?!"

"It's a long story. I'll explain in a minute. Is anyone else here?"

"Just Angelo."

"Where?"

"When we heard knocking on the door, he went to the crawlspace." His eyes drifted to the bandage covering my forehead. "Dad told me Vincent tried to shoot you last night after he whacked you on your head, but a prostitute shot him instead. Judging by your bandage, I'm thinking Dad was actually all there when he told me that story."

"It's the truth."

His hands left my shoulders, finding their way to his hips. "Damn you've been through some shit lately. And to top it off, you're now an escaped prisoner."

"It's been an eventful couple of days."

"I hate to bring it up, but I have to ask— did you kill Davis like they're saying you did?"

"Pretty much."

"Jesus," he mumbled. "Why?"

"He was going to kill Christina."

With a puzzled look he asked, "Who?"

"Delain. Christina is her real name."

"Brother, would you please for the love of God tell me what the hell is going on?"

"Get Dad here and I'll tell y'all everything."

Marcus limped to the kitchen phone while I approached the grandfather clock in the hallway. For anyone outside of the Fabacher family, the grandfather clock built beneath the staircase was just that—an antique clock. For my brother and me growing up, it was the perfect hiding place. According to my grandfather, it was—supposedly—a place for the original owners of the house to hide runaway slaves. Following the incident in the garbage truck at age seven, I could no longer hide in the narrow passage as I found it too restricting. I knocked on the wall next to the clock three times, signaling the coast was clear. After being unlocked from the other side, the heavy clock was soon pushed outward.

"Brother!" An elated Angelo greeted me with a firm hug. The clock slid back into position on its own. "I worry I never see you again."

"It was starting to look that way."

"Why you put in jail?"

"Misunderstanding."

I stepped back, growing less uncomfortable by the sight of my twin. The realization and acceptance that my parents were unfaithful to one another had finally set in.

"Dad's on his way home," Marcus informed us upon limping into the hallway. "I didn't tell him you were here. I just said to get home quickly. You want anything to drink or eat?"

"I haven't eaten since breakfast."

"Are you hungry too, Angelo?"

He nodded. "Always hungry."

Marcus placed various luncheon meats and cheeses on the kitchen table, along with a loaf of French bread, the basic condiments, shredded lettuce, a couple of tomatoes, and a bag of Zapp's potato chips. He proceeded to cut the loaf into three equal pieces. "Angelo, this is how you make a po-boy."

"Poor boy?"

"Po-boy. Sandwich—New Orleans style."

Marcus prepared all three po-boys the same—ham, turkey, and Swiss cheese, topped with lettuce, thin slices of tomato, sliced pickles, mayonnaise and mustard. Angelo was the first to take a bite. He seemed pleased with his first po-boy. It was hard for me to enjoy the sandwich, since every noise I heard outside the house had me racing to the window.

After peering out the window for the fourth time, relief momentarily set in. "Dad's here." Watching him walk towards the side kitchen door from the carport, I felt horrible for the way I had been treating him over the last couple of days. Once he noticed me through the kitchen window, he smiled as big as I had ever seen him smile.

"Jax!"

There were tears in his eyes as we embraced. I was on the verge of crying myself, but once again contained it as I told him, "I'm sorry."

"For what?"

"Everything."

"You don't have to apologize for any of that. How did you get out?"

Marcus shut and locked the side door. "He escaped."

"What?! How?"

"I don't know how much time we have, but I'll start from the beginning."

Angelo began to walk out of the kitchen. "I give you private."

"You might as well stay," I told him. "You're involved now."

A grinning Angelo appeared appreciative as the four of us sat at the kitchen table.

All eyes were on me as I began. "On the morning of my first wedding day, I was clearing space on my video camera when I discovered that Tiffany had cheated on me..." I talked for nearly twenty minutes. No one interrupted me, and I left out nothing.

Marcus was the first to speak upon completion of the story. "I can't believe you saved those girls in Mobile and shot the bad guy. My brother is a hero."

"I knew Mitch was crooked," my dad confessed while aggressively rubbing his hands together, "just like his no-good former partner."

"Does that mean Jackson can't go back to jail?"

"Unless we have proof of what Mitch has done, it's going to be his word against Jackson's. From what I've experienced over the years, a judge is going to take the side of the federal agent every time. The only way to prove his innocence would be to find Thomas Melancon."

"But Jackson was arrested for Davis' death. How will those charges be dropped?"

"Davis blackmailed Christina after convincing her Caleb died in childbirth, and then found a way for his brother to adopt him. Once it's proven Christina is the mother, and Davis did those things to her, especially attempted murder of not only her but Caroline as well, Jackson would more than likely be cleared. No jury would find Jackson guilty after that. Davis would be found guilty along with those who helped orchestrate the elaborate plan."

Marcus shook his head while saying, "I can't believe Christina not only had sex with Davis, but also got pregnant by him."

"I left something out. On the way over here just a little while ago, Christina said Davis wasn't the father. It may be her former boyfriend's child. She wasn't exactly sure though."

"If Davis isn't the father, then we probably can't prove he had cause to do all those things to Christina, right?" Marcus asked our father.

"As long as he's Christina's son, we have a strong case. Jax, are you sure he is Christina's son?"

"Positive. When I saw him in Denver, I had no doubt he was her son. I'm also certain Harley's the guy who kidnapped him, and I know Mitch and his crew are behind it."

"Crew?" My dad stood. He grabbed the pad and pen located next to the phone, before returning to the table. "The Fleur-de-Leans is—or was—the place to be seen at lunchtime on Fridays. Davis and a group of guys—seven total if I'm not mistaken—were there every Friday, and always in the same booth. They were always referring to themselves as 'the Krewe'." My dad wrote the words 'Davis' Krewe' atop the page, along with numbers one through seven listed horizontally beneath it. "Davis was one, and Mitch was two. You said the P.I. mentioned a red-headed man. That would be Redmond Broussard, who makes number three. His uncle, the retired Judge Broussard, makes number four."

"A retired judge would be handy to have around, especially one known for taking bribes over the years."

"You're right about that, Marcus. That man was as corrupt as they got. The same could be said about Redmond too. At twenty-three, he killed a man while under the influence. His blood alcohol level was over .20, and they found cocaine in his blood as well. He never spent a day in jail. His uncle got him off, and now he owns the biggest waste disposal company in New Orleans—which he got by bribing several officials. Now, as for being able to fake the death of a newborn, you would need a doctor, and one was in that booth on most Fridays." He next wrote 'Percy Weller' next to the number five."

"Charlie Guichet was always with them as well," Marcus added.

"Yes, he was," my dad said while writing. "And because he's Harley's lawyer, this whole thing is starting to make perfect sense."

"And there was another guy, kind of nerdy looking," I added. "He didn't look like he belonged in the group. He never seemed to laugh or talk as much as the others did."

"He's Charlie's nephew, and if memory serves me correctly, his name is…something with an 'R'. It'll come to me."

"You think these guys are responsible for what Davis did to Christina?"

My dad added Harley's name to the list before circling all eight names. "I'd bet every dollar I have that each of these people had a hand in it."

"What about Scott Melancon? Do you think he's in on it too?" Marcus asked.

"I never met Scott. Didn't you stay with him and his wife in Denver for a week, Jax?"

"Yes, and I've been asking myself that exact question for the last week. I don't know if he's in on it, but then again, he is related to Davis. I wouldn't put it past him."

Marcus adjusted himself in the chair while saying, "He looked highly emotional on the news broadcast a little while ago. If he's in on it, he's a damn good actor."

"I guess the next thing to do is find Caleb. If Harley has him," my dad spoke," then we need to find Harley."

"Where do we start?"

"His last known residence."

"Are we going to just knock on his door?"

My dad didn't answer as the nausea-inducing sound of police sirens could be faintly heard. He hurried to the kitchen window. The sirens grew louder. "They're here. Jackson, you and Angelo get behind the clock. Marcus, make it look like only you and I were eating those sandwiches."

Angelo grabbed my arm, directing me to the hallway as if I had no idea where we were going. Lights blue and red in color flashed on our faces as he held the swinging pendulum with his left hand, thus unlocking the hidden door. He next pulled the clock forward with his right.

A movie that frightened me more than any other as a young teenager wasn't any of the Friday the 13th movies or anything starring Freddy Kruger or Michael Meyers. It was The Diary of Anne Frank. The scene where it was discovered that Anne and her family were hiding in the attic and the police were on their way to ship them off to concentration camps haunted me for years. My situation felt eerily similar to that one. Not only was I hiding in a confined space, but I was in jeopardy of going to prison—again. On top of that, I had put my family in a position that could put them in jail as well.

Once the clock closed behind us, Angelo locked it. Over twenty years had passed since I last hid in the secret room. It was much smaller than I remembered. The walls seemed to grow thicker and the air much denser as I heard pounding on the front door.

Chapter 126

Mitch stood on the Fabacher's front porch with six police officers and two F.B.I. agents in tow. No longer did he feel in control of the situation, and he very much detested that feeling. Lack of control lead to the inability to maintain his calmness, thus creating irrational thoughts and actions, thus leading to defeat. He felt as if he was standing in a pit of quicksand that was up to his knees. With his right hand hovering over his holstered pistol, the front door opened. "Where is he, Andrew?"

"Who?"

"Jackson."

"What are you talking about? You arrested him a few hours ago."

"We're coming in. Please give me a reason to arrest you for failing to comply." Andrew stepped to the side. Mitch stormed through the cloak room and into hallway. "You four start upstairs," he told the police officers as he stood next to the grandfather clock, "and you two start in the back of the house."

"Dad, what's going on?" Marcus asked, stepping into the hallway with the assistance of his cane.

"Why are you acting as if my son escaped from your custody?"

Mitch approached Andrew, standing nearly nose-to-nose. "Because he did."

"You're saying that my son escaped from federal custody? Your custody?"

Mitch held a black and white photo inches from Andrew's face. "Do you recognize the two individuals in this picture?"

Andrew leaned back, squinting while looking at the picture. "I can't say I do."

"What about you, gimpy? Recognize these two?"

Before Marcus could speak, someone behind Mitch did. "That's not an appropriate nickname, especially coming from someone sporting a ponytail belonging on a 90's porn star."

Mitch turned around to see Logan Besthoff walking through the cloakroom with his hands held high.

"I'm unarmed. Don't shoot me like Thad did to my good friend Mikey. Didn't you work with that murdering scumbag when you were with the N.O.P.D., Mitch?"

With pointed finger, Mitch told him, "You make one more accusation like that and I'll have you arrested."

Logan smirked. "And I'll escape like Jackson just did."

"Cuff him!" a red-faced Mitch yelled.

Logan, grinning while his face was pressed against the wall of the hallway, seemed to find enjoyment while being handcuffed by the agents. "Mr. F is going to have a field day with this, aren't you, Mr. F?"

"Logan, be quiet. Mitch, uncuff him and stop this foolishness. Do you really think I—an assistant to the former district attorney—would help my son escape, and then hide him in my house? Or do you think my son would be dumb enough to come here after escaping from jail? I'm guessing he's with those two individuals whose picture you just showed us."

"Where would he be going?"

"Your guess is as good as mine."

"Aiding and abetting a criminal is a felony."

"We'll keep that under consideration, Federal Agent…douche bag," Logan spoke, his voice trailing off while his face was still pressed against the wall.

"Keep an eye on them," Mitch told the agents. "I need to make a phone call." He walked outside, several steps away from the house, and then dialed the judge's number.

"Is the line secure?"

"Yes."

"Tell me good things, Mitchell."

"Jackson's nowhere to be found. Neither is the girl."

"Mitchell, Mitchell, Mitchell, you are not handling this situation like you said you would."

"I know, Judge."

"You are putting the Krewe at risk."

"I'll have this all sorted out by the day's end."

"How will you do that, Mitchell?"

249

The phone beeped. "I have another call. I'll call you back." Mitch clicked over. "Agent Hennessey."

"You're probably a little ticked off with me right now."

Mitch grew even more furious upon hearing the voice of the gentleman who had thrice gotten the better of him over the last few days. He was also relieved to again be in contact with John. "Why do you say that?"

"Because I didn't deliver the girl to you."

"And because you freed Jackson from my custody."

"I have no idea what you're talking about, Mitch."

"Bullshit. I know what you look like now, John."

"Congratulations. Unfortunately, in about thirty minutes you will no longer be focused on catching me."

"Why do you say that?"

"You're boring. I decided to play games with someone else."

"Who?"

"Harley."

Mitch gripped the phone tighter, pressing it closer to his ear. "Who's Harley?"

"Goodbye, Mitch." The call ended.

"Shit!" The quicksand was inching up to Mitch's waist. He hurried back inside. "You're in charge," he told one of the other agents. "Continue checking the house. Call me if you find anything."

"What do I do with this one?"

Mitch wanted nothing more than to arrest Logan, but knew he had no just cause. "Let him go."

"You're a good man, Mitch," Logan said while being uncuffed. "Jesus loves you."

Mitch hurried to his vehicle, flipped on the dashboard lights and overhead siren, and proceeded to Mid-City. Along the way, he placed several frantic calls to Harley's cell phone. All went to voicemail. "Pick up, dip shit!"

As Mitch grew closer to the shotgun home where Harley was currently residing, he turned off the dashboard lights and siren. With gun drawn and his F.B.I. badge hung around his neck, Mitch approached the canary-colored house. Weeds grew rampant in what used to be a garden, while the grass was in dire need of a mow. Empty beer cans and cigarette butts were scattered about the porch. The house just screamed 'criminal inside'.

Looking over his shoulder for anyone or anything suspicious, Mitch jiggled the front door handle. It was unlocked.

The living room was empty, yet the television was turned on and at a normal decibel level. A bowl of milk sat on the carpeted floor next to the couch. Mitch placed his pinky finger into the bowl. The milk was still cool. He slowly made his way past the kitchen, stopping in front of the bathroom door. Harley's back was to him as he urinated into the toilet. He was without a shirt and shoes, only wearing a pair of faded blue jeans. After holstering his gun, Mitch quietly walked back to the living room. After the toilet flushed, Harley stepped out of the bathroom with a gun aimed at Mitch.

"What are you doing here?"

"Why aren't you answering your phone?"

"I didn't hear it ringing."

"Are you going to stop aiming that gun at me?"

Harley slowly lowered his arm. "What are you doing sneaking around my house?"

"Has a man tried to contact you in the last hour?"

"No."

"No one suspicious has been around here?"

"Just you. Why?" Harley plopped onto the couch and focused his eyes on the chopper being built on the television.

"The girl hired some private investigator to find the kid. He's pretty good. I think they're coming for him."

"Let 'em. They won't find any kid here."

"Where is he?"

"Judge told me not to tell anyone—including you. He's safe and in good hands."

Mitch was surprised at how uncomfortable he still felt in Harley's presence. He was the only person that had such an effect on him. "We need to be extra careful right now."

Harley's eyes remained focused on the television as he said, "I did what I was supposed to do. As soon as one of you sons of bitches tells me to release the kid, I make the call and it's done. As for someone finding me, that would be hard to do considering I'm not listed in the phone book, and there's no record of me living here. That means the only way anyone would know where I live is if they followed you here. You're not that stupid," Harley finally glanced at Mitch, "are you, Federal Agent Hennessey?"

Mitch's pulse skyrocketed. Sweat began to form on his forehead as he was convinced John had gotten the better of him once again. The quicksand was chest-high. Not wanting to let Harley know of his grave mistake, he walked towards the front door. "No, I'm not. See you around, Hitman."

"Hopefully not anytime soon, federal agent."

From behind his sunglasses and without making it obvious, Mitch peered around the block in hopes of spotting someone sitting in a vehicle. He could see nothing. Several minutes after driving off, he returned to the neighborhood and parked four blocks away from Harley's house. *I'm going to catch you at your own game, John!*

Chapter 127

After someone knocked on the grandfather clock three times, Angelo unlocked the grandfather clock and hinged it open. I inhaled deeply once he and I stood in the hallway.

"Y'all okay?" Marcus asked.

Angelo nodded. "Good."

"How long where we in there for?"

"About twenty minutes," my dad informed us.

Logan exited the kitchen with half of a po-boy sandwich in hand. "Holy shit! Is that a panic room?"

"Something like that. When did you get here?"

"Just in time to get handcuffed by that ass clown Mitch." Logan stepped into the hidden room. "It smells old in here. Why didn't y'all tell me about this?" His voice echoed throughout the narrow crawlspace.

"It's kind of a family secret," my dad told him.

Logan exited the space, allowing Marcus to close it. "Y'all got a bunch of those, don't y'all? Now, before anyone says anything," with a grin he looked at me, "I want to know how this one escaped federal custody."

"Two guys pretending to be C.I.A. agents got me out."

"Who are they?"

"One is a private investigator, and the other is Christina's ex-boyfriend." Before Logan could ask, I told him, "Christina is Delain's real name. She's been lying about that since day one."

"I knew she was hiding something! Remember when I told you before you proposed to her that I thought she was hiding something?!"

"You figured it out."

Logan loved being right. With hands thrust in the air, he shouted, "Smartest man alive!" As shredded lettuce fell onto him and the hardwood floors of the hallway, he asked, "What's the ex's name that helped you escape?"

"Tyler."

"You said he was dead."

"I was wrong."

"You see! I told you she was still in love with him!"

"You are absolutely the smartest person alive, Logan. Now, stop gloating and tell me what happened with Jordan."

"She's the stripper from Vegas?" Marcus asked.

"Prostitute, and yes."

"Just like I told you on the phone—she freaked out about killing Vincent and stole my car when I fell asleep."

Angelo pointed towards the front door. "Person!"

He and I hurried back into the crawl space. No sooner than the clock shut behind us, we heard three knocks. A smiling, blonde-haired girl from Southern California stood next to my brother, Dad, and best friend. I wasn't sure if I would ever see Caroline again. We embraced.

"I was so worried about you," she confessed. "I missed you."

I wanted to believe she missed me, but I couldn't stop thinking about Brock's claim that he and Caroline had sex earlier in the day. As we stepped back, her concerned eyes looked above mine. "What happened to your head?"

"Your boyfriend nearly got whacked by a mobster," Logan informed her.

"Vincent?"

"He hit me in the head and was about to kill me, but a prostitute he employs traveled with him and shot Vincent before he could shoot me."

"Oh my God!" She then slapped my arm. "You see what happens when I'm not with you." After shaking her head, she curiously glanced at Angelo. "You were right, Jackson. He looks just like you."

Angelo couldn't stop beaming while shaking and then kissing her hand. "Molto bello."

"This is so…."

"Trippy," Angelo spoke, still clutching to her hand.

"I'm still getting used to it as well."

"How's Mrs. Cecile doing?"

"She's coming around," my dad told her. "We hope to have her home in a few days."

"I'm so glad to hear that."

Despite family members surrounding us, I couldn't hold back from asking, "Where's Brock?"

"He, um…" She appeared uncomfortable. "Could we talk privately for a second?"

"Why don't y'all go to the study?" My dad pried Angelo's hand from Caroline's. "We'll let you know if there are any more visitors."

I pulled her into the study, rolling the door shut behind us. Before I could again ask of Brock's whereabouts, she did something I thought might never happen for me again. Being branded a 'fugitive' was nowhere on my mind as we kissed. My knees felt momentarily weak.

"I didn't know if I would ever get to kiss you again," she told me, her eyes slowly opening. "I know it's only been a day, but I've missed you so much."

I felt the same, but was concerned about someone. "Brock answered your phone when I called this morning. He said y'all were getting back together."

"And once I found out he did that, I ripped him a new one. I would never get back with him."

"Does that mean you two didn't have sex this morning?"

"God no!" Her facial expression was one of disgust.

I believed her. "Why was he down here?"

"He thought we weren't broken up, that we were just taking a little break. He showed up unexpectedly at my uncle's house. I honestly think he's not all there. If I wasn't clear the first time we broke up, I definitely was a little while ago. If he still thinks he has a shot with me, he's officially the stupidest person in the world."

"You're not to leave my side again."

"I know," she replied with a nod. "I saw Delain's son has been kidnapped. I'm sure you heard all about it too. It's all over the news."

"I did. And you were right about her real name. It is Christina."

"Whatever it is, I'm sure she's not doing well right now."

"She didn't look too good a little while ago."

Caroline squinted while asking, "You saw her?"

I nodded. "Her ex-boyfriend, or current boyfriend, and another man helped me escape from federal custody."

"Federal custody?"

"They found out I killed Davis."

After covering her mouth with both hands, she slowly lowered them before asking, "How?"

"An F.B.I. agent named Mitch Hennessey pieced it all together. He was also good friends with Davis, and just as crooked. My dad thinks the only chance I have in clearing my name is to find Caleb before they find Christina. Mitch was just here looking for me."

"And if you don't find Caleb?"

"Then I'll probably be on the run until they find me, and then thrown back in prison."

Caroline looked me dead in the eyes while saying, "And I'll be right there with you—gun and all." She patted her boot.

"You do realize you're committing a crime right now by associating with me."

There was no smile on her face, just a determined look in her eyes as she told me, "Good. They can lock us up together."

We rejoined the others in the kitchen. My dad was on the phone, while Marcus, Logan, and Angelo were gathered around the table. "Who's dad talking to?"

"He's trying to figure out where Harley lives."

"And then we strike," Logan responded with a tight fist. He seemed overly excited.

"This doesn't concern you, Logan."

"It concerns all of us," Marcus chimed in. "We're all helping you, so don't even think about trying to do this on your own anymore."

We all turned around as my dad hung up the phone. "Harley's living in a house in Mid-City. I'm going to check out the scene and see what I can find."

"You're not going alone, Dad. This is my doing."

"I know I'm not going alone. I'm picking Rick up on the way. Besides, you're not to leave this house. If anyone sees you, you're going right back to prison." Rick was a retired detective and my dad's good friend for decades. He could be trusted. "If authorities are to show up here again, Marcus, I need you to hide Jackson and Angelo. I won't be long, and I won't do anything stupid. I'll report back to y'all what we find out."

"Yes, sir."

"No one leaves this house until I get back, understand?" We all answered 'yes' to my dad. "Marcus, call me if anything else happens. I'll see y'all soon." He hurried out the side door, leading to the carport.

"Does anyone else think we should follow him?" Logan asked.

My eyes shifted from Logan, to Marcus, to Angelo, and then Caroline. I suspected we were all thinking the same thing.

"Jackson, you know more about this situation than any of us. You come with me. Logan, you stay here with Caroline and Angelo."

"I want to go," Logan said, pouting like a five-year old. "I never get in on the action."

"You are getting in on the action. Police have been coming by here all day."

I didn't want to leave Caroline, especially after just telling her she wasn't to leave my side. "I think Caroline should come with us."

"No. She stays here." Marcus grabbed my arm and pushed me towards the side door. "Hurry before we lose Dad."

I turned around. Caroline looked concerned. I hated leaving her behind.

Chapter 128

"Are you sure he's in there?" Christina asked from the backseat of the white Tahoe. Across the street and two houses down was the canary-colored shotgun home Mitch visited a half-hour prior.

John, once again wearing his hairpiece, and without his colored contact lenses or Buddy Holly specs, lowered the binoculars from his eyes. "I'm only picking up the thermal scan of one person."

"What does that mean? Caleb's not in there? We have the wrong guy?"

"Caleb could still be in there, perhaps hidden. Or, we indeed have the wrong guy. Maybe Jackson didn't know after all who kidnapped Caleb. Perhaps he threw us a curveball. Or Mitch just tricked us."

"We need to get in there and look around," Tyler suggested. "We still have these C.I.A. badges. It'd be a shame to let them go to waste."

"That's a good idea, but we're being watched right now."

"By who?"

"Mitch is four blocks behind us. He tried to make me think he was leaving the scene, but I saw him pull back around."

"Let's get him out of here then," Tyler suggested. "Call him again and send him on another wild goose chase."

"He's starting to get wise of those. Let me think for a second."

Christina imagined Caleb crying for help while tied up inside a container impervious to John's thermal binoculars. Panicked, she opened the door. John quickly turned around and shut it. "What are you doing?"

"My son could be on death's doorsteps right now." Tears began to trickle down her cheeks. "I can't take this anymore."

"Give me a few seconds, Christina. I promise we're about to find out where he is. Do me a favor and hand me that black satchel behind you."

Christina wiped at her eyes. After handing John the satchel, Tyler grabbed her hand. "We're going to get him back, Chrissy. You're almost there."

"Here's the plan." John handed Tyler the same microphone Christina wore into Davis' condo. "As soon as you see Mitch or anyone approaching the house, you tell me." John placed the earpiece into his ear. "Speak into the microphone, Tyler."

"Can you hear me?"

"We're good. I'm going to be in and out in five minutes."

"What if Mitch comes in?" Tyler asked.

"I'll take care of him. Just let me know if he's getting close. But hopefully he won't see me going in."

"How are you going to do that?"

"Look back there. His car is that black SUV. You see it?"

"On the left? Yes."

As they continued looking, a small car drove from their left to their right on the perpendicular street, half a block away. "I'm going to use a passing car to block his vision while I run in." From the black suitcase, John removed a small bottle and a syringe.

"What's in the bottle?" Christina asked.

"Sodium thiopental."

"What's that?"

"Truth serum," Tyler answered.

"Well done, Marine."

"How are you going to inject him with that?"

"By gunpoint. Hopefully he doesn't—"

Tyler pointed out the back window. "Here comes a moving truck!"

John grabbed the door handle. "You two know what to do." As the truck passed, he hurried out the car, staying low while scampering across the street.

As Tyler kept an observant eye on Mitch's vehicle, Christina watched as John stepped onto the porch, seemingly out of Mitch's view.

"He made it across."

"And there's no movement from Mitch's car."

"Don't take your eyes off of it." Christina's breathing grew heavier as John held his pistol in his right hand while reaching for the door knob.

"What's John doing?"

"He's jiggling the door knob… It's not locked. He just opened the door… He's going in. Shit."

"John seems like a very intelligent man. He knows what he's doing."

While continuing to watch the front door, Christina thought about Jackson and the scene that transpired earlier where she sat. Never had she seen Jackson so upset and furious. She wanted nothing more than to talk to him privately for a few minutes, to explain in depth why she confessed to still being in love with Tyler, why she lied and said Tyler might be the father of Caleb, and how John showed up on her doorstep and told her she had to get in his car immediately before Davis' men showed up to kill her. She wanted desperately to tell him she had no choice but to leave unannounced three days prior or his life would be in danger as well. Now, it seemed Jackson no longer wanted anything to do with her. *He's never going to forgive me for what I did. He's gone and there's no bringing him back.* Christina couldn't get the notion out of her head that she would never speak to, or see him again. With one love seemingly gone from her life, she was determined not to let the other go. "I'm sorry I got you involved in all of this, Tyler. I should have told you earlier what was going on. I really should have told you three years ago instead of breaking up with you. I promise I'll never lie to you again."

Tyler grabbed her hand, keeping an eye on Mitch's vehicle. "It's okay. No matter what happens, I'm just thankful I finally got to know the truth. I didn't mean to freak out earlier. I would do anything for you, no matter how illegal it is."

"I've missed you so much over the last couple of years. What gave me the strength to persevere was believing that today would happen—the day when I'd get to see you again and tell you everything, especially how much I love you and how much I need you in my life."

"You don't know how happy I am to hear that. How about when all of this is over, I take you out to dinner?"

Christina glanced over to see Tyler smiling while staring down the road. "I'd like that."

"And Caleb too."

Christina turned her attention back to Harley's front door. "What if it turns out that Caleb isn't your son?"

Tyler rubbed the back of his neck before saying, "Then I raise him as my own—if you will allow me to."

"That would make me the happiest woman in the world." She gently squeezed his hand. "I really do love you, Tyler."

"I love you too, Chrissy. Always have, always will."

Chapter 129

As we headed east on Tulane Avenue in my brother's truck, Marcus remained far enough behind my dad that we were certain he didn't know we were following him. We were also far enough back that we nearly lost him on two occasions.

"I'm sorry I've gotten you, Melanie, and the boys involved in all of this. It wasn't my intention."

"Stop apologizing." Marcus' eyes remained on the road. "Family has to stick together."

"Even if it means I could be responsible for putting you in jail?"

"I'm not going to jail. You're not going back to jail. Dad's not going to jail. We're the good guys." My brother's optimism, inherited from our dad, was something I wished I had more of.

My dad turned right down a residential street. Marcus slowed down, waiting several seconds before following him down the street. Once their taillights began to flicker, Marcus pulled onto the side of the road. We watched as my dad parallel parked. Neither he nor Rick stepped out of the car.

"He must live close by," Marcus suggested, gazing down the street lined with one shotgun home after another. "I guess they're scoping out the area."

"If Mom knew everything that was going on right now…"

"It's for the best she's in the hospital. Her stroke could be a blessing in disguise."

"But what if she doesn't recover from it?"

"She will recover. I have no doubt." He then placed his hand on my shoulder. "It's my turn to apologize for the way I treated you in the hospital yesterday. I should have never acted the way I did towards you. I'm sorry, brother."

"Everything you said was right—I run away when things don't go my way instead of talking with loved ones. I promise I'm never going to do that again."

"I'm always here for you if you ever need to…what is going on here?" Marcus' stare was aimed in the direction of a bright yellow shotgun home.

A barefooted man wearing nothing more than a pair of blue jeans sprinted from the shotgun house towards the street. He was bald, covered in tattoos, and looked to have a blonde mustache. With a pistol in his left hand, he climbed into an early 90's Chevy Camaro parallel parked on the street. No sooner than the engine started, the black Camaro peeled out, hitting the back bumper of the car parked in front of it.

"That's got to be Harley."

"Don't let him get away!" I shouted.

Marcus followed. It didn't take long to discover we weren't the only ones doing so. My dad was right behind us, as was Logan's truck. Caroline looked to be in the passenger seat with him.

"Shit!" Marcus shouted.

"What?"

"I forgot my gun at Mom and Dad's. I hid it when Mitch was knocking on the door."

"Where's your cell phone?"

Marcus handed me his phone. "He's driving recklessly. Do you think Caleb is in there?"

The thought didn't cross my mind until he mentioned it. "I hope not." I dialed Caroline's number as we sped down Tulane Avenue.

"Hello?"

"Why didn't y'all stay at the house?"

"Logan didn't want to, and frankly, neither did I."

"Where's Angelo?"

"Back at the house. The guy running to the car with the gun— is that him?"

"We think so."

"Do you think Caleb's in the car?"

"I don't know."

The man we assumed to be Harley took a sharp right turn onto a residential street. We were less than a hundred feet behind him.

"Caroline, be careful. I'll call you back in a minute."

"You be careful too."

I hung up.

"They're following us?" My brother asked.

"I'm afraid so."

"I told him to stay back. I'm going to kill Logan."

Marcus's phone rang in my hand. "Dad?"

"I told y'all to stay home."

"We couldn't. We're guessing that was Harley."

"It was."

"Did you see anything?"

"Rick and I heard a loud pop just seconds before Harley ran out of the house. He looked to have blood on his jeans. I don't know what happened, but we assume someone was shot inside the house."

A disturbing thought then popped into my head. "Dad, do you think he killed…"

"I don't think so. I just called the police and told them to send some officers and an ambulance over to the house to see what happened."

Harley came to an abrupt stop on someone's front lawn. He hurried inside. It wasn't more than ten seconds later that he emerged. Any doubt that Harley 'Hitman' Motichek didn't kidnap Christina's son was put to rest by what was held in his left arm.

"That's Caleb!" Marcus shouted as we drove past Harley. "You were right!"

I opened the door with no plan of action. Before I could step onto the pavement, Harley removed a gun from the back of his jeans and took aim in my direction. Marcus grabbed the back of my t-shirt and pulled me backwards before I could react. Once I was in the truck, the back window shattered. Marcus lay on top of me. Broken glass covered the both of us. I was afraid he had been shot. "Are you hit?!"

"I don't think so. You?"

I felt no pain. "No."

While still firmly pressing me against the seat, Marcus slowly sat up. I watched as he peeked out the window before hastily collapsing on top of me once more. "Harley's coming this way."

I could hear the revving of an engine. It sounded as if Harley was right next to us. I held my breath in anticipation of another shot being fired. Marcus and I both flinched as a gun was indeed fired—only it sounded as if it was fired from behind us. I could hear Harley speed off. We sat up to see Logan standing outside his truck with gun in hand.

"He's getting away!" Marcus shouted.

Harley hastily turned a corner. "It's too dangerous to follow him."

"We're so close. We're not giving up." Marcus slammed his foot on the accelerator.

I turned around. Logan and my dad were following closely behind us. A third vehicle was behind us as well—a white Tahoe. I had a hunch it was the same white Tahoe I climbed into following my escape from the F.B.I. building. I dialed Christina's number. It rang, yet she didn't answer.

"We have to rescue Caleb before that asshole does something stupid." Marcus sped up, growing closer to Harley.

"How? He's got a gun."

"We'll find a way."

The phone in my hand rang once more. "Caroline?"

"Are y'all okay?" She sounded worried.

"Yes."

"That guy was about to shoot you. Logan fired my gun and scared him away. Aren't you glad we decided not to stay home now?"

"Yes."

"Where do you think he's going?"

"I don't know, but he definitely has Caleb in the car now. Tell Logan not to shoot at him."

"He won't. What do you want us to do?"

"Keep following us and him. I'll call you back in a minute."

"Okay."

While setting the phone on the seat, a folded piece of paper with my name scribbled upon it caught my attention. I brushed broken glass off of it. "Where did this come from?"

Marcus glanced at it and then back at the road. "I don't know."

I opened it. Delain's name was written on the bottom.

"He's heading toward the interstate."

I briefly looked up then back down at the letter. 'Jackson, right now you're (hopefully) being rescued from federal custody. I know you probably hate me and never want to speak to me again. I don't blame you. Words can't express how much you mean to

265

me, but I'll try: I love you more than you care to believe. There's a reason we met and a reason we are in each other's lives—not just now, but forever.'

"Shit," Marcus mumbled from the corner of his mouth.

My brother's eyes were focused outside my window. I turned to my right. From within a white Crown Vic, two police officers stared back at me. Their lights soon flipped on. Before I could roll down my window and communicate with them about who we were following, they slowed down and merged behind us.

"I'm not pulling over," Marcus spoke over the deafening roar of the sirens. "They're gonna have to ram us off the road if they want to slow us down." We accelerated, putting Harley only a few car lengths ahead as we merged onto I-10.

The phone again rang as we headed east. "Dad, the police saw me. They're trying to pull us over."

"I see them."

"Marcus isn't stopping. We're not letting Harley get away."

"I'm coming up on the left. Tell Marcus to pull out in front of me. I'll try to slow them down."

Once my dad pulled to our left, his lights flashed. "Go!" I yelled.

Marcus changed lanes and sped up. The police were momentarily blocked in by a former assistant to the district attorney.

"It's working." We were able to pull away from the police car and remain close to Harley and Caleb as they veered onto US 90. "How are we going to get Caleb from that car?"

"I don't know. Not only does he have a gun, but he's driving too fast to ram into the wall. We need to let the police know. Call 'em."

"Is that a good idea?"

"Don't give them your name. Tell them Thomas Melancon is in that black Camaro."

I dialed. "911. What's your emergency?"

"I'm currently heading east on US 90," I told the female operator, "and I saw the kidnapped boy, Thomas Melancon, in the back of a black Chevy Camaro. The driver is swerving in and out of traffic and speeding well over the limit. He's heading in the direction of the Crescent City Connection. His license plate is…" I tried to focus on the plate but couldn't read it.

"IBU 323," Marcus told me.

"IBU 323."

"With whom am I speaking?"

I hung up. The Crescent City Connection was quickly approaching. Only two more exits remained before driving across the bridge became the only option. I glanced behind to see if the police car chasing us had just been informed of the location of the kidnapped boy. It didn't appear so as it was again right behind us.

"Driver, pull over now!" a police officer shouted over his loudspeaker.

Marcus remained focused on the task at hand. "Not a chance."

Harley remained in the left lane as we passed the St. Charles exit. "Do you think he's heading across the bridge?"

"It seems so."

It occurred to me that if Harley was to get away, my brother was going to be arrested for aiding a criminal, as well as refusing to pull over. I grabbed the cell phone and again dialed 911.

"911. What's your emergency?"

"My name is Jackson Fabacher. I'm heading east on US 90. I'm forcing my brother against his will at gunpoint to drive me away from the police car that is currently chasing me."

"What are you doing?!" Marcus tried to grab the phone. I swatted his hand away.

"I'm going to shoot him if the police officer following us doesn't back off."

"Sir, I'd advise you to pull over and give yourself over to the police."

"This is a hostage situation, lady. I'm not pulling over." I hung up.

"Are you fucking crazy?! Why did you do that?!"

We passed the Tchoupitoulas Street exit. Harley had no choice but to drive across the bridge. "I don't want you to go to jail."

"I'm not. We're going to catch Harley and the truth will be revealed."

"What if he gets away?"

Marcus was momentarily silent. A short moment passed before a smile appeared on his face. He pointed ahead. "He's not! See!" I could see flashing lights on the other side of the bridge. The chase was nearly over.

As we followed Harley onto the Crescent City Connection in the far-left lane, the police cars at the end of the bridge began to merge together, forming a barricade. Harley's brake lights beamed bright red near the halfway mark of the bridge. He abruptly turned around, coming to a screeching halt in the middle of the four lanes. Marcus drove past him before slamming on the brakes as well. The pursuing police car swerved toward the inside lanes, narrowly avoiding a collision.

I was no longer concerned with the flashing lights of the cruiser in front of us or Harley's Camaro. The deafening sound of tires screeching and metal thunderously clanging together reverberated throughout every nerve ending of my body as several cars—in an attempt to avoid hitting Harley—wrecked into one another. In mere seconds, a pile-up unlike any I had ever seen consumed all four lanes of the Crescent City Connection. Not a single car moved, including Harley's as it sat idle and alone in the middle of the lanes. I placed fingers in both of my ears, wiggling them to reduce the ringing.

At the front of the crash—just on the other side of Harley's Camaro—sat Logan's truck. I couldn't see him or Caroline. I had no clue if they were okay. After swallowing, my ears popped and my hearing returned. The sirens grew louder on both sides of the bridge as more police cars appeared behind the pile-up. The police had Harley—and us—cornered. There was no escape.

Marcus pointed at the Camaro "What's he doing?" Harley was slowly reversing, moving closer towards us.

"Come out of the vehicle with your hands in the air!" a police officer demanded through a loudspeaker.

My attention was diverted forward as the two police officers who had been following us stood behind their doors with guns drawn. They were five to six car lengths away. "Are they talking to us?" I asked Marcus.

"I think so. They're looking this way."

"Maybe they're looking through us at Harley."

Marcus glanced backwards. "Now what's he doing?"

I looked in the passenger-side mirror. Harley was positioning his Camaro sideways in the road. A short moment passed before he revved the engine several times.

"Jesus! Is he going over the side?!"

We were the closest car to Harley and the only ones that could stop him. I opened the car door.

"What are you doing?! He's got a gun! Get back in here!"

I adhered to my brother and shut the door. "What do we do then?"

"Let the police do their thing. Once they find Thomas in the car, all this will be over."

The Camaro remained perpendicular in the middle of the four lanes. The windows were heavily tinted. "Why do I get the feeling something bad is about to go down."

"I have that feeling too." Marcus rolled down his window. While pointing behind us he told the police officers, "That's the guy who kidnapped Thomas Melancon! He's got him in the car with him!"

The officer standing outside the passenger window held the microphone to his mouth. "Will the occupants of both the truck and Camaro please step out of—"

Shots were fired from behind us. I ducked in the seat. Marcus hovered over me once more. "Are you okay?" I asked.

"Yes." He slowly lifted his head and peered in the direction of the lone police car. "One of the officers has been shot."

"Where?"

"Looks like his chest."

"By Harley?"

Marcus glanced into the mirror outside my door. "It appears so." As I tried to see what was transpiring, Marcus pushed me back down. I then heard another shot being fired, followed nearly instantly by a loud clank. The bullet sounded as if it struck metal. Marcus again slowly lifted his head. "The police car is backing up."

"What's Harley doing?"

"I can't tell. I think we should go before he shoots us though."

From a slouched position, Marcus put the ignition into drive. No sooner after we began to slowly roll forward, another shot was fired. The truck began to lean to the left. "He just shot my—" Another shot was fired. Within seconds, both of the back tires had been deflated by bullets. "Jesus!"

The notion that Marcus was going to be shot next incited my heartrate to increase even further, thus causing a temporary loss of hearing. I watched as his lips moved, but all I could hear was my rapidly beating heart. "I can't hear you!"

He grabbed both sides of my face. I focused on his lips as he spoke. It took him saying it three times for my hearing to finally return. "The police are about to take care of him. Just stay low."

"Turn off your engine!" a male's voice yelled from behind us. The demand wasn't spoken over a loudspeaker. "Or I'll shoot the two of you!"

Marcus placed the vehicle in park before killing the engine. "It's Harley," he whispered.

"Driver, throw your keys over the wall now!"

Marcus didn't hesitate in removing the keys from the ignition. It was hard not to notice how the keys shook in his hand just before he tossed them into the Mississippi River. We waited for the next demand from Harley. There were none. Instead, we heard what sounded to be the squeaking of a car door. I couldn't take the anticipation any longer. If Harley was coming to shoot us, I was prepared to charge him and do whatever I could to protect Marcus. I slowly sat up until I could see Harley's car in the mirror. The door was open, but Harley's face was blocked by something. I turned around. "Oh my God!"

"What?!" Marcus quickly sat up. "Holy shit!"

With a gun held in his left hand, Harley walked towards the right lane of the bridge. Hoisted into the air with his right hand was Caleb.

"He's going to throw him into the river!" I shouted.

Harley stood next to the wall of the bridge, where he dangled Caleb over the side. "No, he's not. He's just stalling."

"For what?"

"I don't know."

I cracked my door open. The blood-gurgling scream from a woman caused me to look into the barricade of vehicles behind Harley's Camaro. I immediately located the source of the scream. It belonged to the woman whose note, I was surprised to see, was still held in my hand.

"Is that Christina?"

"Yes."

"Let's hope she doesn't do anything stupid."

With his back to us, Harley began to shake Caleb as Christina approached him. "Take another step and I drop him, bitch! If anyone comes this way, he's going for a swim!"

I breathlessly looked on while waiting for Christina to do as he demanded. She took another step before wisely stopping.

"Please put him down!" Christina pleaded. "He's my son!" Her plea fell on deaf ears. Caleb remained held over the side of the three-foot wall.

My brother's phone rang. He grabbed it from the floor. "Dad."

Oblivious to the phone conversation taking place next to me, I glanced at the police barricade that appeared to have doubled in the last few minutes. It was inevitable that word spread how I had killed one of their former colleagues. I imagined a handful of those officers would enjoy inflicting pain upon me once I was again in custody. If incarceration was my fate, I was prepared to take another route. I faced Harley as the sun began its descent behind him. The sky was bright red in every direction, casting a purplish hue on the scattered clouds. Given the situation taking place, it seemed an inopportune time to notice the surreal setting, but it was hard to ignore. As Harley and I locked eyes with one another, I felt an eerie sense of calm. I didn't focus on the screams of bystanders pleading for Harley to return the kidnapped child to safety, or the blaring police sirens, or the screeching of tires as motorists slammed on their brakes on the adjacent span upon seeing the horrific sight unfolding. I stepped completely out of my brother's truck while coming up with a plan.

"Jackson! He's going to shoot you! Get back in here!"

"He's out of bullets."

"How do you know?"

"Look at his gun. It's a revolver. He already fired it five times."

"Are you sure?"

I had no clue as to how many rounds were fired. I just needed Marcus to believe me. "Yes." I envisioned running to Harley as fast as I could, pulling Caleb from his arms and throwing him safely onto the bridge just before bringing the crazed kidnapper over the side with me. I was certain to die a hero, thus avoiding a trial and most probably incarceration.

"Jackson!" Marcus yelled once more, louder than before. "Get your ass back in here!"

I tucked Christina's note into my back pocket. "We're the only ones that can help. I can save Caleb."

"Bullshit! Get back in here now!"

Harley locked eyes with me. He shook Caleb while yelling, "One more step and he goes overboard!"

Several screams cried out to me from the pile-up, yet one voice was easily recognizable. "Jackson! Please stop!"

I shook my head as if awaking from a trance. I looked to Christina. She was crying as I had never seen her cry before; the kind of crying that can nearly bring one to his or her knees as all hope is gone. I experienced that kind of crying once in my life—when I thought my brother was going to die in a mall parking lot. I stepped backward to the truck.

"Are you crazy? What were you thinking?"

"I don't know. What did Dad say?"

"To stay in the car until the police rescue Caleb and apprehend Harley."

I returned to the passenger seat, sitting with my back to the dashboard while keeping an eye on Harley. "I think I could have grabbed Caleb just now. He's not going to let go of him—you even said it. Caleb is the only reason the police haven't apprehended Harley yet, so why would he let go of his bargaining chip?"

"Is that a chance you really want to take? Besides, I'm starting to have second thoughts about Harley. He just may be crazier than I originally thought. Just wait a minute and this will be over."

My adrenaline began to subside. I watched Harley look to the sky as if he were trying to locate something. After looking myself and seeing nothing, I realized I hadn't finished reading the note from Christina. I reached into my back pocket, giving another glance at Harley before continuing where I left off. 'I don't want to be without you, Jackson. My ex, Tyler, has found his way back into my life, but I think it's only so I can bid a final farewell to him. I said 'yes' to your proposal and I meant it. I love you forever and want nothing more than to call you my husband. Please don't give up on me. –Delain.'

"What are you reading?"

"A letter from Delain."

"Don't you mean Christina? What does it say?"

I glanced at Harley while telling Marcus, "That she loves me and wants to marry me."

"When did she write it?"

"A few hours ago."

"How does that make you feel?"

I told him the truth. "Confused."

"Do you think she's being honest?"

"I don't know." I then felt guilt in the way I treated her in the back of the Tahoe.

The phone again rang. "It's Logan," Marcus said before answering it. "Where?" He turned the speaker phone on before frantically looking towards the sky. "I see it."

I scanned the horizon as well. "What's going on?"

Marcus pointed. "There's a helicopter coming this way."

I soon spotted it. "It must be the police."

"I don't think so," Logan said over the speaker phone. "It doesn't say police on the side."

"Then it's probably the media," Marcus suggested.

"What's he doing now?" Logan asked. Harley appeared to be waiving at the helicopter.

"I don't believe it!" Marcus shouted. "It's his escape!"

My chances of living as a free man again took a drastic nosedive. "He's going to get away with Caleb," I mumbled.

"No, he's not," Logan said over the speaker. "I have a plan. Jackson, once you see me standing next to my truck waving my arm, distract Harley. I need about ten seconds. After those ten seconds, something is going to happen. You and Marcus will then know what to do. I completely trust y'all with my life."

Both the approaching helicopter and Logan's plan had my stomach in knots. "What are you going to do?"

"It's best not to get into details. We're about to be heroes. Get ready."

"Logan! This isn't a game!" The phone went silent. "Shit!"

Marcus called him back. He didn't answer. "If he screws this up…"

As the helicopter grew closer to the bridge, a rope ladder was released out of the side door. It appeared the helicopter was indeed Harley's escape. Time was not on our side.

With a pointed finger, Marcus asked, "What in the hell is Logan doing?"

We watched as he climbed into the back of his truck, gathered something, and then jumped back onto the ground. He was nowhere to be seen. "Where did he go?"

"I think he's slouched behind his truck," Marcus told me.

"What the hell is that idiot doing?"

"I don't know, but it better be quick."

Harley, with Caleb still held over the side of the wall, glanced in the direction of the police barricade behind me and Marcus.

"There's Logan!"

I could see him waving his arm. "Should I do what he told me to do?"

"This might be our only shot. The helicopter's almost here."

I stepped out of the truck. Adrenaline wasn't flowing through my veins as it had done moments earlier when I stood on the bridge, and I didn't feel heroic either. I feared something horrific was about to happen.

"Here." Marcus handed me his cane. "You're quicker than me. You know what's inside—in case you need it. Twist the shaft counter-clockwise while pulling on the handle."

I gripped the handle of the cane. The ladder hanging from the helicopter was a stone's throw away from the bridge, and hastily moving towards Harley. I waved my arms in the air while yelling, "Hey, asshole!" Harley's attention was focused on me. While stepping towards him, I looked for Logan out of the corner of my eye. Again, he had disappeared. "Where are you?" I mumbled to myself.

Harley pointed his gun at me. "Stay back!"

"Why are you doing this?! It's not worth it! He's only two years old!"

"Shut the fuck up and stop right there!"

Logan came into view. With Harley's back to him, Logan jumped over the hood of his truck, landing barefoot onto the ground. In his left hand, he held a baseball bat. Something was wrapped around his waist. I gripped the cane tighter as Logan rose to his feet. It was time for further distraction. As I stood about the length of a Greyhound bus from Harley, I started to jump in place while hollering. Logan began to walk towards Harley. Within a few steps, his walk turned into a jog, which quickly turned into a full-fledged sprint. As he grew closer to Harley, my jumping ceased, but my screaming became louder as it was mostly aimed at my best friend. Once Logan was only a few strides away from Harley, he raised the bat high in the air. I screamed at the top of my lungs as Logan swung the bat forward, striking Harley in the arm holding Caleb. I then watched in horror as Logan thrust himself over the side wall of the bridge with Caleb in his arms. I hurried towards the wall. Logan and Caleb were plummeting towards the water. My disbelief in that Logan had jumped to his death with Caleb in his arms immediately turned to a different disbelief as Logan and Caleb slowed down before being thrust back upward with the assistance of a bungee cord.

"Jackson," Marcus yelled from the truck, "He's cutting the bungee!"

My attention shifted back to Harley. From a kneeling position, he was doing just as Marcus had said. I ran as fast as I had ever run; so fast that there wasn't time to twist and remove the blade from the shaft. I cocked back and swung the Maplewood cane as hard as I could at Harley's back. It knocked him to the ground. He jumped to his feet as I cocked back for another swing. Again, I struck him in the back. He remained on his feet, angry and determined. As I attempted a third swing, he caught the cane with his hand, pulled me towards him, and wrapped both arms around me. I tried to squirm from his grasp. His strength was superior to mine. A head butt was my only option. As I tilted my head back, he lifted me off the ground before throwing me violently against it. Nearly every bone and muscle in my body felt the impact, especially my left arm as it was the first to hit the concrete. As I lay on the ground, momentarily dazed, I could see Harley again attempting to cut the bungee. Ignoring the uncomfortable feeling in my left arm, I climbed to my feet and balled my right hand into a fist. I cocked back, punching as hard as I could into the back of Harley's head. The force was enough to send him stumbling forward, yet he remained on his feet. As he turned around, I stared at the knife in his right hand as he thrust it towards me. There was no time to react. I looked down. The blade struck my abdomen. Harley removed it before flinging it forward once more. I again tried to dodge the knife. For a second time, I was unsuccessful. The blade, several inches long, struck my chest. Shock overcame me upon realizing I had been stabbed twice. After removing the knife, Harley grabbed my neck with his left hand and shoved me against his car. He lifted the knife overhead. While staring at my own blood dripping down the blade of the knife onto the tip, a baseball bat violently struck the side of Harley's head. The 'thump' sound of wood raucously striking his skull was the most unnerving and disturbing sound I had ever heard in my life. Like the massive pile-up that occurred moments earlier, the impact of northern white ash against his skull sent unsettling chills up and down my spine. His grip on my neck lessened. I fell to the ground. Even though I knew I had been stabbed twice, I had yet to feel the effects. I looked up to see another swing of the bat making contact with Harley's back as he was hunched over. Blood dripped down his face as he slowly staggered backwards towards the wall of the bridge. The person holding the bat had their back to me, but I knew to whom the blonde hair belonged. Caroline swung the bat a third time. Harley's chest took the hit. He appeared dazed while leaning against the wall of the bridge. I watched Caroline as she readjusted her grip on the bat. As Harley raised the knife, she cocked back. Harley's eyes grew large as Caroline screamed while stepping into her fourth swing. The bat struck his face. His head flung backwards. The rest of his body followed as momentum carried him over the wall of the bridge. Harley 'Hitman' Motichek had been knocked into the Mississippi River by one of the most beautiful women I had ever known. Caroline ran towards me, dropping the bloodied bat along the way. She squatted next to me. Marcus soon appeared behind her.

With a frown about her face and a look of uneasiness in her eyes, she breathlessly asked, "Are you okay?"

Pain began to radiate throughout my body, but predominately in my left arm. I looked down. Not only was blood trickling from my chest and stomach, but my left elbow was bent backwards. I was quickly becoming nauseous and weak. "I'm fine," I told her. "Where's Logan?"

My brother hurried to the side of the bridge. "You okay, Logan?!"

"Pull us up, dummy!" I faintly heard my best friend yell. Marcus began to pull as Harley's getaway helicopter hastily flew away.

Caroline placed her hands over my wounds. "You're losing a lot of blood, and your arm is…"

A sudden chill overcame me. "I'm cold."

"Help!" she screamed to the crowd of onlookers. "We need an ambulance now!"

My dad appeared. He knelt next to Caroline. "Oh my God." His face lacked any hint of optimism.

"I'm good," I told him. "Help Marcus, Dad." I tried to point, but my arm felt as if it weighed as much as the Camaro I was leaning against. My dad turned around, assisting my brother.

Caroline had begun to cry. "I need you to hang on, Jackson. You hear me?"

I looked downward. Her hands were doused in blood; so much blood that I couldn't see the skin of her hands. My eyelids grew heavy. Keeping my eyes open, all of a sudden, became something I had to consciously attempt to do.

With both hands covering her mouth, Christina stood before me. "Jackson!"

"Caleb," I told her with a nod of my head towards my dad and brother.

She knelt next to me, staring at the wounds on my torso before looking into my eyes. "Are you okay?"

I didn't want to tell the truth. For some reason, I felt embarrassed admitting I wasn't going to make it off of the bridge alive. I smiled. "Of course. I'm tough."

Police officers and bystanders assisted my dad and brother. Logan's bare feet were the first to arrive at the wall. My dad reached over and grabbed Caleb. As an officer tried to grab the young boy, my dad told him, "No. He's her son." He handed him to Christina. She at first seemed reluctant to grab him, but once my dad placed a crying Caleb into her trembling hands, tears poured down her cheeks.

"Please tell me someone got that on video!" Logan exclaimed as he was being helped over the wall. His smile vanished as we made eye contact. He hurried towards me, kneeling next to Caroline, whose hands were still covering my stab wounds. "Dude, are you okay?"

I couldn't lie any longer. "No."

He stood, facing the crowd of onlookers. "Where's the God damn ambulance!"

I watched as Christina held Caleb to her chest while thanking Logan. She then looked to me. "I love you so much, Jackson. I didn't mean to hurt you."

An emotion I had not felt since high school finally got the better of me. My eyes began to water, not from Christina confessing to loving me or the realization that I was on death's doorsteps, but upon seeing Caleb held in his birthmother's arms. Not only Christina's, but Caleb's journey was finally over. I considered repeating what she had just told me, but I couldn't say the words—at least not to her. I replied with, "He's got your eyes." I turned my head. Caroline's mismatched, gorgeous eyes brought a smile to my face. "I love you."

Her crying grew heavier. I could feel her hands applying more pressure to my wounds. "I love you too."

"I'd rather die in the arms of my lover than alone in a nursing home at eighty-five." I attempted to muster a smile.

She shook her head. "How about we die together in about sixty or seventy years?"

Inhaling became extremely difficult. My pulse was slowing dramatically. Everyone and everything around me became blurry. I gave one final look at Logan, Marcus, my dad, Christina and Caleb, and lastly, Caroline. Her tearful face was the last thing I saw before a white light brighter than anything I had ever seen encompassed everything and everyone around me. My eyes shut. The very first breath in which I inhaled upon being born escaped the deepest recesses of my lungs before exiting my lips. I, Andrew Jackson Fabacher the IV, at the age of twenty-nine, died in the arms of the woman I loved.

Chapter 130

While sitting alone at the darkened Fleur-de-Leans bar, Scott Melancon stared at an empty bottle of Bombay Sapphire as it lay on its side. *Goodbye sobriety*. He grabbed the gin and tonic before him—his fifth in the last hour—and placed it to his lips. In a span of just forty-eight hours, Scott's world had come crumbling down. Besides losing custody of his biological son (the second child he had lost custody of in the last ten years), his wife had left him, and the restaurant he was prepared to dedicate his life towards would no longer be opening. Davis Melancon's name and anything linked to it was about to be forever tarnished in not only the city of New Orleans, but throughout the country as word had already begun to spread about what he had done to a young woman from Atlanta, Georgia.

The restaurant door opened. With Scott's back to the door, hope overcame him. *Bridgett's back to apologize for the way she acted hours earlier!* He set the drink on the counter before popping a fresh piece of gum into his mouth to mask the alcohol on his breath. Bridgett knew of his past and vowed to leave him if he ever reverted to his alcoholic tendencies. *Don't act drunk*, he told himself while placing the empty bottle of gin and the full glass behind the bar. *Tell her you just had one drink*. Scott turned around. Optimism escaped him. Hatred took over as he stared at the man standing before him.

"I've been trying to reach you all afternoon, Scottie."

"Haven't you seen me enough already in the last few days, Charlie?" Scott reached back across the bar, grabbing his gin and tonic.

"I was worried about you. I wanted to make sure you were okay following Bridgett's outburst earlier this afternoon."

"Outburst?" Scott's laugh was heavy on sarcasm. "My wife slapped my face repeatedly, kicked me in the groin, and then told me that if she ever saw me again, she'd shoot me between the eyes. That was a little more than an outburst, Charlie." Scott ingested nearly half of the drink with one lengthy sip.

Charlie sat on the stool to Scott's right. "She'll come to. Her emotions got the better of her. I'm sure she's already feeling remorseful for acting the way she did."

Scott slammed his drink on the bar. "The son she had been raising for nearly two years was taken from her in the blink of an eye! And she thinks I'm to blame, Charlie!"

"I understand what it's like to lose a child, Scottie—I really do, however this is far from over. We're going to get Thomas back and—"

"It's over, Charlie! My brother fucked my entire world up, and I had no idea about any of this until you told me about it a few days ago! And then you assured me everything would be all right!"

Charlie held his hands up between himself and Scott. "Please calm down, Scottie. Your anger is not helping the situation."

"When did you find out what my brother was doing to not only me, but that innocent girl as well?"

"Right before he passed away," Charlie immediately answered. "And I assure you that girl was far from innocent. I didn't tell you this earlier, but that 'innocent' girl killed a man behind your brother's restaurant while intoxicated. Your brother saved that young woman from going to jail."

"Why would he protect some random woman he didn't know?"

"Because your brother was an honorable man."

"There's no honor in protecting a murderer, Charlie."

"You have a valid point, Scottie, but the man Christina ran over with her car was trying to extort money from your dear brother. That's why the accident occurred behind this restaurant."

"Why was he extorting money from Davis? What other shady businesses was my brother involved in?"

"None at all. The man was nothing more than a drug dealer, claiming that one of your brother's chefs owed him money. Now, we both know drugs are rampant in the restaurant business, so it was a possibility. He said he wasn't leaving until someone gave him money. Once Davis threatened to call the police, the man took off and Christina hit him. Davis knew the young woman crying in the street would not survive in jail. She made a mistake and her whole life would be affected by something that occurred in the blink of an eye. Davis told the police the man ran into the street and it was entirely his fault. If he hadn't spoken up, they would have checked Christina's blood alcohol level. After the accident, she and your brother became friends. One night at this very bar—and I'm certain the very seat in which you are sitting—Davis, as he often did, talked about you. He eventually arrived on the subject about how you and your wife had difficulty in carrying a fetus. Christina promised to Davis, as a favor for what he did for her, that she would become a surrogate for you and your wife. Now, before you label this woman as a 'saint' for agreeing to carry your future child, know that she was paid $20,000 in addition to the fact that Davis put his reputation on the line in order to protect her from being incarcerated. Your heroic brother confided in me that Christina reminded him so much of his lovely daughter, and that's another reason he helped her. I apologize for not telling you all this earlier, but I didn't think it would get this far. Davis didn't want you to know everything that he had done for you because he didn't want you to ever think that you owed him. Now, everything else I have already told you—how Davis 'borrowed' your sperm sample from the clinic when you were down here years ago and artificially inseminated it into Christina, how she had a change of heart and wanted the baby back several months after giving him up for adoption, and how Davis'…how do we say…monetary donation helped to persuade a certain individual of the adoption agency into seeing that you and Bridgett's name moved up a few spots on the adoption registry. That little move may have been a little deceitful by your brother, but," Charlie laughed while continuing, "after all this is Louisiana. Corruption and bribes are what built this beautiful state of ours."

Scott didn't know whether or not to believe him. "And if my brother never intervened, Bridgett and I would be raising another child that wasn't brought to us by corrupt means."

"I'm not so sure, Scottie. I know several couples that have been waiting well over five years to adopt."

"My point, Charlie, is that Davis screwed up my life. I no longer have a child, my wife will kill me if I try to talk to her, and if I were to open this restaurant, who would come eat here?"

"Part of the reason I came here is to get your wife's cell phone number. I will call her and tell her everything I have told you. She will come running back into your arms once I am done telling her the truth. Don't forget that you are part of the Krewe, and we help one another."

Scott's eyes remained fixed on his drink as he gently slid it back and forth between his hands atop the bar. "Why was my son kidnapped?"

"I already told you—the 'innocent' girl, as you call her, hired that ruthless thug to kidnap him, and then made sure he was killed so he couldn't tell the truth."

"How do you know all of this?"

"At Harley's house, two upstanding, honorable police officers that I have known for several years found a recording of Christina making a deal with Harley to kidnap Thomas. Do you know how much she offered him to perform that horrendous act?"

Scott shook his head.

"$20,000—the exact amount Davis gave her to carry your son in her womb."

"I want to hear that recording."

"I do as well, however it is now property of the New Orleans Police Department and currently they are not letting anyone listen to it. Believe me, I tried to get a hold of it."

Scott drank the remainder of the gin and tonic with another lengthy sip. "So, let's say you call Bridgett and she comes back to me. What's next?"

"We get your son back?"

"How in the hell would that happen?"

"Do you mind if I make myself a drink?"

While using the assistance of the bar, Scott stood. "I'll do it. It'll probably be the last time I get to make someone a drink behind this bar anyway."

Charlie chuckled. "That is far from the truth. You are too pessimistic, Scottie. Even if the newspapers and newscast favor the side of that young woman, your business will not suffer. We make several statements that claim you knew nothing of your brother's actions. Look at you—you're handsome, clean-cut, and honest. People will believe you— especially the women," he spoke with a wink. "The citizens of New Orleans loved your brother's restaurant, and they're going to love your restaurant as well."

"You never answered how I'm going to get Caleb back."

"And you have yet to pour some of that delicious Grand Marnier into a snifter for your thirsty friend," a laughing Charlie said.

A desperate Scott poured the liqueur into a snifter and slid it across the bar. "How do I get him back?"

Charlie held the glass to his nose, inhaling before taking a sip. "A DNA test has already proven that Christina is Thomas' birth mother. Once this goes to court, she will be awarded custody of that boy. You will—more than likely—never be allowed to see him." He paused to take another sip, setting the glass on the bar as he continued. "However, if something were to happen to her, the court would have no choice but to award custody back to you and your wife, provided that we can prove you had no knowledge of your brother's actions."

"Define 'if something were to happen to her'?"

"If Christina was to have an accident, such as a fatal car wreck or a fatal house burglary, then someone else would have to raise that child—his birth father."

"You would have her killed?"

"Of course not. I'm just saying if something tragic were to happen to her, Thomas' father would be next in line to raise him."

Scott was certain Charlie was referring to having her killed, but without actually saying the words. "I don't want her killed. She's already been through enough."

"I don't either, Scottie. But…if something were to happen to her, wouldn't you want your son back?"

Scott felt uneasy each time he was in the presence of the Krewe. His opinion that they were nothing more than ruthless criminals was starting to look factual. He wanted nothing to do with them upon the first meeting, and only did so because he felt pressured to join them. His gut also told him that his brother did not act alone. He couldn't hold back any longer. "Did my brother orchestrate this elaborate plan all by himself?"

Glancing down at the snifter on the bar, Charlie answered, "I'm afraid he did."

"And neither you nor anyone else in the Krewe helped him?"

"That is correct."

Scott doubted Charlie's claim. He was ready to call him out in it. "The last time I was down here in New Orleans, Charlie, was for Tiffany's wedding. Bridgett, Thomas, and I arrived on the Tuesday before the wedding. After checking in at the hotel, we came here to eat. Davis was nowhere to be found. After placing our dinner order, I wandered around the restaurant, eventually finding him in the back standing next to his Ferrari. He was talking to a gentleman whom I could never forget. He was tall, bald, had tattoos all over his body, and looked to be in a friendly conversation with my brother. I clearly saw the man's face that night, and then again two days ago as he held my son over the Mississippi River Bridge. Now, why would someone that my brother knew kidnap my son?"

Charlie shrugged his shoulders, hesitating before telling Scott, "I'm afraid only Harley or your brother could have answer that question."

Scott was certain Charlie was lying to him. In a fit of anger, he forcefully slid his empty drink across the bar, causing it to shatter upon hitting the brick wall several feet away from where he stood. "I hate being lied to, Charlie! There's no way my brother pulled off this entire thing by himself! I thought the Krewe helped each other out! That means he had help!"

Charlie wiped at the broken glass and ice cubes atop the bar with a nearby napkin. He then grabbed another napkin to wipe down his snifter. "There's no need to raise your voice, Scottie. I'm on your side. And we do help each other out. That is why I'm here right now."

"How come your story and the one Christina told the police officers and federal agents are very different?"

"Because the girl has no morals. She was desperate and would do anything to get her son back."

"And now you want to kill her?"

Charlie was slow to answer. "What do you want, Scottie?"

"My brother has ruined my life! I want nothing more to do with him, or his damn club of criminals!"

"What are you saying?"

"I think Harley kidnapped Thomas to hide the truth about what was going on, yet someone got the better of him…and whoever he was working for." Scott looked Charlie square in the eyes while telling him, "I want you to leave my restaurant, and tell your friends to find another place to talk about the next person y'all are going to bully, kidnap, or kill."

Charlie stood from the stool. "Are you sure that's what you want?"

Scott picked up the phone from behind the bar. "If you're not out of here in ten seconds, I'm calling the police."

With his gaze aimed at the ground, Charlie shook his head. "That saddens me."

"Maybe I should call them anyway and tell them what's been going on with some of New Orleans most prominent citizens."

Charlie looked up. An exasperated, lengthy exhalation passed his lips as he tapped his knuckles against the bar. "I really wish you hadn't said that, old friend." Once he turned to walk away, someone firmly grabbed Scott from behind while placing something moist against his lips and nose. Everything around him faded into blackness.

Chapter 131

Tyler signed his name at the bottom of the check before handing it across the desk to John. "You earned every dollar."

John briefly glanced at the check, smiling before placing it into his desk drawer. "I want to thank you again, Tyler, for getting me involved with the most exhilarating case I have ever been involved with."

"I had no idea it was going to be this complex. I'm just sorry you had to take a bullet. How much longer do you have to wear that sling?"

John glanced at his left shoulder and then back at Tyler. "Another two weeks. It's not the first time I've been struck by a bullet, and it probably won't be the last either. Good thing Harley wasn't that good of a shot. Three more inches to my right and I'd be a dead man."

"When Christina and I saw him running out of the house with the gun in his hand, we thought you were a goner. I apologize for leaving you behind, but we couldn't let Harley out of our sight."

"You two did the right thing. And you, my friend, acted brilliantly in the F.B.I. building. When you first opened your mouth, I thought we were in trouble. You proved me wrong."

"I still can't believe I helped someone escape from federal custody. Are you sure they're not going to come looking for me?"

"Positive."

"Isn't the F.B.I. a little embarrassed that someone they took into custody was stolen from beneath their nose?"

"The bureau doesn't know Jackson escaped—only Mitch and a few of his friends do. They still think two C.I.A. agents took him under their custody. I can assure you that Mitch won't be coming after you. He and I talked on the phone this morning."

"What did y'all talk about?"

"I told him that if he attempts to come after you or Christina, I will have no choice but to hand over to every government agency audio tapes of the phone conversations he and I shared over the last few days. Just so he knew I wasn't bluffing, I played a snippet of one of those conversations."

"He's not going to get arrested for what he did? Christina was telling me how he was behind the kidnapping."

"Mitch is definitely dirty. There's no doubt he was responsible for not only the kidnapping, but also Harley's attempted escape via helicopter. However, he and whoever else he is involved with are damn good at covering their footsteps. Harley being killed was the best thing that could have happened to them. He, along with Davis, took the entire blame for what happened."

Tyler felt more at ease. "So, what's next for you? Retirement?" You could probably take a six-month-long vacation to Fiji with the check I just gave you."

"More like a year," John spoke with a smile. "Nah. Retirement is for those who have given up on life and have nothing to live for. I'll lay low until my shoulder heals then take on another case. Next to yours, though, every other job is going to be a bore."

"And probably safer too." Tyler placed both hands on the chair's armrest as he stood. "Can I make you a drink?"

"Why not. Make it—"

"Scotch on the rocks," Tyler spoke on his way toward the bar.

"Good memory. How is Christina doing?"

"Since being awarded temporary custody of Caleb, she's been slowly improving. She still has trouble sleeping through the night. I think she's worried someone is going to take Caleb from her again. It doesn't help that news vans have been camped outside my home for the last few days. I had to sneak out the house and take a cab here."

"Good man. When is the court date?"

"Next month. She's a little on edge about it. I keep telling her they won't take Caleb away from his birth mother."

"They won't. Even though it's been proven Scott is the biological father, the circumstances Davis put her through will be too much to award custody to his wife, especially now that Scott is dead."

"What?!"

"You didn't hear the news?"

"No."

"I guess everything that happened was too much for him. He hung himself yesterday, at the restaurant."

"My God."

"His suicide benefits you and Christina even more."

Tyler handed John his drink "I hope you're right."

"And what's in the future for the three of you?"

"Once this is all behind us, I'm going to propose to her. We talked about moving closer to her parents. They arrived in town two days ago. She told them everything. It was very emotional."

"I have no doubt she's going to accept your proposal."

"I think so too." Tyler then grinned while pouring Jack Daniels Single Barrel into a glass.

"I love that woman so much. I can't thank you enough for what you did, John. I apologize for doubting you at times. I just didn't realize how good you really are…or how real your hair looks."

John held the drink in his left hand, while patting his right against the salt-and-peppered hairpiece. "Why do you think I had to charge you so much?"

Tyler returned to the chair with whiskey in hand. "Now that I got the girl and this case is over, can you answer my question?" He pointed over his left shoulder to the *Starry Night* painting behind the thick glass.

Before he could ask about its authenticity, John told him, "Of course not."

"Then why make it appear that it is real?"

"To offer hope to anyone who sees it."

"How so?"

"Everyone who steps foot in this office for the first time asks the same question. And every one of you wants to believe it's the original. Why do you think that is?"

Tyler shrugged his shoulders. "I don't know."

"Because it's human nature to rebel, to be dangerous, to beat the system. You would have loved to hear that I stole this painting from the Museum of Modern Art, wouldn't you?"

"It would be far more interesting than it being just a replica."

"Exactly. Replicas are, for the most part, worthless. No one wants a copy of something; they want the original. You just did what I had always wanted to do, Tyler. You stole *Starry Night*."

Confused, Tyler asked, "Come again?"

"Christina was going to marry Jackson. You walked right in and stole her from beneath his nose. If it wasn't for you, they would be married right now. On our first meeting I called Christina your masterpiece. You, my friend, just stole your masterpiece. The other women you dated after Christina were just replicas. The original is once again in your possession."

Tyler glanced at the replica.

"You rebelled, you acted dangerously, and you beat the system, Tyler. People died and lives were forever changed. Now, let me ask you a question: was it worth it?"

Tyler slowly turned to John and grinned. "I would do it all again in a heartbeat."

Epilogue

Logan gently slid the Jack and Coke across the bar to Caroline before grabbing a glass from the shelf behind the bar. As she took a sip, Logan noticed her hand shaking as she held the glass to her lips. After setting the drink down, she wiped at her eyes with the tissue that had been permanently attached to her hand since they arrived at the Fabacher house preceding Jackson's funeral. It was well past midnight. Marcus left minutes earlier with his wife. Andrew had just retired to bed, rolling his wife out of the parlour in a wheelchair. Cecile barely spoke to anyone throughout the evening. Every time Logan glanced at her during the funeral, she stared hypnotically at the casket. She never shed a tear at any point throughout the day. Her reaction was much different than at Jackson's previous funeral, in which she cried continuously throughout the funeral as she spoke with loved ones.

"I loved him," Caroline spoke, staring blankly into her drink.

"Me too."

"I loved him more than any man I ever knew." She ingested a lengthy sip before setting the drink back onto the bar. "I was going to marry him. We were going to have three children. And then we were going to die within minutes of each other in a nursing home sixty-five years from now." With a subtle shake of her head and a half-hearted grin she asked Logan, "Does that make me sound crazy?"

While pouring whiskey into the glass, Logan shook his head. "Not at all. There was no one else like him. I have no doubt he would have made you the happiest woman in the world."

Caroline again wiped at her eyes. "Last weekend was the most incredible weekend of my life. It was just me and him. I didn't want it to end."

Logan took a sip of the whiskey before asking her, "What are you going to do now? Go back to San Diego?"

"I'm not ready to go home. I have unfinished business here." Caroline looked to the doors leading to the hallway before locking eyes with Logan, telling him, "Harley isn't the reason Jackson is dead. Other people were behind his death."

"And Mitch is atop the list."

"He and the others need to pay for what they did to Jackson. Don't you agree?"

Logan nodded while glancing at his drink. "What is your definition of 'pay'?"

"I would imagine the same as yours. What do you want to see happen?"

"I want to hurt every one of those fuckers that were behind this. I want to do to them what you did to Harley."

"We have very similar thoughts, Logan."

After ingesting a lengthy sip of the whiskey, he asked Caroline, "When do we start?"

"Now."

"What's our first move?"

Caroline downed the rest of her drink. "First things first, I want to talk to that lying bitch Delain."

Made in the USA
Monee, IL
11 November 2020